Some sec...
forever. It...
time before...
– nine r...

FOR THEIR
CHILD'S SAKE

Two of your favourite writers deliver
two compelling stories

FOR THEIR CHILD'S SAKE

Everyday, Average Jones
SUZANNE BROCKMANN

To a MacAllister Born
JOAN ELLIOTT PICKART

 SILHOUETTE®

Silhouette Books, Eton House, 18-24 Paradise Road,
Richmond, Surrey TW9 1SR

FOR THEIR CHILD'S SAKE © Harlequin Books S.A. 2006

The publisher acknowledges the copyright holders of the
individual works, which have already been published in the UK in
single, separate volumes, as follows:

Everyday, Average Jones © Suzanne Brockmann 1998
To a MacAllister Born © Joan Elliott Pickart 2000

ISBN 0 373 60408 4

064-0606

Printed and bound in Spain
by Litografia Rosés S.A., Barcelona

Everyday, Average Jones

SUZANNE BROCKMANN

SUZANNE BROCKMANN

wrote her first romance novel in 1992 and fell in love with the genre. She writes full-time, along with singing and arranging music for her professional a cappella singing group called Vocomotive, organising a monthly charity event at her church and managing the acting careers of her two young children, Melanie and Jason. She and her family are living happily ever after in a small town outside Boston.

My special thanks to Candace Irvin,
who helped clear up a great deal of confusion
about rank and pay-grade and US Navy life
in general. Thanks also to my online SEAL
buddy, Mike, who in the closed-mouth
tradition of the quiet professionals hasn't
managed to tell me much, yet still can
always make me laugh.

For my big sister, Carolee Brockmann.
And for my mum, Lee Brockmann,
who even likes the ones that never sell.

Chapter 1

It was extremely likely that she was going to die.

And with every hour that passed, her chance of making it out of this godforsaken country any way other than inside a body bag was slipping from slim to none.

Melody Evans sat quietly in the corner of the little windowless office that had become her prison, writing what she hoped would not be her final words in a letter to her sister.

Dear Brittany, I'm scared to death of dying....

She was terrified of the finality of a single bullet to the head. But she was even more afraid of the other sort of death that possibly awaited her. She'd heard of the kinds of torture that were far too prevalent in this part of the world. Torture, and other archaic, monstrous practices. God help her if they found out she was a woman....

Melody felt her pulse kick into overdrive, and she took slow, deep breaths, trying to calm herself.

Remember the time you took me sledding up at the apple orchards? Remember how you got on the sled behind me, and told me in that supertheatrical voice you sometimes used that we were

*either going to steer a straight course down the hill through the
rows of trees—or die trying?*

Her older sister had always been the adventurous one. Yet it
was Brittany who was still at home in Appleton, living in the
same four-story Godzilla of a Victorian house that they'd grown
up in. And it was Melody who, in a moment of sheer insanity,
had accepted the job of administrative assistant to the American
ambassador and had moved overseas to a country she hadn't even
known existed until six months ago.

*I remember thinking as we plunged down the hill—God, I
couldn't have been more than six years old, but I remember thinking—at least we'll die together.*

I wish to God I didn't feel so alone....

"You don't really think they're going to let you *send* that, do
you?" Kurt Matthews's acerbic voice dripped scorn.

"No, I don't." Melody answered him without even looking up.
She knew she was writing this letter not for Brittany, but for
herself. Memories. She was writing down some childhood memories, trying to give herself a sense of that peace and happiness
she'd known once upon a time. She was writing about the way
she'd always tried so desperately to keep up with a sister nearly
nine years older than she was. She skipped over the sibling in-
fighting and petty arguments, choosing to remember only Britt's
patience and kindness.

Britt always used to make such a big deal over Melody's birthday. This year, even though Mel was thousands of miles from the
New England charm of their hometown in Massachusetts, Britt
had sent a huge box of birthday surprises. She'd taken care to
send it far enough in advance, and Melody had received it four
days ago—more than a week before her twenty-fifth birthday.

She was glad now that she hadn't followed Britt's written orders and instead had opened the pile of presents in advance of
the so-called special day. Britt had sent five new pairs of warm
socks, a thick woolen sweater and some new athletic shoes. Those
were the practical gifts. The fun gifts included the newest Garth
Brooks CD, Tami Hoag's latest romantic thriller, a jar of real
peanut butter and two videotapes on which Brittany had recorded

the past three months' episodes of *ER*. It was America-in-a-box, and Melody had both laughed and cried at her older sister's thoughtfulness. It was the best birthday present she'd ever received.

Except now it looked as if she wouldn't live to see those episodes of *ER*. Or her twenty-fifth birthday.

Kurt Matthews was ignoring her again. He'd gone back to his asinine discussion with Chris Sterling. They were trying to figure out just how much CNN would pay them for the exclusive rights to their story after the deal between the terrorists and the U.S. government was made and they were released.

Matthews, the fool, actually had the gall to say that he hoped the talks weren't going too smoothly. He seemed to think that the monetary value of their story would increase with the length of their ordeal. And so far, they'd only been held for two days.

He—or Sterling, either, for that matter—didn't have a clue as to the seriousness of this situation.

Melody, on the other hand, had done research on this particular terrorist group who had overthrown the entire government in an unexpected coup early Wednesday morning. They'd taken the American embassy by storm shortly after that. They were terrorists, and the U.S. didn't negotiate with terrorists. Right now, they were only talking. But if the talking didn't end, and end soon, this group of zealots was not likely to continue to show their three civilian hostages the same amount of respect and creature comfort they had to date. Provided, of course, that one could call being locked in a tiny, nearly airless office with two idiots, irregular deliveries of food and water and a washroom facility that no longer worked "comfortable."

Matthews and Sterling both seemed to think they were being held under rather dire conditions.

But Melody knew better.

She closed her eyes, trying to force away the image of the cold dankness of an underground cell. When she'd left Appleton to take this job at the embassy, she'd had no idea that the desert could be so cold during the winter months. It was March now—early spring—and it could still be chilly at night.

She focused instead on her feet. They were warm, clad in a pair of the socks and the cross trainers Brittany had sent.

They'd be taken from her—both shoes and socks—before she was thrown into that dark cell.

Lord, she had to stop thinking like that. It wasn't going to do her a bit of good.

Still, the image of the prison cell was better than the other picture her overactive imagination cooked up: three American infidels, dead at the hands of their captors.

Cowboy watched the back of the American embassy through high-powered binoculars. The place was jumping with tangos, arriving and leaving at apparently unscheduled times.

"Cat," he said almost silently into his lip microphone.

Capt. Joe Catalanotto, commander of SEAL Team Ten's Alpha Squad, was positioned on the other side of the building. He was cooling his heels with the five other members of the team, having set up temporary camp in an abandoned apartment. The owner of the unit was no doubt some smart son of a bitch who had grabbed his TV and run, realizing the obvious negatives in owning real estate so close to a building that could go up in flames at any moment.

For Alpha Squad's purposes, the apartment was perfect. The master-bedroom window had a nifty view of the front of the embassy. With one of the other SEALs seated in an easy chair in front of that window, and with Cowboy positioned somewhat less comfortably on a rooftop overlooking the back, they could track the tangos'—SEAL slang for terrorists—every move.

"Yeah, Jones." Cat's flat New York accent came in loud and clear over the headphones Ensign Harlan Jones, otherwise known as Cowboy, was wearing.

Cowboy said only one word. "Chaos." He had made himself invisible on the roof, but he was well aware that the windows were opened on the floor directly below him, so when he spoke, he was as concise and as quiet as possible. He kept his binoculars trained on the building, moving from one broken window to the next. He could see movement inside, shadowy figures. The place was huge—one of those old mothers of a building, built during the middle of the previous century. He didn't doubt for a moment that the hostages were secured in one of the inner chambers.

"Copy that," Catalanotto said, a trace of amusement in his voice. "We see it from this side, too. Whoever these clowns are, they're amateurs. We'll go in tonight. At oh-dark-hundred."

Cowboy had to risk a full sentence. "I recommend we move now." He could hear Cat's surprise in the silence that grew longer and longer.

"Jones, the sun'll be going down in less than three hours," the captain finally said. The SEALs worked best at night. They could move almost invisibly under the cover of darkness.

Cowboy switched the powerful lenses to the infrared setting and took another quick scan of the building. "We should go now."

"What do you see that I don't see, kid?" Joe Cat's question was made without even a trace of sarcasm. Yeah, Cat had a wagonload of experience that Cowboy couldn't begin to compete with. And yeah, Cat had recently gotten a pay raise to O-6— captain—while Cowboy was a measly O-1, an ensign. But Captain Joe Catalanotto was the kind of leader who took note of his team's individual strengths and used each man to his full ability. And sometimes even beyond.

Every man on the team could see through walls, provided they had the right equipment. But no one could take the information that equipment provided and interpret it the way Cowboy could. And Cat knew that.

"At least fifty T's inside."

"Yeah, that's what Bobby tells me, too." Cat paused. "What's the big deal?"

"The pattern of movement."

Cowboy heard Cat take over Bobby's place at the bedroom window. There was silence, and then Cat swore. "They're making room for something." He swore again. "Or some*one*."

Cowboy clicked once into his lip mike—an affirmative. That's what he thought, too.

"They're clearing out the entire east side of the building," Joe

Cat continued, now able to see what Cowboy saw. "How many more tangos are they expecting?"

It was a rhetorical question, but Cowboy answered it anyway. "Two hundred?"

Cat swore again and Cowboy knew what he was thinking. Fifty T's were manageable—particularly when they were of the Three Stooges variety, like the ones he'd been watching going in and out of the embassy all day long. But two hundred and fifty against seven SEALs... Those odds were a little skewed. Not to mention the fact that the SEALs didn't know if any of the soon-to-be-arriving tangos were real soldiers, able to tell the difference between their AK-47s and their elbows.

"Get ready to move," he heard Cat tell the rest of Alpha Squad.

"Cat."

"Yeah, Jones?"

"Three heat spots haven't moved much all day."

Catalanotto laughed. "Are you telling me you think you've located our hostages?"

Cowboy clicked once into his lip mike.

Christopher Sterling, Kurt Matthews and Melody Evans. Cowboy had been carrying those names inside his head ever since Alpha Squad was first briefed on this mission in the plane that took them to their insertion point—a high-altitude, low-opening parachute jump from high above the desert just outside the terrorist-controlled city.

He'd seen the hostages' pictures, too.

All of the men in Alpha Squad had held on to the picture of Melody Evans for a little bit longer than necessary. She couldn't have been more than twenty-two, twenty-three at most—hardly more than a kid. In the photo, she was dressed in blue jeans and a plain T-shirt that didn't show off her female figure but didn't quite manage to hide it, either. She was blue-eyed with wavy blond hair that tumbled down her back and a country-fresh, slightly shy smile and sweet face that reminded each and every one of them of their little sisters—even those of 'em like Cowboy who didn't *have* a little sister.

And Cowboy knew they were all thinking the same thing. As they were sitting there on that plane, waiting to reach their destination, that girl was at the mercy of a group of terrorists who weren't known for their humanitarian treatment of hostages. In fact, the opposite was true. This group's record of torture and abuse was well documented, as was their intense hatred of all things American.

He hated to think what they might do—had already done—to this young woman who could've been the poster model for the All-American Girl. But all day long, he'd kept a careful eye on the three heat sources he suspected were the hostages. And all day long, none of them had been moved.

"Fourth floor, interior room," he said quietly into his mike. "Northwest corner."

"I don't suppose in your free time you found us a way into the embassy?" Cat asked.

"Minimal movement on the top floor," Cowboy reported. Those windows were broken, too. "Roof to windows—piece a cake."

"And gettin' to the roof?" The south-of-the-Mason-Dixon-line voice that spoke over his headphones was that of Lt. Blue McCoy, Alpha Squad's point man and Joe Cat's second in command.

"Just a stroll from where I'm at. Connecting roofs. Route's clear—I've already checked."

"Why the hell did I bother bringing along the rest of you guys?" Cat asked. Cowboy could hear the older man's smile in his voice. "Good job, kid."

"Only kind I do," Cowboy drawled.

"That's what I really love about you, Junior." Senior Chief Daryl Becker, also known as Harvard, spoke up, his deep voice dry with humor. "Your humility. It's rare to find such a trait in one so young."

"Permission to move?" Cowboy asked.

"Negative, Jones," Cat replied. "Wait for Harvard. Go in as a team."

Cowboy clicked an affirmative, keeping his infrared glasses glued to the embassy.

It wouldn't be long now until they went inside and got Melody Evans and the others out.

It happened so quickly, Melody wasn't sure where they came from or who they were.

One moment she was sitting in the corner, writing in her notebook, and the next she was lying on her stomach on the linoleum, having been thrown there none too gently by one of the robed men who'd appeared out of thin air.

She felt the barrel of a gun jammed into her throat, just under her jaw, as she tried to make sense of the voices.

"Silence!" she was ordered in more languages than she could keep track of. "Keep your mouths shut or we'll shut 'em for you!"

"Dammit," she heard someone say in very plain English, "the girl's not here. Cat, we've got three pieces of luggage, but none of them's female."

"If none of them's female, one of 'em's a tango. Search 'em and do it right."

English. Yes. They were definitely speaking American English. Still, with that gun in her neck, she didn't dare lift her head to look up at them.

"Lucky, Bobby and Wes," another voice commanded, "search the rest of this floor. Find that girl."

Melody felt rough hands on her body, moving across her shoulders and down her back, sweeping down her legs. She was being searched for a weapon, she realized. One of the hands reached up expertly to feel between her legs as another pushed its way up underneath her arm and around to her chest. She knew the exact instant that each hand encountered either more or less than their owner expected, because whomever those hands belonged to, he froze.

Then he flipped her onto her back, and Melody found herself staring up into the greenest eyes she'd ever seen in her life.

He pulled off her hat and touched her hair, then looked at the black shoe polish that had come off on his fingers. He looked down at the mustache she had made from some of her own cut hair darkened with mascara and glued underneath her nose. He smiled as he looked back into her eyes. It was a smile that lit his entire face and made his eyes sparkle.

"Melody." It was more of a statement than a question.

But she nodded anyway.

"Ma'am, I'm Ensign Harlan Jones of the U.S. Navy SEALs," he said in a soft Western drawl. "We've come to take you home." He looked up then, speaking to one of the other hooded men. "Cat, belay that last order. We've found our female hostage, safe and sound."

"Absolutely not." Kurt Matthews folded his arms across his narrow chest. "They said if any of us attempted an escape, they'd kill us all. They said if we did what we were told, and if the government complied with their modest list of demands, we'd be set free. I say we stay right here."

"There's no way we can get out of here undetected," the other man—Sterling—pointed out. "There's too many of them. They'll stop us and then they'll kill us. I think it's safer to do what they said."

Cowboy shifted impatiently in his seat. Negotiating with damn fools was not one of his strengths, yet Cat had left him here to try to talk some sense into these boneheads as the rest of the squad went to carry out the rest of their mission—the destruction of several extremely confidential files in the ambassador's personal office.

He knew that if worse came to worst, they'd knock 'em over the head if they had to and carry 'em out. But it would be a lot easier to move through the city, working their way toward the extraction point, *without* having to carry three unconscious bodies over their shoulders.

Not for the first time in the past twenty minutes, he found himself staring at Melody Evans.

He had to smile. And admire the hell out of her. There was no doubt in his mind that her quick thinking had saved her own life. She'd disguised herself as a man. She'd cut her long hair short, blackened it with shoe polish to hide its golden color and glued some kind of straggly-looking mustache thing onto her face.

Even with her hair shorn so close to her head and that ridiculous piece of hair stuck underneath her nose, she was pretty. He couldn't imagine that he'd looked at her when they'd first come in and not seen right away that she was a woman. But he hadn't. He'd thrown her onto the floor, for God's sake. And then he'd groped her, searching for hidden weapons.

She glanced at him as if feeling his eyes on her, and he felt it again—that flash of sexual awareness that jolted to life between them. He held her gaze, boldly letting his smile grow wider, letting her take a good long look at this mutual attraction that hovered in the very air around them.

That photo he'd seen had made her look like someone's little sister. But meeting Melody Evans face-to-face made him well aware—and grateful—of the fact that while she may indeed have been someone's little sister, she sure as hell wasn't *his*.

With the exception of the silly mustache, she possessed damn near everything he liked most in a woman. She was tall and slender with a body that he knew firsthand was trim in some places, soft in others. Her face was pretty despite her lack of makeup and the smudges of shoe polish that decorated her forehead and cheeks and hid the shining gold of her hair. She had a small nose, a mouth that looked incredibly soft and crystal blue eyes surrounded by thick, dark lashes. Clear intelligence shone in those eyes. Tears had shown there, too, moments after he'd introduced himself to her. But despite that, she hadn't let herself cry, much to Cowboy's relief.

As he watched, she rubbed her left shoulder, and he knew whatever pain she was experiencing was his fault. That shoulder was where she'd landed when he'd first come in and thrown her onto the floor.

"I'm sorry we had to treat you so roughly, ma'am," he said. "But in our line of work, it doesn't pay to be polite and ask questions first."

"Of course," she murmured, glancing almost shyly at him. "I understand—"

Matthews drowned her out. "Well, *I* don't understand, and you can be damned sure your superiors are going to hear about this little incident. Holding the ambassador's staff at gunpoint and subjecting us to a body search!"

Cowboy didn't get a chance to defend Alpha Squad's actions because Melody Evans stood up and defended them for him. "These men came into this embassy looking for *us*," she said hotly. "They're risking their lives to be here right now—the same way they risked their lives when they opened that locked door and came into this room. They had no idea who or what was on the other side of that door!"

"Surely they could've seen just from looking that we were Americans," Matthews countered.

"Surely there's never been a terrorist who dresses up as a hostage and hides with his captives, waiting to blow away any rescuers," she lit into him. "And of course there's *never* been an American who's been brainwashed or coerced or bribed into defecting to the other side!"

For the first time since they'd let the hostages up off the floor, Kurt Matthews was silent.

Cowboy had to smile. He liked smart women—women who didn't suffer fools. And this one was more than smart. She was strong and clearly courageous, too—able to stand up and defend that which she believed in. He admired the swift action she took to disguise herself in the face of sheer disaster. Surely a woman with that much fight in her could be made to see how important it was that she leave here—and leave soon.

"Melody," he said, then corrected himself. "Miss Evans, it's now or never, ma'am. These tangos aren't gonna let you go, and you know that as well as I do. If you let these gee—*gentlemen,* talk you into staying here, you're all as good as dead. Forgive me for being so blunt, ma'am, but that's the God's truth. It would make *our* job a whole hell of a lot easier if you would simply trust us to get you safely home."

"But Chris is right. There's only a few of you and so many of them."

Count on a woman to play devil's advocate and switch sides

just when he was convinced he had a solid ally. Still, when she fixed those baby blues on him, his exasperation dissolved into sheer admiration. It was true, the odds didn't appear to be in their favor. She had every right to be concerned, and it was up to him to convince her otherwise.

"We're Navy SEALs, ma'am," he said quietly, hoping she'd heard of the special forces teams, hoping word of SEAL Team Ten's counterterrorist training had somehow made its way to whatever small town she'd grown up in.

But his words didn't spark any recognition in her eyes.

The taller man, Chris Sterling, shook his head. "You say that as if it's some kind of answer, but I don't know what that means."

"It means they think they're supermen," Matthews said scornfully.

"Will you *please* let Ensign Jones talk?" Melody said sharply, and Matthews fell silent.

"It means that even with only seven of us and fifty of them, the odds are still on *our* side," Cowboy told them, once again capturing Melody's gaze and holding it tightly. *She* was the one who was going to talk these other idiots into seeing reason. "It also means that the U.S. government has totally given up all hope of getting you out through negotiation or settlement. They don't send us in, Melody," he said, talking directly to her, "unless they're desperate."

She was scared. He could see that in her eyes. He didn't blame her. There was a part of him that was scared, too. Over the past few years, he'd learned to use that fear to hone his senses, to keep him alert and giving a full hundred and fifty percent or more. He'd also learned to hide his fear. Confidence bred confidence, and he tried to give her a solid dose of that feeling as he smiled reassuringly into Melody's ocean blue eyes.

"Trust us," he said again. "Trust *me*."

She turned back to the other hostages. "I believe him," she said bluntly. "I'm going."

Matthews stood up, indignant, menacing. "You stupid bitch. Don't you get it? If you try to escape, they'll kill *us!*"

"Then you better come, too," Melody said coolly.

"No!" His voice got louder. "No, we're staying here, right, Sterling? *All* of us. These steroid-pumped sea lions or whatever they call themselves can go ahead and get themselves killed, but we're staying right here." His voice got even louder. "In fact, since Mr. Jones seems to want so badly to die, I can give him a hand and shout for the guards to come and turn him into hamburger meat with their machine guns *right now!*"

Melody didn't see the broad-shouldered SEAL move, let alone raise his hand, but before she could blink, he was rather gently lowering Kurt Matthews onto the floor.

"By the way, it's *Ensign* Jones," he said to the now unconscious man. He flexed the fingers of the hand he'd used to put Matthews into that state and flashed an apologetic smile in Melody's direction before he looked up at Chris Sterling. "How about you?" he asked the other man as he straightened up to his full height. "You want to walk out of this embassy, or do you want to get carried out like your buddy here?"

"Walk," Sterling managed to say, staring down at Matthews. "I'll walk, thanks."

The door swung silently open, and a big black man—taller even than Ensign Harlan Jones—stepped into the room. Harvard. He was the one Ensign Jones had called Harvard. "You ready, Junior?"

"Zeppo, Harpo and Groucho here need robes," Jones told the other man, sending a quick wink in her direction. "And sandals."

Groucho. She fingered her false mustache. He'd gestured toward Matthews when he'd said Harpo. Harpo. The silent Marx brother. Melody laughed aloud. Chris Sterling looked at her as if she was crazy to laugh when at any moment they could be killed, but Jones gave her another wink and a smile.

Kevin Costner. *That's* who Jones looked like. He looked like a bigger, beefier, much younger version of the Hollywood heartthrob. And she had no doubt he knew it, too. That smile could melt hearts as well as bolster failing courage.

"Melody, I'm afraid I'm going to have to ask you to take off those kicks, hon."

Hon. Honey. Well, she'd certainly gone from being called Miss Evans and ma'am to hon awfully fast. And as far as taking off her shoes... "These are new," she told him. "And warm. I'd rather wear them, if you don't mind."

"I *do* mind," Jones told her apologetically. "Check out the bottoms of my sandals, then look at the bottoms of those things you're wearing."

She did. The brand name of the athletic shoes was emblazoned across the bottoms, worked into the grooved and patterned-to-grip soles of the sneakers.

"Everyone else in this city—and maybe even in this entire country—has sandals like mine," he continued, lifting his foot to show her the smooth leather sole. "If you go out wearing *those*, every time you take a step you'll leave a unique footprint. It will be the equivalent of signing your name in the dirt. And *that* will be like leaving a sign pointing in our direction that says Escaped American Hostages, Thisaway."

Melody took off the sneakers.

"That's my girl," he said, approval and something else warming his voice. He squeezed her shoulder briefly as he turned his attention to several more men who were coming silently into the room.

That's my girl.

His soft words should have made her object and object strenuously. Melody *wasn't* a girl. Jones couldn't have been more than a few years older than she was at most, and he would never have let anyone call him a *boy*.

And yet there was something oddly comforting about his words. She *was* his girl. Her life was totally in his hands. With his help, she could get out of here and return to the safety of Appleton. Without his help, she was as good as dead.

Still, she couldn't help but notice that little bit of something else that she'd heard in his voice. That subtle tone that told her he was a man and she was a woman and he wasn't ever going to forget that.

She watched Ensign Jones as he spoke quietly to the other SEALs. He certainly was a piece of work. She couldn't believe those smiles he kept giving her. Here they were, deep inside an embassy overrun with terrorists, and Jones had been firing off his very best bedroom smile in her direction. He was as relaxed as a man leaning against a bar, offering to buy her a drink, asking for her sign. But this wasn't a bar, this was a war zone. Still, Jones looked and acted as if he were having fun.

Who *was* this guy? He was either very stupid, very brave or totally insane.

Totally insane, she decided, watching him as he took a bundle of robes from another of the SEALs. Underneath his own robe, he wore some kind of dark-colored vest that appeared to be loaded with all kinds of gear and weaponry. He had what looked to be a lightweight, nearly invisible set of headphones on his head, as well as an attached microphone similar to, but smaller than, something a telephone operator would wear. It stretched out on a hinged piece of wire or plastic and could be maneuvered directly in front of his mouth when he needed to talk.

What kind of man did this kind of thing for a living?

Jones tossed one of the robes to Chris Sterling and the other to her, along with another of those smiles.

It was hard to keep from smiling back.

As Melody watched, Jones spoke to someone outside the room through his little mike and headphones as he efficiently and quickly dressed the still-unconscious Kurt Matthews in the third robe.

He was talking about sandals. Sandals, apparently, were a bit harder to procure than the robes had been. At least it was difficult to find something in her size.

"She's going to have to go in her socks," one of the other SEALs finally concluded.

"It's cold out there," Jones protested.

"I don't care," Melody said. "I just want to *go.*"

"Let's do it," the black man said. "Let's move, Cowboy. Cat controls the back door. Now's the time."

Jones turned to Melody. "Put the kicks back on. Quickly."

"But you said—"

He pushed her down into a chair and began putting the sneakers on her feet himself. "Lucky, got your duct tape?"

"You know I do."

"Tape the bottom of her foot," Jones ordered, thrusting the tied shoe on Melody's right foot toward the other SEAL.

The SEAL called Lucky got to work, and Jones himself began taping the bottom of her left sneaker, using a roll of silvery gray duct tape he, too, had been carrying in his vest.

They were covering the tread, making sure that when she walked, she wouldn't leave an unusual footprint behind.

"It might be slippery." Jones was kneeling in front of her, her foot on his thigh, as if he were some kind of fantasy shoe salesman. "And we're going to have to make sure that if you wear it through, we tape 'em up again, okay?"

Melody nodded.

He smiled. "Good girl." He moved his mike so that it was in front of his mouth. "Okay, Cat, we're all set. We're coming out." He turned to Melody. "You're with me, okay? Whatever happens, stick close to me. Do exactly what I say, no questions. Just do it, understand?"

Melody nodded again. She was his girl. She couldn't think of anything else she wanted to be right at that particular moment in time.

"If shots are fired," he continued, and for once his face was serious, his eyes lit with intensity rather than amusement or attraction, "get behind me. I will protect you. In return, I need two hundred percent of your trust."

Melody couldn't tear her gaze away from those neon green eyes. She nodded.

Maybe this man was insane, but he was also incredibly brave. He'd come into this terrorist stronghold to help rescue her. He'd been safe and sound, but he chose to give that up and risk his life for hers. *I will protect you.* As bold and as confident as his words were, the truth was that the next few minutes could see them both killed.

"In case something goes wrong," she began, intending to thank him. God knows if something went wrong, she wouldn't have the chance to thank him. She knew without a doubt that he would die first—taking bullets meant for her.

But he didn't let her finish. ''Nothing's gonna go wrong. Joe Cat's got the door. Getting out of this latrine's gonna be a piece of cake. Trust me, Mel.''

He took her hand, pulling her with him out into the hall.

Piece of cake.

She almost believed him.

Chapter 2

Something was wrong.

Melody could tell from the seriousness with which the man Ensign Jones called Joe Cat was talking to the shorter, blond-haired man named Blue.

They'd made it safely out of the embassy just as Jones had promised. They'd come farther than she'd ever thought possible. They'd traveled across and outside the limits of the city, up into the hills, moving quietly through the darkness.

The danger had not ended when they left the embassy. The city was under military rule, and there was a predusk curfew that was strictly enforced. If they were spotted by one of the squads patrolling the streets, they would be shot without any questions.

More than once, they'd had to hide as a patrol came within inches of them.

"Close your eyes," Jones had murmured into her ear as the soldiers had approached. "Don't look at them. And don't hold your breath. Breathe shallowly, softly. They *won't* see us, I promise."

Melody's shoulder had been pressed against him, and she

leaned even closer, taking strength from his solid warmth. And from the thought that if she died, at least she wouldn't die alone.

After that, each time they had to hide, he'd slipped one arm around her, keeping his other arm free for his deadly-looking assault weapon. Melody had given up her pretense of being strong and independent. She'd let him hold her—let him be big and strong, let herself take comfort from his strength. She'd tucked her head underneath his chin, closing her eyes and listening to the steady beating of his heart kick into overdrive, breathing softly and shallowly as he'd told her.

So far they hadn't been caught.

Jones came and sat next to her now.

"We've got a problem," he said bluntly, not trying to hide the truth from her.

Her trust in him went up to just over a thousand percent. He wasn't trying to pretend everything was hunky-dory when it so obviously was not.

"The chopper's a no-show," he told her. In the moonlight, his expression was serious, his mouth grim instead of curling up into his usual smile. "They're ten minutes late. We're getting ready to split up. We can't keep moving together. Come daybreak, a group this size is going to get noticed. And it won't be long before the tangos realize you and Pete and Linc got away."

Pete and Linc. The men who made up two-thirds of the Mod Squad. Even at his most serious, this man couldn't resist making a joke of sorts. "Ten minutes isn't that long," Melody countered. "Shouldn't we just wait?"

Jones shook his head. "*One* minute isn't that long. Ten is too long. The chopper's not coming, Mel. Something went wrong, and our waiting here is putting us in danger." He lifted one of her feet, looking at the bottom of her sneaker. "How's that duct tape holding up?"

"It's starting to wear through," Melody admitted.

He handed her his roll of tape. "Can you put on another layer yourself? We need to be ready to leave here in about three minutes, but right now I want to put in my two cents about our next move."

Melody took the tape from him as he stood up.

Split up. He'd said they were going to split up. Melody felt a sudden rush of panic. "Jones," she called softly, and he paused, looking back at her. "Please. I want to stay with you."

She couldn't see his eyes in the shadows, but she saw him nod.

Dawn was beginning to light the eastern sky before they stopped moving.

Harvard had the point and he'd traveled twice as far as Cowboy and Melody had during the night. He'd continuously moved ahead, silently scouting out the best route to take, then doubling back to report what he'd seen.

Cowboy was glad to have H. on his team. Moving through hostile territory would've been tricky enough for two SEALs on their own. Add a female civilian into the equation, and that mission got significantly harder. Getting across the border was going to be a real pain in the butt.

He glanced at Melody. The small smile she gave him both worried and elated him.

It was obvious she trusted him. He hadn't been the only one in Alpha Squad to hear her say that she wanted to stay with him. Under normal circumstances, such an overheard remark would've been subject to merciless teasing. Cowboy Jones, notorious lady-killer, strikes again.

But every one of those other men knew that the lady's words only verified that Cowboy had done his job and done it well. It wasn't easy to gain the complete confidence and trust of a former hostage. Kurt Matthews, for instance, hadn't bonded to Cowboy in quite the same way.

Still, the girl trusted him. He saw it in her eyes every time he looked at her. He knew without a doubt that in the course of a few short hours, he had become the most important person in her world.

He'd spent quite a bit of time studying the psychology of hostages and the emotions and fears involved in a rescue mission such as this one. He'd spent twice as much time learning what to expect from himself—his own behavior and psychological reactions when faced with life-and-death situations.

And what worried him most about Melody Evans's smile was not the fact that he'd become the center of her universe. No, what worried him most was that she had somehow managed to become the center of *his*.

He knew it could happen. The danger added to the tremendous responsibility of preserving another's life and multiplied by a very natural and honest sexual attraction sometimes resulted in an emotional response above and beyond the norm.

He'd first been aware of his inappropriate response to this girl when they'd hidden from the city's patrols. She'd huddled close and he'd put his arm around her—nothing wrong with that. She'd rested her head against his chest—and there was nothing wrong with her drawing strength and support from him that way, either.

But then, beneath the pungent odor of the shoe polish she wore on her hair, beneath the more subtle yet no less sharp odor of fear that surrounded all of the former hostages, he'd smelled something sweet, something distinctly female.

And then, right then, when the curfew patrol was inches away from them, when they were nanoseconds away from being discovered and killed, he'd felt Melody relax. The tension among the other hostages and the SEALs could've been cut with a knife, but Melody had damn near fallen asleep in his arms.

He knew in that instant that she trusted him more completely than anyone had ever trusted him before. Her faith in him was strong enough to conquer her fear. Her life was in his hands, and she'd placed it there willingly, trusting that if she died it would be because there was no other way out.

And just like that, as they hid behind trash in one of the city's back alleys, Cowboy's entire life changed. He felt his pulse rate accelerate out of control, felt his body respond to her nearness.

He might've been able to dismiss it as mere sexual desire except that it happened over and over again—even when she wasn't touching him. All this girl had to do was smile at him, and he got that same hot, possessive rush.

Cowboy knew he should have mentioned the way he was feeling to Joe Cat before they split into three smaller groups. But he didn't. He didn't want to risk Cat's pulling him away from Melody. He wanted to make damn sure she got out of this armpit of a country alive. As much as he trusted his teammates, he knew the only way he'd be certain of that was to stay close, to take care of her himself.

With Harvard's help.

As the sun climbed above the horizon, they sat for a moment in the growing warmth outside a shallow cave Harvard had found cut into a desolate outcropping of rocks.

Once they warmed up, they'd spend the daylight hours here, out of the sun and out of sight of anyone wandering the foothills. Come nightfall, they would set out again, heading steadily north.

"I'll take the first watch," Cowboy told Harvard.

Melody was sitting next to him, near the entrance to the cave, her head back, eyes closed, face lifted toward the warmth of the sun. He touched her arm lightly, ready to pass her his canteen, but she didn't move. She was exhausted, but she hadn't complained once, all night long.

"Maybe you should get her settled first," Harvard said in a low voice.

"Am I suddenly not here?" Melody asked, opening her eyes and surprising them both.

Harvard laughed, a low, rich chuckle. "Sorry," he said. "I thought you were asleep."

"Where are we heading?" she asked. Her eyes were nearly the same shade of blue as the cloudless sky. "Up to the coast?" They flashed in Cowboy's direction as he handed her the canteen.

As their fingers touched, he felt an instant connection, a flood of electricity. And he knew damn well she felt it, too.

She was covered with dust from the road, smeared with shoe polish and utterly bone weary. Yet at the same time, she managed to be the most beautiful woman Cowboy could ever remember seeing. Damn, he shouldn't be feeling this way. After this was over, he would have to go in for a psychological review, work with the unit shrink and try to pinpoint what it was, exactly, that he'd done wrong. Find out when it was that he'd let her get under his skin...

Harvard nodded. "We're going for the ocean." He glanced at Cowboy. They hadn't had much time to discuss their route. "I thought it would be easier to leave the country by boat."

"Or plane, Senior Chief," Cowboy interjected. "Get us home a whole hell of a lot faster."

Harvard caught and held his gaze, and Cowboy knew the older man was thinking the same thing he was. They'd both studied a map of this country during the briefing. There was a major city directly between their current position and the ocean. According to the map, that city had an airfield. Maybe instead of skirting the city, they should get close enough to check out that airfield.

"With any luck, it'll be a military base," Cowboy said aloud. "We're the last people they'll be expecting to show up there."

Harvard nodded. "The best defense is a strong offense."

"Do you two always communicate through non sequiturs?" Melody asked.

Harvard stood up. "Junior thinks we should steal a plane tonight, and crazy as it sounds, I agree. But right now I've got a combat nap scheduled." He paused before going into the cave, turning back to Melody. "You've got dibs on whatever soft ground is in there, milady," he said.

But she shook her head. "Thanks, but...I want to get warm first," she told him. She glanced at Cowboy and a faint blush spread along her cheeks as if she realized how transparent she was. No one was fooled. It was clear she wanted to be out here with her own personal hero.

Cowboy felt it again. That hot rush of emotion.

Harvard paused just inside the cave. "Don't let her fall asleep out here," he instructed Cowboy. "And make sure you get your Texan butt in the shade before too long, too. I don't want you two pigment-challenged types unable to move come dusk because of a sunburn."

"Yes, Mother," Cowboy droned.

"And wake me in four." Harvard headed toward the back of the cave. "No more, no less."

Cowboy looked at Melody and smiled. "Hell, I thought he'd *never* leave."

She blushed again.

"You okay?" he asked, both wishing she wasn't sitting quite so far away and glad as hell for the distance between them. God help him if he actually got her into his arms when it *wasn't* a life-and-death situation.

"I wish I could wash my face," she told him.

Cowboy shook his head in apology. "We've got to save the water I've got for drinking," he told her.

"I know," she said. "I just wish it, that's all."

The sun was warming the air considerably, and Cowboy loosened his robe and even unfastened the black combat vest he wore underneath.

Her next words surprised him. "I thought we'd be dead by now."

"Tomorrow at this time, we'll be on America-friendly soil."

She shifted her legs and winced slightly, then pulled her feet closer to untie her sneakers. "You say that with such conviction."

"Have I been wrong yet?" he countered.

She looked up at him, and her eyes were so wide, Cowboy felt as if he might fall into them and drown. "No," she said.

She turned away from him then, looking down as she started to slip off her sneakers.

That was when Cowboy saw the blood on her socks. The entire backs of her socks were stained. She saw it, too, and stopped trying to take off her sneakers. She pulled her feet underneath her as if she intended to hide the blood from him.

"Are you really from Texas?" she asked.

Cowboy was shocked. She was. She was planning to not tell him that her new sneakers had rubbed her heels raw. She wasn't going to mention that her feet were *bleeding,* for God's sake. Every step she'd taken last night had to have been sheer agony, but she hadn't said a word.

"Yeah," he managed to say. "Fort Worth."

She smiled. "You're kidding. How did someone from Fort Worth end up in the navy?"

Cowboy looked her squarely in the eye. "I know that your feet are bleeding," he said bluntly. "Why the hell didn't you tell me about that, like twelve *hours* ago?" His voice came out sounding harsher, sharper than he'd intended.

And although her smile faded and her face went a shade paler, she lifted her chin and met his gaze just as steadily. "Because it wasn't important."

"I have a medical kit. I could have wrapped 'em. All you had to do was say something!"

"I didn't want to slow us down," she said quietly.

Cowboy took his medikit from his combat vest as he stood up. "Are you going to take those sneakers off, or do you want me to do it for you?"

As he knelt in front of Melody, he could see her pain reflected in her face as she silently slid her feet out of her sneakers. Her eyes welled with tears, but she fought them, blinking them back, once again refusing to cry.

Her knuckles were white, hands clasped tightly in her lap, as he pulled off one sock and then the other as gently as he could.

"Actually," he said quietly, hoping to distract her with his words, "I didn't move to Fort Worth until I was about twelve. Before that, I lived damn near everywhere in the world. My old man's career Navy, and wherever he was stationed, that's where we lived."

She had extremely nice feet—long and slender, with straight toes. She had remnants of green polish on her toenails, as if she'd tried hastily to remove it but hadn't gotten it all off. He liked the idea of green nail polish. It was different. Intriguing.

Sexy.

Cowboy pulled his attention back to the task at hand. He rested her feet on his thigh as he opened his canteen and used some of their precious water to clean off the blood. He felt her stiffen as he touched her, and his stomach twisted as he tried his best to be gentle.

"He just made full admiral," he continued, telling her about his father. "He's stationed up in D.C. these days. But Mom still lives in Fort Worth, which just about says it all, considering that Fort Worth is about as landlocked a city as you can get.''

He gave her a quick smile to offset the depressing undertones of his story. Yeah, his home life had sucked. His father had been by-the-book Navy. The old man was a perfectionist—harsh and demanding and cold. He'd run his family the same way he'd commanded his ships, which, to both his young son and his wife, left much to be desired.

''So what made *you* join the Navy?'' she asked, bracing herself for the antibiotic ointment he was about to spread on her raw and broken skin.

''Actually, the old guy manipulated me into it,'' Cowboy told her with a grin, applying the ointment as quickly as he could. ''You don't make admiral without having *some* kind of smarts, and old Harlan the first is nobody's fool.''

He wiped the ointment off his hands on the bottom edge of his robe, then dug in his kit for bandages. ''After I graduated from high school, my old man wanted me to go to college and then into the U.S. Navy's officer's program. I flipped him the bird and set off for my own glowing future—which I was sure I'd find on the rodeo circuit. I spent about a year doing that—during which time the old man squirmed with embarrassment. Even in retrospect, that makes it damn well worth it.''

He smiled up into Melody's eyes. ''He started sending me letters, telling me about the problems he was having with 'those blasted Navy SEALs.' I knew when he was much younger, before I was born, he'd gotten into the BUD/S program and went through the training to become a SEAL. But he was one of the eighty-five percent who couldn't cut it. He was flushed out of the program—he wasn't tough enough. So every time he wrote to me, I could see that he was carrying around this great big grudge against the SEAL units.''

''So you joined the SEALs to tick him off,'' Melody guessed.

Cowboy nodded, his grin widening. ''And to show him that I could do something better than him—to succeed where he'd failed.'' He chuckled. ''The crafty old son of a bitch broke down and cried tears of joy and pride the day I got my budweiser—my

SEAL pin. I was floored—I'd rarely seen the old guy smile, let alone weep. Turns out that by joining the SEALs, I'd put myself exactly where he wanted me to be. He didn't hate the SEAL units the way he'd let me believe. He admired and respected them— and he wanted me to know what it felt like to achieve my potential, to be one of 'em. Turns out dear old Dad loved me after all.''

She was looking at him as if he was some kind of hero. ''You're amazing,'' she said softly. ''For you to realize all that and come to terms with him that way...''

''One of my specialties is psychology,'' he told her with a shrug. ''It's really not that big a deal.''

All he had to do was to lean forward and he could kiss those soft, sweet lips. She wouldn't object. In fact, he could tell from the sudden spark of heat in her eyes that she would welcome the sensation of his mouth on hers.

Instead, he looked away, bandaging her feet in silence. Yes, one of his specialties was psychology, and he knew exactly the kind of problems even just one kiss could cause. But maybe, just maybe, after he'd brought her to safety...

''You should get some sleep,'' he told her quietly.

Melody glanced toward the cave. ''Can I stay here, up near the entrance?''

Near him.

Cowboy nodded. ''Sure,'' he said quietly, moving out of the sun and back into the shade himself. He found a fairly flat, fairly comfortable rock to lean against as he stretched his legs out in front of him, his HK MP5-K held loosely in his arms.

He kept his eyes on the distant horizon as she wrapped herself in her robe and settled down, right on the ground, not far from him. He wished he had a bedroll or a blanket to give her. Hell, he wished he had dinner reservations at some fancy restaurant and the room key to some four-star hotel to give her. He wished he could fall with her back onto some soft hotel bed and...

He pushed that thought far, far away. This wasn't the time or place for such distractions.

It wasn't long before the sound of her breathing turned slow and steady. He glanced at her and his heart clenched.

In sleep, she looked barely more than seventeen, her lashes long and dark against the smoothness of her cheeks. It didn't take much to imagine what she'd look like with that black shoe polish washed out of her hair. The boyishly short cut she'd given herself to hide her femaleness only served to emphasize her slender neck and pretty face.

Cowboy knew with a grim certainty that seemed to flow through him and out into the timeless antiquity of the moonlike landscape that he was going to bring this girl back home where she belonged. Or he was going to die trying.

Melody was sleeping on her side, curled into a ball with the exception of one arm that was stretched out and reaching toward him. And as he looked closer, he saw that in her tightly clasped fist she was holding on to the very edge of his robe.

"Shouldn't he be back by now?"

Melody heard the anxiety in her voice, saw a reflection of it in the darkly patient eyes of the man Jones called Harvard.

"I'm sorry," she murmured.

"Junior's doing his job, Melody," Harvard told her calmly. "This is something he does well—you're going to have to trust him to do it and return in his own good time."

The *this* that Ensign Jones was doing was to creep undetected into a terrorist-held air base. It was only a small air base, he'd told her as if that would reassure her, with only a dozen aircraft of any type out on the field. He was going over the barbed-wire fence to make sure that the dilapidated hangars didn't hold some fancy high-tech machine that could come roaring up into the sky and shoot them down as they made their getaway.

After Jones had checked out the hangar, he was going to sneak out into the airfield and select the biggest, fastest, most powerful plane of all to use for their escape. And after he did that, he was going to meet them here.

Then all three of them would go back over the fence and roar off in a stolen plane into the coming sunrise.

After he came back. *If* he came back.

"You call him Junior," she said, desperate for *some*thing to talk about besides Jones's whereabouts. "But that other man, Joe Cat, he called Ensign Jones *kid*. And everyone else called him Cowboy. Doesn't *any*one call him Harlan?"

Harvard smiled. His straight white teeth flashed, reflecting a beam of moonlight that streamed in through one of the cracks in the boarded-up windows. "His mom does. But that's about it. He *hates* being called Harlan. I only call him that when I want to make him *really* mad. It's his father's name, too. His father is Admiral Harlan Jones."

"I know. He told me."

Harvard lifted his eyebrows. "No kidding. Told you about his old man. I'm surprised, but...I guess I shouldn't be—Junior's always been full of surprises." He paused. "I worked closely with the senior Jones quite a few years ago. I know the admiral quite well. I guess that's why I call his son Junior *Junior*."

"And the other men call him Cowboy because he's from Texas?"

"Legend has it he came to BUD/S wearing an enormous rodeo ring and a cowboy hat." Harvard laughed softly.

"BUD/S," Melody repeated. "That's where SEALs go for training?"

"Not necessarily where, but what," he corrected her. "It's the training program for SEAL wanna-be's. Junior walked into this particular session out in California wearing everything but a pair of spurs, and the instructors took one look at him and named him Cowboy. The nickname stuck."

Melody wished he would come back.

She closed her eyes, remembering the way Jones had gently awakened her as the sun was starting to set. He'd given her a sip of water from his canteen and some kind of high-protein energy bar from a pocket of his vest.

He'd also given her his sandals.

He must've spent most of the time he'd been on watch cutting down the soles and reworking the leather straps to fit her much smaller feet. At first she refused them, but he'd pointed out that they wouldn't fit him now anyway.

Jones was barefoot at this very moment. Barefoot and somewhere on that air base with God only knows how many terrorists—

"Where are you from, Miss Melody Evans?" Harvard's rich voice interrupted her grim thoughts.

"Massachusetts," she told him.

"Oh yeah? Me, too. Where exactly?"

"Appleton. It's west of Boston. West and a little north."

"I grew up in Hingham," Harvard told her. "South shore. My family's still there." He smiled. "Actually, there's not much of my family left. Everyone's gone off to college, with the exception of my littlest sister. And even she heads out this September."

"I don't even know your real name," Melody admitted.

"Becker," he told her. "Senior Chief Daryl Becker."

"Did you really go to Harvard?"

He nodded. "Yes, I did. How about you? Where'd you go to school?"

Melody shook her head. "This isn't working. I know you're trying to distract me, but I'm sorry, it's just not working."

Harvard's brown eyes were sympathetic. "You want me to be quiet?"

"I want Jones to come back."

Silence. It surrounded her, suffocated her, made her want to jump out of her skin.

"Please don't stop talking," she finally blurted.

"First time I worked with the junior Harlan Jones was during a hostage rescue," Harvard told her, "back, oh, I don't know, about six years ago."

Melody nearly choked. "You've been doing this sort of thing for six *years?*"

"More than that."

She gazed into his eyes searchingly, looking for an explanation. *Why?* "Risking your life for a living this way is *not* normal."

Harvard laughed. "Well, none of us ever claimed to be that."

"Are you married?" she asked. "How does your wife stand it?"

"I'm not," he told her. "But some of the guys are. Joe Cat is. And Blue McCoy."

"They're somewhere out in the countryside tonight, hiding from the terrorists, the way we are," she realized. "Their wives must *love* that."

"Their wives don't know where they are."

Melody snorted. "Even better."

"It takes a strong man to become a SEAL," Harvard told her quietly. "And it takes an even stronger woman to love that man."

Love. Who said anything about *love?*

"Does SEAL stand for something, or is it just supposed to be cute?" she asked, trying to get the subject back to safer ground.

"It stands for Sea, Air and Land. We learn to operate effectively in all of those environments." He laughed. "Cute's not a word that comes to mind when *I* think about the SEAL units."

"Sea, air and land," she repeated. "It sounds kind of like the military equivalent of a triathlon."

Harvard's head went up and he held out a hand, motioning for her to be silent.

In a matter of an instant, he had changed from a man casually sitting in the basement entrance of a burned-out building to a warrior, every cell in his body on alert, every muscle tensed to fight. He held his gun aimed at the door, raising it slightly as the door was pushed open and...

It was Jones.

Melody forced herself not to move toward him. She forced herself to sit precisely where she was, forced herself not to say a word. But she couldn't keep her relief from showing in her eyes.

"Let's move," he said to Harvard.

There was blood on his robe—even Harvard noticed it. "Are you all right?" he asked.

Jones nodded dismissively. "I'm fine. Let's do it. Let's get the hell out of here."

Melody didn't want to think about whose blood that was on

his robe. She didn't want to think about what he'd been through, what he'd had to do tonight to guarantee her safety.

There was blood on his bare feet, too.

"Are we going to do this by stealth or by force?" Harvard asked.

"By stealth," Jones answered. His smile was long gone. "Unless they see us. Then we'll use force. And we'll send 'em straight to hell."

He looked directly at her, and in the moonlight his eyes looked tired and old. "Come on, Melody. I want to take you home."

They were halfway to the plane before they were spotted.

Cowboy knew it was really only a question of when—not if— they were seen. It had to happen sooner or later. There was no way they could take a plane from an airfield without *some*one noticing.

He'd just hoped they wouldn't be noticed until they were taxi-ing down the runway.

But nothing else had gone right tonight, starting with his sur-prising four terrorists in the hangar. He'd had *some* luck, though—only one of them had had an automatic weapon, and it had jammed. If it hadn't, he wouldn't be running toward the plane now. He wouldn't be doing much of anything. Instead, he was racing across the sun-cracked concrete. He was both pulling Mel-ody Evans along and trying to shield her with his body from the bullets he knew were sure to accompany the distant cries to halt.

He'd dispatched the four men in the hangar efficiently and si-lently. As a SEAL, he was good at many things, and taking out the enemy was something he never shied from. But he didn't like it. He'd never liked it.

"You want to clue me in as to where we're going?" Harvard shouted.

"Twelve o'clock," Cowboy responded. And then there it was—a tiny Cessna, a mere mosquito compared to the bigger planes on the field.

Harvard's voice went up an octave. "Junior, what the *hell...?*

I thought you were going to swipe us the biggest, meanest, fastest—''

"Did you want to take the 727?" Cowboy asked as he grabbed for the handle of the door, swung it open and gave Melody a boost inside. "It was this or the 727, and *I* sure as hell didn't want to be a sitting duck out on the runway, waiting for those jet engines to warm up."

He'd run the checklist when he'd been out here earlier, so he merely pulled the blocks and started the engine. "This way, I figured we'd be a smaller target in the air, too, in case the tangos want to give their antiaircraft toys a test run."

But Harvard wasn't listening. He was standing, legs spread, feet braced against the ground, firing his AK-47 in a sweeping pattern, keeping the wolves at bay.

"Do you know how to fly a plane?" Melody shouted over the din.

"Between me and H., there's nothing we can't pilot." Cowboy reached back behind him, pushing her head down as a bullet broke the back window. "Stay down!"

He gunned the engine, using the flaps to swing the plane in a tight, quick circle so that the passenger door was within Harvard's grasp.

He took off before H. even had the door fully open, let alone had climbed in. They headed down toward the edge of the field at a speed much too fast to make the necessary U-turn to get onto the main runway.

"I assume you've got another plan in mind," Harvard said, fastening his seat belt. He was a stickler for things like personal safety. It seemed almost absurd. Forty men were shooting at them, and H. was making sure his seat belt was on correctly.

"We're not using the runway," Cowboy shouted, pushing the engine harder, faster. "We're going to take off...right...*now!*"

He pulled back the stick and the engine screamed as they climbed at an impossibly steep angle to avoid hitting the rooftops of nearby buildings.

Cowboy heard Harvard shout, and then, by God, they were up. They were in the air.

He couldn't contain his own whoops of excitement and success. "Melody, honey, I *told* you we were going to get you home!"

Melody cautiously raised her head. "Can I sit up now?"

"No, it's not over yet." Harvard was much too grim as he looked over his shoulder, back at the rapidly disappearing airfield. "They're going to send someone after us—try to force us down."

"No, they're not," Cowboy said, turning to grin at him. God, for the first time in hours, he could smile again.

They were flying without lights, heading due east. This godforsaken country was so tiny that at this rate of speed, with the wind behind them, they'd be in friendly airspace in a matter of minutes. It was true they'd covered a great deal of the distance last night. But this was by far the easiest way of crossing the border.

"Aren't we flying awfully low?" Melody asked.

"We're underneath their radar," Cowboy told her. "As soon as we're across the border, I'll bring 'er up to a higher altitude."

Harvard was still watching their six, waiting for another plane to appear behind them. "I don't know how you can be so convinced they're not going to follow, Jones."

"I *am* convinced," Cowboy told him. "What do you think took me so long earlier tonight? I didn't stop for a sandwich in the food commissary, that's for damn sure."

Harvard's eyes narrowed. "Did you...?"

"I did."

Harvard started to laugh.

"What?" Melody asked. "What did you do?"

"How many were there?" Harvard asked.

Cowboy grinned. "About a dozen. Including the 727."

Melody turned to Harvard. "What did he do?"

He swung around in his seat to face her. "Junior here disabled every other plane on that field. Including the 727. There are a whole bunch of grounded tangos down there right now, hopping mad."

Cowboy glanced back into the shadows, hoping to see her smile. But as far as he could tell, her expression was serious, her eyes subdued.

"We are crossing the border," Harvard announced. "Boys and girls, it looks as if we are nearly home!"

Ensign Harlan Cowboy Junior Kid Jones landed the little airplane much more smoothly and easily than he'd taken off.

Melody could see the array of ambulances and Red Cross trucks zooming out across the runways to meet them in the early dawn light. Within moments, they would taxi to a stop and climb out of the plane.

She wanted four tall glasses of water, no ice, lined up in front of her so that she could drink her fill without stopping. She wanted a shower in a hotel with room service. She wanted the fresh linens and soft pillows of a king-size bed. She wanted clean clothes and a hairdresser to make some sense out of the ragged near scalping she'd given herself.

But before she had any of that, she wanted to hold Harlan Jones in her arms. She wanted to hold him tightly, to thank him with the silence of her embrace for all that he had done for her.

He'd done so much for her. He'd given her so much. His kindness. His comforting arms. His morale-bolstering smiles. His encouraging words. His sandals.

And oh yeah. He'd killed for her, to keep her safe, to deliver her to freedom.

She'd seen the blood on his robe, seen the look in his eyes, on his face. He'd run into trouble out alone on the air base and he'd been forced to take enemy lives. And the key word there was not *enemy*. It was *lives*.

Melody was long familiar with the expression "All's fair in love and war." And this *was* a war. The legal government had been overthrown and the country had been invaded by terrorist forces. They'd threatened American lives. She knew full well that it was a clear-cut case of "them" or "us."

What shook her up the most was that this was what Cowboy Jones did. This was what he *did,* day in, day out. He'd done it for the past six years and he'd continue to do it until he retired. Or was killed.

Melody thought about that blood on Jones's robe, thought about the fact that it just as easily could have been his own blood.

All was fair in love and war.

But what were the rules if you were unlucky enough to fall in love with a warrior?

Jones cut the engine, then pushed the door open with his bare feet. But instead of climbing out, he turned around to face Melody, giving her his hand for support as she moved up through the cramped cabin and toward the door.

He slid down out of the plane, then looked up at her.

He'd taken off his blood-streaked robe, but he still wore that black vest with its array of velcroed pockets. It hung open over a black T-shirt that only barely disguised his sweat and grime. His face was streaked with dirt and dust, his hair matted against his head. There was shoe polish underneath his chin and on his neck—from where she'd burrowed against him, stealing strength and comfort from his arms.

But despite his fatigue, his eyes were as green as ever. He smiled at her. "Do I look as...ready for a bath as you do?"

She had to smile. "Tactfully put. Yes, you certainly do. And as for me—I think I'm more than ready to be a blonde again and wash this stuff out of my hair."

"But before you do, maybe I could send my shoes over to your hotel room for a touch-up...?"

Melody laughed. Until she looked down at his feet. They were still bare. They looked red and sore.

"You and Harvard saved my life," she whispered, her smile fading.

"I don't know about H.," Jones told her, gazing up into her eyes, "but as far as I'm concerned, Miss Evans, it was purely my pleasure."

Melody had to look away. His eyes were hypnotizing. If she didn't look away, she'd do something stupid like leap into his arms and kiss him. She glanced out at the line of cars approaching them. Was it possible that Jones had cut the engine and stopped the plane so far away from the terminal in order to let them have these few moments of privacy?

He reached for her, taking her hands to help her down from the plane.

"What's going to happen next?" she asked.

He pulled just a little too hard, and she fell forward, directly into his arms. He held her close, pressing her against his wide chest, and she held him just as tightly, encircling his waist with her arms and holding on as if she weren't ever going to let go. His arms engulfed her, and she could feel him rest his cheek against the top of her head.

"Jones, will I see you again?" she asked. She needed to know. "Or will they take you away to be debriefed and then send you back to wherever it was you came from?"

She lifted her head to look up at him. The trucks were skidding to a stop. She was going to have to get into one of those trucks, and they would take her someplace, away from Harlan Jones, maybe forever....

Her heart was pounding so hard she could barely hear herself think. She could feel his heart, too, beating at an accelerated rate.

"I'll tell you what's going to happen," he said, gazing into her eyes unsmilingly. "Second thing that's going to happen is that they're going to put you in one ambulance and me and H. in another. They'll take us to the hospital, make sure we're all right. Then we'll go into a short debriefing—probably separately. After that's done, you'll be taken to whatever hotel they're keeping the top brass in these days, and I'll go into a more detailed debriefing. After we both get cleaned up, I'll meet you back at the hotel for dinner—how's that sound?"

Melody nodded. That sounded very good.

"But the first thing that's going to happen," he told her, his mouth curving up into that now familiar smile, "is this."

He lowered his head and kissed her.

It was an amazing kiss, a powerful kiss, a no-holds-barred kind of kiss. It amplified all of the heat she'd seen in Harlan Jones's bedroom eyes over the past forty-eight hours. God, had it only been forty-eight hours? She felt as if she'd known this man for at least a lifetime. She felt, too, as if she'd wanted him for every single second of that time.

He kissed her even harder, deeper, sweeping his tongue into her mouth. It was a kiss that was filled with a promise of ecstasy, of lovemaking the likes of which she'd never known. The entire earth dropped out from under her feet, and she clung to him, giddy and dizzy and happier than she'd ever been in her entire life, returning his kisses with equal abandon. He wanted her. This incredible man honestly, truly *wanted* her.

His lips were warm, his mouth almost hot. He tasted sweet, like one of those energy bars he'd shared with her. Melody realized that she was laughing, and when she pulled back to look at him, he was smiling, too.

And then, just as he'd said, she was tugged gently away from him toward one of the ambulances as he was led toward another.

He kept watching her, though, and she held his gaze right up until the moment that she was helped into the back of the emergency vehicle. But before she went in, she glanced at him one last time. He was still watching her, still smiling. And he mouthed a single word. "Tonight."

Melody couldn't wait.

Chapter 3

Seven months later

Melody couldn't wait.

She had to get home, and she had to get home *now*.

She looked both ways, then ran the red light at the intersection of Route 119 and Hollow Road. But even then, she knew she wasn't going to make that last mile and a half up Potter's Field Road.

Melody pulled over to the side and lost her lunch on the shoulder of the road, about half a mile south of the Webers' mailbox.

This wasn't supposed to be happening anymore. She was supposed to be done with this part of it. The next few months were supposed to be filled with glowing skin and a renewed sense of peace, and yeah, okay, maybe an occasional backache or twinge of a sciatic nerve.

The morning sickness was supposed to have stopped four months ago. Morning sickness. Hah! She didn't have morning sickness—she had every-single-moment-of-the-day sickness.

She pulled herself back into her car and, after only stalling twice, slowly drove the rest of the way home. When she got there, she almost didn't pull into the driveway. She almost turned around and headed back toward town.

There was a Glenzen Bros. truck parked out in front of the house. And Harry Glenzen—one of the original Glenzen brothers' great-great-grandsons—was there with Barney Kingman. Together the two men were affixing a large piece of plywood to the dining-room window. Or rather to the frame of what *used* to be the dining-room window.

Melody had to push her seat all the way back to maneuver her girth out from behind the steering wheel.

From inside the house, she could hear the unmistakable roar of the vacuum cleaner. Andy Marshall, she thought. Had to be. Brittany was going to be mad as a hornet.

"Hiya, Mel," Harry called cheerfully. "How about this heat wave we're having, huh? We've got a real Indian summer this year. If it keeps up, the kids'll be able to go trick-or-treating without their jackets on."

"Hey, Harry." Melody tried not to sound unenthusiastic, but this heat was killing her. She'd suffered all the way through July and August and the first part of September. But it was October now, and October in New England was supposed to be filled with crisp autumn days. There was nothing about today that could be called even remotely crisp.

She dragged herself up the front steps of the enormous Victorian house both she and her sister had grown up in. Melody had moved back in after college, intending to live rent free for a year until she decided what she wanted to do with her life, where she wanted to go. But then her mom had met a man. A very nice man. A very nice, *wealthy* man. Before Melody could even blink, her mother had remarried, packed up her things and moved to Florida, leaving Mel to take care of the sale of the house.

It wasn't long after that that Brittany filed for divorce. After nearly ten years of marriage, she and her husband, Quentin, had called it quits and Britt moved in with Melody.

Melody never did get around to putting the house on the market. And Mom didn't mind. She was happier than Melody had ever seen her, returning to the Northeast for a month each summer and inviting her two daughters down to Sarasota each winter.

They were just two sisters, living together. Melody could imagine them in their nineties, still living in the same house, the old Evans girls, still unmarried, eccentric as hell, the stuff of which town legends were made.

But soon there would be three of them living together in this big old house, breaking with that particular tradition. The baby was due just in time for Christmas. Maybe by then the temperature would have finally dropped below eighty degrees.

Melody opened the front door. As she lugged her briefcase into the house, she heard the vacuum cleaner shut off.

"Mel, is that you?"

"It's me." Melody looked longingly toward the stairs that led to her bedroom. All she wanted to do was lie down. Instead, she took a deep breath and headed for the kitchen. "What happened?"

"Andy Marshall happened, *that's* what happened," Britt fumed, coming into the cheery yellow room through the door that connected to the dining room. "The little juvenile delinquent threw a baseball through the dining-room window. We have to special order the replacement glass because the damn thing's not standard-sized. The little creep claimed the ball slipped out of his hand. He says it was an accident."

Mel set her briefcase on the kitchen table and sank into one of the chairs. "Maybe it was."

Britt gave her such a dark look, Melody had to laugh. "It's not funny," Brittany said. "Ever since the Romanellas took that kid in, it's been chaos. Andy Marshall has a great big Behavior Problem, capital *B,* capital *P.*"

"Even kids with behavior problems have accidents," Melody pointed out mildly, resting her forehead in the palm of her hand. God, she was tired.

Her sister's eyes softened. "Oh, hell. Another bad day?"

Melody nodded. "The entire town is getting used to seeing my car pulled over to the side of the road. Nobody stops to see if I'm okay anymore. It's just, 'Oh, there's Melody Evans hurling

again.' Honk, honk, 'Hey, Mel!' and then they're gone. I feel like
a victim of the boy-who-cried-wolf syndrome. One of these days,
I'm going to be pulled to the side of the road in hard labor, giving
birth to this baby, and no one's going to stop to help me.''

Brittany took a glass down from the cabinet, filling it with a
mixture of soda water and ginger ale. ''Push those fluids. Replace
what you've lost,'' she said, Andy Marshall finally forgotten. ''In
this weather, your number-one goal should be to keep yourself
from becoming dehydrated.''

Melody took the glass her sister was pressing on her. Her stomach was still rolling and queasy, so she only took a small sip
before she set it down on the table. ''Why don't you go upstairs
and change out of your nurse's uniform before you forget you're
not at work any longer and try to give me a sponge bath or
something?'' she suggested.

Britt didn't smile at her pitiful attempt at a joke. ''Only if *you*
promise to lie down and let me take care of dinner.'' Melody's
sister had to be the only person in the world who could make an
offer to cook dinner sound like a dire threat.

''I will,'' Melody promised, pushing herself out of the chair.
''And thank you. I just want to check the answering machine. I
ordered the latest Robert Parker book from the library and Mrs.
B. thought it might be back in today. I want to see if she called.''
She started toward the den.

''My, my, you *do* have quite a wild and crazy lifestyle. Spending Friday night at home with a book again. Honestly, Mel, it's
something of a miracle that you managed to get pregnant in the
first place.''

Mel pretended not to have heard that comment as she approached the answering machine. There were only two messages,
but one of them was a long one. She sat down as the tape took
forever to rewind.

*…it's something of a miracle that you managed to get pregnant
in the first place…something of a miracle…*

She leaned her head back and closed her eyes, remembering
the look in Harlan Jones's eyes as she'd met him at the door to
her hotel room.

Cleaned up and wearing a naval dress uniform, he'd looked like a stranger. His shoulders were broader than she remembered. He seemed taller and harder and thoroughly, impossibly, devastatingly handsome.

She'd felt geeky and plain, dressed in too conservative clothes from the American shop in the hotel. And at the same time, she felt underdressed. The store had had nothing in her bra size except for something in that old-fashioned, cross-your-heart, body-armor style her grandmother used to wear, so she'd opted to go without. Suddenly, the silky fabric of the dress felt much too thin.

At least her hair was blond again, but she'd cut it much too short in her attempt to disguise herself. It would take weeks before she looked like anything other than a punk-rock time traveler from the early 1980s.

"I ordered room service," she'd told him shyly. "I hope you don't mind if we stay in...."

It was the boldest thing she'd ever done. But Jones's smile and the rush of heat in his eyes left no room for doubt. She'd done the right thing.

He'd locked the door behind him and pulled her into his arms and kissed her and kissed her and *kissed* her....

"Hi, Melody, this is Mrs. Beatrice from the Appleton Public Library," said the cheery voice on the tape, interrupting Melody's thoughts. "The book you requested is here. We've got quite a waiting list for this one, so if you aren't interested any longer, please give me a call! Hope you're feeling better, dear. I heard the heat's due to break in a day or two. I know when I was carrying Tommy, my eldest boy, I simply could not handle any temperature higher than seventy-two. Tom Senior actually went out and bought an air conditioner for me! You might want to think about something like that. If you want, I could send both Toms over to help you girls install it. Call me! Bye now!"

Girls. Sheesh.

That's my girl.

With determination, Melody pushed that thought out of her head.

The machine beeped, and a different voice, a male voice with the slightest of drawls, began to talk.

"Yeah, hi, I hope this is the right number. I'm looking for Melody Evans...?"

Melody sat forward. Dear God, it couldn't be, could it? But she knew exactly who it was. This was one voice she was never going to forget. Ever. Not until the day she died.

"This is Lt. Harlan Jones, and Mel, if you're listening, I, uh, I've been thinking about you. I'm going to be stationed here on the East Coast, in Virginia, for a couple of months, and um...well, it's not that far from Boston. I mean, it's closer than California and it's a *whole* hell of a lot closer than the Middle East and..."

On the tape, he cleared his throat. Melody realized she was sitting on the edge of her seat, eager for his every word.

"I know you said what you said before you got on the plane for Boston back in March, but..." He laughed, then swore softly, and she could almost see him rolling his eyes. "Hell, as long as I'm groveling, I might as well be honest about it. Bottom line, honey—I think about you all the time, *all* the time, and I want to see you again. Please call me back." He left a number, repeating it twice, and then hung up.

The answering machine beeped and then was silent.

"Oh. My. God."

Melody looked up to see Brittany standing in the doorway.

"Is this guy trying to win some kind of title as Mr. Romantic, or what?" her sister continued. "He is totally to die for, Mel. That cute little cowboy accent—where's he from anyway?"

"Texas," Melody said faintly. Lieutenant. He'd called himself Lt. Harlan Jones. He'd gotten a promotion, been awarded a higher rank.

"That's right. Texas. You told me that." Britt sat down across from her. "Mel, he wants to see you again. This is *so* great!"

"This is *not* so great!" Melody countered. "I can't see him— are you kidding? God, Britt, he'll take one look at me and..."

Brittany was looking at her as if she'd just confessed to murdering the neighbors and burying them in their basement. "Oh, Melody, you didn't—"

"He'll know," Melody finished more softly.

"You didn't tell him you're pregnant?"

Mel shook her head. "No."

"You didn't tell him you're having his baby—that he's fathered your child?"

"What was I supposed to do? Write him a postcard? And where was I supposed to send it? Until he called, I didn't even know where he was!" Until he called, she didn't even know if he was still alive. But he was. He was still alive....

"Melody, that was a very, very, *very* bad thing to do," Brittany said as if she were five years old again and had broken their mother's favorite lamp by playing ball in the house. "A man has a right to know he's *knocked up* his girlfriend!"

"I'm not his girlfriend. I never was his girlfriend."

"Sweetie, you're having this man's baby. You may not have been his girlfriend, but you weren't exactly strangers!"

Melody closed her eyes. No, they were anything but strangers. They'd spent three days in that hotel room in that Middle Eastern city whose name she couldn't pronounce, and another three days in Paris. In the course of those six amazing days, they'd made love more times than she could count—including once in the miniature bathroom on board the commercial flight that had taken them north to France.

That was her doing. She'd wanted him so badly, she couldn't bear to wait until they touched down and took a taxi to their hotel. The plane was nearly empty—she'd thought no one would notice if they weren't in their seats for just a little while.

So she'd lured Jones to the back of the plane and pulled him into the tiny bathroom with her.

After three days, she had learned enough of his secrets to drive him wild with just a touch. And Jones—he could light her on fire with no more than a single look. It wasn't long before the temperature in that little room skyrocketed out of control.

But Jones didn't have a condom. He'd packed his supply in his luggage. And she didn't have one, either....

Making love that way was not the smartest thing either of them had ever done.

Brittany went to the answering machine and rewound the message, playing it again and writing down the phone number he left. "What does he mean by 'I know you said what you said before you got on the plane for Boston....'? What's he talking about?"

Melody stood up. "He's talking about a *private* conversation we had before I came home."

Brittany followed her out of the room. "He's implying that *you* were the one who broke off whatever it was you had going."

Melody started up the stairs. "Britt, what I said to him is not your business."

"I always just assumed that he dumped you, you know. 'So long, babe, it's been fun. Time for me to go rescue some other chick who's being held hostage.'"

Melody turned and faced her sister, looking down at her from her elevated position on the stairs. "He's not that type of man," she said fiercely.

She could practically see the wheels turning in Brittany's head. "Now you're defending him. Very interesting. Fess up, Sis. Were you the one who dumped him? Jeez, I never thought you'd turn out to be the love-'em-and-leave-'em type."

"I'm not!" Melody started up the stairs again, exhaling noisily in frustration. "Look, nobody dumped *any*one, all right? It was just a...fling! God, Britt, it wasn't real—we hardly even knew each other. It was just...sex, and lust, and *relief.* A whole *lot* of very passionate relief. The man saved my life."

"So naturally you decide to bear his child."

Melody went into her bedroom and turned to shut the door, but Brittany blocked her.

"That's what you told him before you got on the plane home, isn't it? That crap about sex and lust and passionate relief? You told him you didn't want to see him again, didn't you?"

Mel gave up and sat down wearily on her bed. "It's not crap. It's true."

"What if you're wrong? What if this man is your missing half, your one true love?"

She shook her head vehemently. "He's *not.*" God, over the

past seven months, she'd asked herself the same question. What if...?

It was true that she missed her Navy SEAL. She missed him more than she was willing to admit. There were nights that she ached for his touch, that she would have died for a glimpse of his smile. And those amazing green eyes of his haunted her dreams.

But what she felt wasn't love. It *wasn't*.

Brittany sat next to her on the bed. "As much as you talk about passionate relief, sweetie, I just don't see you as the type to lock yourself in a hotel room with any man for six solid days unless he means something special to you."

Melody sank back against her pillows. "Yeah, well, you haven't met Harlan Jones."

"I'd *like* to meet Harlan Jones. Everything you've told me about him makes him sound like some kind of superman."

"There you go," Melody said triumphantly, sitting back up again. "That's my point exactly. He's some kind of superhero. And I'm just a mere mortal. What I felt for him wasn't love. It was hero worship. Jones saved my life. I've never met anyone like him before—I probably never will again. He was amazing. He could do *any*thing. Pilot a plane. Bandage my feet. Cut his sandals down to fit me yet make them look like new. He spoke four different languages, *four!* He knew how to scuba dive and skydive and move through the center of an enemy compound without being seen. He was smarter and braver and—God!—*sexier* than any man I've ever known, Britt. You're right, he *is* a superman, and I couldn't resist him—not for one day, not for six days. If he hadn't been called back to the States, I would've stayed with him for *sixteen* days. But that has nothing to do with real love. That was hero worship. I couldn't resist Harlan Jones any more than Lois Lane could resist Superman—and *that's* one relationship that could never be called healthy, or normal, either."

Brittany was silent.

"I still think it's wrong not to tell him about the baby," she finally said, setting the paper with Jones's phone number on Melody's bedside table. She stood up and crossed the room, pausing with her hand on the doorknob. "Call him and tell him the truth. He deserves to know."

Brittany left the room, closing the door behind her.

Melody closed her eyes. Call Jones.

The sound of his voice on her answering machine had sparked all sorts of memories.

Like finding the bandage he wore under his shirt on the back of his arm. They had been in her hotel room and she had been in the process of ridding him of that crisp white dress uniform, trailing her lips across every piece of skin she exposed. She'd pushed his jacket and then his shirt over his shoulders and down his arms, and there it was—big and white and gauze and covering a "little" gash he'd had stitched up at the hospital that morning.

When she pressed, he told her he'd been slashed with a knife, fighting off the men he'd surprised in the hangar at the air base.

He'd been *stabbed*, and he hadn't bothered to mention it to either Harvard or Melody. He'd simply bandaged the wound himself, right then and there, and forgotten about it.

When she asked to see it, he'd lifted the gauze and shown her the stitches with a shrug and a smile. It was no big deal.

Except the "little" gash was four *inches* long. It was angry and inflamed—which also was no big deal to Jones, since the doctor had given him antibiotics. He'd be fine in a matter of days. Hours.

He'd pulled her back on top of him, claiming her mouth with a gentleness astonishing for a man so strong, intertwining their legs as he took a turn ridding her of more of *her* clothes.

And it was then Melody knew for dead certain their love affair was not going to be long-term.

Because there was no way this incredible man—for whom rescuing strangers deep inside a terrorist stronghold and getting sliced open in a knife fight was all in a casual day's work—would ever remain interested in someone like drab little Melody Evans for long.

He would be far better off with a woman reminiscent of Mata Hari. Someone who would scuba dive and parasail with him. Someone strong and mysterious and daring.

And Melody would be better off with an everyday, average guy. Someone who would never *forget* to mention it when he was slashed by a knife. Someone whose idea of excitement was mowing the lawn and watching the Sunday afternoon football game on TV.

She curled up on her side on her bed, staring at the piece of paper that Brittany had left on her bedside table.

Still, she had to call him back.

If she didn't call him, he'd call here again, she was sure of it. And God help her if he spoke to Brittany and she let slip Melody's secret.

Taking a deep breath, Melody reached for the paper and the phone.

Cowboy was in Alpha Squad's makeshift office, trying to get some work done.

Seven desks—one for each member of the squad—had been set up haphazardly down at one end of an echoy metal Quonset hut. This hut was a temporary home base to work out the details of a training mission. Except this time, the members of Alpha Squad were the trainers, not the trainees. Within a few months, a group of elite FinCOM agents were being sent down from D.C. to learn as much as they could of SEAL Team Ten's successful counterterrorist operations.

They needed the desks, and the computers and equipment set up on top of them, to plan out their own little version of BUD/S training for these Finks.

Joe Catalanotto had pulled strings with his admiral pal, Mac Forrest, to make arrangements for Lt. Alan Francisco, one of the top BUD/S training instructors, to meet them out here in Virginia. Joe Cat was hoping Frisco would be able to organize the jumble of notes and training ideas the squad had come up with to date.

Frisco was a former member of Alpha Squad who had been pulled off the active duty list with a knee injury more than five years ago. Cowboy had been filling in for a missing member of the squad when Frisco had been injured. That had been Cowboy's first time in the field, his first time in a real war zone—and he'd been sure that it was going to be his last. Cowboy was certain that Joe Cat, the squad's commander, had seen his hands shaking as they set a bomb to blow a hole in the side of an embassy.

It had been another embassy rescue....

Melody Evans's wide blue eyes flashed into his head, but Cowboy gently pushed the image away. He'd been thinking about Mel too much lately, and right now he was writing up a summary of the information he was intending to share with the FinCOM agents. At Cat's request, he was in charge of presenting the psychological profile of a terrorist to the Finks. The key to success when dealing with terrorists lay in understanding their reasoning and motivation—how their minds worked. And with all of the cultural, environmental and religious differences, their minds worked very differently from the average white-bread American FinCOM agent.

Frisco was going to arrive Monday morning, and although it was only Friday, Cowboy was pushing to get his report finished today. After working nearly nonstop over the past seven months, he was hoping to take a few days of leave this weekend.

Mel's face popped into his thoughts again. He'd left a message on an answering machine he'd hoped was hers. Please, dear Lord, let her call him back.

Again he took a deep breath and focused his thoughts on his report. It was important to him that this summary be as complete as possible. Alan "Frisco" Francisco was going to be the man to read it, and Cowboy wanted to make the best impression he could.

Because when it was determined that Frisco's injury was permanent, Cowboy had been assigned to Alpha Squad at Joe Cat's request, as the man's replacement.

Cowboy still felt a little uncomfortable when Frisco was around. He knew the man missed being in the action, and here he was, his official replacement. And if Frisco hadn't been hurt, Cowboy probably wouldn't be working with the elite seven-member Alpha Squad. Cowboy had benefited from Frisco's tragedy, and both men damn well knew it. As a result, when they were together, they tippytoed around each other, acting especially polite. Cowboy was hoping that would change as the two men worked closely together over the next few months.

Right now, he appeared to be the only man in the room who was actually working. Blue McCoy and Harvard were checking out the Web site for Heckler and Koch, the German weapon manufacturer. Even Joe Catalanotto had his feet up on his desk as he talked on the phone with his wife, Veronica. Their son's first birthday was quickly approaching, but from what Cowboy couldn't help but overhear, it sounded as if Joe was more interested in planning a separate, very different, very *private* party for the parents of the birthday boy, to be held after all the guests had gone home and little Frankie Catalanotto was tucked into his crib.

The rest of the guys were sitting around the "office," trying to come up with ways to truly torment the poor Finks.

"We start the whole thing off with a twenty-five-mile run," Wesley was suggesting.

One desk over, Lucky O'Donlon was playing some kind of computer game complete with aliens and exploding starships and roaring sound effects.

"No, I read the rule book," Bobby countered loudly to be heard over the sound of the alien horde. "These guys—and gals—are going to be put up at the Marriott while they're here. I don't think they're going to let us run 'em for five miles, let alone twenty-five."

That got Lucky's attention. "FinCOM's sending *women* out here?"

"That's what I heard," Bobby said. "Just one or two out of the bunch of them."

Lucky smiled. "One or two is all we need. One for me and one for Cowboy. Oh, but wait. I almost forgot. Cowboy's sworn off women. He's decided to become a priest—or at least live like one. But then again, maybe a little one-on-one with a pretty young FinCOM agent is all he needs to get him back in the game."

Cowboy couldn't let that go. Lucky had been teasing him mercilessly about his current celibacy for months. "I don't criticize the way you live, O'Donlon," he said tightly. "I'd appreciate it if you'd show me the same courtesy."

"I'm just curious, Cowboy, that's all. What's going on? Did you honestly find God or something?" Lucky's eyes were dancing with mischief. He didn't realize that he'd pushed Cowboy to his limit. "I seem to remember a certain Middle Eastern country and a certain pretty little former hostage you seemed intent upon setting some kind of world record with. I mean, come on. It was kind of obvious what you were up to when you went to meet her for dinner and then didn't come back for six days." Lucky laughed. "She sure must've been one hell of a good—"

Cowboy stood up, his chair screeching across the concrete floor. "That's enough," he said hotly. "You say one more word about that girl and you're going to find the very next word you say is going to be said without any teeth."

Lucky stared at him. "God, Jones, you're serious! What the hell did this girl do to you?" But then he grinned, quick to turn anything and everything into a joke. "Do you think if I asked real nice, I could get her to do it to me, too?"

Cowboy was moments from launching himself at the blond-haired SEAL when Harvard stepped between them, holding up one hand, silently telling Cowboy to freeze.

The big man fixed Lucky with a steady, dangerous gaze. "You're nicknamed Lucky because with all the truly asinine things that come out of your mouth, you're lucky to still be alive, is that right, O'Donlon?"

Lucky wisely returned his attention to his computer game, glancing up at Cowboy with disbelief still glimmering in his eyes. "Sorry, Jones. Jeez."

Cowboy slowly sat back down, and as Joe Cat hung up the phone, a complete silence fell, broken only by the sounds of Lucky's computer game.

What the hell did this girl do to you?

Cowboy honestly didn't know.

Surely it was some kind of witchcraft. Some kind of enchantment or spell. It had been seven months, seven *months,* and he couldn't so much as glance at another woman without comparing her, unfavorably, to Melody Evans.

Melody. Shoot, she'd had his head spinning from the moment she'd opened her hotel-room door for him.

Her hair was so light, he'd nearly laughed aloud. He knew she was a blonde from her picture, but until he saw her, he really hadn't been able to imagine it. Cut short the way it was, it accentuated the delicate shape of her face and drew attention to her long, graceful neck.

She was gorgeous. She'd gotten hold of some makeup and wore just a trace of it on her eyes and a touch of lipstick on her sweet lips. It highlighted her natural beauty. And it told him without a doubt that she had anticipated and prepared for this dinner as much as he had.

She was wearing some kind of boxy, shapeless, too large dress that she must've had sent up from one of the hotel shops. On any other woman, it would've looked as if she was playing dress-up in her mother's clothes. But on Mel, it looked sexy. The neckline revealed her delicate collarbone, and the silky material managed to cling to her slender body, revealing every soft curve, every heart-stopping detail. Her legs were bare, and she wore the sandals he'd made for her on her feet.

Nail polish. She had pink nail polish on her toes. Probably hadn't been able to get any green.

He'd stood there in the doorway, just looking at her, knowing that despite all he'd silently told himself about the basis for the emotion behind hostage-and-rescuer relationships, he was lost. He was truly and desperately lost.

He'd wanted this woman more than he'd ever wanted anyone....

Wes's voice broke the silence. "You think they're gonna put *us* up in the Marriott, too?" the shortest member of Alpha Squad wondered aloud.

Bobby, Wes's swim buddy, built like a restaurant refrigerator, shook his head. "I didn't see anything about that in the FinCOM rule book."

"What FinCOM rule book?" Joe Cat's husky New York accent cut through the noise of exploding spacecraft. "Blue, you know anything about a *rule* book?"

"No, sir."

"This morning, FinCOM sent over something they're calling a rule book," Bobby told their commanding officer.

"Let me see it," Cat ordered. "O'Donlon, kill the volume on that damn thing."

The computer sounds disappeared as Bobby sifted through the piles of paper on his desk. He uncovered the carefully stapled booklet FinCOM had sent via courier and tossed the entire express envelope across the room to Cat. Cat caught it with one hand.

The phone rang and Wesley picked it up. "Alpha Squad Pizza. We deliver."

Catalanotto pulled out the booklet and the cover letter. He quickly skimmed the letter, then opened the booklet to the first page and did the same. Then he laughed—a snort of derision—and ripped both the book and the letter in half. He stuffed it back into the envelope and tossed it back to Bob.

"Send this back to Maryland with a letter that tells the good people of FinCOM no rule books. No rules. Sign my name and send it express."

"Yes, sir."

"Hey, Cowboy."

Cowboy looked up to see Wes holding up the telephone receiver, hand securely over the mouthpiece. "For you," Wesley said. "A lady. Someone named Melody Evans."

Suddenly, the room was so quiet, Cowboy could have heard a pin drop.

But then Harvard clapped his hands together. "Okay, coffee break," he announced loudly. "Everyone but Junior outside. Let's go. On the double."

Cowboy held the phone that Wes had handed him until the echo from the slamming door had faded away. Taking a deep breath, he put the receiver to his ear.

"Melody?"

He heard her laugh. It was a thin, shaky laugh, but he didn't care. Laughter was good, wasn't it? "Yeah, it's me," she said. "Congratulations on making lieutenant, Jones."

"Thanks," he said. "And thanks for calling me back. You

sound...great. How are you?" He closed his eyes tightly. Damn, he sounded like some kind of fool.

"Busy," she said without hesitation, as if it was something she'd planned to say if he asked. "I've been incredibly busy. I'm working full-time as an AA for the town attorney, Ted Shepherd. He's running for state representative, so it's been crazy lately."

"Look, Mel, I don't want to play games with you," he told her. "I mean, we've never been anything but honest with each other, and I know you said you didn't want to see me again, but I can't get you out of my head. I want to get together."

There. He'd said it.

He waited for her to say something, but there was only silence.

"I can get a weekend pass and be up in Massachusetts in five hours."

More silence. Then, "Jones, this weekend is really bad for me. The election's only a few weeks away and... It's not a good time."

Now the silence belonged to him.

He had two options here. He could either accept her excuses and hang up the phone, or he could beg.

He hadn't begged back in March. He hadn't dropped to his knees and pleaded with her to reconsider. He hadn't tried to convince her that everything she'd told him about their passion being false, about their relationship being based on the adrenaline rush of her rescue, was wrong.

He was a psych specialist. Everything she said made sense—everything but the incredible intensity of his feelings for her. If those feelings weren't real, he didn't know what real was.

But his pride had kept him from saying everything he should have said. Maybe if he'd said it then, she wouldn't have walked away.

So maybe he should beg. It wouldn't kill him to beg, would it? But if he was going to beg, it would have to be face-to-face. No way was he going to do it over the phone.

"Nothing's changed," Melody said softly. "Ours wasn't a relationship that could ever go anywhere."

I miss you, Mel. Cowboy closed his eyes, unable to say the words aloud.

"It was nice hearing your voice, though," Melody said.

She said she was busy this weekend. Maybe it wasn't just a transparent excuse. Maybe she *was* busy. But even busy people had to grab a sandwich for lunch. He'd take that weekend pass, head up to Boston, rent a car and drive out to Appleton.

And then, face-to-face, he'd get down on the ground and beg.

"Yeah," Cowboy said, "yeah—it was nice talking to you."

"I'm sorry, Jones," she said quietly, and the line was disconnected.

Cowboy slowly hung up the phone.

For all these months, he'd sat around, waiting to get over this girl. It was definitely time to stop waiting and take some action.

He saved his file on the computer, then set it up to print. As the laser printer started spewing out his psych summary, Cowboy pushed his chair back from his desk.

He left the Quonset hut and headed toward the barracks where the unmarried members of Alpha Squad were being housed. He would pack a quick bag, do the necessary paperwork for a weekend pass, then bum a ride to the air base.

As Cowboy pulled open the screen door, the inner door opened, too, and he nearly walked into Harvard. The older man took one look at the grim set to Cowboy's mouth, then sighed.

"No good, huh?" Harvard stepped back to let Cowboy into the spartanly decorated bunk room.

Cowboy shook his head. "Senior Chief, I need a weekend pass and information on flights heading north to Boston."

Harvard smiled. "Way to go, Junior. You pack your things, I'll handle the paperwork. Meet you by the gate in fifteen."

Cowboy forced a smile of his own. "Thanks, H."

First thing tomorrow, he'd be face-to-face with Melody Evans.

She didn't want to see him because she knew damn well that if she saw him, she wouldn't be able to resist the pull of the attraction that lingered between them. Face-to-face, she wouldn't be able to resist him any more than he could resist her.

And by this time tomorrow, he'd have her back in his arms.

And maybe, if he played his cards right, if he got humble and got down on his knees and begged, maybe then he'd have her back in his life for as long as it took for him to be satisfied—to get over her once and for all.

For the first time in a long time, Cowboy's smile actually felt real.

Chapter 4

Melody spotted him from across the town common and her heart nearly stopped.

The Romanellas' new foster kid, Andy Marshall, was fighting with two boys who had to be at least three years older and a foot and a half taller than he was.

The three kids were in the shadows of the trees at the edge of the town playground. As Melody watched, Andy was knocked almost playfully to the ground as the two older boys laughed. But the kid rolled into the fall like an accomplished stunt fighter and came up swinging. His fist connected with the nose of one of the other boys, sending the taller one staggering back.

Melody could hear the bellow of pain from inside her car. She heard the shouts change from taunting laughter to genuine anger, and she knew that Andy was on the verge of getting the spit kicked out of him.

She took a quick left onto Huntington Street and another left the wrong way into the Exit Only marked drive of the playground parking lot, leaning on her horn as she went.

"Hey!" she shouted out the car window. "You boys! Stop that! Stop fighting *right now!*"

One of the older boys—Alex Parks—savagely backhanded Andy with enough force to make Melody's own teeth rattle before he and his friend turned and ran.

As Melody scrambled to pull her girth from the front seat of her car, Andy tried to run, too, but he couldn't. He couldn't do better than to push himself up onto his hands and knees on the grass.

"Oh, Andy!" Melody crouched down next to him. "Oh, God! Are you all right?"

She reached for him, but he jerked away and she backed off.

His knees and elbows were raw, and his nose was bleeding pretty steadily. He had a scrape on his cheek underneath his left eye, and his lip was already swollen and split. His brown hair was messy and clotted with dirt and bits of grass, and his T-shirt was bloody and torn.

He'd had the wind knocked out of him and he struggled to regain his breath as tears of pain and humiliation filled his eyes.

"Go away," he growled. "Just leave me alone!"

"I can't do that," Melody told him evenly. "Because we're neighbors. And here in Appleton, neighbors look out for each other."

She sat down in the grass, crossing her legs tailor-style, fighting a familiar wave of nausea, thankful they were sitting in the shade.

He was checking the watch he wore on his skinny left wrist, examining the protective surface over the clock face and holding it to his ear to be sure it was still ticking.

"Did they break it?" Melody asked.

"What's it to you?" he sneered.

"Well, you seem more concerned with your watch than with the fact that you're bleeding, so I thought—"

"You're the unwed mother, right?"

Melody refused to acknowledge the tone of his voice. He was being purposely rude so that she wouldn't know he was on the verge of dissolving into tears. She ignored both the rudeness and the threatening tears. "In a nutshell, yeah, I guess I am. My name's Melody Evans. I live next door to the Romanellas. We met last week, when Vince and Kirsty brought you home with them.''

He sat down, still catching his breath. ''You know, they talk about you. They wonder exactly who knocked you up. Everyone in town talks about you all the time.''

''Except when they're talking about you,'' Melody pointed out. ''Between the two of us, we've got the gossips working full-time, haven't we? A foster child from the big, bad city who blows up lawn mowers. There's probably a betting pool guessing how long it'll be before the police become involved in your discipline.''

Her bluntly honest words surprised him, and he actually looked at her. For a brief moment, he actually met her eyes. His own were brown and angry—far too angry and bitter for a twelve-year-old. But then he looked away.

''The hell with them,'' he said harshly. ''I won't be here long anyway.''

Melody feigned surprise. ''Really? Vince told me you were going to be staying with him and Kirsty at least until next September—that's almost a year.'' She fished in her handbag for some tissues. She wished she had a can of ginger ale in her bag, too. She was trying to make friends with this kid, and God knows throwing up on him wouldn't win her big points.

''A year.'' Andy snorted. ''Yeah, right. I'll be gone in a month. Less. A week. That's all most people can take of me.''

She handed him a wad of tissues for his nose. ''Gee, maybe you should try a different brand of mouthwash.''

There was another flash of surprise in his eyes. ''You're a laugh riot,'' he said scornfully, expertly stemming the flow of blood. He seemed to be a pro at repairing the damage done him in fistfights.

''You're a sweet little bundle of charm and good cheer yourself, munchkin.''

He held her gaze insolently. He was James Dean and Marlon Brando rolled into one with his heavily lidded eyes and curled lip. He'd successfully concealed all of his pain and angry tears behind a "who cares?" facade. "I broke your window yester-day."

"I know." Melody could play the "who cares?" game, too. "Accidents happen."

"Your sister didn't think it was an accident."

"Brittany wasn't born with a lot of patience."

"She's a witch."

Melody had to laugh. "No, she's not. She's got something of a volatile temper, though."

He looked away. "Whatever."

"Volatile means hot. Quick to go off."

"Duh. I know *that*," he lied.

She handed him more tissues, wishing she could pull him into her arms and give him a hug. He was skinny for a twelve-year-old, just a narrow slip of a little boy. His injuries from the fight—and probably from the battles he'd been fighting all of his life—went far deeper than a split lip, a bloody nose and a few scrapes and scratches. Still, although he may have looked like a child, his attitude was pure jaded adolescent, and she gave him a smile instead.

"You're prettier than what's-her-name, the witch," he said, then snorted again. "But look what being prettier got you. Preggo."

"Actually, being careless got me...preggo. And to tell you the truth," Melody said seriously, "not using a condom could've gotten me far more than just pregnant. These days, you have to use a condom to protect yourself against AIDS. But I'm sure you already know that. Smart men never forget—not even for a min-ute."

Andy nodded, acting ultracool, as if sitting around and talking about condoms was something he did every day. It was clear he liked being spoken to as if he were an adult.

"What was the fight about?"

"They insulted me." He shrugged. "I jumped them."

"You jumped *them?* Andy, together those boys weigh four times more than you."

He bristled. "They insulted me. They were making up stories

about my mother, saying how she was a whore, turning tricks for a living, and she didn't even know who my father was—like I was some kind of lousy bastard.'' He glanced down at her belly. "Sorry."

"I know who the father of my baby is."

"Some soldier who saved your life."

Melody laughed. "Gee, you're up to speed on the town gossip after only a few days, aren't you?"

Another shrug. "I pay attention. My father's a soldier, too. He doesn't give a damn about me, either."

Doesn't give a damn. Melody closed her eyes, fighting another wave of nausea. She hadn't exactly given Harlan Jones a chance to give a damn, had she?

"So you gonna keep it or give it away?"

The baby. Andy was talking about the baby. "I'm going to keep it. Him." Melody forced a smile. "I think he's a boy. But I don't know for sure. I had an ultrasound, but I didn't want to know. Still, it just...*he* feels like a boy to me."

As if on cue, the baby began his familiar acrobatic routine, stretching and turning and kicking hard.

Melody laughed, pressing her hand against her taut belly and feeling the ripple of movement from both inside and out. It was an amazing miracle—she'd never get used to the joy of the sensation. It made her sour stomach and her dizziness fade far away.

"He's kicking," she told Andy. "Give me your hand—you've got to feel this."

Andy gave her a skeptical look.

"Come on," she urged him. "It feels *so* cool."

He wiped the palm of his hand on his grubby shorts before holding it out to her. She held it down on the bulge close to her belly button just as the baby did what felt like a complete somersault.

Andy pulled back his hand in alarm. "Whoa!" But then he hesitantly reached for her again, his eyes wide.

Melody covered his hand with hers, pressing it down once again on the playground-ball tightness of her protruding stomach.

Andy laughed, revealing crooked front teeth, one of which was endearingly chipped. ''It feels like there's some kind of alien inside of you!''

''Well, there sort of is,'' Melody said. ''I mean, think about it. There's a person inside of me. A human being.'' She smiled. ''A little, wonderful, *lovely* human being.'' And if she was lucky, that little human being would take after his mother. Her smile faded. If she was really lucky, she wouldn't have to spend the rest of her life gazing into emerald green eyes and remembering....

''Are you okay?'' Andy asked.

It was ironic, really. *He* was the one who looked as if he'd been hit by a train. Yet he was asking if *she* was all right. Underneath the tough-guy exterior, Andy Marshall was an okay kid.

''Yeah, I'm fine.'' Melody forced another smile. ''I just get dizzy and...kind of queasy sometimes.''

''You gonna barf?''

''No.'' Melody took a deep breath. ''Why don't we go get you cleaned up?'' she suggested. ''Maybe I should take you over to the hospital...?''

He pulled away, slipping instantly back into surly James Dean mode. ''No way.''

''You've got dirt ground into your knee.'' Melody tried to sound reasonable. ''It's got to be washed. All of your scrapes have to be washed. My sister's a nurse. She could—''

''Yeah, like I'd ever let the Wicked Witch of the West touch *me*.''

''Then let me take you home to Kirsty—''

''No!'' Beneath his suntan and the dirt, Andy's face had gone pale. ''I can't go there looking like this. Vince said...'' He turned abruptly away from her.

''He told you no more fighting,'' Melody guessed. Violence wasn't in her next-door neighbor's vocabulary.

''He said I got into another fight, I'd get it.'' Andy's chin went out as he pushed himself to his feet. ''No way am I gonna let him take his belt to me! Hell, I just won't go back!''

Melody laughed aloud. ''Vince? Take his belt to you?''

''I'm outta here,'' Andy said. ''It's not like anyone's gonna miss me, right?''

"Andy, Vince doesn't even *wear* a belt." Vince Romanella might've looked like the kind of guy who would react with one of his big, beefy fists rather than think things through, but in the three years he and his wife had been foster parents, he'd never raised a hand to a child. What Andy was going to "get" was a trip to his bedroom tonight, where he would sit alone, writing a five-page essay on nonviolent alternatives to fighting.

But before she could tell Andy that, he was gone, walking quickly across the field, trying his best to hide a limp.

"Andy, wait!"

She started after him. He glanced back at her and began to run.

"Shoot, Andy, wait for me!"

Melody broke into a waddling trot, supporting her stomach with her arms.

He had to stop at Main Street and wait for a break in the traffic before he could cross.

"Andy, Vince isn't going to *hit* you!"

But he didn't hear her. He darted across the road and started running down the street.

Melody picked up her own pace, feeling like one of the running dinosaurs in *Jurassic Park*. With each step she took, the sky should have rumbled and the earth should have shook.

"Andy! Wait! Somebody stop Andy Marshall—please!"

She was light-headed and dizzy and within nanoseconds of losing what little breakfast she'd forced down earlier this morning. But no one seemed to notice her calls of help. No one seemed to be paying one bit of attention to the gigantically pregnant woman chasing the twelve-year-old boy.

No one except the exceptionally tall, exceptionally broad-shouldered man on the corner. Sunlight gleamed off sun-streaked brown hair that was pulled back into a ponytail at the nape of his neck. He was dressed similarly to just about all the other Saturday-morning antique shoppers who crowded the quaint little stores that surrounded the common. He wore a muted green polo shirt and a pair of khaki Dockers that fit sinfully well.

Seemingly effortlessly, he reached out and grabbed Andy around the waist. He moved with the fluid grace of a trained warrior, and as he moved, Melody recognized him instantly. He didn't have to come any closer for Melody to know that his shirt accentuated the brilliant green of his eyes.

Lt. Harlan "Cowboy" Jones had come to Appleton to find her. Blackness pressed around Melody, taking out her peripheral vision and giving her the illusion of looking at Jones through a long, dark tunnel.

"Is this the kid you wanted, ma'am?" he called across the street to her, his voice carrying faintly over the roaring in her ears. He didn't realize he'd found her. He didn't recognize her new, extralarge, two-for-the-price-of-one size.

Melody felt nausea churning inside of her, felt dizziness swirling around her, and she did the only thing she could possibly do, given the circumstances.

She carefully lowered herself down onto the grass of the Appleton Common and fainted.

"What's wrong with you?" Cowboy scolded the squirming kid as he carried him across the street. "Making your mama chase after you like that."

"She's not my mother," the kid spit. "And you're not my father, so let go of me!"

Cowboy looked up and blinked. That was odd. The woman had been standing right behind the blue Honda sedan. She was blond and hugely, heavily pregnant, but somehow she had managed to vanish.

He took a few more steps and then he saw her. She was on the ground, on the grass behind the parked cars, lying on her side as if she'd stopped to take a nap, her long hair hanging like a curtain over her face.

The kid saw her, too, and stopped struggling. "God, is she dead?" His face twisted. "Oh, God, did I kill her?"

Cowboy let go of the kid and moved fast, kneeling next to the woman. He slid his hand underneath her hair and up to the softness of her neck, searching for a pulse. He found one, but it was going much too fast. "She's not dead."

The kid was no longer trying to run away. "Should I find a phone and call 911?"

Cowboy put his hand on the woman's abdomen, wondering if she was in labor, wondering if he'd even be able to feel her contractions if she was. He knew quite a bit about first aid—enough to qualify as a medic in most units. He knew the drill when it came to knife wounds, gunshot wounds and third-degree burns. But unconscious pregnant women were way out of his league. Still, he knew enough to recognize shock when he saw it. He brushed her hair out of her face to check her eyes, glancing up at the kid. "Is the hospital far away?"

"No, it's right here in town—just a few blocks north."

Cowboy looked back to check the woman's eyes, and for several long, timeless seconds, he couldn't move.

Dear, dear God, it was Melody. It was *Melody*. This immensely pregnant woman was *Melody*. *His* Melody. *His*...

He couldn't breathe, couldn't speak, could hardly even think. Melody. *Pregnant?*

The implication nearly knocked him over, but then his training kicked in. Keep going, keep moving. Don't analyze more than you have to. Don't think if it's gonna slow you down. Act. Act and react.

His rental car was on the corner of Main Street. "We can probably get her to the hospital faster ourselves." His voice sounded hoarse. It was a wonder he could speak at all. He handed his car keys to the kid with the split lip. "I'll carry Mel, you unlock the car door."

The kid stared at him as he lifted Melody up and into his arms. "You know her?"

A hell of a question, considering he'd gone and gotten her pregnant. "Yeah. I know her."

She roused slightly as he carried her down the street toward his car. "Jones...?"

"Yeah, honey, I'm here."

The kid dropped the keys twice but finally managed to get the passenger door open.

"Oh, God, you are, aren't you?" Melody closed her eyes as he affixed the seat belt around her girth.

Cowboy felt light-headed himself. She looked as if she were hiding a watermelon underneath her dress. And he'd done that to her. He'd sent his seed deep inside of her and now she was going to have his baby. And if he didn't hurry, she was going to have his baby in the front seat of this car.

"Hang on, Mel. I'm taking you to the hospital."

Cowboy turned around to order the kid into the back seat, but the kid was gone. He did a quick sweep of the area and spotted the boy at ten o'clock, running full speed across the common.

Melody had no doubt been chasing him for a reason, but no matter what that reason was, getting her to the hospital had to take priority.

The kid had left Cowboy's car keys on the front seat, thank God. Cowboy scooped them up as he slid behind the wheel, then started the engine with a roar.

Melody was *pregnant* and the baby had to be his. Didn't it? Had it truly been nine months since the hostage rescue at the embassy? He did a quick count but came up with only seven months. He must have counted wrong. He pushed all thoughts away as he searched the street for a familiar blue hospital sign. Don't think. Act. He'd have plenty of time to think after he was certain Mel was going to be okay.

The kid had been right—the hospital was nearby. Within moments, Cowboy pulled up to the emergency-room entrance.

He took the shortest route to the automatic ER doors—over the hood of the car—and helped the sliding doors open faster with his hands. "I need some help," he shouted into the empty corridor. "A wheelchair, a stretcher, *some*thing! I've got a lady about to have a baby here!"

The startled face of a nurse appeared, and Cowboy moved quickly back to the car, opening the door and lifting Melody into his arms. Even with the added weight of her pregnancy, she still felt impossibly light, improbably slender. She still felt so familiar. She still fit perfectly in his arms. God, how he'd missed her.

He was met at the door by a gray-haired nurse with a wheelchair who took one look at Mel and called out, "It's Melody Evans. Someone call Brittany down here, stat!"

"She's unconscious," Cowboy reported. "She's come out of it once but slipped back."

The nurse pushed the chair away. "She'd only fall out of this. Can you carry her?"

"Absolutely." He tossed his car keys to a security guard. "Move my car for me, will you, please?"

He followed the woman through a set of doors and into the emergency room where they were joined by another woman—this one a doctor.

"She's preregistered, but we will need your signature on a form before you go," the nurse told him as they moved briskly toward a hospital bed separated from a row of other beds by only a thin, sliding curtain.

"I'm not going anywhere," Cowboy said.

"Can you tell me when the contractions started?" the doctor asked. "How far apart they are?"

"I don't know," he admitted as he set Melody on the bed. "She was out cold when I found her. She must have just keeled over, right by the side of the road."

"Did she hit her head when she fell?" The doctor examined Melody quickly, lifting her eyelids, checking her eyes and feeling the back of her head for possible injury.

"I don't know," Cowboy said again, feeling a surge of frustration. "I didn't see her fall."

The nurse had already slipped a blood-pressure cuff on Mel's arm. She pumped it up and took a reading. "Blood pressure's fine. Pulse seems steady."

Melody looked so helpless lying there on that narrow bed. Her face was so pale. Her hair was so much longer than it had been in Paris. Of course, his hair was a lot longer, too.

It had been a long time since he'd seen her.

But it had only been seven months. Not nine.

Was it possible that she'd already been two months pregnant in Paris? He couldn't believe that. He *wouldn't* believe that. Of course the baby was his. She'd told him it had been close to a year since she'd broken up with her last serious boyfriend and...

Melody's eyelashes flickered.

"Well, hello," the doctor said to her. "Welcome back."

As Cowboy watched, Melody gazed up at the doctor, her brow wrinkled slightly with confusion. "Where am I?" she breathed.

"At County Hospital. Do you remember blacking out?"

Melody closed her eyes briefly. "I remember..." She opened them, sitting up suddenly, turning to look around the room until her gaze fell directly on Cowboy. "Oh, God. You're real."

"I'd say hi, how are you, but that's kind of obvious." Cowboy did his best to keep his voice low and even. She was in no condition to be yelled at—even if she damn well deserved it. "It looks as if you have some news you forgot to tell me yesterday when we spoke on the phone."

Her cheeks flushed, but she lifted her chin. "I'm pregnant."

He moved closer. "I noticed. When were you planning to tell me?"

She lowered her voice. "I thought you told me SEALs were trained never to assume anything. Yet here you are, assuming my condition has something to do with you."

"Are you telling me it doesn't?" He knew without a doubt that that baby was his. He couldn't imagine her with somebody else. The idea was ludicrous—and unbearable.

"How far apart are the contractions?" the doctor asked as the nurse gently pushed Melody back down on the hospital bed.

"Are you telling me it doesn't?" Cowboy said again, knowing he should just step back and give the doctor space but needing to know if Melody was actually going to look him in the eye and lie to him.

She looked from the doctor to Cowboy and back. "The... what?"

"Contractions." The doctor spoke slowly and clearly. "How far apart are they?"

"Sir, I'm going to have to ask you to wait outside," the nurse murmured to him.

"And, ma'am, I'm going to have to decline that request. I'm staying right here until I know for sure Melody's all right."

Melody was shaking her head. "But I'm not—"

"Mel, what happened?" Another nurse came bursting through the door. She didn't wait for an answer before turning to the doctor. "It's nearly two months too soon. Have you given her something to stop the contractions? How far is she dilated?"

"I'm not having—"

"I've given her nothing," the doctor reported calmly. "If she's having contractions, they're *very* far apart. I haven't even done a pelvic exam."

"Sir, her sister's here now. Please wait outside," the older nurse murmured, trying to push him gently toward the door.

Cowboy didn't budge. So this was Mel's sister. Of course. Mel had told him she was a nurse.

"I don't *need* a pelvic exam," Melody protested loudly. "I'm not having contractions at all. I was running after Andy Marshall and I got a little dizzy, that's all."

Her sister nearly jumped down her throat. "You were *running!*"

Melody sat up again, turning toward Cowboy. "You caught Andy for me. I saw you. Is he here?"

"No. I'm sorry. He ran away while I was getting you into my car."

"Shoot! *Shoot!*" Melody turned toward her sister. "Brittany, you've got to call the Romanellas for me. Andy's going to run away because he thinks Vince is going to take his belt to him for getting into another fight!"

But Brittany was looking at Cowboy, noticing him for the first time. Her eyes were a different shade of blue than Mel's. Her face was sharper, more angular, too, but it was clear the two women were closely related. "Who the hell are you?"

"That depends on the baby's due date," he answered.

"What?"

"He brought Melody in," the other nurse told her. "I've been trying to tell him—"

"Can we focus on *Melody* for a minute?" the doctor asked,

gently trying to push Melody back down onto the bed. "I'd like to do that pelvic anyway—make sure that fall didn't do anything it shouldn't have."

The gray-haired nurse was persistent. "Sir, now you *really* must wait outside."

Brittany was still looking at him, her eyes narrowed in speculation. "Her due date, huh?"

Melody sat up again. "If we don't hurry, Andy Marshall will be gone!"

"December 1st," Brittany told Cowboy. She looked him over more carefully, from the tips of his boots to the end of his ponytail. "My God, you're what's-his-name, the SEAL, aren't you?"

December 1st. That made more sense. Melody *wasn't* due now—she *wasn't* about to have the baby. With her slender frame and petite build she only *looked* as if she were going to pop any minute.

December... Cowboy quickly counted back nine months to... March. He'd been in the Middle East in March performing that hostage rescue. And after that, he'd spent six solid days in heaven.

He met Melody's eyes. She knew without a doubt that he'd done the easy math and put two and two together—or, more accurately, one and one. And in this case, one and one had very definitely made three.

"I'm Lt. Harlan Jones," he said, holding Melody's gaze, daring her to deny what he was about to say. "I'm the baby's father."

Jones was waiting for her in the hospital lounge.

Melody took a deep breath when she saw him, afraid that she might pass out again. She'd more than half expected him to be long gone.

Brittany tightened her grip on her arm. "Are you okay?" her sister whispered.

"I'm scared," Melody whispered back.

Britt nodded. "This isn't going to be easy for either of you. Are you sure you don't want me to stick around?"

Jones was standing by the windows, leaning against the frame, looking out over the new housing development going up on Sycamore Street. He looked so tall, so imposing, so stern.

So impossibly handsome.

Melody could see the muscles in the side of his jaw jumping as he clenched his teeth. She saw the muscles in his forearms tighten and flex as he slipped his hands into the back pockets of his pants. She knew firsthand the strength and power of those arms. She knew how incredibly gentle he could be, as well.

Jones looked so odd in civilian clothes—particularly these pants and this shirt that had such a blandly yuppie style. But she realized that she'd never seen him out of uniform. He'd worn black BDUs under his robe during the rescue. And after that, she'd only seen him in—or out of—his dress uniform.

These oddly conservative clothes might be the way he dressed all the time when he was off duty. Or they might have been something he'd specially chosen to wear for this surprise visit.

Talking about surprises...

As she watched, he closed his eyes and rubbed his forehead with one hand, as if he had a headache and a half. And why shouldn't he? He'd come here obviously hoping to sweet-talk his way back into her bed. He'd gotten far more than he'd bargained for—that was for sure.

She could see the lines of stress clearly etched on his face.

He'd smiled and laughed his way through the six days they'd spent together. But then his pager had gone off, and he'd told her he needed to return to California. He'd smiled as he kissed her in the airport, making promises she knew he wouldn't keep. He'd smiled—right up until the point where she told him she didn't want to see him again. And as he struggled to understand her many reasons for making a clean break, he looked so grim and imposing—rather like the way he looked right now.

It was as if no time had passed at all. It was as if they were right back where they'd left off.

Except for the obvious differences. His hair was longer. Hers was, too. And instead of being three days pregnant and ignorant of the fact, she was now seven months along.

Melody rubbed her extended belly nervously, afraid of what he was going to say, afraid of the tension she could see in his face and in the tightness of his shoulders.

The early-afternoon sunshine lit his face, giving his hair an even more sun-streaked look.

She remembered how soft his hair had felt beneath her fingers. It had grown down past his shoulders now—rich and gleamingly golden brown. Freed from its restraint, it would hang wavy and thick around his face, making him look like one of those exotic men who graced the covers of the historical romances she liked to read so much.

He straightened up as he saw her coming. A flick of his green eyes took in Brittany, too, and Melody knew he was wondering if they were going to have this conversation with an audience. She saw him straighten his shoulders and clench his teeth a little more tightly, and she knew he intended to say what he had to say whether or not her sister was listening.

But, "I've got to get back to work," Britt announced. She narrowed her eyes at Jones. "Will you see that she gets home safely?"

Jones nodded, managing only a ghost of his usual five-thousand-watt smile. "That's my specialty."

"Okay," Brittany said, backing away. "Then I'm out of here. It was nice finally meeting you, Lieutenant Jones."

"Likewise, ma'am."

Melody had forgotten how polite Cowboy Jones could be. She'd forgotten how green his eyes were, how good he smelled, how sweet his lips had tasted... No, she hadn't forgotten that. She had simply tried to forget.

"Are you really all right?" Jones asked. His smile was gone again, and he gazed searchingly into her eyes, looking for what, she didn't know. "They don't want to keep you here overnight or anything? Do more tests...?"

She shook her head, suddenly shy, suddenly wishing that Brittany hadn't walked away. "I didn't have much breakfast, and being hungry combined with chasing Andy across the common made me light-headed. It hasn't been an easy pregnancy—I've had trouble keeping food down almost right from the start.''

''I'm sorry.''

Melody glanced up at him. *I'll bet you are.* She forced a smile. ''Brittany wouldn't let me leave until I had lunch. Did you have something to eat?''

''Yeah. I grabbed a sandwich from the cafeteria.'' He was uncomfortable, too. ''Do you want to sit down?''

''No, I want to... I want to go home. If you don't mind.''

He shook his head. ''I don't mind. It might be easier to talk someplace less public.'' He led the way toward the double doors. ''My car's out this way.''

''Are you still with SEAL Team Ten?'' she asked, realizing as they stepped out into the warm afternoon sunshine that she had about a million questions to ask him.

''Yes, ma'am.''

God, they'd regressed all the way back to ''ma'am.'' ''How's Harvard?''

''He's fine. He's good. The entire squad's in Virginia—for the next few months, at least.''

''Say hello for me next time you see him.''

''I will.'' He gestured with his head. ''Car's over here.''

''Have you heard from Crash?'' Melody waited as he unlocked and opened her door for her.

Cowboy's swim buddy, Crash, was as dark and mysterious as his odd nickname implied. They'd met him by chance at the hotel in Paris. Crash wasn't a member of Alpha Squad, or even SEAL Team Ten. In fact, Cowboy hadn't been absolutely certain *where* the SEAL he'd called his best friend back in BUD/S training was assigned. Except for the accidental meeting, it had been years since they'd even seen each other, but the ongoing mutual trust and respect between the two men had been obvious.

''I got some E-mail from him just last week. Nothing much— just a hi, how are ya, I'm still alive. But when I wrote to him, the mail all bounced back, undeliverable. Need help getting in?'' He watched her maneuver her unwieldy body into the bucket seat.

She shook her head. "It looks more awkward than it really is. Although ask me again when we get to my house—I won't refuse a hand getting out."

Jones leaned over so that he was at her eye level. "I can't believe you still have two more months to go." He quickly back-pedaled. "Not to imply that you're not telling the truth or..." He closed his eyes, swearing softly. When he opened them again, his eyes were a startling shade of green against the tan of his face. "What I was *trying* to say was that if that baby gets much bigger, it's going to be a real struggle for you to give birth." He paused. "I want you to know that from the moment I saw you, Mel, I didn't doubt for a minute that the baby was mine."

"Jones, you don't have to—"

"You haven't denied that I'm right."

"I haven't said anything either way!"

"You don't have to." Jones straightened up and closed the car door. As Melody watched, he crossed around the front and unlocked the driver's-side door. "I called your neighbor—Vince Romanella—about that kid. He said to relax—that he'd find him. Andy. That's the kid's name."

The subject of whose baby she was carrying seemed to have been temporarily and quite intentionally dropped. "I know," Melody said as he climbed in and started the car. "Brittany told me you called Information to get Vince's number. Thank you for doing that."

"It was no problem." He took a left as he pulled out of the driveway.

"Don't you want me to give you directions?"

Jones glanced at her. "I know where you live. I checked a map and went out there this morning, but you weren't home." He smiled slightly, politely, as if they were strangers. "Obviously."

Melody couldn't stand it anymore. "Look, I think you should just drop me off and drive away." He was silent, so she took a deep breath and went on. "You can pretend you don't know. Pretend you never came to Appleton. Just...drive into Boston and catch the next flight to Virginia and don't look back. *Don't* say hi to Harvard for me. Don't say anything. You can tell the guys I wouldn't see you and..."

She had to stop and clear her throat. He was holding on to the steering wheel so tightly, his knuckles were white, but he still didn't speak.

"I know you didn't ask for this, Jones. I know this was not what you were thinking when we spent that time together. It wasn't what I was thinking, either, but I've had a chance to deal with it. I've had time to fall in love with this little baby, and I'm okay about it now. I'm *excited* about it. It may not have been what I wanted seven months ago, but I do want it now. But your being here messes things up."

He pulled into her driveway and, leaving the engine running, turned toward her. "It was on the flight to Paris, wasn't it? That's when it happened."

The look in his eyes was so intense, Melody felt as if he had X-ray vision and could see deep inside of her. She prayed that he couldn't. She prayed that he wouldn't know how close she was to throwing up even as she desperately tried to send him away forever.

"Drive away," she said again, steeling herself, purposely making her words as harsh as she possibly could. "And don't look back. I don't need you, Jones. And I don't want you."

He looked away, but not before she saw a flare of hurt in his eyes. Her heart nearly broke, but she forced herself to go on. It was better this way. It had to be better this way.

"I know for a fact that the last thing *you* need is this baby and me, tying you down in any way at all. All you can possibly do by sticking around is to complicate things. I have money. I have enough saved so that I can spend the next four years at home with the baby. My mother's already started a trust fund for him, for college. There's nothing you can give him that I haven't already thought of and provided."

He tried to cover his hurt with a cynical smile. "Well, hell, honey. Don't hold back. Tell me how you *really* feel."

She felt like a total bitch. But she had to do this. She had to make him leave before he got some crazy idea of "doing right"

When she returned and sat back down, she looked through her handbag in the pretense of searching for some chewing gum. She opened her bag carefully, revealing its contents—including a white bit of satin and lace—only to Jones and not the general. While she'd been gone, she'd once again removed her panties, knowing full well Jones would recognize the same article of clothing he'd taken such pains to remove earlier that morning, causing them to have to rush to get to the airport on time.

Melody felt her blush deepen. Who would've thought she'd have done such things, such daring, provocative, sexually aggressive things like that?

She'd liked it, though. She'd loved the way Jones had made her feel as if she was the sexiest woman in the world. She loved the way he'd needed her so desperately, the way he couldn't seem to get enough of her.

On that flight to Paris, she'd lured him into the tiny bathroom. She hadn't realized he wasn't carrying any condoms. And he had thought she had some in her purse. But once they were together in that hot little closet of a room, the need to sate their searing desire had taken priority over the fact they had no protection.

Jones had roughly pushed her skirt up her thighs and she had wrapped her legs around him as he thrust deeply inside her and took her to heaven. He'd pulled out in an attempt to keep her from getting pregnant, but Melody was well aware that as a form of birth control, the withdrawal method was far less than foolproof.

Still, she'd convinced herself that one time wouldn't matter. Surely they could cheat just once. Surely the odds were in their favor. And heck, luck had been on their side so far. Besides, she'd told herself, she wanted Jones badly enough to be willing to face the consequences.

As she glanced at him now, she knew he was remembering that little airplane bathroom, too. He was remembering the taste of her, the scent of her, the slick heat that surrounded him, carrying them both to ecstasy.

God knows *she'd* never forget the incredible waves of pleasure that engulfed her as he gritted his teeth, fighting to keep himself from releasing all of his seed deep inside her.

He cleared his throat not once but twice before he could speak. "At least the sex was the greatest I've ever had in my life. I mean, it would've been real anticlimactic—no pun intended—to find out that I got you pregnant after having only mediocre sex."

Melody laughed. She couldn't stop herself. It was so like Jones to search for the positives in a no-win situation. But then her eyes filled up and she opened the car door, afraid she was going to burst into tears.

Somehow she managed to scramble up and out of the bucket seat. She closed the door, then he climbed out, too. But he stood with his door open, engine still running, as he looked at her over the top of the car.

"Jones, we had fun together. I can't deny that. But I told you back in March and I'm telling you again—what we shared is not enough to base any kind of real relationship on." Her voice shook slightly, and she fought to steady it. "So good luck. God bless. Don't think I won't remember you. I will." She forced a smile. "I brought home a souvenir."

Jones shook his head. "Melody, I can't—"

"Please. Do me a favor and don't say anything," she begged him. "Just…leave and think about it for a week or two. Don't say anything until you've given yourself time to really think it through. This whole concept—my pregnancy—is still so new to you. I'm giving you a chance to walk away. No strings attached. Give yourself time to think about what that means before you say or do anything rash." She turned and headed toward the house.

He didn't follow, thank God.

She nearly dropped her keys as she unlocked the door. As she went inside, he was still standing there, half in and half out of his car.

As she shut the door behind her, she heard the car door slam. And then, through the window, she saw him drive away.

With any luck at all, he'd do as she asked and think about his options. And if her luck held, he would realize that she was dead

serious about this easy way out she was giving him. And that
would be that. He wouldn't call, he wouldn't write.

She would never see Lt. Harlan Jones of the U.S. Navy SEALs
again.

The baby kicked her, hard.

Chapter 5

Cowboy thought Mel was going to faint again, merely at the sight of him.

He opened the screen door, ready to catch her, but Melody stepped out on the porch rather than let him into the house.

"What are you doing here?" She sounded breathless, shocked, as if she'd actually expected him to take her advice and leave town.

He met her eyes squarely, forcing himself to keep breathing as the enormity of what he was about to do seemed to set itself down directly on his chest. "I think you can probably figure it out."

Melody sat on the edge of one of the plastic lounge chairs that hadn't yet been moved inside for the coming winter. "Oh, God."

He'd put on his white dress uniform, hat and all. He'd even shined his shoes for the occasion. This was not your everyday, average social call.

"Sweetie, who's...?" Brittany's voice trailed off as she came to look out the screen.

"Good evening, ma'am." Cowboy was uncertain if the covered porch was considered indoors or out. He took off his hat, deciding that the ceiling above his head had to count for something. And he didn't want to risk being rude. God knows he was going into this with enough points against him already.

Brittany did a double take. "Are those all *medals?*" she asked.

"Yes, ma'am."

Melody wasn't looking at him. She was staring off into space, across the front yard and down the road that led into town. She looked worn-out and about as unhappy as he'd ever seen her. Even in the Middle East, in the midst of all the danger and death, she hadn't looked this defeated.

Her sister pushed open the screen door. "God, you've got—there must be...*how* many?"

"Lucky thirteen, ma'am."

"*Thirteen* medals. My God."

She leaned even closer to look and Cowboy cleared his throat. "If you'll excuse us, Brittany...? You see, I came over here tonight to ask Melody to marry me."

He managed to get the words out without choking. Dear God, what was he doing here? The answer came swiftly: he was doing the only thing he could do now. He was doing the right thing.

Melody looked up at him, clearly surprised he'd be so forthcoming.

He smiled at her, praying he didn't look as terrified as he felt. She'd told him back in Paris that she couldn't resist his smile. He held out his hand, too. "What do you say we go for a walk?"

But she didn't reach for him. In fact, she all but slapped at his hand. "Didn't you hear *any*thing I said this afternoon?"

It seemed as if over the past seven months, she'd somehow learned to resist him.

"I'll just go and, um, go." Brittany faded back into the house.

"You don't need me." Cowboy repeated Melody's words. "You don't want me. You've got it all figured out. You and you alone can give this baby everything he or she needs. Except you're wrong. Without me, you can't give this child legitimacy. And you can't be his father."

His words came out sounding a whole lot more bitter than he'd intended, and as he watched, her eyes filled with tears.

"I didn't say those things purposely to hurt you, Jones," she told him quietly. "I just thought... I wanted to give you a chance to escape. To get away from here free and clear. I wanted to keep you from doing exactly what you're doing right now. I thought if I could make you see that I truly, honestly don't need you to support me or the baby—"

"You actually thought I'd just walk away?" Cowboy felt sick to his stomach.

Her tears almost overflowed, but she fiercely blinked them back. "I thought if I could convince you that I'm absolutely not your responsibility—"

"You truly believed I'd just turn around and go back to the Alpha Squad and never even *think* of you again?" Cowboy sat down heavily in the chair directly across from hers. "Honey, you don't know me very well."

Melody leaned forward. "That's the point. We don't know each other at all. We were together for...what? Eight days? During which time we actually *talked* for all of eight hours? That's not enough to build a relationship on, let alone a *marriage!*"

Even tired, even with the seriousness of this argument keeping her from smiling, she was lovely.

There was a trail of freckles across her nose and cheeks, making her look as if she had slowly ripened in the summer sun. Her pregnancy had added a lushness to her body, a womanly fullness to breasts and hips that had been almost boyishly slender before.

Even her face was fuller, less little-girl cute and more grown-woman beautiful.

Cowboy wanted to touch her. He was dying to press his hand against the tautness of her stomach, to feel the reality of her baby—*his* baby—beneath his fingers.

They'd done this together. They'd created this baby in the cramped bathroom of that 747 to Paris. It had to have happened then. It was the only time they hadn't used protection. Hell, it was the only time in thirteen years he'd had sex without a condom.

He could still remember the dizzying swiftness with which he had thrown aside a lifetime of precaution and control. And he could also remember the heart-stoppingly exquisite sensation when he'd driven himself deeply inside her.

Damn, but he wanted to do that again. And over and over again...

Cowboy cleared his throat, unable to hide the heat he knew was in his eyes as he looked at her. "It's just that, well, let me put it this way. I could think of far worse ways to spend the rest of my life than being married to you."

Married. Damn, the word still made him feel faint.

She held his gaze with eyes the color of a perfect summer sky. They were so familiar, those eyes. He'd dreamed about her eyes more times than he could count. He'd dreamed about sitting right here, across from her on the front porch of her house and gazing at her.

He'd dreamed that he'd touch her. He'd trail one finger down the silky smoothness of her cheek and she would smile and open her arms to him. And then, finally, after all these months of starving for the taste of her lips, he would kiss her and...

But here in real life, he didn't dare reach for her. And she didn't smile. She simply looked away.

But not before he saw it—the undeniable answering heat of attraction that flashed across her face. There was still a spark between them. Despite everything she'd said, she was not unaffected by his presence. But it just wasn't enough.

"I can't think of anything worse," she said softly, "than to get married for the wrong reason."

"And you don't think that little baby you're carrying is a right enough reason?"

Melody lifted her chin in the air in that gesture of defiance that was so familiar. "No, I don't. Love is the only reason two people should get married."

He was about to speak, but she stopped him. "And I *know* you don't love me, so don't insult my intelligence by even trying to pretend that you do. People don't really fall in love at first sight— or even after eight days. Lust, yes, but not love. Love takes time.

The kind of love you base a long-term relationship on—a relationship like marriage—needs to grow over a course of weeks and months and even *years*. What we experienced during my rescue and those days following it had nothing to do with love. Love is about normal things—about sharing breakfast and then going off to work. It's about working in the yard together on the weekend. It's about sitting on the back porch and watching the sunset.''

"When I go off to work, I don't come back for four weeks," Cowboy said quietly.

"I know." She gave him a very sad smile. "That's not what I want from a husband. If I'm going to get married, it's going to be to a man whose idea of risking his life is to mow the lawn near the hornet's nest."

Cowboy was silent. He'd never been one for long speeches. He'd never been the type for philosophizing or debating some minute detail of an issue the way Harvard could do for hours at a time.

But at this crucial moment, Cowboy wished he had Harvard's talent for waxing eloquent. Because he knew how he felt—he just wasn't certain he'd be able to find the right words to explain.

"Sometimes, Mel," he started slowly, hesitantly, "you've got to take what life dishes out. And sometimes that's real different from what you hoped for or what you expected. I mean, I didn't exactly picture myself getting married and starting a family for a whole hell of a lot of years, but here I am, sitting here with a diamond ring in a box in my pocket."

"I'm not going to marry you," she interrupted. "I don't want to marry you!"

His voice rose despite his intentions to stay calm. "Yeah, well, honey, I'm not that excited about it myself." He took a deep breath and when he spoke again his voice was softer. "But it's the right thing to do."

She pressed the palm of her hand against her forehead. "I knew it. I knew you were going to start with 'the right thing.'"

"You bet I'm starting with it. Because *I* believe that baby— *my* baby as well as yours, Mel—deserves a name."

"He'll have a name. He'll have *my* name!"

"And he'll grow up in this little town with everyone knowing he's a bastard. Yeah, you're really looking out for him, aren't you?"

Anger flashed in her eyes. "Stop with the Middle Ages mentality. Women are single mothers all the time these days. I can take care of this baby by my—"

"I know. I heard you. You've got it all figured out. You've got his college education handled. But you know, there *is* one thing you can't provide for this kid, and that's a chance for him to know his father. *I'm* the only one who can make sure this kid grows up knowing that he's got a father who cares."

Cowboy couldn't believe the words that had come out of his mouth. He was glad he was sitting down. A father who cared. Hell, he actually sounded as if he knew what he was talking about—as if he knew anything at all about how to make sure this unborn child would grow up believing that he was loved.

In truth, he was clueless. His own father had been a dismal failure in that regard. By-the-book U.S. Navy, Admiral Jones was a perfectionist. He was harsh and demanding and cold and—with the exception of Cowboy's joining the SEALS—was never happy with anything he ever did. With the old man as his only real role model, Cowboy wasn't sure he was ready to get within a hundred feet of an impressionable child.

Still, he didn't have any choice, did he? He drew the ring box from his pocket and snapped the lid open. He held it out to her. "Mel, you gotta marry me. This isn't just about you and me anymore."

Melody couldn't bring herself even to look at the ring.

She clumsily pushed herself to her feet, fighting to keep from crying. She'd made a mistake—assuming Jones wouldn't care. She'd misjudged him—thinking his good-time, pleasure-seeking, no-strings disposition would win out over his sense of responsibility.

But a sense of responsibility didn't make for a happy home.

"The worst thing we can do for this baby is enter into a marriage neither one of us wants," she said. "What kind of home life could we possibly give him when we don't even know if we like each other?''

That seemed to floor Jones. He swore softly, shaking his head. "I like you. I sort of thought you liked me, too." He laughed in disbelief. "I mean, come on..."

She stopped, her hand on the screen door. "I did like you," she told him. "I liked you a whole lot when you were the only thing standing between me and death when we were inside that embassy. And I liked you even more when you made love to me, after we were back and safe. But there's a whole lot more to you besides your abilities as a Navy SEAL and your considerable talent in bed. And I don't know *that* part of you at all. And you don't know me, either. Let's be honest—you don't.''

Let's be honest. Except she wasn't—not really. She *did* like Cowboy Jones. She admired and respected him, and every time he opened his mouth, every minute longer he hung around, she liked him more and more.

It wouldn't take much for her feelings to grow into something stronger.

And that would be trouble, because adventure and excitement were this man's middle names. There was no way he would be satisfied with a marriage to someone as unadventurous and unexciting as Melody Evans. And after the novelty of doing the right thing wore off, they'd both be miserable.

By then, he'd be bored with her, and she—fool that she was—would be hopelessly in love with him.

Melody looked up at him as she opened the door and stepped inside. "So, no, Lieutenant Jones, I'm not going to marry you."

"I need a room."

The elderly woman behind the counter at the local inn could have been a SEAL team's point man. Cowboy could tell that she missed nothing with her shrewd, sweeping gaze. She quickly took in his naval uniform, his perfectly shined shoes, the pile of medals that decorated his chest. No doubt she was memorizing the color of his eyes and hair and taking a mental picture of his face—probably for reference later when she watched *Top Cops* or another of those reality-based TV shows just to make sure the uniform wasn't an elaborate disguise when, in fact, he was wanted for heinous crimes in seven different states.

He gave her his hundred-dollar smile.

She didn't blink. "How many nights?"

"Just one, ma'am."

She pursed her lips, making her face look even longer and narrower, and slid a standard hotel-room registration form across the counter to him. "You're from Texas?"

Cowboy paused before picking up the pen. His accent wasn't that obvious. "You have a good ear, ma'am."

"That was a question, young man," she told him sternly. "I was asking. But you are, aren't you? You're that sailor from Texas."

Another elderly woman, this one as round and short as the other was tall and narrow, came out of the back room.

"Oh, my," she said, stopping short at the sight of him. "It's him, isn't it? Melody's navy fellow."

"He wants to stay the night, Peggy," the stern-faced woman intoned, disapproval thickening her voice. "I'm not sure I want his type in our establishment. Having all kinds of rowdy parties. Getting all of the local girls pregnant."

All of the...?

"Hannah Shelton called to say he just bought a diamond ring at Front Street Jeweler's," the round lady—Peggy—said. "On credit."

Both women turned to look at him.

"About time," the tall one sniffed.

"Did he give it to her?" Peggy wondered.

It was odd—the way they talked about him as if he weren't there, even as they stood staring directly at him.

He decided the best course would simply be to ignore their comments. "I'd like a room with a telephone, if possible," he said as he filled out the registration form. "I need to make some out-of-state calls. I have a calling card, of course."

"None of our rooms have private phones," the tall lady informed him.

"Our guests are welcome to use the lobby phone." Peggy gestured across the room toward an antique sideboard upon which sat an equally antique-looking rotary phone.

The lobby phone. Of course. God forbid a conversation go on in this building that Peggy and the bird lady not know about.

"You *did* buy it as an engagement ring, didn't you?" the tall woman asked, narrowing her eyes, finally confronting him directly. "With the intention of giving it to Melody Evans?"

Cowboy tried his best to be pleasant. "That's private business between Ms. Evans and me."

"Thank God, Lieutenant! You're still here!" Brittany came bursting through the inn's lobby door. "I have to talk to you."

"It's Brittany Evans." Peggy stated the obvious to her dour-faced companion.

"I can see that. She wants to talk to the sailor."

"Do you have a few minutes?" Mel's sister asked Cowboy.

He shrugged. "Yeah, sure. Although I'm not sure if the Spanish Inquisition has finished with me."

She laughed, and he could see traces of Melody in her face. The wave of longing that hit him was overpowering. Why couldn't this have been easy? Why couldn't he have arrived in Appleton to find Melody happy to see him—and not seven months pregnant?

But "why couldn't" scenarios were of no help to him now. He couldn't change the past—that wasn't in his control. And difficult as it seemed, he somehow had to change Mel's mind. He had to make her see that they really only had one choice here.

As he'd walked away with that diamond ring still in his pocket, it occurred to him that he'd been taking the wrong tack. He shouldn't have tried to argue with Melody. He should've spent all of his energy sweet-talking her instead. He should've tried to seduce his way back into her life.

Yeah, sure, great sex probably *wasn't* enough to base a long-term relationship on. But great sex combined with a soon-to-be-born baby were grounds for a definite start.

Brittany turned to the two old ladies, fixing them with a pointed finger and a glare. "Peggy. Estelle. If either one of you breathes so much as a word about the fact that I came here to talk to Lieutenant Jones, and my sister hears about it, I swear I will take my chain saw to your rosebushes. Is that understood?''

Estelle didn't seem convinced, lifting a hawklike nose into the air. ''She'd never do it.''

Peggy wasn't quite so certain. ''She might.''

Brittany grabbed Cowboy's arm. ''Come on, Lieutenant. Let's take a walk.''

He scooped his duffel bag off the floor and followed her out into the early-evening dusk.

There was a chill in the air as the sun dipped below the horizon. After weeks of unseasonably warm weather, autumn was definitely on its way.

Melody's sister marched in silence until they were a good fifty feet away from the front porch of the inn. At that point, Cowboy ventured to speak. ''I doubt they can hear us from this distance. Although I suppose they could be tracking us via some KH-12 SATCOM.'' At her frown of confusion, he explained, ''Spy satellite. It'd be right up their alley.''

Brittany laughed, rolling her eyes and crossing the street, taking them onto the town common. ''God, I can just picture Peggy and Estelle down in some high-tech studio in their basement, with little headsets on over their purple hair, gleefully monitoring the private conversations going on all over town.''

''Seems they do pretty well all by themselves. In fact, they could probably teach the staff at NAVINTEL a thing or two about information gathering.''

Appleton was a perfect little New England town, complete with eighteenth-century clapboard houses that surrounded a picture-perfect, rectangular-shaped common. The common was covered with thick green grass and crisscrossed with sidewalks. Benches and stately trees were scattered here and there. Brittany led the way toward one of the benches.

''This town has a gossip network like you wouldn't believe. We've got the highest busybody per capita ratio in the entire state.''

Cowboy swore softly. ''That must've been really tough on

Melody—I mean, when her pregnancy started to show. There was probably a lot of talk.''

''Actually, she didn't give anyone a chance to talk. Come on, let's sit. I've been on my feet, running all day.'' Brittany sank onto the white-painted bench, and Cowboy sat beside her.

From a playground, way down at the other end of the green, he could hear the sounds of children laughing. Someday his kid would play there. His *kid.* He felt a cold streak of fear run down his spine. How could he have a kid? He wasn't ready to stop being a kid himself.

''Melody went all the way into the city to buy a home pregnancy test,'' Brittany continued. ''She knew if she bought it here in town, word would've been out within two minutes of leaving the store. When the test turned up positive, she didn't have to think for very long before deciding that an abortion wasn't the right choice for her. And giving the child up for adoption was also out of the question. So there she was, pregnant, about to be a single mother. She realized that sooner or later her condition was going to be obvious to the entire town, so she…''

She broke off, chuckling and shaking her head. ''I'm sorry— I still can't quite believe she did this. But my little sister crashed one of Estelle Warner's Ladies' Club meetings. The Ladies' Club is really just a cover name for Gossipers Anonymous. I usually don't go—Estelle and I aren't exactly friends—but I was there that day, drumming up support for the hospital's AIDS awareness program.

''At first I thought Melody was there to give me support, but when Hazel Parks opened the floor for new topics of discussion, Mel stood up. She cleared her throat and said, 'I would like you all to know that I have no intention of getting married, but I am, however, two months pregnant.' She didn't even give anyone time to gasp in shock. She just kept going. She gave 'em the facts— that you were the father and that she intended to keep the baby.''

''She stood there,'' Brittany went on, ''looking all those gossipmongers in the eye, and offered to answer any questions they might have about her condition and her plans. She even passed around a picture of you."

Cowboy shook his head in admiration. "She told them the truth. And once the truth was out, no one could speculate." He paused. "God, I wish she'd told me, too. I wish..."

He should've called her at the beginning of the summer. He should have swallowed his pride a whole hell of a lot sooner and picked up the phone. He should have been there. He should have known right from the start.

"Although Estelle and Peggy pretend to disapprove, I've got to admit even *they've* been pretty supportive. They even threw Mel a baby shower that the entire Ladies' Club turned out for." Brittany gazed at him. "There's been some talk, but not a lot. And most of it's concerned you."

Cowboy sighed. "And here I am, showing up in town, throwing the gossip squad into an uproar. No wonder Melody wanted me to leave as quickly as possible. I'm just making things worse for her, aren't I?"

"I heard what you said to my sister this evening out on the porch," Brittany said baldly. "And I heard what she said to you, about not needing you. Don't you believe her for a second, Lieutenant. She pretends to be so tough and resilient. But I know better.

"She's been depressed and unhappy ever since she came back from Paris," Brittany told him. "And she may believe with all of her heart that marrying you won't make her any happier, but I've got to tell you, today in the hospital, I watched her when she looked at you. And for the first time in more than half a year, she actually seemed alive again. Don't let her chase you away, Lieutenant."

Cowboy looked at the woman sitting next to him and smiled. "I wasn't about to go anywhere. In fact, I was planning to knock on your door again first thing in the morning."

Brittany took a deep breath. "Good. Okay. I'll plan not to be home."

"And, by the way, since I'm getting a strong hint here that we're allies, you should know that my friends call me Cowboy."

She lifted one eyebrow. "Cowboy. Is that because you're from Texas or because you're some kind of hotshot?"

"A little of each."

Brittany laughed. "Doesn't it figure? Somehow I always imagined Melody spending the rest of her life with an accountant—not one of the X-Men."

Cowboy smiled ruefully. He wished he could feel as certain that Melody was going to see things his way. And despite his belief that getting married was the only solution, he wished that the thought of vowing to remain faithful and true to one woman for the rest of his life didn't scare him half to death.

He'd been so enchanted by Melody that he hadn't been able to stop thinking about her those months they'd been apart. He'd loved making love to her. But she was right. He hadn't come all the way to Appleton to pledge his undying love. He'd come to renew their affair. He'd come to have sex, not to get married.

But now he had to convince Mel to marry him.

That would be hard enough to do even if he didn't have his own doubts and fears. And he was running out of time. His leave was up at 0900 Monday morning.

Cowboy closed his eyes at the sheer impossibility of this situation. Compared to this mess, a hostage rescue was a piece of cake.

Chapter 6

Melody was a hostage in her own home.

Of course, she was a hostage to her own stupidity and foolishness, but knowing that didn't make it any better. In fact, it made it worse.

Cowboy Jones had been sitting out on her front porch for more than two hours now. He'd rung her doorbell while she was getting dressed to go to the late service at the Congregational Church. She'd wrapped her robe around herself and rushed into Brittany's room, intending to beg her sister to tell him she wasn't home.

But Brittany's bed was neatly made. She was long gone. There was a note on the kitchen table saying that she'd forgotten to tell Melody, but she'd promised to work a friend's shift at the hospital. She wouldn't be home until late.

So Melody had hidden from Jones. She'd taken the chicken's way out and she hadn't answered the door at all. And Jones had made himself comfortable out on the porch, apparently determined to wait all day for her to come back home.

So if she went out now, she'd be forced to admit that she truly had been home all this time. Assuming, of course, that he didn't already know that.

She tried to catch up on her reading, tried not to let herself be unnerved by the fact that this man she had shared such intimacies with was sitting within shouting distance. She tried to convince herself that those twinges of frustration and longing she felt were the result of her being unable to work in her garden. She'd planned to spend the afternoon out in the sunshine and fresh air.

Instead, she was here. Locked inside her house.

Melody slowly opened the window in the room she was making into a nursery, careful not to make any noise. It *was* a glorious day—cool and crisp. She pressed her nose to the screen and took a deep breath.

There was no way she could possibly have caught a whiff of Harlan Jones's hauntingly familiar and utterly masculine scent, was there? Of course not. Not all the way up here on the third floor. She was imagining things. She was remembering—

"Hey."

The sound of a voice in the yard made her jump back, away from the window. But it was only Andy Marshall, crossing over from the Romanellas' yard.

"That's not an Army uniform, is it?" He wasn't talking to her. He hadn't even seen her, and she moved closer to the window to peer down at the boy. "My old man's in the Army."

"I'm Navy," Jones replied from beneath the roof of the porch.

"Oh." There was disappointment in Andy's voice. "Then I guess you don't know my father."

"I guess not." Jones sounded sleepy, his Western drawl more pronounced. Melody could picture him sitting back in one of her lounge chairs, feet up and eyes half-closed, like a lion sunning himself. Relaxed, but dangerously aware of everything going on around him.

"Looks pretty damn uncomfortable, buttoned all the way up like that," Andy commented.

"It's not that bad."

"Yeah, well, you look like a monkey. You'd never get me into one of those things, not in a million years."

"Probably not. Only the smartest, toughest and strongest men get into the SEAL teams. You probably wouldn't come close."

Out on the lawn, Andy took a step back. "The hell with you."

Jones yawned. "The hell with you too. If you don't want to be insulted, don't insult *me*. But the fact is, SEAL training is tough. Most guys don't have what it takes and they end up dropping out of the program. They run away—the way you did yesterday."

Melody winced. Ouch. Jones wasn't pulling his punches.

"And you're like some kind of god, right?" Andy bristled with outrage. "Because you made it through—?"

Jones laughed. "That's right. My pay grade is O-3, but my rank is God. Anytime you feel like it, just go right ahead and grovel and bow down to my magnificence. And if you don't believe me, go to the library and read anything you can get your hands on about BUD/S—the SEAL training program. Of course, in your case, you're probably going to have to learn to read first."

Melody watched Andy, certain that he was going to turn and run away. But to her surprise, the boy laughed and sat down on the steps leading up to the porch.

"You think you're pretty funny, don't you?" he retorted.

"Hey, I'm a god—I don't need to be funny. The mortals laugh even when I make a bad joke."

"Is it really that tough—you know, the training?"

"It's insane," Jones said. "But you know what I learned from doing it?"

"What?"

"I can do anything." Jones paused and Melody could picture his smile. "There's no job that's too tough. There's no task that's impossible. If I can't climb over it, I'll swim around it. If I can't swim around it, I'll blow the damn thing up and wade through the rubble."

Melody closed her eyes. Jones had already done the very same thing to her life. He'd blown it up and now was wading through the rubble.

"So you're the guy who knocked up Melody Evans, huh?" Andy asked.

Jones was silent for several long seconds. And when he spoke, there wasn't even the slightest trace of amusement or laughter in his voice. "You want to rephrase that question so that I'm certain you meant absolutely no disrespect to the woman I intend to marry? You can dis me all you want, but don't you ever, *ever* dis Melody. Not behind her back and not to her face. Do you read what I'm saying?"

"But she doesn't want you around."

"Tell me something I don't know."

"So why are you even bothering?" Andy asked. "You should be grateful and leave while you've got the chance. That's what *my* father did. He left before I was born even. I've never met him, you know. The closest I've ever gotten to him is this stupid watch."

Andy's watch. Melody remembered how carefully he'd checked it after fighting with Alex Parks in the playground. That had been his father's watch. She had guessed it was important to him in some way.

Jones's voice was quiet. "I'm sorry."

"Yeah, well, you know, he probably had things to do. My mother told me he was stationed overseas and she didn't want to go. He didn't have a choice, though. When you're in the Army, you've got to go where you're sent. You don't have a lot of extra time to spend on having kids." His words were almost recited— as if this was something he'd said over and over in an attempt to justify his father's actions.

Jones was silent, and Melody knew that he didn't want to say anything that would contradict Andy.

But then Andy himself laughed—a scornful expulsion of air. "Yeah, right. I don't know why I'm sticking up for him. Like he didn't *run* to get away from us."

Melody's heart broke for the boy. He was at the age where he was starting to doubt the fairy tales his mother had told him. He still knew all the words, but he was starting to see through them to the truth beneath the surface.

It was a moment before either Jones or Andy spoke again.

''Melody's home, you know,'' Andy finally said. ''Her car's in the garage.''

''I know.''

Melody closed her eyes. Jones knew.

''I figure sooner or later she'll get tired of hiding and she'll come out and talk to me.''

''She'll have to come out tomorrow morning,'' Andy pointed out. ''She's got to go to work.''

''Well, there you go,'' Jones said. ''Of course, by Monday morning, I'll be AWOL. Unless I can arrange more leave. Hell, with the amount of vacation time coming to me, I figure I could sit out here on this porch until Thanksgiving.''

More leave? Melody closed her eyes. Oh, God, no...

''That would be a stupid way to spend your vacation.''

''Yeah, it would be,'' Jones agreed. ''But if that's what I've got to do...''

''But you don't,'' Andy argued. ''She doesn't want you to stay. She doesn't want to marry you. If I were you, I'd've been out of here a long time ago. 'Cause, like, what do you get out of this anyway? I mean, seven months ago, yeah, she was probably pretty hot. But now she's all...well, no disrespect intended, but she's all fat and funny-looking.''

Melody grimaced in despair. Andy was only a kid—what should she care what he thought of her physical attractiveness? But she *did* care. She cared what Jones thought and she braced herself, waiting for his response.

''She's 'fat and funny-looking,' as you so tactlessly put it, because *I* made her that way,'' Jones countered. ''I did this, I got her pregnant, and *I've* got to make it right. I don't deal with my problems by running and hiding like some kind of frightened girl.''

Melody couldn't stand it any longer. Not only was she some awful fat and funny-looking *problem,* but she was cowardly, as well.

She headed downstairs and threw open the front door before she gave herself a chance to think.

"I am *not* hiding," she announced as she stepped out onto the porch.

Andy looked startled at her sudden appearance, but Jones just smiled as if he'd been expecting her.

"I knew that one would get you out here," he drawled.

He was sitting back in one of the lounge chairs, legs crossed at the ankles, hands behind his head, elbows out, just the way she'd pictured him.

"You were listening?" Andy actually had the sense to look embarrassed.

"Yes," Melody told him tartly. "I was listening. With my fat and funny-looking ears. I was practicing the age-old Appleton skill of eavesdropping."

"I didn't mean—"

"For me to overhear. Yeah, no kidding, Einstein. And you still owe me an apology for making me chase you across the world yesterday."

"I'm sorry," Andy said.

His quick and seemingly sincere apology caught her off guard. "Well, good," she said. "You should be."

Jones smiled at Andy. "Thanks for keeping me company, but I think you'll probably understand when I say *scat*."

Andy was gone before Melody could blink.

Jones sat up, putting one leg on either side of the lounge chair, leaving space on the cushion in front of him. He patted the cushion. "Sit down. You look like you could use a back rub."

He was right. The tension of the past few hours had turned her shoulders into knots. But there was no way she was going to let him touch her. That would be sheer insanity.

"Come on," he whispered, holding out his hand for her. His impossibly sexy smile almost did her in.

But she sat down on the other lounge chair instead. "You know darn well where we'd end up if I let you give me a back rub."

His smile didn't falter. "I was hoping we'd end up having dinner."

"Right. And we've never had dinner without it leading directly back to my bed,'' she said bluntly. ''Jones, what possible good could come of our sleeping together?''

The warmth in his eyes got hotter. ''I can think of one hell of a reason—to remind you how really good we were together.''

''When we had sex,'' she clarified.

''The rest of the time, too.''

Melody had to laugh. ''There was no rest of the time. We were either having sex or unconscious.''

''We spent two days together behind enemy lines and I hardly even touched you the entire time.''

''That was foreplay,'' she told him. ''For you, anyway.''

His smile was gone and his eyes were nearly neon green in their intensity. ''You don't really believe that.''

She shook her head. ''I don't know *what* to believe—I don't know you well enough to do more than guess. But it sure seemed to me that while I was scared to death, *you* were having fun.''

''I was doing my job. And part of that job was to keep you from losing faith.''

''You did it well,'' she told him. ''I had total faith in you. God, I would have followed you into hell if you'd told me to.''

''So where's your faith in me now?'' he asked quietly.

Without his smile to light him up, Jones looked tired. He looked as if he'd slept about as well as she had last night—which was not well at all.

''The faith I have in you is still as strong,'' Melody said just as softly. ''I believe—absolutely—that you think you're doing the right thing. But I also believe that getting married would be a total disaster.'' She sat up, her conviction making her voice louder. ''You'd never be happy married to someone like me. Jones, I work with the local Brownie troop, going around picking up trash on the side of the road for excitement. And when I'm feeling *really* adventurous, I volunteer down at the Audubon Bird Refuge. Believe me, I'm *really boring.*''

''I'm not looking to recruit you to join the Alpha Squad,'' he argued. ''I have six teammates—I don't need to be married to a SEAL.''

''And I don't need to be married to a SEAL, either,'' she countered. She leaned forward. "Don't you see, Jones? I don't want to be married to someone like you. I want to find a boring, regular, average, *normal* man."

"I'm as average and normal as the next guy—"

She cut him off. "Oh, *please!*"

"I am."

"Yeah, I can just picture you in the yard with an edge trimmer or cleaning out the gutters. Or helping me shop for baby furniture—oh, that's *right* up your alley! You can 'take the point' when we go to the mall," she said, using some of the military terminology he'd taught her during their brief time together.

Jones shook his head, trying to hide his smile. "Come on, Mel. You said yourself you don't know me well enough to—"

"I know enough to be convinced that you're the polar opposite of average."

"How can you be so sure?" He threw her own words back at her. "We were either having sex or unconscious."

Jones stood up, and she knew she was in trouble. She held up one hand before he could move any closer. "Please don't touch me."

He sat down next to her anyway, invading her personal space, invading her senses. God, he smelled so good. "Please don't tell me not to touch you," he countered in that slight Western drawl that melted her insides and weakened her resolve.

He lightly trailed his fingers through her hair, not quite touching her. "We can make this work," he whispered. His eyes were a very persuasive shade of green, but there was something in his face that told her he was trying to persuade himself as well. "I know we can. Come on, Mel, say you'll marry me, and let's go upstairs and make love."

"No." Melody pushed herself up and off the chair, desperate to get away from the hypnotizing warmth in his eyes. God, he made her dizzy. She pulled open the screen door and reached for the knob....

Locked.

The door was locked.

She tried it again, praying it was only temporarily stuck. But it didn't budge. Somehow it had swung shut behind her and now was tightly locked.

She and Brittany kept a spare key hidden beneath a loose board under the front welcome mat, but when she lifted it up, there was no key to be found. Of course not. She'd used that key the *last* time she'd locked herself out. And it was sitting where she'd left it—on the foyer sideboard. She could see it through the window, gleaming mockingly at her from among the piles of junk mail.

She could feel Jones watching as she fought the waves of nausea that hit her one after another.

She was locked out.

None of the downstairs windows was open—Brittany had just finished reading a heart-stoppingly scary serial-killer suspense novel and had been making a point to lock the windows at night. Even the mudroom windows were tightly shut. The only open window in the house was the one in the baby's nursery—the tower room, way up on the third floor.

She was going to have to ask for Jones's help.

She turned toward him, taking a deep, steadying breath. "Will you help me, please? I need a ride to the hospital."

He was up out of the chair and next to her in a fraction of a second. "Are you all right?"

Melody felt a twinge of regret. For the span of a heartbeat, she allowed herself to wish that the concern darkening his eyes was the result of love rather than responsibility. But she wasn't into playing make-believe, so she quickly pushed those errant thoughts aside and forced a smile.

"I'm locked out. I need to go get Brittany's key. I think she's probably still at work." Please God, let her be there...

"As long as we're going downtown, why don't we stop and have some lunch?"

"Because I don't *want* to have lunch with you, thank you very much."

He inched a little closer, reaching out to play with the edge of her sleeve. Touching, but not touching. "So, okay, we'll skip lunch, drive into Boston and catch the next flight to Vegas instead. We can get married before sundown at the Wayne Newton Wedding Chapel or someplace equally thrilling. No, don't answer right away, honey. I know the thought overwhelms you and leaves you all choked up with emotion.''

Melody laughed despite herself. "God, you're never going to give up, are you?''

"No, ma'am.''

The tips of his fingers brushed her arm, and she pulled away, straightening her back. "I can be as stubborn as you can.''

"No, you can't. You dull, boring types are never as stubborn as us wild adventurers.''

Another wave of dizziness hit, and she reached behind her, suddenly needing to sit.

Jones held her elbow, helping her down into one of the chairs. "Is this normal?''

She pulled her hand free from his grasp. "It's normal for me.''

"As long as we're going to the hospital, maybe we should get you checked out. You know, make sure everything's okay…?''

She sat back in the chair, closing her eyes. "Everything's okay.''

"You're looking a little green.''

She felt him sit down next to her, felt the warmth of his leg against her thigh, felt his hand press against the clamminess of her forehead. But she didn't have the strength to move. "I *feel* a little green. But that's normal—for me, or so my doctor tells me. Every now and then, I throw up. It's part of my particular pregnancy package. I just sip some ginger ale and nibble on a cracker and then—if I'm lucky—I feel a little better.''

"And the ginger ale and crackers are…?''

"Conveniently stored in the kitchen," she finished for him. "Inside the locked house.''

"Hang on—I'll get 'em.''

She felt him stand up and she opened her eyes to see him step off the porch.

"Jones…''

He flashed her a smile. "There's no such thing as locked," he told her and disappeared from sight.

* * *

Cowboy unfastened the screen and pushed the window up even higher. He slipped into the house and looked around as he slid the screen back into place.

This room had recently been painted. The walls were white and the window frames were bright primary colors. There was a band of dancing animals stenciled across the walls in those same brilliant hues.

He was standing in a nursery.

Some kind of baby dresser thing was against the wall and a gleaming white crib was set up in one corner of the room. Several silly-looking teddy bears were already waiting in the crib, their mouths set in expressions of blissful happiness.

Cowboy picked one of them up. It was as soft and furry as it looked, and he held it as he took in the rest of the room.

A rocking chair sat near the open window. It, too, had been painted white, with several of the same dancing animals carefully stenciled on the back. A package of what looked to be brightly patterned curtains and several curtain rods had been set on the dresser—a project yet to be completed.

It was obvious that Melody had already spent a great deal of time getting this room ready for her baby.

Their baby.

What had she been thinking about as she painted those yellow, red and blue animals on the walls? Had she thought of him at all? Had she wondered where he was, what he was doing?

He gazed into the teddy bear's plastic eyes, unable to keep from smiling back at its loopy grin. But then his smile faded. If Melody had her way, his son was going to know this bear's face better than Cowboy's. This bear was going to be the kid's constant companion while Cowboy would be a stranger.

He felt a rush of anger and frustration that quickly turned to despair. He couldn't blame Melody for her mistrust. Everything she'd said was based in truth.

They didn't know each other very well at all. And marriage *did* need more than sex and physical attraction to make it work. Growing up in a household filled with arguments, anger and ten-

sion could well be worse than growing up in a household without
a father.

And it wasn't as if he was any kind of major prize. Sure, he'd
made the maverick jump from enlisted seaman to officer, but it
wasn't as if he had any great aspirations to follow in his own
father's footsteps and become an admiral.

He had a little money saved, but not a lot. In fact, it was barely
enough to pay for that ring he'd bought at the local jeweler's.
He'd spent most of his disposable income on his car and that
sweet little powerboat that was docked down in Virginia Beach
right this minute. He liked things that went fast and he'd spent
his money accordingly.

He hadn't even considered saving up. The need for financial
security hadn't crossed his mind. He'd had no intention of settling
down and starting a family for a good, long time.

But now here he was. Standing in his soon-to-be-born son's
nursery, his insides tied in a knot because there was no way out,
no easy solution.

There was only the obvious solution—the grit-your-teeth and
shoulder-your-responsibility solution that involved marriage vows
and a shockingly abrupt change in life-style.

But hell, he'd made this baby; now he was going to have to
live with it. Literally.

Cowboy gently set the bear back in the crib.

Right now, he had to go downstairs and fetch Melody some
ginger ale and crackers from the kitchen. And then, despite his
own doubts, he had to go out on that porch and convince her to
do right by this baby and marry him.

Except every time he sat down next to her, every time he gazed
into her heaven-blue eyes, every time he as much as *thought* about
her, he wanted to skip the negotiations. He wanted nothing more
than to swing her up into his arms and carry her into the house.
He wanted to take her into her bedroom and show her exactly
how well they could get along. He wanted to bury himself inside
her, to lose himself in the sweetness he'd only known in his
dreams for the past seven months.

Despite the fact that her near-perfect body was swollen with child, he wanted her so much he could barely breathe. He'd never even glanced twice at a pregnant woman before—in fact, he'd considered the lack of an hourglass figure to be something of a major turnoff. But now he found himself fascinated by the changes in Melody's body. And he couldn't deny the extremely primitive rush of masculine pride he felt every time he saw her.

He had done that. He had possessed her and made her his own.

In everything but name.

Of course, that insane sense of pride was accompanied by a healthy dollop of toe-curling fear. How on earth was he going to be a good father when he didn't have a clue as to how a good father acted? And how the *hell* was that enormous, destined-to-be-six-feet-three-inches, Harlan Jones-sized baby going to be delivered from petite little Melody Evans without putting her at risk and endangering her life?

And how was he going to react on his next counterterrorist mission with Alpha Squad, knowing he had a wife and son waiting for him—depending on him—at home?

He went down a few steps and pushed the nursery door open, then found himself in what had to be Melody's bedroom.

It smelled like the perfume he'd caught a whiff of both yesterday and today. It smelled like Melody—sweet and fresh. The room was a little messy, with clothes flung over the back of a chair, and the bed less than perfectly made.

Her sheets had a floral print that matched the bedspread. Throw pillows spilled over onto the hardwood floor. Her bedside table was cluttered with all kinds of things—books, a tape player, CDs, bottles of lotion and nail polish.

It was a nice room, pretty and comfortable and welcoming—a lot like Melody herself.

Cowboy caught sight of his reflection in the full-length mirror attached to the closet door. The starkness of his dress uniform accentuated his height and the width of his shoulders, and surrounded by the tiny rose-colored flowers and the lacy curtains, he looked undeniably out of place.

He tried to picture himself dressed down in civilian clothes, in jeans and a T-shirt, with his hair loosened from its rather austere-looking ponytail, but even then, he didn't seem to fit into the pretty picture this room made. He was too big. Too muscular. Too male.

Cowboy squared his shoulders. That was just too damn bad. Melody was going to have to get used to him. Or redecorate. Because neither of them had any choice. He was here to stay.

He went down the stairs and found the kitchen.

The entire house was decorated in a pleasant mixture of both antiques and more modern furnishings. It was neat, but not obsessively so.

He searched the cabinets for some crackers and found a box that boasted unsalted tops. He grabbed the package and a can of ginger ale from a refrigerator that was nearly filled with fresh vegetables and went down the hall to the front door. He opened it, making sure it was unlocked before he stepped out onto the porch.

Melody was sitting, bent practically in half, her head between her knees. The position was awkward—her belly made it difficult to execute.

"Sometimes this helps if I feel as if I'm going to faint," she told him without even looking up.

Cowboy crouched next to her. "Do you feel like you're gonna faint?"

"I think it was the thought of you climbing all the way up to that third-floor window," she admitted. "I figured that's how you got into the house." She turned to look at him through a veil of golden hair, her eyes wide and her lips questioningly pursed. "Am I right?"

"It was no big deal." Cowboy wanted to kiss her, but he opened the can of soda instead.

She sat up, pulling her hair back from her face. "Except if you slipped and fell. Then it would be a *very* big deal."

He had to laugh, handing her the can. "There's no way I would slip. It just wasn't that tough a climb."

Her eyebrow went up into a delicate, quizzical arch as she took a sip of the ginger ale. "No? What exactly *is* a tough climb?"

Cowboy found himself looking at the freckles that were sprinkled liberally across her cheeks and nose. Her skin looked so soft and smooth, and he could smell the sweet freshness of her clean hair. Great big God, he wanted to kiss her. But she'd asked him a question.

"Let's see...." He cleared his throat. "Tough is going up the side of an oil rig in freezing weather, coming out of a forty-five degree ocean, carrying more than a hundred pounds of wet gear on my back. Compared to that, this was nothing. Piece a cake." He looked down at his uniform. "I didn't even get dirty."

She took another sip of her soda, gazing at him pensively. "Well, you've certainly proved *my* point."

Cowboy didn't follow. "Your point...?"

"Climbing three stories up the outside of a house *isn't* a 'piece a cake.' It's dangerous. And it's on the absolute opposite end of the spectrum from average and normal."

He laughed. "Oh, come on. Are you saying I should have just let you lie here and feel sick even though I knew it wouldn't take me more than three minutes tops to get inside the house and get you the ginger ale and crackers?"

Melody pressed the cold can against the side of her face. "Yes. No. I don't know!"

"So what? So I can do some things that other guys can't do," he countered.

She stood up. "That's like Superman saying 'So what—I can leap tall buildings in a single bound.'"

She was preparing to go inside. He should have locked the door behind him when he came outside. "Melody, please. You've got to give me a chance—"

"A chance?" Her laughter was tinged with hysteria. "Asking someone to fly to Vegas to marry you isn't exactly what *I'd* call a *chance!*"

He straightened up. "I can't believe you don't even want to try."

"What's to try? Your leave is up tomorrow morning. God only knows where you'll be going and for how long! If I marry you tonight, I could be a..." She stopped herself, closing her eyes and shaking her head. "No," she said, "forget it. Forget I said that.

That doesn't matter, because I'm *not* going to marry you.'' She opened the screen door. "Not now, not ever. It's as simple as that, Jones. And there's nothing you can do to make me change my mind, short of mutating into a nearsighted accountant or a balding computer programmer.''

Cowboy stopped himself from taking a step toward her, afraid to push her farther into the house. "I'll make arrangements to get more leave.''

"No," she said, and she actually had tears in her eyes. "Don't. I'm sorry, Jones, but please don't. The next time I need rescuing, I'll call you, all right? But until then, do us both a favor and stay away.''

"Mel, wait—''

She closed the door firmly in his face and he resisted the urge to swear and kick it down.

Now what?

Short of going inside after her, Cowboy was stuck waiting for her to come back out. And something told him that she wasn't likely to do that again today.

He needed more time. *Lots* more time.

And he knew exactly the man who could help him.

Chapter 7

"Will *some*body spend the damn hundred bucks to get me more memory for this thing? It's like trying to surf the net on one of those kiddie kickboards. I swear to my sweet Lord above, if this takes much longer, I'm not going to be responsible for my actions!" Wes was giving the computer screen his best psychotic-killer glare when Cowboy tapped him on the shoulder.

"Have you seen the senior chief?"

Wes didn't even look up. "Yo, Bobby—is H. here?" he shouted across the busy Quonset hut before muttering to the computer, "Don't you hang on me. Don't you dare."

"Nope," Bobby shouted back.

"Nope." Wes finally glanced up. "Oh, hey, Cowman! You're back. Feeling better?" His smile turned knowing. "Finally get some?"

Cowboy swatted the smaller man on the back of the head. "None of your damned business, gutterbrain. And by the way, I could see with my own eyes that Harvard isn't here. I was wondering if you knew where I could find him."

"Cowboy didn't get any," Wes announced in a megaphone

voice that belied his compact size as Cowboy moved farther into the Quonset hut, searching for a free desk and a telephone. *Some-*body on this base had to know where Harvard was. "Look out, guys. It's like the groundhog seeing his shadow. Cowboy goes on leave and doesn't score and we're in for another six months of winter."

"It's October," Blue McCoy pointed out in his slow Southern drawl. "Winter's coming anyway."

"Good thing *some*thing's coming." Lucky cracked himself up.

Cowboy pretended not to hear as he picked up the phone and dialed Joe Cat's home number.

"Maybe it's the hair," Wes suggested. "Maybe she'd go for you if you got it cut."

"Maybe you need a distraction," Bobby chimed in. "Wes and I hooked up with some really amazing-looking girls who hang out at the Western Bar. Problem is, there's *three* of 'em, so you'd actually be doing us a favor if—"

"No, thanks," Cowboy said, listening to the phone ring. "I'm not interested."

"Yeah, that's what I said, too." Lucky put his feet up on his desk. "I figured since it was Bobby and Wes, they didn't mean amazing-looking like a *Sports Illustrated* swimsuit model, but amazing-looking like someone from the bar scene in *Star Wars.*"

Bobby shook his head. "You're wrong about this one, O'Donlon. I'm talking potential supermodels."

"Potential. That means either they're twelve or in need of plastic surgery." Lucky rolled his eyes.

"One of these days, O'Donlon," Blue said in his soft voice, "you're going to come face-to-face with the one woman on this earth who alone has the ability to make your sorry life complete, and you're going to walk away from her because she's not an eleven on a scale from one to ten."

"Yeah, yeah, I know. Poor, pitiful me." Lucky pretended to wipe tears from his eyes. "I'm going to die alone—an old and broken man."

Over at Joe Cat's house, an answering machine picked up. "Capt. Joe Catalanotto," Cat's New Yawk-accented voice growled into Cowboy's ear. "I'm not available. Leave a message at the beep."

"Yeah, Skipper, this is Jones. If you see the senior chief, tell him I'm looking to find him ASAP."

"This ol' bar we go to is right up your alley, Texas-boy," Wesley said with an exaggerated Western drawl when Cowboy hung up the phone. "There's line dancin' and boot scootin' and everything short of a rodeo bull."

"Including Staci, Tiffani and pretty little Savannah Lee," Bobby said with a sigh. "Course with our luck, Wes, Jones'll hit the dance floor and walk out with all three of 'em on his arm."

"I'm not interested," Cowboy said again. *"Really."*

On the other side of the Quonset hut, the door burst open.

Joe Cat entered with Harvard right behind him. Neither of the two men looked very happy. "Pack it all up, guys, we've been reassigned. We're getting the hell out of here."

Reassigned. Cowboy felt his heart sink. Damn, the last thing he wanted to do was be forced to ask for a transfer away from the Alpha Squad. But if they were being sent overseas...

He had responsibilities now. Responsibilities and different priorities.

Two days ago, his number-one goal would've been to stay with Alpha Squad for as long as he possibly could, no matter where they went, no matter what they did.

Today, his number-one goal was very different.

"What the hell, Cat?" Bobby spoke up. "I thought this FinCOM agent training gig was our silver bullet."

"Yeah, this was the perfect cushy assignment," Lucky added. "Lots of R and R with the added bonus of a chance to really mess with some Finks' minds."

Joe Cat was steamed. "Yes, pulling this assignment was supposed to be a reward," he told them. "But silver bullet or not, our job was to train a team of FinCOM agents in counterterrorist techniques. We can't possibly train these people effectively if our hands are completely tied—which is the only way the top brass will let us do it."

"Aw, come on, Cat. So we let the Finks sleep in their fancy

hotel and we let them do their twenty-mile run from the back seat of a limo,'' Wes urged. ''It's no skin off our noses.''

''Yeah, Captain, we can cope with their rule book.'' Lucky pulled his feet down off his desk. ''It's no big deal.''

''It'll probably make the job that much easier for us,'' Bobby argued.

''These agents we were supposed to train,'' Harvard countered in his rich bass voice, ''are going to be used in the field to back up or work with SEAL units. *I* sure as hell wouldn't want to go up against a crazy-assed pack of 'Brothers of the Light' terrorists with some badly trained FinCOM team of fools as the only thing preventing Alpha Squad from being shipped home in body bags.''

There was no argument anyone could make against *that*.

''So where's Alpha Squad going, Cat?'' Cowboy broke the gloomy silence.

The dark-haired captain looked up at his men and exhaled a single burst of extremely nonhumorous laughter. ''Barrow,'' he enunciated with extra clarity.

''*Alaska?*'' Wesley's voice cracked. ''In the *winter?*''

''You got it,'' Cat said, smiling grimly. ''The pencil pushers upstairs are not happy with me right now, and they're making sure I know it—and you poor bastards pay.''

Alaska. Cowboy closed his eyes and swore.

''Not planning to come with us, Junior?'' Harvard never missed a thing, no matter how subtle the comment. And Cowboy had said ''Alpha Squad,'' not ''we.''

Cowboy lowered his voice. ''I have a situation, Senior Chief. I was hoping to talk to you privately. I need to take an extended leave. A full thirty days if possible.''

Wesley overheard. ''Leave? Hell, yeah, H., I need to take some, too. Anything to get out of going to *Alaska.*''

''Let's get this gear packed and stored,'' Joe Cat ordered. ''Our new assignment has us going wheels up in less than two hours.''

Harvard shook his head. ''Sorry, Jones. There's no time. We'll have to deal with it after we get to Barrow.''

''Senior Chief, wait.'' Cowboy stopped him short. Suddenly,

the answer to this top-brass-induced snafu seemed obvious. "Don't you see? That's the solution. Leave. For *everyone.*"

Understanding sparked in Harvard's dark brown eyes and then he laughed. "Harlan Jones Jr., you have the devious soul of a master chief. Cat, guess what Junior here thought up all by himself? The Answer, with a capital *A.*"

"We've probably all got lots of time coming to us. Hell, I've got a full 120 days on the books," Cowboy continued. "And if we stall long enough, say maybe two or three weeks, they won't want to ship us up to northern Alaska because of the risk of bad weather. There's no way they'd send Alpha Squad someplace we could be snowed in—I've heard of people going up there and not able to get back until spring. No matter how ticked off they are at the skipper, they won't do that to SEAL Team Ten's top counterterrorist squad."

Everyone else in the room was listening now, too, including Joe Cat.

Blue McCoy laughed softly, shaking his head. "What do you think, Joe?" he said to the captain. "A vacation in the Virgin Islands with your wife and kid, or cold-water exercises for the squad in Barrow, Alaska?"

Joe Cat looked at Cowboy and smiled. "I'm gonna get hammered for this, but...who wants leave?"

The curtains were up and hanging in the nursery windows.

Melody had meant to do that project before she got too large to stand on a chair. She'd put it off for too long, of course, and had been meaning to ask Brittany to help.

It looked as if Britt had beaten her to the punch.

Melody went back into her bedroom and quickly dialed her sister's number at the hospital. As she waited for Brittany to come to the phone, she sat on her bed and wriggled out of her panty hose. Even with the stretch panel in the front, they were hellish to wear for more than an hour or two.

"Brittany Evans."

"Hi, it's me," Melody said. "I wanted to let you know that I'm home from Ted's photo op."

"It took longer than you thought."

"It was late getting started."

"You weren't standing up that entire time, were you?" Brittany asked.

"No, I wasn't," Melody said. She hadn't been standing, she'd been running. She lay back on the bed, exhausted. "Thank you for hanging the curtains."

"You're purposely changing the subject," Brittany accused her. "It was awful, wasn't it?" she guessed. "You spent half the time with your ankles swelling and the other half of the time in the ladies' room, throwing up."

"Not *half* the time."

"Sweetie, you've got to give Ted Shepherd your notice. This is crazy."

"I told him I'd work up to the election. I *promised* him." Melody *liked* the hectic busyness of her job. All day today, she'd only thought about Harlan Jones a few dozen times rather than the few million times she'd caught herself thinking about him yesterday.

She closed her eyes, feeling a familiar surge of regret. Jones had left. He'd actually gotten into his car and driven away. But that was what she'd wanted, she reminded herself. It was for the best.

"Look, I'm bringing home Chinese for dinner tonight," Brittany told her, "so don't even *think* about cooking. I want you to be in bed, napping, when I get home."

"Believe me, I'm not going anywhere."

"I'll be home around six. I've got some errands to run."

"Britt, wait. Thanks—really—for hanging those curtains."

There was a pause on the other end of the phone. "Yeah, you said that before, didn't you? *What* curtains?"

"The ones in the nursery."

"Mel, I haven't had the time or energy to even go *into* the nursery over the past few days, let alone hang up any curtains."

"But..." Melody sat up. From her vantage point on the bed, she could see up the stairs into the tower room she'd made into a nursery. The bright colored curtains she'd bought to match the animals she'd stenciled on the nursery walls were moving gently in a breeze from an open window.

An open window...?

Melody stood up. "Brittany, my God, I think he's back!"

"*Who's* back?"

"Jones."

"Oh, thank you, Almighty Father!"

"Hey, whose side are you on here?" Melody asked her sister indignantly.

"*Yours.* The man is to die for, Mel. He's clearly got his priorities straight when it comes to his responsibilities, he's impossibly polite, he seems *very* sweet, he's got excellent taste in jewelry and he's built like a Greek statue. And oh, yeah. As if that wasn't enough, he just happens to look like Kevin Costner on a *good* hair day! Marry him. The rest will sort itself out."

"I'm *not* marrying him. He doesn't love me. And *I* don't love *him.*"

"Why not? I'm half in love with him myself already."

Melody crossed to her bedroom window and looked down into the yard. "Oh, God, Britt, I've got to go! There's a tent in the backyard!"

"A *what?*"

"A *tent.*"

"Like a circus tent—?"

"No," Melody said. "Like a camping tent. Like..."

Jones pushed his way out of the tent and into the yard. The sun glistened off his bare chest and shoulders. He wore only faded jeans, a pair of worn-out cowboy boots and a beat-up baseball cap. His hair was down loose around his tanned shoulders.

"Like an army tent," she finished weakly.

Melody knew that the Dockers and polo shirt Jones had worn the day he'd arrived in Appleton had been similar to his gleaming white dress uniform. He'd worn both outfits in an attempt to be more formal, more conservative. But these clothes he was wearing now—this was the real Jones.

His message was clear. He was done playing games.

As Melody watched, he bent and made an adjustment to the

tent, and the muscles in his back and arms stood out in sharp relief. He looked dangerous and hard and incredibly, mind-blowingly sexy.

Despite his long hair, he looked much more like the man she'd first come face-to-face with in the middle of a terrorist-controlled embassy all those months ago.

"A *tent?*" Brittany was saying. "In our yard?"

"Brittany, look, I have to go. He's definitely here." As she watched, Jones straightened up and said something. Said something to whom? But then, Andy Marshall scrambled out from inside the tent, laughing—apparently at whatever Jones had said.

"Sweetie, don't be too quick to—"

"Goodbye, Britt!"

Melody cut the connection, and taking a deep breath she headed downstairs.

She went out the kitchen door and stood on the back porch, just watching until Jones looked up. He glanced at Andy but didn't have to say a word. The kid disappeared.

Jones wiped his hands on the thighs of his jeans as he came toward her. He was smiling, but his eyes were guarded—as if he wasn't quite certain of his welcome.

He was correct to be uncertain. "What do you think you're doing?" Melody asked.

He turned to glance back at the tent as if double-checking exactly what he'd erected there. "The inn's a bit pricey," he told her. "I figured since I'm going to stay awhile, it'd be more economical to—"

"How long, exactly, are you planning to stay?" Melody couldn't keep her voice from shaking. How *dare* he just set up camp in her backyard where she would be forced to look at him, to notice him, to *talk* to him if she wanted to tend to her gardening?

Jones propped a foot up on one of the back steps and rested his arms on his knees as he gave her his best smile. "As long as it takes for you to agree to marry me."

She sat down on the top step. "Gonna get pretty cold in a

couple of months, living in a tent. But after a few years, you'll probably get used to it.''

He laughed. ''Honey, there's no way you and I could live this close to each other for even a few weeks, let alone a few years, without one or both of us spontaneously combusting.''

Melody snorted. ''Get real, Jones. Have you looked at me lately? Unless you have a fetish involving beach balls, I'm not likely to set your world on fire any time soon.''

''Are you kidding? You're *gorgeous*. It's very sexy....''

Melody closed her eyes. ''Jones, *please* don't do this.''

She never should have closed her eyes. She didn't see him settle on the step next to her, and by the time she felt him put his arms around her, it was too late. She was trapped.

She hadn't forgotten how strong his arms felt, how safe she felt inside his embrace. And when she looked up at him, she found she hadn't forgotten the little flecks of brown and gold floating in the always changing green ocean of his eyes either. And she hadn't forgotten the way the mysterious darkness of his pupils widened, seemingly enough to swallow her whole, right before he bent to kiss her.

He tasted like coffee, two sugars, no cream. He tasted like Paris in the moonlight, like the rough feel of bricks as he covered her mouth with his and pressed her up against a house that had been built four hundred years before Columbus had sailed west to reach the Far East and discovered America instead.

He tasted like chocolate, like expensive wine, like a second helping of dessert. He tasted like everything she'd ever wanted but had taught herself to refuse for her own sake.

He kissed her so gently, so sweetly, almost reverently as if he had missed her as much as she'd pretended not to miss him. And, God, she *had* missed him. There was a place in her chest that had felt hollow and cold for all these months—until now. Now she felt infused by warmth, both inside and out.

She felt him touch her, the warmth of his palm lightly pressing against her extended belly.

''My God,'' he breathed. ''It's really all you, isn't it?''

Melody saw it then. Jones made an effort to smile as she looked up at him, but he couldn't hide the fact that he was thoroughly unnerved. She was having his baby, and as long as he was with her, there was no way he was going to forget that. She could see from his eyes how disconcerted he was, how unsettled he felt.

And just like that, the hollowness was back, making her feel emptier than ever.

She knew with a dead certainty that if Jones were granted only one wish, it would be that he'd had a condom on that flight to Paris. She knew that being tied down with a wife and a child was the last thing on earth that this man wanted. She knew that the last place in the world that he wanted to be was here, sitting on her porch, talking her into doing something he himself didn't want to do.

And yet here he was. She had to admire him for that.

She could see the determination in his eyes as he leaned toward her one more time. His lips were so soft as he kissed her again. She was reminded just how very astute he was when it came to reading her needs. He somehow knew that these gentle, almost delicate kisses would get him much further than the intensely passionate, soul-sucking inhalations of desire they'd shared time and again in Paris.

Of course, it was entirely possible that he was kissing her without that explosion of passion because he no longer felt passion for her.

And why should he? She was a constant reminder of his obligations and responsibilities. And on top of that, she was about as sexy as a double-wide trailer.

Still, he kissed her so sweetly, she felt like melting.

Melody was in deep trouble here. Lt. Cowboy Jones was a warrior and a psych expert. While other men might well have been put off by her constant rejections, he was unswervable. And it was more than obvious that he had a battle plan as far as she was concerned. He'd figured out that she wasn't immune to him. He'd realized that he was still firmly entrenched under her skin and he'd dug in to wait her out. Time and her traitorous hormones were on his side. She was going to have to be even stronger.

She was going to have to start by pulling away from this delicious kiss that was making her knees feel even more rubbery than usual. She was going to have to unlock her fingers from the thick softness of his hair. She was going to have to be tougher than this.

Melody stood up, slipping free from his embrace. "Excuse me," she said. It was amazing how she could sound so calm when inside she was experiencing an emotional tornado. "I have to go inside." He stood up, too. "Alone," she added.

He tried to hide his frustration by taking a deep breath and smiling. "Mel, honey, what do I have to do to convince you—"

"I think the presence of your tent on my property constitutes trespassing. I'll thank you very much to remove it."

He laughed at that. "I figured this way it was hidden behind the house. I thought the fewer people who knew about it, the better. But if you insist, I'll move the tent over into the Romanellas' yard. Vince said that would be okay. Of course, then everyone in town will be able to see it from the street."

"I don't care," Melody said. "Odds are everyone in town knows it's there already."

He took a step toward her and she took a step back. "Mel." He held out his hands, palms facing down as if he were calming a wild animal. "Think about this for a minute. We're both on the same side here. We're both trying to find the best solution for this situation."

"Jones, I *know* you don't really want to marry me," she said. "What I don't know is how you'd be able to make yourself say those wedding vows. It would all be a lie. 'Til death us do part. Yeah, right. Until divorce us do part is more like it. You know it as well as I do."

He leaned back against the porch rail, folding his arms across his chest. "You're right about the fact that I don't want to get married," he admitted. "But if I've got to marry *some*one, I'd just as soon have it be you."

"And *I'd* just as soon have it be someone normal—" She cut herself off. "God, haven't we had this conversation already?"

"Yes," he said. "And I'm going to say it again. I'm no different from any other man."

"Except for the fact that when you get in a knife fight with four-to-one odds against you, you win." Melody shook her head. "Jones, don't you see how incredibly out of place you are here?"

"I'm a SEAL," he said. "I've been trained to adapt to any environment or culture. Appleton, Massachusetts, shouldn't be that big a deal." He straightened up. "Where's the edge trimmer? In the garage?"

She blinked. "What? Why?"

He adjusted his baseball cap as he went down the steps and started walking backward along the path toward the garage as he talked. "You said you couldn't picture me using an edge trimmer. I'm going to help you out by actually letting you watch me use one."

Melody's laughter was on the verge of being hysterical. "You're not going to leave, are you? You're just going to stay here forever and torment me."

He stopped walking. With the sun shining down on him, glistening off his tanned skin, gleaming off his gold-streaked hair, he looked invincible. "That depends on your definition of 'torment.'"

Melody sat down on the steps, fighting the urge to burst into tears. She was *so* tired. She had all that she could handle working three-quarters time during these past few months of a difficult pregnancy. There was no way she could do that *and* go one-on-one in a battle of wills with a man who didn't know what it meant to quit.

Jones came back toward the porch, his eyes darkening with concern. "Honey, you look a little tuckered out." His voice was soft. "Maybe we should skip the lawn-care demonstration so you can go on upstairs and catch a nap before dinner, huh?"

She knew what he was doing. He was trying to show her that he knew the words and music to the middle-class, suburban song. He was trying to be normal. His words sounded as if they'd been married for years.

But all he'd proved was that he'd watched a few dozen reruns of *The Cosby Show,* or *Family Ties.* It was one thing to mimic and play pretend games. It was another thing entirely to keep up the pretense of being happily married for the rest of his life.

Melody hauled herself to her feet. "You are not normal," she told him. "You'll *never* be normal. And don't kiss me," she added. "Ever again."

Another of his smiles slipped out as he reached for her again, but she escaped into the house, locking the screen door behind her.

"Thank you for hanging the curtains in the nursery," she told him stiffly through the protection of the screen. "But the next time you come into my house uninvited, I *will* have you arrested."

If Jones's smile faltered at all, she didn't see it.

Chapter 8

"**Y**ou did *what?*"

"I gave him a key," Brittany repeated calmly as she checked the rice and turned on the burner underneath the wok, bending over to adjust the gas flame.

Melody's knees were so weak she had to sit down. "To the *house?*"

"Of course to the house." Brittany added some oil to the pan and went back to cutting up the vegetables for the stir-fry. "What good would an open invitation to use the bathroom and the shower be without a key to the house?"

Melody put her head in her hands. "Brittany, what are you doing to me?"

"Sweetie, your SEAL's been living in the backyard for almost a week now—"

"Thanks to your *first* asinine invitation!" Melody proceeded to give a ridiculously unflattering imitation of her sister's voice: "No, Lieutenant, of *course* we don't mind your tent in our back-yard. Of *course,* Lieutenant, you're welcome to stay as long as you like.' I was waiting for you to offer to do his laundry and lay a chocolate out on his pillow each night. Jeez Louise, Britt, didn't you even consider the fact that I might not want him underfoot twenty-four hours a day?''

Her sister was not fazed. ''I'm not convinced you know what you want.''

''Whereas you do?''

The oil was hot enough, and Brittany tossed thin slices of celery into the wok. ''No.''

''Yet you insist on encouraging him to stay.''

''My encouragement hardly makes up for your *dis*couragement. But since he hasn't gone away yet,'' Brittany said, ''I think it's a pretty strong indication that he intends to stay until you give in.''

''I'm not going to give in.''

Brittany turned to face her, knife in hand. ''That's right. You're *not* going to give in—if you keep doing what you're doing. When you leave for work in the morning, you make a beeline for your car. When you come home, you make a beeline for your room. You haven't let the poor man say more than three sentences to you in the past four days.''

Melody lifted her head. ''The 'poor man'?''

Brittany returned some of her attention to her cooking, adding broccoli and thinly cut strips of zucchini squash to the wok. ''I'm with Estelle and Peggy on this one, Mel. I know that's hard to believe—those two seeing eye to eye with me—but it's true. We think you should stop thinking only of yourself and marry the man.''

Melody sat up even straighter. ''You swore when I first told you that I was pregnant that you wouldn't lecture me. You said you'd support me whatever I decided to do.''

''What I just told you wasn't a lecture,'' Brittany said firmly, stirring the vegetables. ''It was an opinion. And I *am* supporting you, the best way I know how.''

''By giving Jones a key to the house and an open invitation to just walk in whenever the mood strikes him?''

''The man is a gem, Mel. This yard has never looked so good!''

Of course the yard looked good. Every time Melody turned

around, Jones was outside her window, raking the leaves or tinkering under the hood of Brittany's car or lifting enormous amounts of weights. Every time she turned around, she caught a flash of sunlight reflecting off smooth, deeply tanned muscles.

Whether it was sunny and sixty degrees or drizzling and barely fifty, Jones went outside without a shirt on. Whether he was working in the yard or sitting and reading a book, he was naked from the waist up. You'd think that after a while she'd get used to the sight of all those muscles rippling enticingly in the sunshine or gleaming wet from the rain.

Yeah, right. Maybe in her next lifetime...

"And I don't know what your lieutenant's done to my car, but it hasn't run this well in years," Brittany added. "You really should let him look at yours."

"He's not *my* lieutenant. And if a smoothly running car is what you're after," Melody said hotly, "maybe I should marry Joe Hewlitt from the Sunoco station instead."

"You're impossibly stubborn," Brittany complained.

"Can we talk about something else?" Melody pleaded. "Isn't there something going on in the world that's more interesting than my nonrelationship with Harlan Jones?"

Brittany made room at the bottom of the sizzling wok for the cubes of tofu she'd cut. "Well, there's always the latest installment in the Andy Marshall adventure."

Melody braced herself. "Oh, no. What did he do this time?"

The stove timer buzzed, and Brittany turned off both it and the heat beneath the rice. "Tom Beatrice caught him outside the liquor store on Summer Street. He'd just given Kevin Thorpe ten bucks to buy him a six-pack of beer and a pack of cigarettes."

"Oh, Andy, you didn't..." Melody sighed, resting her chin in the palm of one hand. "Damn, I thought he was finally adjusting to Appleton."

She'd seen Andy out in the yard, hanging around Jones while he worked. Jones always had time to talk. Sometimes he even stopped to toss a ball around with the kid. She'd been secretly impressed with his patience and hoped that Andy had finally latched on to a man who was, indeed, a worthy role model.

There was no doubt about it. The boy was starved for affection and attention. Melody had run into him a few times downtown over the past week.

The first time they talked, he'd hesitantly reached out to touch her belly again, smiling almost shyly when the baby kicked.

The second time, she'd bumped into him—literally. His cheek was scraped and his lip was swollen, and although he'd insisted he'd fallen off his bicycle, she knew Alex Parks and his friends had been giving the younger boy trouble again. The third time, he'd actually greeted Melody with a hug. He'd said hello to the baby by pressing his face against Mel's stomach—and got kicked in the nose for his trouble. That sent him rolling on the ground with giddy laughter.

He was a good kid. Melody was convinced that deep inside he had a sweet, caring soul. He shouldn't be trying to grow up so fast, drinking beer and smoking cigarettes. "He's only twelve. He probably doesn't even like the *taste* of beer."

"He's twelve going on thirty," Brittany said grimly, "which, at the rate he's going, is how old he'll be when he finally gets out of jail. It's a wonder Tom didn't lock the little jerk up."

"Who's Tom and which little jerk didn't he lock up?"

Melody's shoulders tensed. Just like that, merely at the sound of Jones's voice, she was an instant bundle of screaming nerves.

He was standing on the other side of the screen door, looking into the kitchen.

"Tom Beatrice is the Appleton chief of police. And the little jerk is the kid who's running for Troublemaker of the Year—Andy Marshall. Come on in," Brittany called from the stove. "Dinner's almost ready."

Melody stood up, crossing to stand next to her sister. "You invited him to dinner?" she whispered through clenched teeth.

"Yes, I invited him to dinner," Brittany said evenly. "There's beer in the fridge," she told Jones. "Help yourself. And if you don't mind, would you grab one for me and pour a glass of milk for Mel?"

"It'd be my pleasure. Hey, Mel." Jones had dressed for the occasion. He was actually wearing a T-shirt with his jeans, and his hair was pulled back from his face in a single neat braid. "How're you feeling?"

Betrayed. Melody sat down at the kitchen table and forced a smile. "Fine, thanks."

"Really?" He sat down directly across from her, of course, where she wouldn't be able to keep from looking at him while they ate. *Why* did he have to be so utterly good-looking? And why did he have to smile at her that way all the time, as if they were constantly sharing a secret or a very personal private joke?

"Mel's been having trouble with backaches again," Brittany announced as she set the wok on a hot pad in the middle of the table.

Jones took a sip of his beer directly from the bottle as he gazed at Melody. "I'm available any time you want a back rub."

She remembered his back rubs. She remembered them too well. She looked everywhere but into his eyes. "Thanks, but a soak in the tub'll take care of it."

Jones took the serving bowl filled with steaming rice that Brittany handed to him. "Thanks. This looks delicious. What's up with Andy Marshall?"

"The little fool was caught trying to get his hands on beer and cigarettes," Melody told him.

Jones paused as he dished out the rice onto his plate, stopping to look up at her. "Shoplifting?"

She shook her head. "No. He paid Kevin Thorpe to buy them for him."

Jones nodded, passing her the heavy bowl. "At least he wasn't stealing."

Their fingers touched, and Melody knew damn well it wasn't an accident. Still, she ignored it. Her heart could not leap when he touched her. She simply would not let it. Still, she had to work to keep her voice even. "He shouldn't be drinking or smoking. Whether or not he stole the beer and cigarettes is a moot point."

"No, it's not. It's—"

The phone rang, interrupting him.

Brittany excused herself and stood up to answer it. "Hello?"

Jones lowered his voice. "I think the fact that Andy didn't

simply go into the store and walk out with a stolen can of beer in his pocket says a lot about him.''

"Yeah, it says that he wanted more than one can of beer. He wanted an entire six-pack.''

"It says he's not a thief.''

"I'm sorry," Brittany interrupted. "That was Edie Myerson up at the hospital. Both Brenda and Sharon called in sick with the flu. I'm going to have to go over and cover for at least two hours—until Betty McCreedy can come in.''

Melody looked up at her sister in shock. She was leaving her alone with Jones? "But—"

"I'm sorry. I've got to run." Brittany grabbed her bag and was already out the door.

"Where's Andy now? Do you know?" Jones asked, barely missing a beat in their conversation, as if the situation hadn't just moved from embarrassingly awkward to downright impossible to deal with. He took a mouthful of the stir-fry. "Man, this is good. After a week of Burger King and KFC, my body is craving vegetables.''

Melody set down her fork. "Did you and Brittany plan this?''

He washed down his mouthful of food with a sip directly from his bottle of beer. "You really think I'd stoop to lying and subterfuge just for a chance to talk to you?''

"Yes.''

Jones grinned. "Yeah, you're right. I would. But that's not what this is. I swear. Your sister invited me for dinner. That's all.''

The stupid thing was, she believed him. Brittany, on the other hand, had probably planned to leave right from the start.

Melody picked up her fork but couldn't seem to do more than push the food around on her plate as Jones had a second helping. Her appetite had vanished, replaced by a nervous flock of butterflies that took up every available inch of space in her rolling stomach.

"So how's work?" he asked. "Are you always this busy?''

"It's going to get frantic as the election gets closer.''

"Are you going to be able to keep up?" He gazed at her

steadily. "I got some books about pregnancy and prenatal care out of the library, and they all seem to agree that you should take care not to push yourself too hard these last few months. You know, you look tired."

Melody took a sip of her milk, wishing he would stop looking at her so closely, feeling as if she were under a microscope. She *knew* she looked tired. She *was* tired and bedraggled, and this dress she had on made her resemble a circus tent. How had Andy described her? Fat and funny-looking. "I'll be fine."

"Maybe I could come to work with you—act as your assistant or gofer."

Melody nearly sprayed him with milk. Come to work with her? God, wouldn't *that* be perfect? "That's really not a very good idea." It was the understatement of the century.

"Maybe we should compromise," he suggested. "I won't come to work with you, if you stop ignoring me."

He was smiling, but there was a certain something in his eyes that told her he wasn't quite kidding.

"I haven't been ignoring you," she protested. "I've been practicing self-restraint."

He leaned forward, eyebrows rising. "Self-restraint?"

She backed off, aware that she'd already slipped and told him too much. She had to get out of here before she did something really stupid—like throw herself into his arms. "Excuse me." She pushed her chair back from the table and stood up, then carried her plate to the kitchen sink.

Cowboy took another long sip of his beer, hiding the relief that was streaming through him. He could do this. He could actually succeed in this mission.

He'd been starting to doubt his ability to get through to her, starting to think she just plain disliked him, but in fact the opposite was true. Self-restraint, she'd said.

Hell, she liked him so much she couldn't stand to be in the same room with him, for fear she wouldn't be able to resist his attempts to seduce her.

Yes, he could win this war. He could—and he would—convince her to marry him before his leave was up.

His relief was edged with something else. Something sharp and pointed. Something an awful lot like fear. Yeah, he could take his time and make her see that marrying him was the only option. But then where would he be?

Saddled with a wife and a baby. Shackled with a ball and chain. Tied down, tied up, out of circulation, out of the action. A husband and a father. Two roles he'd never thought he would ever be ready to play.

But he had no choice. Not if he wanted to live with himself for the rest of his life.

Cowboy took a deep breath. ''Mel, wait.''

She turned to look warily back at him.

Cowboy didn't stand up, knowing that if he so much as moved, she'd run for the stairs. Damn, she was that afraid of him—and that afraid of the spark that was always ready to ignite between them.

Still, he'd made her trust him before, under even more difficult circumstances. He could do it again. He *had* to do it again, no matter how hard, no matter how much fear of his own he felt. This was too important to him.

He took a deep breath. ''What if I promised...?'' What? That he wouldn't pull her into his arms? Wouldn't try to kiss her? He needed to do both of those things as much as he needed to keep breathing. Keeping his distance from this woman was going to be hard to do. Nevertheless, he had no choice. It was gonna hurt, but he'd done hard and painful things before. ''What if I swore I wouldn't touch you? You pick a distance. Two feet, three feet, six feet, whatever, and I promise I won't cross that line.''

She wasn't convinced. He could see her about to turn him down, but he didn't give her a chance to speak.

''I also promise that I won't say a single word tonight about weddings or obligations or responsibilities or anything heavy. We'll talk about something entirely different. We'll talk about—'' he was grasping at straws here, but she hadn't left the room yet ''—Andy Marshall, all right? We'll figure out what we're going to do about him.''

She turned to face him. ''What *can* we do?''

Cowboy already knew the best way to deal with Andy—directly, ruthlessly and mercilessly. He'd been intending to call on Vince Romanella later tonight and ask his permission to spend part of tomorrow with the kid.

But why not teach Andy his lesson tonight?

"There's a place in the woods, up by the old quarry," he told Melody, willing her to sit back down at the table, "that's always littered with beer bottles and cigarette butts. My guess is that's where Andy was going to go with his six-pack."

Melody actually sat down, and Cowboy used all of his self-control to keep from reacting. He had to play it really cool or she'd run.

"I know the place you mean," she said. "It was a popular hangout spot back when I was in high school, too. But Andy's only twelve. He wouldn't exactly be welcome there."

"He would if he showed up with a six-pack of brew under his arm."

"Why on earth would Andy want to make friends with high school seniors?" Melody wondered.

"That kid he's always fighting with," Cowboy said. "What's his name? Parks?"

"Alex Parks."

"He's only a freshman or a sophomore, right?"

Melody nodded. She was actually looking into his eyes. She was actually sitting there and talking to him. He knew it was only a small victory, but he'd take 'em where he found 'em.

"Well, there you go," he concluded. "It seems like a pretty sound strategy to me. Make friends with people who can crush—or at least control—your enemy. Andy's not stupid."

"Then the six-pack was really just an offering to the gods, so to speak. Andy wasn't really going to drink it."

Her eyes begged him to tell her she was right. He wished he could agree so that she would smile at him, but he couldn't.

"I'd bet he wasn't planning to drink all of it," he told her, "but he was certainly intending to drink some. Probably enough to give him a good buzz. And to come out of it thinking the entire evening was a positive experience. Which would leave him wanting to go back and do it again.''

Melody nodded, her face so serious, her eyes still glued to his as if he held all the wisdom and knowledge in the universe.

"So what we've got to do," Cowboy continued, "is make sure his first experience with a six-pack of beer is a nightmare."

She blinked. And then she leaned forward. "I'm not sure I understand."

"Remember Crash?" Cowboy asked. "William Hawk? My swim buddy?"

"Of course."

"To this day, he doesn't drink. At least I assume he still doesn't. He didn't during the time we were going through BUD/S training. Anyway, he told me he wasn't much older than Andy when his uncle caught him sneaking a beer from the downstairs refrigerator." It was one of the few stories about his childhood that Crash had told Cowboy. And he'd told it only to convince Cowboy that no, he didn't want a beer, thank you very much. "Crash's uncle taught him a thing or two that day, and we, in turn, are going to run the same drill with Andy." He smiled ruefully. "It's a lesson I could've used myself, but the admiral wasn't around enough to know what kind of trouble I was getting myself into."

She was watching him. "I thought you told me your father was really strict."

"He was—when he was home. But after we moved to Texas, he was hardly ever home. There were a few years he even missed Christmas."

He had her full attention and he kept going. She claimed they didn't know each other. And as hard as it was to talk about his less-than-perfect childhood, it was important that she understood where he came from—and why walking away from her and this baby was not an option for him.

"You know, I used to be like Andy," he continued, "always making excuses for my old man. He had to go where he was needed. He was very important. He had to be where the action was. Even though—during the Vietnam conflict—he'd more than earned the chance to sit back and relax, he wouldn't ask to be assigned to a cushy post like Hawaii. Hawaii wasn't exactly what my mother wanted, but she would have settled for it. But old Harlan wanted to keep moving forward in his career.

"I always used to think he had such a tough job—going out to sea for all those months, being in charge of all those men, knowing that if an aggressive action started, he'd be right in the middle of it. But the fact is, that stuff was easy for him. *We* were the hard stuff. A wife who honestly didn't understand why he didn't retire from the Navy and take a job selling cars with her Uncle Harold. A kid who needed more than constantly being told that B's and B pluses weren't good enough. You know, I could work my butt off, cleaning my room for him, making it shipshape, and he would focus on the one spot of dust I'd missed. Yeah," he repeated softly, "we were the hard stuff, and he ran away from us."

She didn't say anything, but he knew she read his message loud and clear. *He* wasn't going to run away.

Cowboy pushed back his chair, still careful to move slowly. "Mind if I use your phone?"

She shook her head, distracted, as if she were still absorbing all that he'd told her. But then she looked up. "Wait. You haven't told me exactly what Crash's uncle did that day."

"Do you have Vince Romanella's number—?" Cowboy scanned the list of neighbors' and friends' numbers posted on a corkboard near the kitchen phone. "Here it is. And as for Crash's uncle..." He smiled at her. "You're just going to have to wait and see." He dialed Vince's number.

She laughed in disbelief. "Jones. Just tell me."

"Hey, Vince," he said into the phone, "it's Jones—you know, from the Evanses next door? I heard about the trouble Andy got into this evening. Is he there?"

"He's probably in his room, grounded for a week and writing a twenty-page paper on why he shouldn't drink beer," Melody said, rolling her eyes. "Vince's heart is in the right place, but something tells me all the essay writing in the world isn't going to have any impact on a kid like Andy Marshall."

Across the room, Jones smiled again. "You're right," he mouthed to her, shaking his head as he listened to Vince recount the evening's excitement—and the subsequent ineffective punishment.

"Yeah," Jones said into the phone, "I know he's grounded, Vince, but I think I know a way to make sure he doesn't drink again—at least not until he's old enough to handle it." He laughed. "You heard of that method, too? Well, a friend of mine told me that when he was a kid... Yeah, I can understand that. As his official foster parents, the state might not approve of... But I'm not his foster parent, so..." He laughed again.

The way he was standing, leaning against the kitchen counter, phone receiver held easily under his chin, reminded Melody of Paris. He'd stood the same way in the hotel lobby, leaning back against the concierge's desk as he took a call. Except back then, he'd been wearing a U.S. Navy uniform, he'd been speaking flawless French and he'd been looking at her with heat simmering in his eyes.

There was still heat there now, but it was tempered by a great deal of reserve and caution. In Paris, the idea of an unwanted, unplanned pregnancy had been the furthest thing from either of their minds. But here in Appleton, the fact that they'd made an error in judgment was kind of hard to avoid. She carried an extremely obvious and constant reminder with her everywhere she went.

And as much as he was pretending otherwise, Melody knew that Jones didn't really want to marry her.

"Okay," he said into the telephone now. His slightly twangy Western drawl still had the power to send chills down her spine. "That'd be great. There's no time like the present, so send him over." He hung up the phone. "Andy's on his way."

Melody forced the chills away. "What are you planning to do?"

Jones smiled. "I'm going to wait and tell you at the same time I tell Andy. That way, we can get a good-cop, bad-cop thing going that'll sound really sincere."

"Jones, for crying out loud..."

His smile turned to a grin. "I thought pregnant women were supposed to be really patient."

"Oh yeah? Guess again. With all these extra hormones flying around in my system, I sometimes feel like Lizzie Borden's crazier sister."

"One of the books I was reading said that during pregnancy most women feel infused with a sense of calm."

"Someone forgot to give me my infusion," Melody told him.

Jones opened the door to the pantry. "I'm ready with a back rub at any time. Just say the word."

She narrowed her eyes at him. "Hey, you promised—"

"I did, and I'm sorry. Please accept my apology." He pulled the string and the pantry light went on. "Do you have any beer that's not in the fridge?"

"Brittany keeps it in there, on the bottom shelf," Melody directed him. "Why?"

"Yup, here it is." He emerged from the pantry with a six-pack of tallboys. "Nice and warm, so the flavor is...especially enhanced. Tell your sister I'll replace these. But right now, Andy needs it more than she does."

"Andy needs...? Jones, what are you—"

"We better go out on the patio." He flipped the light switches next to the kitchen door until he found the one that lit the old-fashioned stone patio out back. "This *will* get messy. It's better to be outside."

"*Please* just tell me—"

Melody broke off as she saw Andy standing defiantly at the bottom of the porch stairs. "Vince said you want to see me."

"Yes, we certainly do." Jones held open the back door for Melody.

"He said to give you this." The boy spoke in a near monotone as he held out a half-empty pack of cigarettes. "He said they're from three months ago, when his brother came to visit. He said to tell you that they're probably stale but that he didn't think you'd mind."

Andy tossed the pack into the air, and Jones caught it effortlessly in his left hand. "Thanks. Heard you were hoping to do some partying tonight."

Melody grabbed her jacket from the hook by the door and slipped it on as she went out into the cool evening air. "Hello, Andy." The boy wouldn't meet her gaze. He wouldn't even glance up at her.

"So what? It's not that big a deal," Andy sullenly told Jones.

"Yeah, that's what I figured you'd say." Jones set the beer down on the picnic table that sat in the center of the patio. He brushed a few stray leaves from one of the chairs for Melody. "You just wanted to have some fun. And it was only beer. What's the fuss, right?"

There was a flash of surprise in Andy's eyes before he caught himself and settled back into sullen mode. "Well, yeah," he said. "Right. It's only beer."

Melody didn't sit. "Jones, what are you doing?" she whispered. "Are you actually *agreeing* with him?"

"All I'm saying is that people get uptight about the littlest things. Sit down, Andy," Jones commanded. "So you're a beer drinker, huh?"

Andy slouched into a chair, a picture of feigned nonchalance. His nervousness was betrayed by the way he kept fiddling with the wide leather band of his beloved wristwatch. "It's all right. I've had it a few times. Like I said, it's no big deal."

Jones took one of the cans off the plastic loop that held the six-pack together. "Drinking some brew and having a few smokes. Just a regular old, no-big-deal Saturday night. You were planning to go up to the quarry, huh?"

Andy gave Jones a perfect poker face. "Up where?"

"To the quarry." Jones exaggerated his enunciation.

Andy shrugged. "Never heard of it."

"Don't try to con a con artist. I know you know where the quarry is. You've been up there while I was doing laps. You don't really think I didn't notice you—sneaking up on me like a herd of stampeding elephants."

"I was quiet!" Andy was insulted.

"You were thunderous."

"I was *not!*"

"Well, okay, so you were relatively quiet," Jones conceded, "but not quiet enough. There's no SEAL on earth who would've missed hearing you."

Melody couldn't stay silent a moment longer. "You swim *laps* in the *quarry?*"

"First he runs five miles," Andy told her. "I know, because I clocked it on my bike. Then he swims—sometimes for half an hour without stopping, sometimes with all of his clothes on."

It was Jones's turn to shrug. "Every so often in the units, you take an unplanned swim and end up in the water, weighed down with all your clothes and gear. It's good to stay in practice for any situation."

"But the water up there's cold in August," Melody argued. "It's October, and lately we've had frost at night. It must be *freezing.*"

Jones grinned. "Yeah, well, lately I've been swimming a little faster."

"And then after you swim, you run another five miles back here," Andy said, "where you work out with your weights."

Melody knew about the weights. She'd been getting dressed each morning for the past week to the sound of clinking as Jones bench-pressed and lifted enormous-looking weights. But she'd had no idea that he ran and swam before that. He must've been up every morning at the very first light of dawn.

"Even though I'm on vacation, it's important to me that I stay in shape," he explained.

She nearly laughed out loud. This was the man who was going to prove to her how average and normal he truly was?

"But we're getting sidetracked here," Jones continued. "We were talking about beer, right?" He held one of the cans out to Andy. "You want one?"

Andy sat straight up in surprise.

Melody nearly fell over. "Jones! You can't offer him that— he's twelve years old."

"He's clearly been around the block a few times," Jones answered, his eyes never leaving Andy. "Do you want it, Andy?

It's not particularly a great brand, but it's not bad, either—at least as far as American beers go. But you probably already know that, right? Being a beer drinker.''

"Well, yeah. Sure." Andy reached for the can, but Jones wouldn't let go.

"There's a catch," the SEAL told the boy. "You can't have just one. You have to drink the entire six-pack right now. In the next hour."

Melody couldn't believe what she was hearing. "There's no way Andy could *possibly* drink an entire six-pack by himself in an hour."

Andy bristled. "Could, too."

Cowboy leaned forward. "Is that a yes?"

"Damn straight!" the boy replied.

Cowboy popped the top open and handed him the can. "Then chug it on down, my friend."

"Jones," Melody hissed, "there's no way Andy could drink that much without getting..." She stopped herself, and Cowboy knew that she'd finally caught on.

She was right. There *was* no way this kid could drink two cans of warm beer, let alone an entire six-pack, in an hour without getting totally, miserably, horrifically sick.

And that was the point.

Cowboy was going to make damn sure that Andy would associate the overpoweringly bitter taste of beer with one of the most unpleasant side effects of drunkenness.

He watched as Andy took a tentative sip from the can, then as the kid wrinkled his nose at the strong beer taste.

"Gross. It's warm!"

"That's how they serve beer in England," Cowboy told him. "Chilling it hides the taste. Only sissies drink beer cold." He glanced at Mel. She was giving him an "Oh yeah?" look, complete with raised eyebrow. He'd had a chilled beer with dinner tonight himself. He shot her a quick wink. "Come on, Andrew. Bottoms up. Time's a-wasting, and you've got five more cans to drink."

Andy looked a little less certain as he took a deep breath and a long slug of beer, and then another, and another. The kid was tougher than Cowboy had thought—he was actively fighting his urge to gag and spit out the harsh-tasting, room-temperature, totally unappealing beverage.

But Andy wasn't tough enough. He set the empty can on the table, burping loudly, looking as if he was about to protest as Cowboy opened another can and pushed it in front of him.

"You don't have time to talk," Cowboy said. "You only have time to drink."

Andy looked even more uncertain, but he picked up the can and started to drink.

"Are you sure this is going to work?" Melody asked softly, sliding into the seat next to him.

It was already working far better than he'd hoped. Melody was sitting beside him, talking to him, watching him, interacting with him. He was aware of her presence, aware of the heavenly blue of her eyes, aware of her sweet perfume—and more than well aware that he still had a hell of a long way to go before he gained her total trust.

But that wasn't what she'd meant. She'd been talking about Andy.

"Yes," he told her with complete confidence. It would work. Especially with the cigarette factor.

Taking a lighter from the pocket of his jeans, he picked up the half-empty pack Vince had sent over. They were old and stale, Andy had said. Yes, this was definitely going to work.

Cowboy held out the pack to Andy, shaking it slightly so that one cigarette appeared invitingly.

Andy thankfully set down the can of beer and reached for the smoke. He may or may not have wanted it—but Cowboy knew what he was thinking. Anything, *any*thing to take a break from having to drink that god-awful beer.

Cowboy could hear Melody's disbelieving laughter as he leaned across the table to give Andy a light. "Good Lord," she said, "I can't believe I'm sitting here giving beer and cigarettes to a child."

Andy couldn't argue with her use of the word *child*. He'd taken a drag of tobacco smoke and was now coughing as if he was on the verge of asphyxiation.

Cowboy handed him his can of beer. "Here, maybe this'll help."

He knew damn well it wouldn't. It only served to turn Andy a darker shade of green.

"I can't...drink any more," he gasped when he finally found some air.

"Are you kidding?" Cowboy said. "You've got to finish that one and drink four more. We had a deal, remember?"

"Four more?" Now Andy looked as if he was on the verge of tears.

Cowboy opened another can. "Four more."

Melody put her hand on his arm. "Jones, he's just a kid...."

"That's the whole point." He lowered his voice, leaning closer to her so Andy couldn't hear. "He's a kid—who wants to hang out with high school seniors who are too young to drink themselves. It's dangerous in those woods, the way that quarry's flooded. If those kids are going to be walking around up there in the dark, they should be doing it sober, not drunk." He turned to Andy. "You're not even a third done. Get busy, Marshall."

Melody's grip on his arm tightened. "But he's—"

"On the verge of learning an important lesson," Cowboy interrupted. "I don't want him to stop until he's *got* to stop. Believe me, it won't be long now." She was about to protest and he covered her hand with his. "Honey, I know this seems harsh to you, but the alternative is far harsher. Imagine how awful you'll feel if some Sunday morning we've got to go and drag that quarry because the boy genius over there was out staggering around drunk and stupid the night before and fell in and drowned."

She hadn't considered such dire possibilities, and he could see the shock in her eyes. She was close enough for him to count the freckles on her nose, close enough to kiss....

Her thoughts must've been moving in the same direction because she quickly straightened up, pulling her hand out from underneath his.

She'd touched *him.* He saw her realize that as a flush of pink tinged her cheeks. All that talk about keeping his distance—and she was the one who couldn't keep her hands off him.

"I'm sorry," she murmured.

"I know that wasn't about you and me," he quickly reassured her. "That was about your concern for Andy. I didn't read it the wrong way, so don't worry, all right?"

But before she could reply, Andy bolted from the table and lunged for the bushes.

Cowboy stood up. "Go on inside, Mel. I'll take care of him from here on in. I think it's probably best not to have an audience—you know, save the last shreds of his manly pride."

The sound of Andy throwing up a second time seemed to echo in the stillness of the night. Melody winced as she got up and moved toward the kitchen door. "I guess I should go in before I join him in sympathy."

"Oh, hell, I'm sorry—I didn't even think of that possibility."

"I was making a joke. Granted it was a bad one, but..." She smiled at him. It was just a little smile, but it was a smile just the same. His heart leaped crazily at the sight of it. "Are you sure I can't get you anything? A towel or maybe some wet washcloths?"

"No. Thanks. I've got a spare towel in my tent. No sense making you do extra laundry." A joke. She made a joke. He managed to make her feel comfortable enough to make a joke. "Go on, Andy'll be fine. I'll see you later."

Still, she hesitated, looking down at him from the back porch of the house. Cowboy would've liked to believe it was because she was loathe to leave his sparkling good company. But he knew better, and when he looked again, she was gone.

"Hey, Andy," he said as he gently picked the boy up from the dirt under the shrubbery. "Are we having fun yet, kid?"

Andy turned his head and, with a groan, emptied the rest of his stomach down the front of Cowboy's shirt and jeans.

It was the perfect topper to a week that had already gone outrageously wrong.

But Cowboy didn't care. He didn't give a damn. All he could think about was Melody's smile.

Chapter 9

The baby was working hard on his tap-dancing routine.

Melody looked at the clock for the four millionth time that night. It read 1:24.

Her back was aching, her breasts were tender, she had to pee *again,* and every now and then the baby would twist a certain way and trigger sciatic nerve pain that would shoot a lightning bolt all the way down her right leg from her buttocks to her calf.

Melody swung her legs out of bed. The only way she was going to get some sleep was if she got up and walked around. With any luck, the rocking movement would lull the baby to sleep.

She shrugged her arms into her robe and slipped her feet into her slippers and, after a brief stop in the bathroom, headed downstairs. She actually had a craving for a corned beef sandwich *and* she knew there was half a pound of sliced corned beef in the fridge. If she was really lucky, she'd manage to make herself a sandwich and eat half of it before the craving disappeared.

But the light was already on in the kitchen, and she stopped in the doorway, squinting against the brightness. "Brittany?"

"No, it's me." Jones. He was sitting at the kitchen table, shirtless, of course. "I'm sorry, I was trying to be quiet—did I wake you?"

"No, I was just...I couldn't sleep and..." Melody tried to close her robe to hide the revealingly thin cotton of her nightgown, but it was useless. The robe barely even met in the front.

Her urge to flee was tempered by the fact that she no longer was merely hungry—she was starving. Her craving for that sandwich had grown out of control. She eyed the refrigerator and gauged the distance between it and Jones.

It was too close for comfort. Heck, anything that put her within a mile of this man was too close for comfort. She turned to go back upstairs, aware of the irony of the situation. The baby had been quieted simply by her walk down the stairs, but now she wouldn't be able to sleep because *she* was restless.

But Jones stood up. "I can clear out if you want. I was just waiting for my laundry to dry."

She realized that he was wearing only a towel. It was fastened loosely around his lean hips, and as she watched nearly hypnotized, it began to slip free.

"Andy did the psychedelic yawn on my last clean pair of jeans," Jones continued, catching the towel at the last split second and attaching it again around his waist.

Melody had to laugh, both relieved and oddly, stupidly disappointed that he wasn't now standing naked in front of her. "I've never heard it called that before. As far as euphemisms go, it sounds almost pleasant."

He smiled as if he could read her mind. "Believe me, it wasn't even *close* to pleasant. In fact, it was about four hundred yards beneath *un*pleasant, way down in the category of awful. But it was necessary."

She was lingering in the doorway. She knew she was, but she couldn't seem to walk away. The towel was slipping again, and he finally gave up and just held it on with one hand.

"How *is* Andy?" she asked.

"Feeling pretty bad, but finally asleep. He had the added bonus of the dry heaves after Vince and I got him cleaned off and into bed."

His hair was still wet from his own shower. If she moved closer, she knew exactly how he would smell. Deliciously clean and dangerously sweet. Jones had the power to make even the everyday smell of cheap soap seem exotic and mysterious.

"Why don't you come sit down?" he said quietly. "If you're hungry, I could make you something to eat. Same rules apply as during dinner. We talk, that's all."

Melody could remember staying up far later into the night with this man, feeding each other room-service food and talking about anything that popped into their heads. Books, movies, music. She knew he liked Stephen King, Harrison Ford action flicks and the country sounds of Diamond Rio. But she didn't know why. Their conversations had never been that serious. He'd often interrupted himself midsentence to kiss her until the room spun and to bury himself deeply inside her so that all talk was soon forgotten.

He'd told her more about himself this evening than he'd had the entire time they'd been in Paris. She could picture him as a boy, looking a lot like Andy Marshall, desperate for his father's approval. She could imagine him, too, getting into the kind of trouble that Andy attracted like a high-powered magnet. She was dying to find out how he'd turned himself around. How had he gone from near juvenile delinquent to this confident, well-adjusted man?

Melody stepped into the room. "Why don't you sit down?" she told him. "I'm just going to make myself a sandwich."

"Are you sure I can't help?"

"I'd rather you sat down. That way, I know your towel won't fall off."

He laughed. "I'm sorry about this. I honestly didn't have anything clean to put on."

"Just sit, Jones," she ordered him. She could feel him watching her as she got the cold cuts and mustard from the refrigerator. She set them on the table. "What I really want is a Reuben—you know, a grilled sandwich with corned beef, sauerkraut and Swiss cheese on rye? Thousand Island dressing dripping out the sides. Except we don't have any Swiss cheese or Thousand Island dressing."

"Salt," he said. "What you crave is salt. But I read that you're not supposed to have a lot of salt while you're pregnant."

"Every now and then, you've just got to break the rules," Melody told him as she took two plates from the cabinet.

"If you want, I'll run out to the store," he volunteered. "There's got to be a supermarket around here that's open twenty-four hours."

She glanced at him as she got the bread from the cupboard. "I can picture you at the Stop and Shop wearing only your towel."

He stood up. "I'll put my jeans on wet. It doesn't bother me. Believe me, I've worn far worse."

"No," Melody said. "Thanks, but no. By the time you got back, the craving would be gone."

"Are you sure?"

"Yeah. It's weird. I get these cravings, and then as soon as I'm face-to-face with the food, I get queasy—particularly if it's something that takes me awhile to prepare. Suddenly, the food I was craving becomes absolutely the last thing I want to get anywhere near my mouth. I stand a better chance if I can make it and start eating it quickly." She sat across from him at the table to do just that. "Help yourself."

"Thanks." Jones sat back down. He pulled one of the plates in his direction and took several slices of bread from the bag.

"So what happens next with Andy?" Melody asked.

"I'm going to get him up early," Jones told her, reaching for the mustard. "Let him experience the joys of a hangover. And then we're going to go over to the library and get some statistics on the correlation between starting to drink at age twelve and alcoholism." He glanced up at her, licking his fingers. "I think it would be a really good idea if you came along."

"What possible good can I do for Andy by coming with you?"

"Oh, it's not for Andy. It's for me. I want you to come because I enjoy your company." He smiled as he took a bite of his sandwich.

Melody tried not to feel pleased. She knew his words were just part of his effort to charm her.

"I don't know," she said. "Saturday's really the only morning I have to sleep late."

"Andy and I'll be at the library for a while," he told her. "You could meet us over there."

"I don't know..."

"You don't have to tell me now. Just think about it. See how you feel in the morning." He watched as she took a tentative bite of her own sandwich. "How is it?"

It tasted...delicious. "It's good," she admitted. "At least that bite was good."

"It must be so bizarre to be pregnant," Jones mused. "I can't even imagine what it would feel like to have another person inside me."

"It was really strange at first, back when I first felt the baby move," Melody said between bites. "I wasn't even really showing that much, but I could feel this fluttering inside me—kind of as if the grilled cheese sandwich I had for lunch had come alive and was doing a little dance."

Jones laughed. "I've felt that. It's called indigestion."

"No, this is different. This doesn't hurt. It just feels *really* strange—and kind of miraculous." She couldn't keep from smiling as she rested her hand on her belly—on the baby. "Definitely miraculous."

"The entire concept is pretty damn amazing," Jones agreed. "*And* terrifying. I mean, you've still got a month and a half to go before that baby decides he wants to get shaken loose. But by then, he's going to be three inches taller than you. I swear, I look at you, Melody, and I get scared to death. You're so tiny and that baby's so huge. How exactly is this going to work?"

"It's natural, Jones. Women have been having babies since the beginning of time."

He was silent for a moment. "I'm sorry," he finally said. "I promised we wouldn't talk about this. It's just...I don't like it when things are out of my control."

Melody put her half-eaten sandwich back down on her plate. Her appetite was gone. "I know how hard this must be for you," she told him. "I know it must seem as if—in just one split second—your entire life's been derailed."

"But it happened," Jones pointed out, "and now there's no turning back. There's only moving ahead."

"That's right," Melody agreed. "And what lies ahead for you and what lies ahead for me are two entirely different paths."

He laughed, breaking the somber mood they'd somehow fallen into. "Yeah, yeah, different paths, yada, yada, yada. We've talked about this before, honey. What I want to know is, who's going to be your labor coach? You *are* planning to use Lamaze, aren't you?"

Melody blinked. "You know so much about this...."

"I've been reading up. I'd like to be considered for position of coach. That is, if you're still accepting applications."

"Brittany's already agreed to do it," she told him, adding a silent thank God. She could just imagine having Cowboy Jones present in the delivery room when she was giving birth. Talking about double torture.

"Yeah, I figured. I was just hoping..." He looked down at her unfinished food. "I guess you hit the wall with your sandwich, huh?"

Melody nodded as she stood up. "I better get to bed."

"You go on up. I'll take care of the mess." Jones smiled. "This was nice. Let's do it again sometime—like every night for the rest of our lives." He smacked himself on the top of his head. "Damn, there I go again. Of course, as you pointed out yourself—every now and then you've got to break the rules."

"Good night, Jones." She let her voice drip with exaggerated exasperation.

He chuckled. "Good night, honey."

As Melody went up the stairs, she didn't look back. She knew if she looked, she'd see Jones smiling at her, watching as she walked away.

But she knew that his smile would be a mask, covering his frustration and despair. This was hard enough for him, considering that marrying her was not truly what he wanted to do. It would've been hard enough to set the wheels in motion and simply follow through. But for him to sit there night after night, day after night, and try to convince her that marriage was for the best when he didn't quite believe it himself...

She felt sorry for him.

Almost as sorry as she felt for herself.

"Hey, guys. Find out anything good?"

Cowboy glanced up from the library computer to see Brittany Evans standing behind Andy's chair. He turned, looking past her, making a quick sweep of the library, searching for her sister. But if Melody was there, she was out of sight, hiding among the stacks.

"She's outside," Brittany answered his unspoken question. "She was feeling a little faint, so she's taking a minute, sitting on one of the benches out front."

"You left her alone?"

"Only for a minute. But I figured, instead of me sitting with her... Well, I thought you might want to switch baby-sitting jobs."

"Yeah," Cowboy said as he stood up. "Thanks."

Andy glared. "Hey. I don't need no *baby*-sitter."

"That's right," Brittany said tartly to him as she slid into the seat Cowboy had left empty. "You don't. You need a *warden*. And a grammar instructor, apparently. So what are you researching here? The statistics of alcohol overdoses among minors, resulting in fatalities? Kids who've died from drinking too much. Fascinating subject, huh? How's your stomach feeling this morning, by the way?"

Cowboy didn't wait to hear Andy's retort as he crossed the library foyer, pushed open the heavy wooden door and stepped outside.

Mel was sitting on a bench, just as Brittany had said. The sight of her still had the power to make him pause. She was beautiful. Her golden hair cascaded down around her shoulders, reflecting the bright autumn sun. And although the air was cool, she'd taken off her sweater and wore only a sleeveless dress. Her arms were lightly tanned and as slender as they'd ever been. In fact, he was certain he could encircle both of her wrists with the thumb and forefinger of one hand. That is, if she would let him get close enough to touch her.

As he moved toward the bench, he was surprised that she didn't leap up and back away—until he realized that behind her sunglasses, her eyes were closed.

Her face was pale, too.

"Honey, are you all right?" He sat down beside her.

She didn't open her eyes. "I get so dizzy," she admitted. "Even just the walk from the car..." She opened her eyes and looked at him. "It's totally not fair. My mother was one of those ridiculously healthy people who played tennis the day before I was born. Two kids, and she didn't throw up once."

"But you have more than just your mother's genes," Cowboy pointed out. "You're half your father, too."

She smiled wanly. "Yeah, well, he never had morning sickness, either."

The breeze ruffled her hair, blowing a strand across her cheek. He wanted to touch her hair, to brush it back and run his fingers through its silk.

"You don't talk about him much." Cowboy reached down and picked up a perfect red maple leaf that the wind had brought right to their feet. "I remember when we were in Paris, you told me about your mother getting remarried and moving to Florida, but you never even mentioned your father."

"He died the summer I was sixteen." Melody paused. "I never really knew him. I mean, I lived in the same house with him for sixteen years, but we weren't very close. He worked seven days a week, eighteen hours a day. He was an investment broker. If you want to know the awful truth, I don't know what my mother saw in him."

"Maybe he was dynamite in bed."

Melody nearly choked. "God, what a thought!"

"Hey, you and Brittany came from somewhere, right? Parents are people, too." He smiled. "Although I have to admit that the idea of my mom and the admiral together is one very scary concept."

Melody was chewing on her lower lip speculatively as she gazed at him. "How come we always end up talking about sex?"

"Maybe because it's been more than seven months now since I've had some," he admitted. "It's kind of on my mind a lot."

"You can't be serious." She was shocked.

Cowboy shrugged. He hadn't meant for it to be such a big deal. "You want me to get you a soda or something to help settle your stomach?"

Melody wouldn't let herself be distracted. "You're telling me honestly that since we were together in Paris, you haven't...? Not even once?"

"No." He was starting to get embarrassed. He stood up. "Why don't I run down the street and get us a couple ginger ales?"

"Jones, *why?*" Her eyes were wide. "I can't believe you didn't have plenty of opportunities to... I mean..." She laughed nervously. "Well, I've seen the way women look at you."

Cowboy sighed as he sat down again. He should have known she wouldn't simply let this go. "Yeah, you're right. Over the past months, I've been in bars where I've known for a fact that I could've gone home with some girl." He held her gaze. "But I didn't want just some girl. I wanted *you.*" He twisted his mouth into a crooked smile, aware that he'd revealed far more than he'd intended. "Pretty powerful for a feeling based only on lust and relief, don't you think?"

He saw the confusion in her eyes as she tried to process all that he'd just told her. He willed her to reach for him, to surrender to the truth, to admit that he was right—that there *was* more between them than pure physical attraction. He wanted her to whisper that she, too, hadn't taken another lover since they'd last been together. He couldn't believe that she had, but he didn't know for certain, and he wanted to hear her say it.

But most of all, he wanted her to kiss him.

She didn't.

So Cowboy did the next best thing. He leaned forward and kissed her.

She didn't pull away, so he kissed her again, coaxing her mouth open, pulling her closer, pressing the palm of his hand against the sensual fullness of her belly. She was so sweet, her lips so soft. He felt himself melt inside, felt his muscles turn liquid with desire, felt his soul became infused with new hope.

He *was* going to have another chance to make love to her. Maybe soon. Maybe even—please, God—today.

"I've dreamed about kissing you like this." He lifted his head to whisper, hoping to see a mirror image of his own breathless passion in her eyes.

She was breathless all right, but when he lowered his head to kiss her again, she stopped him. "God, you're good, aren't you?"

"I'm what...?" But he understood what she meant the moment the words left his lips. Melody thought that everything he'd said, everything he'd done, was all just part of his elaborate plan to seduce her.

In a way, she was right. But she was wrong, too. It was more than that. It was much more.

But before he could open his mouth to argue, he felt it. Beneath his hand, Melody's baby—his baby—moved.

"Oh, my God," he said, his mouth dropping open as he gazed into Mel's eyes, all other thoughts leaving his head. "Mel, I felt him move."

She laughed at his expression of amazement, her accusations forgotten, too. She slid his hand around to the side of her belly. "Here, feel this," she told him. "That's one of his knees."

It was amazing. There was a hard little knob protruding slightly out from the otherwise round smoothness of her abdomen. It was his knee. It was their baby's knee.

"He's got a knee," Cowboy breathed. "Oh, my God."

He hadn't thought about this baby in terms of knees and elbows and arms and legs. But this kid definitely had a knee.

"Here." Melody brought his other hand up to press against her other side. "This is his head, over here."

But just like that, the baby shifted, and Cowboy felt a flurry of motion beneath his hands. That was not Melody doing that. That was...someone else. Someone who hadn't existed before he and Melody had made love on that plane to Paris. He felt out of breath and tremendously off balance as the enormity of the situation once again nearly knocked him over.

"Scary, huh?" Melody whispered.

He met her eyes and nodded. "Yeah."

"Finally," she said, smiling slightly, sadly. "Real honesty."

"I've never even really *seen* a baby before, you know, except in pictures," Cowboy admitted. He wet his suddenly dry lips. "And you're right, the idea of there being one that belongs to me scares me to death." But the baby moved again and he couldn't keep from smiling. "But God, that is so cool." He laughed with amazement. "He's swimming around in there, isn't he?"

She nodded.

He was still touching her, but she didn't seem to mind. He wished they were alone in the privacy of her kitchen rather than here on a bench outside the very public library.

She closed her eyes again, and he knew she liked the sensation of his hands on her body.

"I know you think you're winning, but you're not," she said suddenly, opening her eyes and looking at him. "I'm as stubborn as you are, Jones."

He smiled. "Yeah, well, as a rule, I don't quit and I don't lose. So that leaves really only one other option. And that's winning."

"Maybe there's a way we can both win."

He tightened his grip on her, leaning closer to nuzzle the softness of her neck. "I know there is. And it involves going back to your house and locking ourselves in your bedroom for another six days straight."

Melody pulled away from him. "I'm serious."

"I am, too."

She shook her head impatiently. "Jones, what if I acknowledge you as the father and grant you visitation rights?"

"Visits?" he said in disbelief. "You're going to give me permission to *visit* the kid two or three times a year, and I'm supposed to think that means I've *won?*"

"It's a compromise," she told him, her eyes a very earnest shade of blue. "It wouldn't be a whole lot of fun for me, either.

So much for the clean end to our relationship I'd hoped for. And imagine how awful it's going to be for the man I finally do marry—you showing up, flashing all your big muscles around two or three times each year.''

Cowboy shook his head. ''No deal. I'm the baby's father. And a baby's father should be married to that baby's mother.''

Melody's eyes sparked. ''Too bad you weren't feeling quite so moral on that flight to Paris. If I remember correctly, there was no talk of marriage then. If I remember, just about all that you had to say concerned how and where I should touch you, and the most efficient way to rid ourselves of our clothing in that tiny bathroom.''

He couldn't hide a laugh. ''Don't forget our three point five seconds discussion about our lack of condoms.''

She frowned at him. ''This *isn't* funny.''

''I'm sorry. And you're right. I've picked a hell of a time to join the moral majority.'' He picked up her hand and gently laced their fingers together. ''But, honey, I can't help the way I feel. And I feel—particularly after spending the morning with Andy—that it's our responsibility, for the sake of that baby, at least to give marriage a try.''

''Why?'' She turned slightly to face him as she gently pulled her hand free from his grasp. ''Why is this so important to you?''

''I don't want this kid to grow up like Andy,'' Cowboy told her soberly. ''Or me. Honey, I don't want him growing up the way I did, thinking my old man simply didn't give a damn.'' He gave in to the urge to touch her hair, pulling a strand free from where it had caught on her eyelashes and wrapping it around one finger. ''You know, I honestly think this morning is the first time Andy's ever been inside a library. He didn't know what a library card was—I'm not sure he can read half of what we pulled up on that computer screen. And I know for a fact that boy has never held a book in his hands outside of school. *Tom Sawyer,* Mel. The kid's never read it, never even heard of it. 'Mark Twain, who's he?' Andy said. *Damn.* And I'm not saying that if his father was around, it'd be any different, but fact is, it's hard to like yourself when one of the two most important people in your life deserts you. And it's hard as hell to get ahead when you don't like yourself very much.''

Cowboy took a deep breath and continued. ''I want that baby you're carrying to like himself. I want him to know without a shadow of a doubt that his daddy likes him, too—enough to insist upon marrying his mom and giving him a legitimate name.''

Melody met his gaze as she pulled herself to her feet, and he hoped his plea had made an impact.

''Think about it,'' he told her. ''Please.''

She nodded. And changed the subject as he followed her into the library. ''We better go rescue Andy. Britt's not one of his all-time favorite people.''

But as Cowboy looked, he saw Andy and Mel's sister sitting where he'd left them, in front of the computer, heads close together.

The two of them barely glanced up as Cowboy and Melody approached. They were playing some kind of bloodthirsty-looking computer game they'd no doubt found while surfing the Net.

''This would be *so* much better on my computer at home,'' Britt was telling Andy as she skillfully used the computer keyboard to engage a pack of trolls in mortal combat. ''The graphics would be much clearer. You should drop by some time—I'll show it to you if you want.''

''Can your computer do an Internet search like this one did?'' Andy asked.

Brittany snorted. ''Yeah, in about one-sixteenth the time, too. Wait'll you see the difference. I swear, this library computer is from the Stone Age.''

Melody looked at Cowboy, her eyebrows slightly raised.

He had to smile. If Brittany and Andy could form a tentative alliance, there was definite hope that he and Melody could do the same.

As Melody moved off to glance at a shelf filled with new books, Cowboy watched her.

She had no idea how beautiful she was.

She had no idea how badly he wanted her.

She also had no idea how patient he could be.

He'd once gone on a sneak and peek—an information-gathering expedition—with Blue McCoy, Alpha Squad's XO. They'd been assigned to scope out a vacation *Haus* in Germany's Schwarzwald that was, according to FinCOM sources, to be inhabited at the end of the week by a terrorist wanted in connection with a number of fatal bombings in London.

The Fink sources had been wrong—the tango showed up five days early, leaving McCoy and Cowboy pinned down in the bushes next to the front door and directly beneath the living-room window. They'd been trapped between the house and the brightly lit driveway, hidden by the shadow of the foliage but unable to move without immediate detection from the teams of security guards and professional soldiers that constantly patrolled the premises.

They'd lain on their bellies for three and a half days, counting soldiers and guards and listening to conversations *auf deutsch* and in various Arabic dialects from the living room. They'd relayed all the information to Joe Cat over their radio headsets and they'd waited—and waited and waited—for Alpha Squad to be given permission to apprehend the terrorists and to liberate McCoy's and Cowboy's butts.

He'd come away from that little exercise smelling really bad and hungry beyond belief, but knowing that he could outwait damn near anything.

Melody Evans didn't know it, but she didn't stand a chance.

Chapter 10

Melody woke up, aware that her afternoon nap had stretched on far past the late afternoon. It was dark in her room and dark outside, as well. Her alarm clock read 11:14 p.m.

Someone had come into her room while she was asleep and covered her with a blanket. But that someone couldn't have been her sister, who had been called away to the hospital before Melody had gone up for a nap, and who, from the obvious emptiness of Britt's room and the quietness of the house, had not yet returned home.

Melody glanced out the window at the tent in the backyard. It was dark. No doubt Jones had gone to sleep himself after he'd tucked her in.

Either that, or it had been Andy. The boy had been spending a great deal of time over at their house, working—or playing—with Britt on her computer. In the week since Jones had done his "tough love" Intro to Drinking 101 session, Andy had been acting less like a twenty-three-year-old ex-con and more like a twelve-year-old boy.

He and Brittany had really hit it off—which was good for both of them. Ever since Britt's divorce, she'd been more likely to focus on the negative instead of the positive. But when Andy was around, Melody heard far more of her sister's musical laughter.

Oh, Britt complained about him. Crumbs around the computer. Dishes left out on the kitchen table. But she gave the kid his own screen name on her computer account and let him use it even while she was doing the evening or night shift at work.

He *was* a nice kid, despite his bad reputation. He had a natural charm and a genuine sense of humor. But there was no way he would've left Britt's computer long enough to come upstairs and throw a blanket over her. It had to have been Jones who'd done that.

In the past week, he'd been up every morning, sitting in the kitchen while she'd had her breakfast before going to work. After watching her halfheartedly eat dry toast for several days in a row, he'd actually cooked her bacon, eggs, pancakes and oatmeal in the hopes that one of those foods would be something that she would want.

He'd been waiting when she'd returned home from work, as well. She'd gotten into the habit of sitting on the front porch with him, talking quietly and watching the setting sun turn the brilliant autumn leaves even more vivid shades of red and orange.

Jones was always around for dinner, too. Just like Andy, he'd managed to totally charm Brittany. And as for Melody, well, she was getting used to him smiling at her from across the kitchen table.

She was waiting for him to kiss her again—the way he'd done out in front of the library. But as if he sensed her trepidation, he was keeping his distance, giving her plenty of space.

But more often than not, when their eyes met, there was a heart-stoppingly hot spark, and Jones's gaze would linger on her mouth. His message was very clear. He wanted to kiss her again and he wanted to make sure that she knew it.

The thought of Jones up in her room, covering her with a blanket and watching her as she slept was a disconcerting one, and she tried to push it far away. She didn't want to think about that. She didn't want to think about Jones at all. She focused instead on her hunger as she went downstairs to the kitchen. She was, as they said in Boston, *wicked* hungry.

Melody nibbled on a soda cracker as she searched the refrigerator, then the pantry, for something, *any*thing to eat. With the flu still running rampant through the nursing staff at the hospital, Brittany hadn't had time to pick up groceries. There was nothing in the house to eat. Correction—nothing Melody *wanted* to eat.

She would've gone shopping herself, but Britt had made her promise under pain of death that she wouldn't try to wrestle both the shopping cart and the crowds at the Stop and Shop until after the baby was born.

Of course, if Britt had her way, Melody would spend the next few months in bed. And from the way he'd been talking last week outside the library, Jones was of the same mind-set. But *he* wanted her to stay in bed for an entirely different reason.

Melody couldn't quite believe that his motive was pure passion. She wasn't exactly looking her sexiest these days—unless, of course, one was turned on by a pumpkin. Andy's words, "fat and funny-looking," sprang immediately and quite accurately to mind. No, she had to believe that Jones wanted her in bed only because he knew that once he got her there, he'd be that much closer to his goal of marrying her.

For the baby's sake.

With a sigh, she took her jacket from the hook by the door, checking to make sure her car keys and her wallet were in the pockets. Brittany may have made the supermarket off-limits, but the convenience store up by the highway was fair game.

Maybe if Melody wandered through the aisles she'd see something she actually wanted to eat—something besides an entire sleeve of chocolate chip cookies, that is.

She unlocked the door and stepped out onto the porch, nearly colliding with Jones. He caught her with both arms, holding her tightly against him to keep them both from falling down the stairs.

His body was warm and his hair was disheveled as if he, too, had just woken up. She'd seen him look exactly like this in Paris. She couldn't remember how many times she'd slowly awakened underneath warm covers, opening her eyes to see his lazy smile and sleepy green eyes.

Time had lost all meaning back then. They'd slept when they were tired, eaten when they were hungry and made love the rest of the time. Sometimes when they woke, it was in the dark hours of the early morning. Sometimes the warm light of the afternoon sun slipped in beneath the curtains.

But it never mattered. The rest of the world had ceased to exist. What was important was right there, in that room, in that bed.

"I saw the light go on," he said, his voice still husky from sleep, his drawl more pronounced. "I thought I'd come over, make sure you were okay."

"I'm okay." Melody stepped back, and he let her go. The night air had a crisp chill to it, and she missed his warmth almost immediately. "I'm hungry, though. I'm making a run to the criminal."

He blinked. "You're...what?"

She started down the steps. "Going to the Honey Farms—the convenience store on Connecticut Road."

Jones followed her. "Yeah. But...what did you call it?"

"The criminal. You know, because the prices they charge are criminal."

He laughed, genuine amusement in his voice. "Cool. I like that. The criminal."

Melody couldn't help but smile. "Boy, it doesn't take much to make you happy, does it, Jones?"

"No, ma'am. And right now it would make me downright ecstatic to go to the criminal for you. Just hand me the keys to your car, tell me what you want and I'll have it back here for you inside ten minutes."

Melody looked around. "Where's *your* car?"

"It was, um, getting costly to keep a rental car for all this time." He fished a ponytail holder out of the front pocket of his jeans. Raking his hair into some semblance of order with his fingers, he tied it back at the nape of his neck. "I returned it about a week and a half ago."

"God, and I didn't even notice."

Jones held out his hand. "Come on. Give me the keys and your dinner order."

She stepped past him, heading toward her car. "Thanks, but no thanks. I don't know what I want. I was intending to go and browse."

"Do you mind if I come along?"

"No," Melody said, surprised that it was true. "I don't mind."

She opened the front door of her car, but he moved to block her way. "How about I drive?"

"Do you know how to drive a stick shift?"

Jones just looked at her.

"Right," she said, handing him the keys. "Navy SEAL. God, can you believe I almost forgot? If you can fly a plane, you can certainly handle my car, as particular as it is."

It was much easier getting in the passenger side without the steering wheel in her way. Jones waited to start the engine until after she closed the door behind her and fastened her seat belt.

"The clutch can be really temperamental," she started to say, but stopped when he gave her another pointed look.

But he smiled then, and she found herself smiling, too. She always found herself smiling when he was around.

Jones managed to get the car down the driveway and onto the main road without stalling, without even hiccuping. He drove easily, comfortably, with one hand on the wheel and the other resting lightly on the gearshift. He had nice hands. They were strong and capable-looking, just like the man himself.

"I was thinking," he said, finally breaking the silence as they approached the store, "that tomorrow might be a good day to put your garden to bed for the winter. It's supposed to be in the high fifties and sunny." He glanced at her. "I could help you do it after church, if you want."

Melody didn't know what to say.

"I'm afraid I've never been much of a gardener. I'm not really sure what needs to be done." He cleared his throat. "I figure the best way to do the job is for me to act as your hands and back. You tell me what to do, what to lift, what to carry, and I'll do it for you."

There was only one other car in the convenience-store parking lot and it was idling over by the telephones. Jones slid Melody's car neatly into one of the spots near the doors and turned off the engine. But he shifted slightly to face her rather than climb out.

"What do you think?" he asked.

Melody looked into his eyes and smiled. "I think you heard about the charity apple picking that's going on up at Hetterman's Orchards tomorrow after church, and you want to make sure you have a really good reason not to go."

Jones laughed. "No, I haven't heard anything about anything. What's the deal? Apple picking?"

"Hetterman's has always had a problem hiring temporary help to pick the last of the apples. It's a self-service farm, and people come out from the city all season long to pick their own apples, but there's always a lot left over. About seven years ago, they made a deal with one of the local Girl Scout troops. If the girls could get twenty people to come out and pick apples for a day, Hetterman's promised to award one of the high school kids a five-hundred-dollar scholarship. Well, the girls outdid themselves. They got a hundred people to come and got the job done in about three hours instead of an entire day. And in the seven years since then, it's become a town tradition. Last year, four hundred people turned out for the event, and they finished in less than two hours. And the five hundred dollars from Hetterman's has been matched by Glenzen Brothers Hardware, the Congregational Church, The First City Bank and a handful of private benefactors, making the scholarship a full five *thousand* dollars."

She laughed at herself. "Listen to me. I sound like such a Pollyanna. I can't help it, though. The thought of all those people working together like that for such a good cause just makes me all goose bumpy and shivery. I know, I know, I'm a sap."

"No, you're not." Jones was smiling at her very slightly. "I think it's cool, too. It's real teamwork in action." He was watching her closely, paying careful attention, as if what she had told him was the most important piece of news in the universe. Being the center of the tight focus of all his intensity was somewhat overwhelming, though.

The yellowish parking-lot lamps shone dimly through the car windows, creating intricate patterns of shadow and light on the dashboard. It was quiet and far too intimate. She should get out of the car. She knew she should.

"This year, they're trying to get six hundred people to participate and do the whole thing in under an hour. They want to try to set a record."

He reached forward to play with one of her curls. Touching but not touching. "Then we better plan to show up, huh?"

Melody laughed, gently pulling her hair free from his grasp, trying to break the mood, knowing that she *had* to. She had no choice. If she didn't do *some*thing, it wasn't going to be long before he leaned over and kissed her. "Somehow I just can't see you spending even half an hour picking apples." She unfastened her seat belt, but Jones still made no move to get out of the car.

"Why not?"

"Get serious, Jones."

"I *am* serious. It sounds like fun. Serious fun."

"Apple picking isn't exactly your speed."

"Yeah, well, maybe I don't know anything about that," he drawled, "but I *do* know all about working in a team, and it sounds as if this is one team I'd be proud to be a part of."

Melody got out of the car, fast. She had to, or else she was going to do something really stupid—like kiss *him*.

But he must've been able to read her mind because he followed and caught her hand before she even reached the convenience-store door.

"Come on," he said, his eyes daring her to take a chance. "Let's make this a plan. We'll do the apple-picking thing, have lunch, then come home and tackle the garden." He smiled. "And then in the evening, if you're feeling really adventurous, we can take a walk down at the Audubon Bird Refuge."

Melody laughed, and Jones leaned forward and kissed her.

She knew exactly what he was doing, what he had been doing over the past week. He was wearing her down little by little, piece by piece. He was actively trying to make her fall in love with him. He was taking everything really slowly. He was making a point to be extraordinarily gentle.

Except this was no languorous, gentle kiss. This time, he took her by storm, claiming her mouth with a hunger that stole her breath away. She could taste his passion along with the sweet mint toothpaste he must've used right before he came out of his tent to meet her.

She could feel his hands in her hair, on her back, sliding down to cup the soft fullness of her rear end. He'd held her that way in Paris, pressing her tightly against him so that she would be sure to feel the evidence of his arousal, nestled tightly between them.

But the only thing nestled between them now was her watermelon-sized stomach.

She heard him half growl, half laugh with frustration. "Making love to you is going to be *really* interesting. We're going to have to get kind of creative, aren't we?"

Melody could feel her heart pounding. She was breathing hard as she looked up into his eyes, but she couldn't seem to pull away. She didn't *want* to pull away. She actually *wanted* him to take her home and kiss her that way again. She wanted to make love to him. God, she was weak. He'd broken down her defenses in just a little over fourteen days. But maybe she had been crazy ever to think she could resist this man.

But instead of pulling her back toward the car, Jones reached for the criminal door. "Let's get what we came for."

He stood back to let her go through first.

Melody reached up to touch her lips as she went into the store. That kiss had been so scalding it should, by all rights, have marked her. But as far as she could tell, her lips were still attached.

The overhead lights were glaring compared to the dim parking lot, and she squinted slightly as she looked around the depressingly bleak little store.

Isaac Forte was clerking tonight. He always handled the night shift—which seemed appropriate. With his pale, gaunt face and painfully thin, almost skeletal frame, he reminded her of a vampire. If daylight ever actually came in contact with him, no doubt he would crumble into dust. But she, too, had become a creature of the night over the past few months. And her odd cravings had made her a frequent customer of the Honey Farms, so she'd come to know Isaac rather well. He had his problems, but having to drink human blood to stay alive *wasn't* one of them, thank goodness.

"Hi, Isaac," she said.

Two men in black jackets were at the checkout counter. Isaac was waiting on them and—

Jones moved so fast he was almost a total blur.

He kicked, and something went flying to the other side of the room.

A *gun*. One of these men had had a gun, and Jones had disarmed him, knocking it out of reach before Melody had barely even noticed it.

"Get out of here!" he shouted as he slammed one of the men down onto the floor, forcing the one to trip up the other.

The first man was dazed, but the second scrambled away, trying to reach the fallen gun. Melody could see it, gleaming and deadly, on the floor in front of the popcorn and corn chips.

"Melody, dammit, *go!*" Jones bellowed even as he grabbed for the second man, his hand closing around the leather of the thug's jacket.

He was talking to *her*. He wanted her to get to safety.

A rack of paperback books crashed to the floor as the man furiously fought to get free, to reach the gun. Melody watched, hypnotized with icy fear, as Jones fought just as hard to hang on, not even stopping for a second as he placed a well-aimed kick behind him that dropped the first man, the dazed man, to the floor with a final-sounding thud.

There was nothing even remotely fair about this wrestling match. No rules were being followed, no courtesies allowed, no time-outs granted. Jones slammed the gunman's head against the floor even as the man continued his own barrage of blows. Elbows, knees, hands, feet—it was meant to drive Jones back, but the SEAL was unstoppable. He just kept on coming.

The look on Jones's face transformed him, and his eyes sparked with an unholy light. He looked more like beast than man, his lips pulled back in a terrifying snarl of rage.

He kicked the gun even farther away as he flung the man violently in the opposite direction. Cheerios boxes exploded everywhere as he followed, pounding the man, hitting him hard again and again until there was no doubt in anyone's mind that the robber wasn't going to get up. At least not right away.

Outside in the parking lot, the car that had been idling sped away with a squeal of tires.

Even though both men were down and still, Jones moved quickly, going for the gun. Melody nearly collapsed with relief as his hands closed around it. He was safe. She wasn't going to have to stand there and watch him get pumped full of bullets.

She could hear police sirens in the distance. Isaac, no doubt, had triggered the alarm when the fight had started. He now peered warily over the top of the counter, his eyes wide as he gazed at Jones.

Jones checked the gun, removing the clip and releasing the chambered round. And then he looked at her, his eyes still lit from within with the devil's own anger.

"The next time I give you an order, dammit, you *do* it!" He was breathing hard, his chest still heaving as he fought to suck in enough air. His nose was bleeding and the front of his T-shirt was stained bright red with blood, but he didn't even notice.

"An order? But—"

"No buts." He slammed the empty gun down on the checkout counter. Melody had never seen him like this. Not even during the hostage rescue. He was furious. With *her.* "These scumbags had a weapon, Melody. If that dirtwad over there—" he gestured toward the man who'd put up a fight "—had managed to get his hands on it, he damn well would've used it! And these days, honey, you aren't exactly the tiniest of targets!"

Stung, Melody turned and walked out of the criminal.

"*Now* you leave," he said, pulling the door open to follow her. "*Perfect.*"

She spun back to face him. "I don't take orders from *you.* I'm not one of your SEAL buddies—I don't know *how* to take orders!''

"You managed just fine in the Middle East."

"Yeah, well, look around you, Lieutenant. This *isn't* the Middle East. This is Appleton, Massachusetts. And *I* haven't trained myself to react instantly when I walk into the middle of a convenience-store stickup." Her voice caught on something that was half laughter, half sob. "God, and I was just starting to think that maybe you *were* just a normal guy. Yeah, you're normal—and I stand a shot at winning the Miss America swimsuit competition. What a joke!''

The night was getting downright frosty. Or maybe it wasn't the chill in the air that was making her start to shake.

"I'd like my car keys," she said, lifting her chin, determined to keep from crumbling in front of him. "I want to go home now."

He ran his hands back through his rumpled hair, closing his eyes and pressing the heels of his hands against his temples, visibly trying to bring himself out of combat mode. And when he spoke, his voice was more even. "I don't think I can just leave. They're going to want a statement—"

"I'm not asking you to leave. I'm sure one of the police officers can give you a lift when you're done."

Jones reached for her. "Melody..."

She stiffened, closing her eyes and refusing to feel anything as he put his arms around her. "I don't want you to touch me," she told him through clenched teeth.

He backed off, but only a little. He took a deep breath, forcing even more of his anger to dissipate. "Honey, you gotta understand. I saw that revolver and—"

"You did what you had to do," she finished for him. "What you've been trained to do. You attacked. You're very good at that, I'll give you that much." She stepped out of his embrace. "Please tell Chief Beatrice that I'll stop by the station tomorrow to give my statement. But right now, I have to go home."

He held the car keys in his hand. "Why don't you let me drive you?" He glanced up as the first of the police cars pulled into the lot, and he raised his voice to be heard over the wailing siren. "I'll just tell these guys that I'll be back in a second." The siren cut off, leaving him shouting in the stillness, "I don't want you to have to drive."

She took the keys from him. "I'm fine. I can drive myself."

Isaac Forte came out to meet the policemen and all three men approached Jones. Melody used the opportunity to get into her car. But she should have known Jones wasn't going to let her just drive away. He came to the side of the car and waited until she opened her window.

"I won't be too long," he told her. He looked down as if noticing the blood on his shirt for the first time. He had an angry-looking scratch on his arm, as well, and he was gingerly touching the inside of his lips with his tongue as if he'd cut himself on his own teeth. "Can we talk when I get back?"

She looked out the windshield, afraid to meet his eyes. "I don't think that's a good idea."

"Mel, please? I know I had no right to speak to you that way, but I was scared to death you were gonna get hurt—"

"I'm tired, Jones," she lied. "I'm going to grab a bowl of soup and go back to sleep." He was leaning with both hands braced on the top of her car, so she couldn't just drive away. She did put the car into gear, though. She knew he could see that the reverse lights had come on. But when he still didn't step back, she finally looked up at him. "I want to go now," she said, fighting to keep her voice from shaking.

All of his earlier anger was gone, and he looked worn-out and beaten—as if he'd lost the fight instead of won.

"I'm sorry," he told her, straightening up. If she didn't know better, she might've thought those were tears in his eyes. "Mel, I'm deeply sorry."

"I am, too," she whispered.

Melody released the clutch and backed out of the parking lot. She only stalled once as she pulled onto the road that took her home.

"What's up?"

Cowboy glanced up from his book to smile at Andy. "Hey,

kid. I'm getting Mel's garden ready for winter.''

"No, you're not," Andy scoffed. "You're sitting there reading a book."

Andy had a swollen lip and a nasty-looking scrape on his jawline. He'd been in another fight, probably with that older kid— Alex Parks—who took such pleasure in tormenting him.

Andy's brown eyes dared him to comment on his injuries.

"Well, yeah, I'm reading a book," Cowboy said, purposely saying nothing. "That's the first step. See, first I have to learn how to do it—you know, figure out what kind of tools and supplies I need."

"That book tells you all that?"

"It does. Believe it or not, all the information I need to do damn near anything is two miles down that road in the town library. Need your refrigerator fixed? Piece a cake. Just get me a book. I can learn another language, build a house from the foundation up, shoe a horse—you name it, the knowledge I need to get the job done is in the library, guaranteed. Especially now that they're plugged into the Internet."

Andy looked at the garden bed, at the plants that had shriveled and turned brown in the cool night air, then at the last of the beans that were still clinging stubbornly to life. He looked back at Cowboy, clearly unimpressed. "So what's there to do? Everything's dead. You can't plant anything new until spring anyway."

"Ever hear of mulching?" Cowboy asked.

"No."

"Me, neither. At least not more than really vaguely before I picked up this book. But apparently, it's good to do. I haven't quite reached the part that tells me why, but I'm getting there."

Andy rolled his eyes. "You know, there's a much easier way to do all this."

"Oh yeah?"

"Yeah. Just ask Melody what she wants done."

Ask Melody. That was a damned fine idea. But unfortunately, Cowboy couldn't ask Melody anything until she stopped hiding from him again.

It had been nearly three days since the incident at the Honey Farms convenience store. The criminal, she'd called the place. And the name fit. They'd certainly run into some criminal activity, that was for sure.

God, he'd never known fear like that hot-and-cold streak of terror that had shot through him when he'd seen that revolver. He'd had about one-tenth of a second to decide what to do, and in that fraction of a moment, for the first time in his life, he'd actually considered backing down. He'd actually thought about surrendering.

But he couldn't tell in that heartbeat of time if the men were using or not. He didn't know for sure from that one quick glance if they were out of their minds, high on some chemical substance, or strung out, desperate and ready to eliminate anyone who so much as looked at them crooked.

All he knew was that in his experience, when he carried a weapon, *he* was always prepared to use it. He had to assume the same was true for these clowns. So he'd attacked in that one split second when the revolver was pointing away from the clerk, catching the assailants off guard.

The entire fight had lasted all of eighty-five seconds.

But it had been eighty-five seconds of sheer hell.

Melody had just stood there, staring at him. She hadn't even ducked for cover. She just *stood* there, a target, ready to be knocked over or shot full of lead if that bastard had gotten hold of his revolver.

It had taken Cowboy twice as long as it should have to subdue the enemy and gain control of the weapon. His fear that Melody would be hurt or killed had gotten in the way. And he'd lashed out at her afterward because of it. He'd shouted at her when all he really wanted to do was drag her into his arms and hold her until the end of time.

But she'd been less than thrilled with his performance—in more ways than one. And she'd run away again.

Before they'd gone into that store, Melody had been ready to invite him up to her bedroom to spend the night—he'd been almost certain of that. He'd been so close to relief from this hellish frustration.

Of course, now the frustration was ten times as bad. He hadn't even *seen* her in three days. The hell with the lack of sex. Just not seeing her was driving him damn near crazy.

"You want me to ask Melody for you?" Andy asked. "I'm going inside—Britt said it was okay if I used her computer to do an Internet search."

"What are you searching for?"

Andy shrugged. "Just some stuff about the Army."

"Oh yeah? What kind of stuff?"

Another shrug. "I dunno."

Cowboy gazed at the boy. "You thinking about enlisting?"

"Maybe."

"Only way to become a SEAL is to join the U.S. Navy, not the Army."

"Yeah," Andy said, "I know. You running again tonight?"

Cowboy had taken to working out both in the evening as well as the early morning in an attempt to run some of his frustration into the ground. "Why? You want to try again?" Andy had run along with him yesterday evening. The kid had only made it about two miles before he'd dropped out.

"Yeah, I do."

"You know, if you start getting in shape now, you'll be a monster by the time you graduate high school."

Andy kicked at a clump of grass. "I wish I could be a monster now."

Cowboy acknowledged the boy's scraped face. "Alex Parks again, huh?"

"He's such a *jerk.*"

"If you want, I can help you out with your PT," Cowboy volunteered. "You know, physical training. And, if you want, I can also help you learn to fight."

Andy nodded slowly. "Maybe," he said. "What's the catch?"

Cowboy grinned. This boy was a fast learner. "You're right. There *is* a condition."

The kid groaned. "I'm going to hate this, aren't I?"

"You have to promise that after I teach you to beat the crap out of Alex Parks, you use what you've learned only to defend yourself. And after he figures out that you're ready and able to kick his butt, you turn and walk away."

Andy looked incredulous. "What good is *that?*"

"That's my deal. Take it or leave it."

"How do you know I'll even keep my promise?"

"Because if you don't, I'll break you in half," Cowboy said with a smile. "Oh, and there is one other catch. You need to learn a little self-discipline. You need to learn to follow *orders.* My orders. When I say jump, you jump. When I say chill, you cool it. You give me any attitude, any garbage, any whining, any moaning of *any* kind, and the deal's off."

"Gee, you're making this sound too good to pass up," Andy said, rolling his eyes.

"Oh yeah. One other thing. If I ask you a question, you answer me straight. You say, 'Yes, sir,' or 'No, sir.'"

"You want me to call you *sir?*"

"Yes, I do." God knows Andy could learn a thing or two about showing respect.

Andy was silent.

"So do we have a deal?" Cowboy asked.

Andy swore. "Yeah, all right."

"Yes, *sir,*" Cowboy corrected him.

"Yes, sir. *Jeez.*" Andy turned toward the house. "I'll tell Melody you could use her help with the garden."

"Thanks, kid, but that's not going to get her out here. She's been hiding from me for days."

"I'll tell her you're sorry, too. Sir. God."

"Sir is good enough, Marshall. You don't have to call me God, too," Cowboy teased.

"Sheesh." Andy rolled his eyes again as he headed toward the kitchen door.

In truth, Cowboy *was* sorry. He was sorry about a lot of things. He was sorry that he hadn't gone into the house and hammered on Melody's bedroom door after he'd gotten home that night. He was sorry he still hadn't found a way to force the issue, to make her sit down and talk to him.

He wasn't quite sure what he would tell her, though. Cowboy wasn't sure he was ready to share the fact that after she'd left the Honey Farms, right as he was giving his statement to Tom Beatrice, the Appleton chief of police, he'd had to excuse himself. He'd gone into the men's room and gotten horribly, violently sick.

At first, he'd thought it might've been the flu—people all over town were falling victim to a virulent strain of the bug. But as the night wore on and he didn't get sick again, he'd been forced to confront the truth.

It was the residual of his fear that had made him bow to the porcelain god. His fear for Melody's safety had squeezed him tight and hadn't let go, making his gut churn and his blood pressure rise until he'd forcefully emptied his stomach.

It was weird. His career as a SEAL involved a huge amount of risk taking. And he was fine about that. He knew he would survive damn near anything if surviving entailed fighting. But if his survival depended on something outside his control—like the intrinsic danger they all faced every time they jumped out of a plane, knowing that if their chute failed, if the lines got tangled or the cells didn't open right, they would end up as a mostly unrecognizable stain on the ground—if his survival depended on a twist of fate like that, Cowboy knew he would either live or die as the gods saw fit. No amount of fear or worry would change that, so he rarely bothered with either.

But he found he couldn't be quite so blasé when it came to Melody's safety. Whenever he thought about that revolver aimed in her direction, even now, three days later, he *still* felt sick to his stomach.

It was similar to the sensation he felt when he thought about her having to give birth to that baby she was carrying.

As was his usual method of operation when forced to deal with something he knew nothing about, he'd taken a pile of books about pregnancy out of the library. He'd read nearly every one from cover to cover, and frankly, the list of possible life-threatening complications resulting from pregnancy or childbirth made his blood run cold.

Women went into shock from pregnancy-related diabetes. Or they had strokes caused by the strain on their system. Some women simply bled to death. The mortality rates reported in the books shocked Cowboy. It seemed impossible that even in this day and age of enlightened, modern medicine, women died simply as a result of bearing children.

He'd wanted to go into the hospital and donate blood to be set aside and used specifically for Melody in case she needed it. He was a universal donor, but he knew that all of the inoculations he'd had as he'd traveled around the world would make him ineligible.

He'd just approached Brittany to find out if her blood type matched her sister's—to see if she might be willing to donate blood and help soothe some of his fear. She'd looked at him as if he was crazy, but she'd agreed to do it.

Cowboy looked toward the house, up at the window he knew was Melody's room. He willed the curtain to shift. He hoped to see a shadowy form backing away or a hint of moving light, but he saw nothing.

Melody was staying far from the window.

And his patience was running out.

Chapter 11

Melody heard the doorbell ring from up in her bedroom.

She focused all of her attention on her book, determined to keep reading. It was Jones. It had to be Jones.

It had been five days since she'd driven away from him at the Honey Farms, and she'd been bracing herself, waiting for him to run out of patience and come confront her.

Andy was downstairs, using Britt's computer. Melody had told him she was going to take a nap. She closed her eyes for a moment, praying that he would send Jones away.

But then she heard voices—a deep voice that didn't sound very much like Jones, and then Andy's, higher-pitched and loud. She couldn't hear the words, but he sounded as if he was angry or upset.

The lower voice rumbled again, and she heard what sounded like a chair being knocked over. No, that was definitely not Jones down there with Andy.

Melody unlocked her bedroom door and hurried down the stairs to the kitchen.

"It *wasn't* me," Andy was shouting. "I didn't do *nothin'*."

Tom Beatrice, the police chief, stood between Andy and the door, ready to catch the boy if he ran. "It'll go easier on you, son, if you just tell the truth."

Andy was shaking with anger. "I *am* telling the truth."

"You're going to have to come with me, son."

"Stop calling me that! I'm *not* your son!"

Neither of them had noticed that Melody stood in the doorway. She raised her voice to be heard. "What's going on here?"

"That's what I was wondering, too." Jones opened the screen door and stepped into the kitchen.

The police chief glanced at them both apologetically. "Vince Romanella said I'd find the boy over here. I'm afraid I need to bring him down to the station for questioning."

"What?" Melody looked at Andy, but he was silent and stony-faced. She tried not to look at Jones at all, but she could feel his eyes on her from across the room. "Why?"

"House up on Looking Glass Road was broken into and vandalized several nights ago," Tom explained. "Andy here was seen up in that area at about 9:00—about the time the break-in occurred."

"That's pretty circumstantial, don't you think, Chief?" Jones voiced Melody's own disbelief.

"Oh, there's other evidence, too, that points in his direction." Tom shook his head. "The place is trashed. It's a real mess. Windows and mirrors broken. Spray paint everywhere."

Jones briefly met Melody's gaze, then he turned to the boy. "Marshall, did you do it?" His voice was soft, almost matter-of-fact.

Andy straightened his shoulders. "No, sir."

Jones turned back to Tom. "Chief, he didn't do it."

Tom scratched the back of his head. "Well, Lieutenant, I appreciate your faith in the boy, but his fingerprints are all over the place. He's going to have to come down to the station with me."

"*Finger*prints?" Jones echoed.

"Inside and out."

Jones's eyes pinned the boy in place. This time when he spoke, his voice was harder, more demanding. "Marshall, I'm going to ask you that question again. Did you have anything to do with vandalizing that house?''

Andy's eyes had filled with tears. "I should've known you wouldn't believe me," he whispered. "You're really no different from the rest of them.''

"Answer my question.''

Andy answered with a blisteringly foul suggestion. Like an afterthought, he added, "sir.'' He turned to Tom Beatrice. "Let's get this over with.''

"Andy, I'm on your side...'' Jones started to say, but Andy just pushed past him, Tom's hand on his arm.

Melody stepped forward. "Go with him,'' she urged Jones. "He's going to need you.''

Jones nodded, taking in her tentlike dress, her unbrushed hair, the blue nail polish on her toes, before looking in her eyes. "I was scared I'd lose you, Mel,'' he said. "That night—I shouted at you because I was more scared than I've ever been in my life. It was wrong, but so's not letting me apologize.''

He turned and went out the door.

"Jones.''

Cowboy sat up in his tent, suddenly wide-awake, wondering if his mind was finally starting to snap. He could've sworn he'd heard Melody's voice calling his name. Of course, he *had* been dreaming a particularly satisfying and sinfully erotic dream about her....

"Jones?''

It *was* her. He could see her unmistakable silhouette outside of the tent. He reached up to unzip the flap. "Mel, are you all right?''

"I'm fine.'' She was wearing only a nightgown and a robe and she shivered slightly in the chill night air. "But we just got a phone call from Vince Romanella.'' She peered into the darkness of his tent. He was glad for the darkness, and glad for the sleeping bag that still covered most of him—including an extremely healthy arousal, the direct by-product of that dream. "Jones, Andy's not in here with you, is he?''

"No." He opened the flap a little wider. "Honey, it's freezing outside. Come on in."

"It feels like it's freezing in there, too," she pointed out, not moving any closer. He couldn't quite see her eyes in the darkness. "I don't know how you stand it."

"It's not that bad." His sleeping bag was nice and warm. And the dream he'd been having about Melody had been hot enough to heat the entire state of Massachusetts.

"Jones, Andy's missing. Vince said he heard a noise, and when he got up to check it out, he looked in on Andy, and his bed was empty."

Cowboy reached for his jeans, swiftly slipping them on, wrestling with the zipper, willing his arousal away. "What time is it?"

"Nearly 4:00. Vince thinks Andy's been gone since around midnight, when he and Kirsty went to bed. Tom Beatrice is organizing a search party."

He pulled on his boots and grabbed a T-shirt and a jacket. "Can I use your phone?"

"Of course." She moved aside to let him come out of the tent. "Do you know where he might've gone?"

He sealed the flap to keep any stray animals out, then straightened up, pulling on his T-shirt as they walked toward the house. "No. He wouldn't talk to me down at the police station. And all he said to the chief was that he'd been set up and framed." With impatient fingers, he tried to untangle a knot that was in his hair. "I might've believed it if his fingerprints had only been found on, you know, something like a single can of soda, or a few things here and there." He gave up on his hair as he opened the door for Melody, then followed her into the brightly lit warmth of the kitchen. Brittany was awake, too, and talking on the phone. "But according to the police report, his prints were on the furniture, on the walls, in every single room. He was in that house, there's no denying it."

"But he *is* denying it," Melody said, her blue eyes wide. "And rather vehemently, I've heard." She lowered herself into one of the kitchen chairs, shifting uncomfortably, as if her back was hurting again. What else was new? Never mind the fact that he knew how to give a killer back rub—she wouldn't let him near enough to give her one.

But despite her obvious discomfort, she looked particularly lovely tonight. She'd put her hair in a single braid down her back, but while she'd slept, several tendrils had escaped. They floated gracefully, delicately, around her face. Without any makeup on at all, she looked fresh and sweet—barely old enough to baby-sit, let alone have a baby of her own.

As he watched, she chewed on her lower lip. She had gorgeous lips—so full and red even without the help of cosmetics. In his dream, she'd smiled at him almost wickedly before she'd lowered her head and...

Don't go there, Cowboy admonished himself. As much as he would've liked to, he couldn't let his thoughts continue in that direction right now. He had to think about Andy Marshall instead. Damn fool kid. What the hell was he trying to prove?

"Running away like this is a pretty strong admission of guilt," Cowboy pointed out.

"Sometimes people run because they're afraid." Melody was talking about more than Andy—he knew because she suddenly wouldn't meet his gaze.

"Sometimes people don't realize that everyone in the world is afraid of *some*thing," he countered. "Best thing to do is face your fear. Learn all you can about it. Then learn to live with it. Knowledge goes a long way when it comes to declawing even the scariest monsters."

"Is that what you've been doing here with me?" she asked, no longer even pretending to talk about Andy. "Learning to live with your fear? Facing the terrors of a lifetime commitment? And don't try to pretend that the thought of marrying me doesn't scare you to death—I *know* it does."

He went for the truth. Why not? He had nothing to lose. "You're right," he said. "It *does* frighten me. But I've done frightening things before and come out a better man because of them."

Before Melody could respond, Brittany grimly hung up the

phone. "They're starting the search up by the quarry," she announced. "Alex Parks just told his father that Andy had called him and told him to meet him in the woods up there just after midnight. Alex is claiming he never went, but my gut feeling is that we haven't gotten the full story from this kid yet. Anyone who's willing and able is supposed to meet out at the end of Quarry Road."

Melody stood up. "I'm going to go change."

"Willing and able, sweetie," Brittany said. "Not willing and seven and a half months pregnant."

"But I *want* to help!"

"Help by giving the lieutenant your car keys and waving goodbye," Brittany told her sister. "You don't really think Cowboy'll be able to give the search for Andy his full attention if you're there for him to worry about, do you?"

Melody looked directly at him. "So...just don't worry about me."

Cowboy smiled ruefully. "Honey, that's kind of like telling me don't breathe."

She looked as if she was going to cry. "My keys are by the door," she told him. "Take my car. But call as soon as you hear *any*thing."

By 7:45, Melody had gotten tired of waiting. Jones hadn't called. He *still* hadn't called. Fortunately, Brittany had gotten tired of waiting, too.

By 8:00, Britt was driving her down to the end of Quarry Road. The narrow road was lined on both sides with parked cars for about a good half mile.

"You get out here," Britt told her. "I'll park and walk back."

"Are you sure?" Melody asked.

Brittany raised her eyebrows. "Do you honestly believe that I would bring you up here in the cold, and then make you walk an *extra* half mile? I should have my head examined for driving you over here in the first place—and all for the sake of some stupid kid."

"He's not stupid." Melody opened the door.

"He's incredibly stupid," Britt argued. "He didn't call *me* before he ran away. I know he didn't vandalize that house."

Melody stared at her sister. "You *do?*"

"Yeah, and I realized as we were driving here that I can prove it, too. The kid's been on-line, using my computer every night this week, right? I was working the night of the break-in, and you were probably already in bed, but Andy *was* at our house, at my computer. I just realized I got E-mail from him at work that night. Unless he scheduled a flash session, I can give him a solid alibi. And whether or not there was a flash session scheduled should be easy enough to prove. I just have to access my account information. It'll prove he was logged on and actively using the Net that night."

"You seriously believe Andy's innocent—?"

Brittany shrugged. "Well, yeah. He said he didn't do it. The kid may be a royal pain the butt, but I've gotten to know him pretty well over the past few weeks, and he's *not* a liar."

"But all those fingerprints..."

"I know. I haven't figured that out yet, but if Andy says he didn't do it, he didn't do it."

"I think you should tell this to Tom Beatrice right now," Melody said. She had to smile. "Of all people, I wouldn't have thought *you'd* be Andy's champion."

"Yeah, well, I was wrong about him. He's an okay kid." Worry flickered across her face. "I hope he's okay."

"Jones'll find him," Melody told her sister as she hauled herself out of the car. She had total faith in the SEAL. This was what he was good at. Rescuing hostages and disarming gunmen and finding missing little boys would all fall under the category labeled "piece a cake."

"Don't go any farther than the quarry," Brittany said threateningly, leaning across the seat to look up at her. "If I get back here and find out that you've done something insane, like join a search party, I swear I'll never let you leave the house again."

"I won't join a search party. I promise." It was then that Melody saw them. "Oh, God!"

"You all right?"

"Boats, Britt." There were two trucks parked at haphazard angles, both of which had boat trailers behind them. They were empty, which meant the boats were in use. "They're dragging the quarry."

Brittany put the car in park and shut off the engine. She opened the door, then stood looking across the roof of the car at the telltale trailers. Her face was pale, but she shook her head in denial. "It doesn't mean that. Not necessarily."

Melody blinked back tears. "Yes, it does. You know it."

Brittany slammed the car door, leaving the vehicle right there, blocking in at least four other cars. "No, it doesn't." Her voice rang with determination.

Mel followed her sister down the trail that led to the flooded quarry.

A crowd had gathered. She could see Estelle Warner and Peggy Rogers, surrounded by other members of the Ladies' Club decked out in their hiking boots and jeans. Tom Beatrice and nearly all of Appleton's police force were talking to several state troopers as Vince and Kirsty Romanella hovered nearby. Even Alex Parks was there, sitting on a rock, looking as if he'd been crying. And standing off to the sides were all the people who had volunteered to help search the woods for Andy. The turnout was nearly bigger than last weekend's apple picking at Hetterman's. They were talking in hushed voices, somberly watching the boats.

"They're not dragging the water." Brittany shielded her eyes with her hand, trying to see past the glare of the early-morning sun. "What *are* they doing?"

Jones was out on one of the boats. Although he was too far away to see clearly, Melody recognized him from his easygoing posture. That, the baseball cap he wore on his head and the fact that, even though it was only forty chilly degrees out, he wore his jacket unbuttoned more than tipped her off.

The man was totally immune to the cold.

"The water's too deep to drag in many places." Melody turned to see Estelle Warner standing behind them. "They're using some kind of sonar contraption to try to get a reading on anything that might be a body down at the bottom of the pit," the elderly woman said. "This old quarry's three hundred feet deep in some places. Maybe even deeper in others."

"They can't be sure he's in there." Melody's heart was in her throat. "Aren't they searching anywhere else?"

"Considering the fact that an eyewitness saw the boy go into the water, and that the searchers found his clothes exactly where that witness said they'd be..."

"Oh, no..." Brittany reached for Melody's hand.

Estelle looked even more dour than usual. "I'm afraid so. It seems the Parks boy met Andy Marshall up here late last night. From what he says, Andy was always trying to pick a fight, and this time was no different. Andy dared the Parks boy to swim across the quarry, and when the Parks boy backed down, Andy took of his own clothes and dove into the water. Had to have been close to freezing, but that wild kid just dove right in."

Both boats were heading to shore. Jones took off his baseball cap and raked his hair back out of his face, refastening his ponytail. As Melody watched, he put his hat back on, making sure it was securely on his head. As he got closer, she could see that his face was decidedly grim.

"Apparently, the Parks boy didn't see young Andy come back up," Estelle told them. "He says he searched for a while, calling to Andy, but there was no reply. Of course, it was dark and hard to see much of anything. It's likely the boy dove in the wrong spot, hit his head on a rock. Or maybe the cold just got to him."

Brittany was squeezing Melody's fingers. "Please don't let them have found something," she whispered.

"That lieutenant of yours," Estelle told Melody. "He took one look at Andy's clothes—left right where the Parks boy had said they were—and he made a few phone calls to Boston. And this other man, the tall black fellow, he was out here within a few hours with this sonar whatever. Brought diving gear with him, too."

Harvard. Harvard was on that boat with Jones. Melody could see him now, towering over everyone—even Jones. His shaved head gleamed exotically in the sunlight. His expression, like Jones's, was less than pleased.

Melody saw Jones spot her as he climbed out of the boat. She saw him hesitate, glancing quickly back at Harvard, and she knew. He hadn't told his friend that she was pregnant.

It would have been funny if the situation weren't so deadly serious.

Still, he came toward her, and Melody knew when she looked into his eyes that Harvard's reaction to her pregnancy was the least of his worries.

He didn't say hello, didn't mince his words. "Honey, we think he's down there."

Brittany sank to the ground. Estelle knelt next to her, holding her tightly—two mortal enemies allied once again, this time through the death of a child.

"No," Melody whispered. But she could see the truth written clearly in the stormy green of Jones's eyes. He was stony-faced, sternly angry.

"It's my fault." His voice was raspy and as dry as his eyes. "I thought he was ready to learn some discipline. I'd been taking him out, running him through some PT. I told him that SEALs had to condition themselves against cold water. I told him about Hell Week—about having to sit in that freezing surf and just hang on. He wanted to try it—try swimming in the quarry, so I let him do it. We just jumped in and jumped out. I thought I'd let him get a taste of what cold *really* was."

He stopped, taking a deep breath before he continued. "That was my mistake. I didn't let him stay in. I just pulled him back out. I didn't let him cramp up or find out how hard it is to swim when every muscle in your body is cold and stiff. I think I must've given him the false confidence to try it again."

"That still doesn't make this your fault." Melody wanted to reach for him, to put her arms around him, but he seemed so distant, so unanimated and still, so grim and hard and unreachable.

Harvard had come to stand beside them, and she could feel his curious eyes on her, but she didn't look away from Jones. She *couldn't* look away. He truly blamed himself for this tragedy.

"It *is* my fault. I told him about swim buddies—about how

SEALs never swim or dive without another team member, but I know he saw me breaking the rules by swimming alone in the quarry.''

"Junior, we should probably make that dive," Harvard said quietly. "If we've got to go down to 175 feet, it's going to take awhile." When Melody finally glanced at him, he nodded. "How are you, Melody? You're looking very...healthy."

"Will you tell him, please, that this is not his fault?"

"The lady says it's not your fault, Jones."

Jones's expression didn't change as he turned away. "Yeah, right. Let's get this over with."

Melody couldn't stand it a second longer. She reached for him, catching his hand in hers. "Harlan—"

There was a flash of surprise in his eyes, surprise that she'd actually used his given name, surprise that she'd actually touched him, but that emotion was quickly turned into stone, along with everything else he was feeling. Even his fingers felt cold.

She knew this stony anger was his defense against having to go down into that water and possibly—probably—bring up the lifeless body of the boy they'd all come to love over the past few weeks. But she knew just as well that everything he felt—all the blame and the fear and the awful, paralyzing grief—was there inside him. His anger didn't cancel his feelings out; it merely covered them.

She knew him quite well, she realized. Over the past few weeks, despite her attempts to keep her distance, she'd come to know this man's vast repertoire of minutely different smiles—what they meant, how they broadcast exactly how and what he was feeling. She'd come to know his silences, too. And she'd had a firsthand look at his method of dealing with fear.

He hid it behind icy cold anger.

"Be careful," she whispered. A local diving club had frequented the quarry several years ago—until someone had gotten killed and it had been deemed too dangerous a place to dive.

His eyes told her nothing—nothing but the fact that underneath all that chill, he was hurting. He nodded and even tried to force a smile. "Piece a cake."

"We'll be down for a while," Harvard told her. "Diving at this depth requires regular stops both on the way down and coming back up. It's time-consuming, and for you, waiting up here on the surface, it'll seem as if it takes forever. You might want to go home and wait for a phone call."

"Jones has forgotten how to use the phone," Melody said, still gazing into his eyes.

"I'm sorry I didn't call you," he said quietly, "but all I kept getting was bad news." Emotion shifted across his face, and for a heartbeat, Melody thought he was about to give in to all of his pain and crumple to the ground just as Brittany had. But he didn't. "It seemed senseless to make you worry until I knew for sure Andy was dead." He said the word flatly, bluntly, using it to bring back his anger and put his other emotions in check.

"We still don't know that for sure." Melody squeezed his hand. But her words were pure bravado. She could see Jones's certainty in his eyes.

"Go home," he told her.

"No," she said. If he did find Andy down there, he was going to need her to be here—as badly as she was going to need him. "I'll wait for you to come back up. We can go home together."

She couldn't believe the words that were coming out of her mouth. *Go home together...*

His expression didn't change. For a moment, he didn't even move. But then, in one swift movement, he pulled her into his arms and kissed her hard on the mouth. She clung to him, kissing him back just as ferociously, wanting him, needing him—and needing him to know it.

He pulled away, breathing hard. He didn't say a word about that incredible kiss. He just took off his jacket and handed it to her. "Spread this on the ground so you'll have something dry to sit on." His voice was harsh, and his eyes were still so angry, but he gently touched the side of her face with one finger. "I don't want you catching cold."

It was almost as if he loved her. It was almost as if they were lovers who had been together for years.

"Be careful," Melody said again.

As he gazed at her, his eyes suddenly looked bleak. "It's too late," he told her quietly. "When it came to dealing with Andy, I wasn't careful enough, and now it's too damn late."

Melody tried not to cry as he turned and walked away.

Chapter 12

Cowboy usually loved to dive, but this was sheer hell. He and H. were heading nearly straight down, using a marked rope to gauge their distance, stopping at regular intervals to let their bodies adjust to the increasing pressure of the water.

The time spent stopping and waiting dragged on interminably.

It was necessary, though. If they moved too quickly from the surface to a depth below a hundred feet, and then back, they could—and would—get the bends.

Cowboy had seen a guy who hadn't believed how crippling the bends could actually be. The stupid SOB had gotten brain damage from bubbles of nitrogen expanding in his system. He still couldn't walk to this day.

Despite the fact that SEALs were known for breaking the rules, this was one rule they never even bent. Even when they were in as big a hurry as he was.

Contrary to what he'd told Melody, this dive was anything but a piece of cake. At this depth, he and Harvard had to breathe from special tanks of mixed gas to prevent nitrogen narcosis— also known as the rapture of the deep. As if that wasn't dangerous enough, there was a definite time limit to how long they could remain at that depth. And the number and lengths of decompression stops they would have to make on the way back to the surface were intensely complicated.

With the scuba gear on, he and Harvard couldn't talk. And at this depth beneath the surface, it was very, very cold and very, very dark. He couldn't even see Harvard next to him. He could only sense his presence.

Out of all the men in Alpha Squad, Cowboy was glad it was the senior chief who'd been just a short drive away, visiting his family in his hometown just outside Boston. Unlike some of the guys, Harvard knew when *not* to talk.

As they'd pulled on their cold-water diving suits, Harvard had had only a brief comment to make about Melody's pregnancy. He'd said, "When you told me you had a situation to deal with, you weren't kidding. You don't do anything halfway, do you, Junior?"

"No," Cowboy had replied.

"I assume you're going to do right by the girl?"

"Yeah," Cowboy had answered automatically. For so long now, his single-most goal had been to marry Melody and be a real father to their baby. But that was before he'd failed so utterly with Andy. Who was he trying to fool here anyway? He knew less than nothing about parenting. The fact that he was diving in this quarry in hopes of recovering Andy's drowned body was proof of that.

Cowboy floated in the darkness, uncertain of what to wish for. He hoped they weren't going to find Andy's body, but at the same time, if the kid *had* drowned in this quarry, he hoped that they'd find him right away. It would end the waiting and wondering. And it would be far better than never finding him, never quite knowing for sure.

He shone his flashlight straight down, knowing that the light couldn't possibly cut through the murky depths to that place where the sonar camera had found an object the approximate size and density of a human body.

Cowboy turned off the light, sending both Harvard and himself back into the deprivation-tank-like darkness. They had to save their flashlight batteries for when they were really needed.

He closed his eyes. He knew he could do anything if he had to. But watching the beam from his light reflect off Andy Marshall's pale, water-swollen face was going to be one of the hardest things he would ever have to do.

It was going to be almost as hard as admitting that maybe Melody had been right all along, almost as hard as it would be to walk away from her sweet smile.

Cowboy *was* going to do right by her. Only now that he knew better, he was going to do it by leaving her alone.

"It was only a bundle of trash," Melody heard Jones report to Tom Beatrice as she inched closer to the group of men. "There *was* an outcropping of rocks. We searched that area as extensively as possible, given our time limit at that depth." His mouth was still a grim, straight line. "However, that was only one part of the quarry."

She had nearly fainted with relief when she'd seen Jones's and Harvard's heads break the surface of the water.

Jones must've known she'd be watching, worried out of her mind, because he'd turned to search for her, picking her out in the crowd on the shore. As he'd treaded the icy quarry water, he'd looked at her, touching the top of his head with the tips of his fingers, giving her the diver's signal for okay. He was okay, thank God. And the blip they'd picked up on the sonar wasn't Andy's body. It was only a bag of trash.

"How long do you have to wait before you can make another dive?" Tom Beatrice asked.

"The earliest we could do it would be late tonight," Jones told the police chief.

"But it would be smarter and safer to wait until morning," Harvard added. He met the other SEAL's eyes. "You know as well as I do, Jones—a four-or five-hour delay isn't going to matter one bit to that boy if he's down there."

Jones glanced around the somber crowd, at the Romanellas, at Estelle Warner and Brittany. His gaze lingered on Melody before he turned back to the police chief. "I'm sorry, Tom," he said. "Senior Chief Becker's right. We'd better wait and continue the search in the morning."

"That's fine, son," Tom told him. "It's risky enough diving down there in daylight." He looked around at the men who'd brought the boats. "We'll meet back here at 8:00 a.m. Let's get those boats up and out of the water!"

Brittany touched Melody's arm, pulling her aside. "I'm leaving."

"I'm waiting for Jones," Mel told her sister.

"I know," Brittany said. Her eyes were rimmed with red, but she managed a watery smile. "It's nice to know that something good will come of this."

Melody shook her head. "Britt, don't get the wrong idea here. Just because I care about Jones doesn't mean I intend to marry him. Because I don't. This isn't about that. We're friends."

She wasn't certain herself what it *was* about. Friendship, maybe. Or comfort. Comfort and friendship with a healthy dose of attraction. Yeah, when it came to Cowboy Jones, her intense attraction to him was always a part of the equation.

Brittany was looking at her with one eyebrow elevated skeptically. *"Friends?"*

Melody blushed, remembering how he'd kissed her, right there in front of everyone, remembering the way she'd clung to him—returning all of his passion and then some. But whatever she'd been thinking, whatever she'd been feeling, the moment had passed. Her sanity has returned.

She hoped. "I'd like Jones to be my friend. Of course, based on our history, it's bound to be a little confusing as we iron things out...."

Brittany didn't look convinced. "Whatever. I'm going in to work—try to keep my mind off Andy. I have the afternoon shift. You and your 'friend' will have the house to yourselves."

Melody sighed. "Britt, I'm not going to..."

But her sister was already gone.

The crowd had moved off, too, leaving Jones and Harvard to stow their diving gear and strip out of their bulky dry suits.

For the first time since Melody had met him, Jones actually looked cold. The water had been icy, and he'd been submerged in it an endlessly long time. He was shivering despite a blanket someone had put around him.

His fingers fumbled on the zipper, and she moved toward him. "Do you want me to get that?"

He smiled tightly. "The irony here is incredible. It's only *after* I screw up beyond belief that you want to undress me."

"I was...I thought..." She blushed. The truth was that she'd wanted to undress him from the moment she saw him again. But God help her if he ever realized that.

His smile faded with the last of his anger, and he looked dreadfully tired and impossibly unhappy. "I'm not sure exactly what's happening here between us, honey, but I've got to tell you—I sure as hell don't deserve any kind of consolation prize today."

"I didn't hear any of that," Harvard singsonged, peeling his own dry suit off his well-muscled body and nearly jumping into his jeans, pulling them on directly over the long woolen underwear he'd worn underneath. "I am so not listening. Got water in my ears, can't hear a damn thing." In his haste, he didn't bother with his shirt. He just yanked his winter coat over his undershirt. "In fact, I'm so outta here, I've already been gone for ten minutes. I've got all the gear except for your suit, Junior. You get that dried out, and I'll get the tanks filled for tomorrow."

"Thanks, H."

"Melody, girl, you don't need my admonishment to be careful around this man. Clearly, you two have already taken the concept of being careful, packed it in a box and tied a big red ribbon around it." Harvard took one look at Jones's face and backed away. "Like I said, though, I'm gone. I'll be back in the morning."

And then he *was* gone, leaving Jones and Melody alone.

"Jones, I didn't mean to imply..." she started lamely. She took a deep breath. "When I said that about us going home, I'm not sure I really meant to make it sound as if—"

"Okay," he said. "That's okay. I misinterpreted. I'm sorry. That kiss was my mistake."

No, it wasn't. And he *hadn't* misinterpreted. At the time, Melody *had* meant what she'd said. She was just too cowardly to admit it now. Obviously, she'd been swept along by the rush of high emotions. Now that she was thinking clearly again, the thought of taking him home and bringing him up to her room scared her to death.

She could not let herself fall in love with him. She absolutely couldn't.

"One step forward, two steps back," Jones added softly, almost as if he was talking to himself, almost as if he was able to read her mind. "This is your game, honey. You make up the rules and I'll follow them."

He had managed to unzip his diving suit and he pushed it off his body. Like Harvard, he had long underwear on underneath. He pulled that off, too, covering himself rather halfheartedly with the blanket, uncaring of who might be watching.

Melody quickly turned away and picked up his jeans from the rock he'd left them on. But when she started to hold them out to him, still carefully averting her eyes, she realized that they were at least six sizes too small.

She knew what must have happened even before Jones spoke. She was holding Andy's jeans.

"Someone must've put those over here by mistake," he said.

Andy's jeans and Andy's sweatshirt. The clothes Andy had been wearing before he'd jumped into the quarry. The clothes he had taken off just moments before he'd drowned.

Jones found his own jeans and pulled them on as Melody slowly sat down on the rock.

The woods around the quarry had been searched for quite some distance. If Andy *had* managed somehow to crawl out of the quarry and collapse in the bushes, he would have been found. And if he'd crawled out of the quarry and *hadn't* collapsed— well, it was hard to imagine him running around the woods in only his underwear.

Andy *had* drowned. He'd gone into the water and he hadn't come back out. As she sat holding his clothes, the reality hit her hard. Andy Marshall was dead.

Melody had been hanging pretty tough all day, but now the realization hit her, and she couldn't hold back her tears. Try as she might, she couldn't keep them from escaping. One after another, they rolled down her face.

Jones sat down next to her, close but not quite touching. He'd put on his T-shirt and pulled on his cowboy boots. He still had that blanket wrapped around his shoulders for warmth, and without a word, he drew it around her shoulders, too.

They sat for a moment, watching the noonday sun reflecting off the surface of the flooded quarry.

"I feel like I'm never going to be warm again," he admitted.

Melody wiped ineffectively at her tears. She couldn't stop them—they just kept on coming. "We should go home, get you something warm to drink."

It was as if he hadn't heard her. "Melody, I'm so sorry." He turned to her, and she saw that he had tears in his eyes, too. "If I hadn't come to town, this never would've happened."

She took his hand underneath the blanket. His fingers were icy. "You don't know that for certain."

"I thought I could help him," Jones told her. His eyes were luminous as he held her hand tightly. "I thought all he really needed was someone who cared enough to help get him in line. Someone to set some limits, and at the same time, make some demands that were above and beyond what he'd been asked to do in the past." He stared back out at the water, his jaw muscles jumping. "I remembered what joining the Navy—joining the SEALs—had done for me, and I thought I could give him a taste of that. I thought..."

He trailed off, and Melody finished for him. "Piece of cake?"

Jones looked at her and laughed, half in disbelief, half in despair. He wiped at his eyes with the back of his free hand. "Sweet Lord, was I ever wrong about that." He shook his head. "I can't believe he lied to me about breaking into that house on Looking Glass Road."

"He wasn't lying," Melody told him. "At least Britt doesn't think so. She thinks she can prove that he was using her computer that night. She claims he was at our house, surfing the Net on the night the vandalism took place.''

"If he didn't do it, how did his fingerprints get all over the place?''

Melody shook her head. "I don't know. But I *do* know that he stuck to his story. He insisted he didn't do it. What *I'd* like to know is why he called Alex Parks. And why would Alex agree to meet Andy out here after midnight?''

"I should've believed the kid. Why didn't I?'' The muscles in Jones's jaw were clenching again. "He said he didn't do it. I asked, and he answered me. I should've stuck by him. I should have trusted him unconditionally.''

Now it was Melody's turn to gaze out at the water. "It's hard to trust someone unconditionally,'' she told him. "Even the most powerful trust has its limits. I should know.'' She forced herself to look at him, to meet his eyes. "I would—and I did—trust you with my life. But I found myself unable to trust you with my heart. I expected you to hurt me and I couldn't get past that.''

His eyes were so green in the early-afternoon light. "You really expected me to hurt you?''

Melody nodded. "Not intentionally, but yeah.''

"That's why you didn't want to see me again. That's why you didn't give what we had going a chance.''

"Yes,'' she admitted.

"I probably would've,'' he admitted, too. "Hurt you, I mean. Like you said, not intentionally, but...''

She didn't want to talk about this. Nodding again, she pushed on, hoping he would follow. "In the same way, you expected Andy to mess up. So when it seemed as if he was lying, you went with your expectations.''

"God, I really blew it.'' The tears were back in Jones's eyes. "I thought I knew what I was doing, but the truth is, I was really unprepared to deal with this kid. I did *every*thing wrong.''

"That's just not true.''

But he wasn't listening. "When we hit 175 feet, we weren't quite on target and had to search for the object that the sonar picked up.'' He was talking about the dive he'd made in the quarry with Harvard. "It took us so long to get down there with all the stopping and waiting, but once we were there, I was scared to death. I just wanted to close my eyes and sink to the bottom myself. I didn't want to look, I didn't want to know. And then my light hit something, and it reflected back at me, and for one split second, Mel, I saw him. My eyes played a nasty trick on me, and I saw Andy's face down there."

Melody didn't know what to say, so she said nothing. She just kept holding his hand.

"Tomorrow, I'm going to have to go back down there," he continued. "And tomorrow, I probably *am* going to find him."

He was shaking. Whether it was from the wintery chill of the air or the darkness of his thoughts, Melody wasn't sure. She *did* know it was time to bring him home, though.

She stood up, tugging him gently to his feet, escaping from the confines of his blanket. "Let's go, Jones." She paused. "Do you still have my car keys?"

"Yeah." He gathered up his diving suit. "They're in my pocket."

Melody folded Andy's jeans, putting them back on the rock. "I wonder if we should try to contact Andy's father. Andy was running some searches on the Internet—he told me he thought he might've located his father at an Army base up in New Hampshire and—"

She realized what she was saying at the exact same moment Jones did.

"What did you just say?" he asked, turning to face her.

"He was looking for his father on the Net."

"And he thought he found him in *New Hampshire*."

Transfixed, Melody stared into the sudden glaring intensity of Jones's eyes. "Do you think...?" she breathed.

Jones grabbed Andy's jeans, searching quickly through the pockets. "Honey, did you see his watch? Was his watch here with the rest of his clothes?"

"No." Melody was afraid to get too excited. Although Andy never went anywhere without that watch, he certainly wouldn't have worn it into the water. So why wasn't it here? "It's possible

Alex Parks took it. I wouldn't trust that kid any farther than I could throw him.''

"Yeah, you're right. It's possible Alex has it. But..." Jones ran his hands through his damp hair. "Last week at the library, I talked Andy into checking out a copy of *Tom Sawyer*. He told me that he liked it—so he must've been reading it.''

"Oh, my God.'' Melody turned to look at the quarry. "He might've set this whole thing up to make it look as if he'd drowned.''

Jones grabbed her hand. "Come on.''

"Where are we going?''

"You're going home. *I'm* going to New Hampshire.''

Melody's back was killing her.

Cowboy shook his head in disgust, amazed that he'd let her talk him into coming along with him. It was an hour-and-a-half drive up to New Hampshire—each way.

She was careful not to mention her discomfort. Of course not. This was the woman who had walked for eight hours across the desert, the back of her heels raw from blisters, without complaining even once. No, she didn't say a word, but her constant shifting in her seat gave her away.

"We're almost there,'' she said, looking up from the map into the midafternoon glare.

The town was small, clearly built as an afterthought to the neighboring U.S. Army base. There were a series of bars and pool halls along the main strip, along with a tired-looking supermarket, a cheap motel, a tattoo parlor, a liquor store and a bus station with a sputtering neon sign.

Cowboy did a U-turn, right there in the middle of town.

"What are you doing? The base is in the other direction.''

"Just following a hunch.''

"But—''

"This whole thing—driving all the way up here without even being able to talk to Private Marshall on the phone—is a long shot, right?'' He'd used a contact he had at the Pentagon to locate

Andy's father, Pvt. David Marshall, here at the Plainfield, New Hampshire, Army Base.

Plainfield wasn't any kind of cushy silver-bullet assignment. In fact, it was the opposite. Men were assigned to Plainfield as a punishment just short of a jail sentence. And according to Cowboy's Pentagon friend, David Marshall had had plenty of reasons to be reprimanded. He had a rap sheet a mile long, filled with unsavory charges including sexual harassment and use of excessive violence in dealing with civilians.

When Cowboy had called Plainfield, he was told that Private Marshall was not available. He couldn't even get the unfriendly voice on the other end of the line to verify if the man was still stationed at the base. From the tone of the phone call, though, he suspected the elder Marshall was currently in the middle of a severe dressing-down—or maybe even in the lockup.

If Private Marshall *was* at Plainfield, assuming Andy had even been able to see him, it wasn't too hard to imagine his reaction as he came face-to-face with the son he'd abandoned twelve years earlier. There weren't going to be many kisses and hugs, that much was for sure.

Cowboy pulled into the potholed parking lot next to the bus station.

"You think Andy's father won't want anything to do with him," Melody guessed correctly. "But do you really think Andy would have enough money to buy a bus ticket out of here? He probably spent everything he had getting here from Appleton."

"I think he probably doesn't even have enough to buy himself dinner, but the bus station's warm and dry. He can stay here all night if he needs to. He can even sleep on one of the benches if he pretends he's waiting for an arriving bus."

She was watching him closely in the shadowy dusk as he pulled up the parking brake and turned off the engine. "You sound as if you're speaking from experience."

Cowboy gazed into her eyes. It felt as if it had been a million years since they shared a smile. The trip from Massachusetts had been a quiet one. In fact, this entire day had been the furthest

thing from a laughfest he'd ever known. "I think maybe you
know me a little too well."

"How many times exactly did you run away when you were
a kid?"

"I don't know—I lost count. The dumb thing was, no one ever
really missed me. So I finally stopped running. I figured I could
tick my parents off more by being around."

Melody shifted in her seat. "But you ran away again when you
were sixteen, right? You told me you went to see a rodeo and
just never went home."

"That wasn't running away. That was growing up and leaving
home." He managed a wan smile. "Well, maybe not growing
up. I'm still not sure I've managed to do that yet."

"I think you've done just fine." Her eyes were soft in the
rapidly fading light, and Cowboy knew with a sudden certainty
that all he had to do was lean forward and she would let him kiss
her. Despite everything that she'd said about misinterpretation and
mistakes, with very little effort on his part, she would belong to
him.

He couldn't figure it out. Certainly if Andy was dead, but even
if the kid was alive, Cowboy had proven himself to be irresponsible and incapable of dealing with a child. It didn't make sense.
He screws up and *now* he gets the girl? What he'd done should've
made her want to put even more distance between them. He just
didn't get it.

Maybe it *was* only based on comfort, on shared grief—or hope.
Or hell, maybe it was only his imagination. He'd find out soon
enough by kissing her again, by lowering his mouth to hers and…

It was funny. All this time, he would've risked damn near anything for a chance to take this woman into his arms and lose
himself in her sweet kisses. But now, as badly as he wanted to
feel her arms around him, he was going to have to deny himself
the pleasure. They'd come here hoping to find Andy. He should
be looking for the kid, not kissing Melody.

But God, he wanted to kiss her. He was drowning in the ocean
blue of her eyes, wondering just how much comfort she'd be

willing to give him, how much comfort she'd be willing to take in return....

"We're stalling," she told him, breaking the spell. "We should go inside."

Cowboy nodded, realizing he was gripping the steering wheel so hard his knuckles had turned white. He pried his fingers free. "I know." He *was* stalling. Truth was, he was afraid of going into that bus station and finding out his hunch was wrong. He was afraid this entire trip was just the result of wishful thinking and that Andy really *was* down at the bottom of that quarry.

Melody unfastened her seat belt. "I'll go. You stay here."

Cowboy snorted at that. "I don't think so."

He helped her out of the car, and as he closed the door behind her, she held on to his hand. He'd been on quite a few difficult missions since he'd become a SEAL, but this was the first time he'd had a hand to hold as he took the point. And odd as it was, he was glad for it, glad she was there.

"Please, God, let him be here," she murmured as they started toward the door.

"If he *is* here," Cowboy told her, "do me a favor. Don't let me kill him."

She squeezed his hand. "I won't."

He took a deep breath, pushed open the door and together they went inside.

It was vintage run-down bus station. The odor of cigarette smoke and urine wasn't completely masked by the cloyingly sweet chemical scent of air freshener. The bleak walls were a hopeless shade of beige, and the industrial-bland floor tiles were cracked and chipped in some places, revealing triangles of the dirty gray concrete beneath. The men's room had a sign on the door saying Out Of Order—Use Facilities Near Ticket Agents. The snack bar had been permanently shut down, replaced by vending machines. The cheery orange and yellow of the hard plastic chairs had long since been dulled by thousands of grimy fingers.

And Andy Marshall, a picture of dejection, sat in one of them, shoulders slumped, elbows on knees, forehead resting in the palms of his hands.

Relief roared in Cowboy's ears. It made the bus station, and the entire world with it, seem to shift and tilt on its axis.

The relief was followed by an icy surge of anger. How could Andy have done this? The little bastard! He'd had them all worried damned sick!

"Jones." He turned and looked down into Melody's eyes. They were brimming with tears. But she blinked, pushing them back as she smiled up at him. "I think he's already been punished enough," she said as if she could read his mind, as if everything he was feeling was written on his face.

Cowboy nodded. It was obvious that the kid's last hope had been ripped from him without any anesthetic. It wasn't going to do either Andy *or* Cowboy the slightest bit of good to foam at the mouth and rage at him.

"I'm going to go call Tom Beatrice," he told Melody, knowing that he had to attempt to regain his equilibrium before he confronted the boy. "I want to give Harvard a call, too. Tell him we found Andy alive."

She held on to his hand until the last possible moment. "Call Brittany, will you? Please?"

"I will." He went to a row of beat-up pay phones, punching in his calling-card number and watching as Melody approached Andy.

She sat down next to him, and even then the kid didn't look up until she spoke. Cowboy was too far away to hear what she said, but Andy didn't seem surprised by her presence.

He watched them talk as he made his calls. Tom was quietly thankful. Harvard was out, and Cowboy left a message for him with his father. Brittany cried and then cursed the boy for his stupidity in the same breath in which she thanked God for keeping him safe.

As Cowboy hung up the phone, Andy glanced warily in his direction. The flash of his pale face called to mind that other ghastly image he'd thought he'd seen 175 feet beneath the surface of the flooded quarry.

Andy's face looked much better with life glistening in his eyes.

And just like that, Cowboy's anger faded. The kid was alive. Yeah, he'd made a pile of very huge mistakes, but who was Cowboy to talk? He'd made some whopping mistakes here himself.

Starting seven and a half months ago in that 747 bathroom with Melody. With barely a thought, he'd gambled with fate and lost—and changed her life irrevocably.

She looked up at him as he approached, and he could see trepidation in her eyes. He tried to smile to reassure her, but it came out little better than a grimace. Great big God, he was tired, but he couldn't even consider slowing down. He had a ninety-minute drive back to Appleton that he had to make before he could even *think* about climbing into bed.

Climbing into Melody's bed.

If she let him. Hell, if he let himself, knowing what he now knew for certain—that he had no right to be anyone's father.

He laughed silently and scornfully at himself. Yeah, right. Like he'd *ever* turn Melody down. Whether it was comfort, true love or sheer lust that drove her into his arms, he wasn't going to push her away. Not in *this* lifetime.

"I'm sorry," Andy said before Cowboy even sat down.

"Yeah," Cowboy told him, "I know. I'm glad you're okay, kid."

"I thought maybe my father would be like you." Andy kicked once at the metal leg of the chair. "He wasn't."

"I wish you had told me what you were planning to do." Cowboy was glad he'd made those phone calls first. His voice came out even and matter-of-fact rather than harsh and shaking with anger. "I would've come up here with you."

"No, you wouldn't've." The boy's words were spoken without his usual cheeky attitude or resentment. They were flat, expressionlessly hopeless. "You didn't believe me when I said I didn't mess up that house."

"Yeah," Cowboy said. He cleared his throat. "Lookit, Andy, I owe you a major apology on that one. I know now that you didn't do it. Of course, now is a little bit late. Still, I hope you can forgive me."

There was a tiny flare of surprise in Andy's eyes. "You know I didn't...?"

"Brittany believed you," Melody told him. "And she figured out a way to prove you were telling the truth. The account information from her computer is going to show that someone—you— were on-line that night. And although that probably wouldn't hold up as an alibi in a court of law, it'll go far in convincing Tom Beatrice he's caught the wrong kid."

"Brittany believed me, huh?" Andy looked bemused. "Man, there was a time when she would've been organizing a lynch mob." He looked up at Cowboy and squared his narrow shoulders. "Maybe I *am* at least partly guilty, though. I *did* go into that house about two weeks ago. One of the upstairs windows was open a crack. I knew the place was empty, so I climbed up and went inside. I didn't break anything, though, and I didn't steal anything. I just looked."

"And touched," Cowboy added.

Andy rolled his eyes. "Yeah. I left my fingerprints everywhere. What a fool. Someone must've seen me go in and told Alex Parks. He did the spray painting and broke the windows and mirrors and stuff. He told me last night up by the quarry. He told me he'd made sure I was going to leave town. He told me he'd reserved a room for me at juvy hall." He smiled grimly. "I scared the hell out of him when I jumped into the quarry."

"You scared the hell out of *all* of us."

"It was a stupid, *dangerous* thing to do," Melody admonished him hotly. "You might have really drowned."

Andy slouched in his seat. "Yeah, like anyone would've missed me. Like anyone in the world gives a damn. My father doesn't—that's for sure. You know, he didn't even know my name? He kept calling me Anthony. *Anthony.* And he stood and talked with me for five lousy minutes. That's all he could spare me in all of twelve years."

"Forget about your father," Melody said fiercely. "He's an idiot, Andy. You don't need him because you have us. You've got me and Brittany and Jones—"

"Yeah, for how long?" There were actually tears in Andy's

eyes. He couldn't keep up the expressionless act any longer. His voice shook. "Because after this mess, Social Services is going to pull me out of the Romanellas' house so fast I won't even have time to wave goodbye."

"We won't let them," Melody said. "I'll talk to Vince Romanella and—"

"What are you going tell him to do?" Andy sneered. "*Adopt* me? That's about the only thing I can think of that would keep me around. And I'm *so* sure that would go over *really* well." He shook his head, swearing softly. "I bet Vince already has my stuff packed into boxes."

"Someone at Social Services must have the authority to give you a second chance," Cowboy said. "Alex Parks is the one who should be thrown into the brig for this, not you."

Andy wiped savagely at his tears. "What do *you* care? You're going to leave town yourself in a few weeks!"

Cowboy didn't know what to say. The kid was right. He *wasn't* going to stay. He was a SEAL. His job pulled him all over the world. Even under the best of circumstances, he'd often be gone for weeks at a time. He glanced up, and Melody made a point of not meeting his gaze.

"I don't know why you're so hot to marry her," Andy continued, gesturing with a thumb toward Melody, "when you're only going to see her and the kid a few times a year. My father might've been a real jerk, but at least he didn't pretend he was doing anything besides giving me his name when he married my mother."

Melody stood up. "I think we'd better get going," she said. "It's getting late."

"You know, Ted Shepherd's got a thing for you," Andy said to Melody.

"Andy, I changed the subject." Melody's voice sounded strained. "We need to go, and we need to stop talking about this now."

Andy turned to Cowboy. "The guy she works for has the hots for her. You didn't know that, did you? The guy's got money, too. He could take care of her and the kid, no problem. Brittany told me he's going to be governor some day. But as long as you're around, she doesn't stand a chance of getting anything started with him. And if *you* marry her—''

"Home, Andrew," Melody said in that tone that she used when she had reached the absolute end of her rope. *"Now."*

Chapter 13

"**Y**our Lamaze class starts tonight." Brittany was in the dining room, rifling through the sideboard drawers, searching for something. "Seven o'clock. At the hospital. In the West Lounge."

Melody sank into a chair at the kitchen table, aware of Jones watching her from the other side of the room. Lamaze class. God. It was nearly six. She would barely have enough time to take a shower. "Britt, I'm beat. I'm just going to stay home."

Brittany stopped her search long enough to poke her head through the door. "Abigail Cloutier has a waiting list a mile long for this class. If you don't show up, she'll fill your slot, and then you'll be stuck waiting for the next session, which doesn't start until next month. You'll probably end up having your baby before you're halfway through." She disappeared again. "I made some pea soup—it's on the stove. And there's bread warming in the oven."

"Wait a minute," Melody said, sitting up straight. "Aren't you coming with me?"

"*Here's* my passport," Brittany said triumphantly. She

slammed the drawer shut and came into the kitchen, adjusting her hair. "I need it as a second form of ID."

"You *aren't* coming with me, are you?" Melody looked at her sister, fighting her panic. If Brittany didn't come as her coach, then that left Melody going solo, or... She didn't look at Jones. She refused to look at Jones.

But Britt was all dressed up, and it was obvious it wasn't for Abigail Cloutier's benefit. She was wearing a dark suit, complete with panty hose and her black heels that meant business. Her blond hair was pulled up into a French braid and she actually wore makeup.

"Sweetie, Social Services is intending to take Andy back to Boston tonight. I've been on the phone with Vince Romanella and at least twelve different social workers since Cowboy called this afternoon. There's a meeting at 6:00 at the Romanellas'," she told them, turning to look at Jones, who was silently leaning against the kitchen counter. "I expect it to drag on until quite late, so no, Mel, I can't go to the Lamaze class with you tonight."

"I'll go," Jones said. Melody closed her eyes.

Britt laughed. "I figured you'd be willing to volunteer as temporary coach."

God, the last thing Melody wanted to do was sit with Jones in a room with a dozen other expectant, *married* couples. But that wasn't the worst of it. She'd seen childbirth classes portrayed on TV, and all of them had demanded a certain amount of physical intimacy—touching at the very least—between the mother-to-be and her coach.

It was obviously all she could do to keep from throwing herself at Jones even under normal circumstances. Add any strong emotions into the churning pot of passion, and she would be on the verge of meltdown. Add a situation in which Jones would be *forced* to touch her, and she would be lost.

"Jones, you look even more exhausted than I feel," Melody countered, knowing that no matter what she said, he wouldn't quit. He didn't know how to quit. He'd never quit before in his entire life.

He gave her a crooked smile. "Honey, is it going to be harder than diving to 175 feet?"

"No." Melody realized that for the first time since he'd arrived in Appleton all those weeks ago, he was wearing a sweatshirt. She'd honestly thought he didn't have one. Before today, she'd thought he wasn't capable of feeling the cold.

"Well, there you go. As long as it doesn't involve breathing a tank of mixed gas, it'll be a—"

"Piece of cake," Melody finished for him with a sigh. "Speak for yourself," she muttered.

He straightened up, concern darkening his eyes. "Mel, if you're really feeling too tired to go, I'll go for you. I can take notes and tomorrow I can tell you everything you missed."

He was serious. He looked a total mess, but he stood ready to help her however he could, and the effect was touching. She tried to look away. When it came to Jones, she shouldn't be thinking words like "touching."

But his chin glinted with golden brown stubble, and although he looked exhausted to the bone, and as if by all rights he should be sitting rather than standing, he looked...undeniably touchingly adorable. Melody couldn't help but glance at him, and he mustered a tired smile. She knew him well enough to believe he would be ready and willing to run ten miles if it was asked of him. Twenty if *she* asked him.

Brittany pulled on her overcoat. Her purse was by the door, and she gathered it up. "If you're not going to go, call Abby now," her sister told her.

Melody closed her eyes. "I'm going to go." With Jones. Oh, God. The feeling that gripped her was more than pure dread. In fact, the dread was laced with stomach-flipping, roller-coaster-style excitement.

Brittany opened the door, but as a seeming afterthought, she turned back. "Oh, just so you know, I'm planning to begin the preliminary paperwork tonight to adopt Andy."

Melody nearly fell out of her chair. *"What?"*

"You heard me."

"I can't believe you're serious."

Britt bristled. "If you can be a single mother, then I can, too. And it's not as if we don't have four empty bedrooms in this house."

Melody shook her head. "I'm not criticizing you," she told her sister. "I'm just...amazed. A few weeks ago, Andy's name was interchangeable with Satan's."

"Well, yes, but that was before I got to know him."

"Britt, you don't really know Andy Marshall," Melody countered. "I mean, you might *think* you do, but—"

"I know all that I need to know," Brittany said quietly. "I know that right now the one thing that boy needs more than anything in the world is someone who loves him and wants him, *truly* wants him. I know he's not perfect. I know he's going to give me headaches over things I can't even imagine, but I don't care. I don't care! Because you know what? The thought of my life without that kid around...well, it just feels cold—like spring will never come again. I've thought about it long and hard. I honestly want him, Mel."

"It's not going to be that easy to cut through the red tape," Melody cautioned. "A single woman trying to adopt a kid who's a known troublemaker... I can imagine Social Services deciding that he's going to need a strong father figure and turning you down."

"Even if it doesn't work out," Brittany told her, "at least Andy will know that *some*one wanted him. At least I can give him *that* much."

Melody stood up and gave her sister a hug. "You go and fight for him," she whispered, blinking back tears.

And then Brittany was gone, leaving her alone in the kitchen with Jones. Jones and his stormy green eyes...

"I better shower and change if we're going out," he said.

She nodded. "I have to, too."

"Are you certain you just don't want to let me go?" he asked.

Melody was certain of nothing anymore. "The class is only an hour and a half," she told him. "It'll be over before we know it."

She hoped.

* * *

Jones was helping himself to a cup of coffee as Melody returned from the ladies' room. Abby Cloutier, the Lamaze instructor, had called a ten-minute washroom break—a definite necessity for a class filled with hugely pregnant women.

So far, they'd sat on folding chairs in a darkened room and watched a movie that focused on giving birth. She'd barely been able to pay attention with Jones sitting so close to her. Having him here was a thorough distraction. He smelled good and looked even better.

But he hadn't had to touch her.

Not yet.

Jones was smiling as he listened to another man talk. He was standing in a group of about five men, most of whom were helping themselves to cookies from the snack table. He'd broken out his Dockers and polo shirt for the occasion, and with his hair neatly pulled back into a ponytail at the nape of his neck, and his chin freshly shaven, he looked impossibly handsome. But even though he was dressed nearly the same as the other men, he stood out in the crowd. He might as well have been wearing his dress whites.

"Is that your Navy SEAL?" a voice behind Melody asked. She turned to see Janette Dennison, one of Brittany's high school friends who was pregnant with her fourth child. Janette peered across the room at Jones. "Dear Lord, he's bigger than Hank Forsythe!"

Hank owned the local gym. His wife, Sandy, was pregnant with their first. "Jones *is* taller," Melody pointed out.

"Your Lieutenant Jones is more than taller," Janette countered. "Your Lieutenant Jones is...beyond description, Mel. Haven't you noticed every single woman in this place looking at you as if you've won the lottery?"

Melody *had* noticed. But she was well aware that everyone's envy would fade rapidly as soon they were told exactly what a U.S. Navy SEAL did for a living. She'd heard several women complaining in the ladies' room about husbands who had to fly to Boulder or Los Angeles or Seattle on business and were gone for days, sometimes even weeks, at a time.

They didn't know how lucky they were. Their husbands weren't going to be parachuting out of airplanes or helocasting—jumping from low-flying helicopters into the ocean below—as they inserted into enemy territory. Their husbands carried briefcases, not submachine guns. Their work didn't expose them to physical dangers. Their husbands would always be returning safe and sound. There was no chance of their being brought back home strapped to some medic's stretcher, bleeding from gunshot wounds, or—worse yet—zipped inside a body bag.

"Did he really rescue you from that embassy where you were being held hostage?" Janette asked. "That is *so* romantic."

Melody smiled. But Janette was wrong. Yes, Jones had saved her life. But he'd saved Chris Sterling's and Kurt Matthews's lives, as well. He would've saved anyone's life. It wasn't personal—it was his job. And because of that, the fact that he'd saved her wasn't particularly romantic.

What *Melody* found truly romantic was the image of Jones, up on a step stool in the baby's nursery, hanging curtains patterned with brightly colored bunnies and teddy bears.

Romantic was the wondrous look in his eyes that she'd seen when he'd touched her and felt their baby move.

Romantic was Jones, driving home from New Hampshire after they'd found Andy, furtively wiping tears of relief from his eyes when he thought she wasn't looking.

Romantic was the way he could gaze at her from across the room—the way he was gazing at her right now—as if she were the most beautiful, most desirable woman on the entire planet. His eyelids were slightly lowered, and the intensity of the expression on his face would be a little frightening if not for the small smile playing around the corners of his lips.

She'd seen that smile before. In Paris. And she knew for a fact that Jones had the ability and the wherewithal to make everything that little smile promised come true.

She turned away, her cheeks heating with a blush. She didn't want this man, she reminded herself. She didn't love him. God help her, she didn't *want* to love him....

"Gentlemen," Abby Cloutier announced, "grab a floor mat

and some pillows and find your ladies. We're going to do some simple breathing and relaxation exercises to get you started.''

Across the room, Jones waited patiently for a chance to take a mat from the pile. As if he felt Melody watching him, he looked up at her again and smiled. It was a tentative, apologetic smile, as if he knew what was coming and how much the thought of his touching her scared her.

Scared her and exhilarated her.

''Gentlemen, sit down on the mat and use your bodies and the pillows to make as comfortable a nest as you possibly can for your ladies,'' Abby continued.

Jones set the mat and the pillows toward the back of the room, giving them what little privacy he could. No doubt he was well aware of the curious glances they'd been receiving all evening long. Appleton was a fairly conservative community, and they were the only unmarried pair in the group—although a few of the younger couples looked as if there had been a shotgun present at their nuptials.

He sat down, imitating their classmates as he spread his long legs for her to sit nestled against him, as if they were riding a toboggan.

Knowing it would be far worse if she hesitated and stood there gaping at him like some landed fish, Melody lowered herself to the mat. At least this way, she would keep her back to him. At least this way, he wouldn't see the blush that was heating her cheeks. At least this way, she wouldn't have to gaze into his eyes or watch his lips curve up into one of his smiles. At least this way, she wouldn't be tempted to do something foolish, such as kiss him.

She gingerly inched her way back, bumping against the inside of his knee. ''Oh, I'm sorry!''

''That's all right, honey. Keep coming on back.''

She didn't dare look at him. ''Are you sure? It's a little warm in here, and I'm not exactly a lightweight these days.''

''Mel. You're *supposed* to lean against me. How're you going to relax if you're not leaning back?''

How was she supposed to relax, leaning back against this outrageously sexy man's solid chest, her legs against the inside of his thighs?

"Come on," he whispered. "I promise it won't be that bad."

Bad wasn't what she was afraid of. She was afraid it was going to be irresistibly *good*.

"Get comfortable, ladies," Abby ordered.

Melody inched farther back, closing her eyes as Jones took control and pulled her in close. Too close. He put his arms around her, the palms of his hands against her belly, and she felt both impossibly safe and in terrible peril. She felt his breath, soft against her ear. She felt his heart beating against her back. She didn't want to move, didn't want to talk. She just wanted to sit there with him like this. Forever.

And that was absolutely the wrong thing to be thinking.

"This makes me really uncomfortable," she whispered. It was both a lie *and* the understatement of the year.

"Sorry—I'm sorry." He removed his hands but then didn't know quite where to put them.

God, now she'd gone and made *him* tense, too.

Abby's voice was just a drone in the background. She was saying something about breathing, about the importance of taking a deep cleansing breath before and after contractions. Melody inhaled deeply through her nose, releasing her breath through her mouth, along with the rest of the class.

She tried her best to follow the breathing exercises but knew without a doubt that she was retaining absolutely nothing. Come tomorrow morning, she would remember none of this—except for the way Jones smelled, and the warmth of his body pressed against her, and...

"...back rub while she's doing this." Abby's voice cut into her thoughts. "Come on, guys, make her feel good."

"At last," Jones said, trying to make light of it. "I'm finally going to get a chance to give you a back rub."

Melody closed her eyes. There was nothing even remotely funny here. She remembered his back rubs far too well. They had involved a great deal more of both of their anatomies than simply her back and his hands.

She felt him move aside the mass of her long hair, felt his hands touch her shoulders, his fingers gently massaging the too tense muscles in her upper back and neck. She tried to focus on her breathing, but with him touching her that way, she could barely get a breath in, let alone push one out.

"Tell her how wonderfully she's doing, gentlemen," Abby urged. "Tell her how beautiful she is. Tell her how much you love her. Don't hold back. Practice letting her know. When she's in labor, she's going to need to hear all these little things you take for granted."

"Don't you dare say anything," Melody said from between clenched teeth.

His husky laughter moved the hair next to her ear. "Are you kidding?" he asked. "I wouldn't dream of it. I'm supposed to be relaxing you, not getting you more tense. I know you pretty well by now, Mel—enough to know that when you look into a mirror, you don't see what I see. I happen to think you're crazy, but this is not the time to debate the issue."

"...called *effleurage,*" Abby was saying. "It's a French word, meaning to stroke or lightly massage. Gentlemen, when your lady is in labor, it may comfort her to stroke her abdomen very lightly in a circular motion. Ladies, let him know the right amount of pressure. Tell him what feels good. Don't be shy."

Melody closed her eyes tightly as Jones's long fingers caressed the mountain that was her belly. Somehow he knew exactly how to touch her. Watching those powerful-looking hands touch her so exquisitely gently was enough to make her dizzy.

"Is this all right?" he asked. "Am I doing this right?"

She managed to nod. Right was not quite the word for what he was doing.

"How's your lower back?" he asked, using his other hand to reach between them and massage her. "This is where you're always hurting the most, isn't it?"

She nodded again, unable to speak.

"Are you focusing on the breathing?" he asked, his voice soft and soothing in her ear. "If I know you, you're not. You're thinking about something else entirely—about Brittany and Andy, about what's going on over at the Romanellas'. You're always thinking and worrying about someone else, but right now, you've got to clear your mind and think only about yourself. Relax and breathe and just shut everything else out.'' He laughed softly. ''I know that's hard because I'm probably the one problem you'd like to shut out the most, right?''

Wrong. Jones was wrong. He was incredibly, impossibly, amazingly, *totally* wrong. Melody realized with a sudden startling clarity that she didn't want to shut him out. She'd tried, but he'd been doggedly persistent, and somehow, someway, over the past few weeks, he'd gone from former lover and near stranger to dear friend.

He'd been patient and he'd let her see that although he would never be called average or normal, there *was* a part of him that could be content just sitting on the porch, talking and watching the sunset. He'd taken his time and told her stories about himself as a boy, about growing up, so she felt she had a good sense of him, of why he did the things he did. And his dealings with Andy had told her even more about the kind of man he'd become.

He was the kind of man she could fall in love with.

The kind of man she *had* fallen in love with.

I know you pretty well by now, he'd said. *If I know you...* He *did* know her. And she knew him.

Oh, she didn't know him completely. Even if she spent the rest of her life with him, there'd still be secrets she knew he'd never share with her. And even the parts of him she *did* know, she'd never totally understand. His need to risk his life, to be a SEAL. But even though she didn't understand it, she could appreciate it. And God knows he was good at what he did.

She was starting to believe that if he *did* marry her, he *would* stick by her—for the rest of his life, if need be. If he made a vow, he wouldn't break it. He had the strength and the willpower to keep to his word, no matter how hard.

But would that be enough for her? Knowing that he was with her not out of love, but out of duty? Was it possible that her own feelings for him were strong enough to sustain them both?

She didn't think so.

She knew he liked her. And although she couldn't quite believe it, he seemed to desire her. But unless he loved her, *truly* loved her, she couldn't *marry* him. Could she?

"Mel, you're tightening up again," Jones whispered. "Just let it go. Whatever you're wrestling with, just give it up, throw it away."

"We're out of time," Abby announced. "The next class is about to break down the doors, so just leave your mats and pillows where they are. Next week, we're going to work on Modified-Paced Breathing and the Progressive Relaxation Exercise, so read over those sections in your books—it'll save us a little time. Ladies, remember to do your stretches and your Kegels!"

Jones helped Melody to her feet. He would've held on to her hand, but she pulled away, afraid he would somehow know the awful truth just from touching her. She'd done what she'd sworn she wouldn't do. She'd fallen in love with him. She was doomed.

A shadow flickered in his eyes, and all at once he looked about as tired as she felt. "You're never going be able to relax around me, are you?" It was a rhetorical question, and he didn't wait for her to answer. "It was stupid to think I could be your labor coach. Come on, let's get you home. You look beat."

He was careful not to touch her again as he opened the door for her. And he was noticeably silent in the car on the way home. And it wasn't until they pulled into the driveway that Melody gathered up the nerve to speak.

"Jones, I'm sorry...I, um..." What could she possibly say? I love you? She wasn't sure she'd ever be able to tell him that. Not with words anyway. Not in *this* lifetime.

He pulled up the parking brake and turned to face her. "Mel, look, I've been thinking about...a lot of things. Andy. Our baby. You and me. You—what you want and what you don't want." The muscle in his jaw was jumping. "As in *me*."

"Jones—"

He stopped her by holding up one hand. "I need to say this, so please let me talk. I think it's kind of obvious that my parenting skills need a lot of work. I'm not sure anymore that I should help you raise our child.

"But I keep coming back to the fact that I don't want this kid growing up thinking I don't give a damn. Because I do. I do." His voice broke, and he took a deep breath, steadying himself. "I care about him, but I care about you, too. And what Andy said is right. If you marry me, you'll never find someone that you can really love, someone who can be a real father to our baby."

"Jones—"

"Hush and let me finish. I'm giving you your deal, Melody. You acknowledge that the baby's mine, put my name on his birth certificate, let me come and visit a couple times a year. I'll want to pay child support, too, but we can have our lawyers work that out."

He cleared his throat. "My only other condition is that I'd like to be there when the baby's born. I know there's no real way to be certain when that's going to take place, but it's not likely to happen within the next three weeks. So I figure what I'll do is pack up and head back to base as soon as possible. I'll apply for additional leave at the start of December, and then we'll just cross our fingers and hope it happens sooner rather than later."

Melody was speechless. He was accepting her deal. He had it all figured out, down to being there when the baby was born. He was capitulating, backing down, giving in. She could barely believe it.

Didn't he realize that she was on the verge of surrender herself?

But there was no need to worry anymore. She'd won.

So why did she feel as if she'd lost?

Chapter 14

Cowboy stood on the steps of the porch, waiting while Melody unlocked the front door. He was making sure she got safely inside before he returned to his tent. He'd grab a combat nap—just enough to refresh him—and then he'd pack up and walk over to the gas station by the highway, bum a ride off someone heading into Boston. Once in town, he'd take the T to Logan Airport. By sunup, he'd be wheels up, heading back to base.

Harvard had told him most of Alpha Squad had long since returned to Virginia. After a great deal of bitching and moaning, FinCOM was ready to negotiate with Joe Cat about the counter-terrorist training session. It looked as if FinCOM would keep its rule book with the understanding that the program was going to happen on a trial basis only. Although latest word was that the combined SEAL/FinCOM training program wouldn't happen until spring—May or June at the earliest.

Which left Alpha Squad with a *looong* time to prepare. But as they waited, of course, they were ready to go wherever they were needed at a moment's notice.

The moon had risen above the trees, and its silvery light made

Melody's face seem exquisitely otherworldly as she pushed open the door and then turned to face him. "Good night."

"You *are* beautiful, you know."

She closed her eyes. "Jones, we're done. We've come to an agreement. There's no need for you to—"

"Yeah, I know," he interrupted. "I figure that's why I can say it. I don't have to worry anymore about you freaking out and running away. Hell, I don't have to stop there. I can tell you that despite what you think, you're the sexiest lady I've ever known."

She tried to make a joke of it. "Well, sure, you're a SEAL. After spending all that time in the ocean, it's no wonder you'd be attracted to someone who reminds you of a whale."

Cowboy didn't laugh. "You know what you remind me of?"

"A circus tent?"

He refused to acknowledge her attempts at humor. He continued as if she hadn't spoken. "You remind me of the hottest, most powerful sex I've ever had in my life. Every time I see you, I think about what we did to make you look that way. I think about locking myself in that bathroom with you on board that 747. I think about the way you made me feel, about the fact that for the first time in my entire life, I honest to God didn't care that I didn't have a condom."

He lowered his voice. "I think about the way you kissed me when you climaxed so you wouldn't cry out. I look at you, Melody, and I remember every stroke, every touch, every kiss. I look at you, and all I can think about is how badly I want another chance to make love to you like that again."

Melody was silent, just staring at him, her eyes wide.

"So," Cowboy said, "now you know."

She still didn't say a word. But she didn't run away, either.

He took a step toward her, and then another step, and she still didn't move. "I may be way out of line here—no, I *know* I'm way out of line, but I figure as long as I'm being brutally honest, I have to tell you that I've spent these past few weeks damn near tied in knots from wanting you so badly. I wanted you and I thought I needed you, but I found out today that wanting and needing aren't the same thing. Need's not about sex, is it? Not really. Because today I needed you more than I've ever needed anyone, and you were there for me." He forced a smile. "And what do you know? We had our clothes on the entire time."

He touched her hair, touched the softness of her cheek. "Look at me," he said. "Still putting the moves on you. We've reached an understanding, made an agreement. We've achieved a friend-ship of sorts, and I still can't seem to back away. I still want you more than I've ever wanted any woman."

She was trembling. He knew damn well that kissing her wasn't the gallant, gentlemanly thing to do, but he couldn't keep himself from lowering his mouth to hers.

She tasted so sweet, so perfect. Her lips were deliciously soft, exquisitely inviting. He pulled her closer, and the tautness of her belly pressed against him. He loved the way she felt beneath his hands, loved the way she seemed to sigh and melt against him as he kissed her again, deeper, longer, but just as slowly and gently.

"Come inside," she whispered. Her eyes were soft and dreamy as she gazed up at him. "Please?" Her fingers were laced through his hair, and she tugged his head down toward her to kiss him again.

She kissed *him.*

Cowboy knew he should turn and walk away. He knew nothing had changed. He was still going to have to leave tomorrow. But hell, it was entirely possible that she was doing this *because* he was leaving.

He broke free from her kiss. "Mel, are you sure?"

"Yes."

Yes. It wasn't something he needed to hear twice.

She took his hand and drew him into the house. She didn't say another word as she led him toward the stairs and up to her bed-room.

Cowboy felt compelled to speak. "Honey, I don't have any condoms. Again."

She glanced back at him. "Jones, it's not as if you're going to get me pregnant," she said. "Again."

"Still, I was reading this whole huge debate about whether or not women should have sexual relations in the eighth and ninth

months of their pregnancies,'' he told her. ''The consensus was
unless the pregnancy was high risk, anything goes. Except there
was a minority who seemed to think unprotected sex increased
the risk of potential infection to the baby.''

She'd gone into her room without turning the light on and now
stood there in the moonlight, gazing at him. ''Sometimes I think
you go a teeny bit overboard with your research. My garden, for
instance. It looks as if it's ready for a Siberian winter. All I really
needed was someone to clear out the dead plants and throw down
a little mulch.'' A smile softened her words. ''Thank you for
taking care of it, by the way.''

''You're welcome. But yeah,'' he agreed, ''I've definitely read
far more than I should have about the potential dangers of pregnancy. Eclampsia. God. Just the thought of it scares me to death.''

Damn, he was nervous. He'd wanted her for so long, but now
all he could do was stand here and talk. Yada, yada, yada. He
couldn't seem to make himself shut up. He cleared his throat,
fighting the urge to ask her about her blood pressure. She was
fine. He knew she was fine. With the exception of the relentless
morning sickness she suffered, she was healthy. Melody's was
not a high-risk pregnancy. He'd already discussed it with Brittany,
and she'd reassured him. She was a nurse; she should know.

He cleared his throat again. ''May I lock your door?''

Melody nodded. ''Please.''

The door had an old-fashioned hook-and-eye lock, and he fastened it. It wouldn't do much against an invading horde, but for
privacy, it would work just fine. When he turned around, she was
closing the curtains. Without the moonlight, the room was very,
very dark. He switched on the light.

''Oh,'' she said, ''please don't.''

He turned it off. She must've had some kind of room-darkening
shades because it was nearly as dark in there as it had been down
at 175 feet in the quarry. ''Mel, I'm going to need night-vision
glasses to see you.''

She was a disembodied voice, lost in the shadows on the other
side of the room. ''That's the idea.''

"Oh, come on. Weren't you paying attention to *any*thing I said downstairs on the porch?"

"Yes," she said. "And it got you this far. It was...very nice. But... You know that cover Demi Moore did for *Vanity Fair* when she was pregnant?"

"You mean the one where she was naked?"

"Yeah. Pregnant and naked. She looked amazingly beautiful." She paused. "I don't look anything like that."

Cowboy had to laugh. "How will I ever know?"

She laughed, too. She had a musical laugh that brushed over him like velvet in the darkness. "My point exactly."

"How about we turn on the light in the bathroom? Nothing *too* bright?"

"How about you come over here?"

It was an invitation he couldn't refuse. He moved toward her, sensing more than seeing that she'd climbed into bed. He reached for her, and with an explosion of pleasure, discovered that in the darkness she'd rid herself of her clothes. Every last little stitch was gone.

It was a total surprise, and as he touched her, he realized that with the lights off and the room so very dark, his other senses were heightened. Making love in the dark this way might not have been exactly what he'd wanted, but it was going to be very, very, *very* good.

He kissed her, her skin smooth beneath his still-exploring fingers. Her breasts were so full, they rested on the enormous bulge of her belly—the bulge that held their baby.

She moaned as he kissed her harder, deeper, filling her mouth with his tongue and his hands with the softness of her breasts. Her nipples were hard peaks pressed against the palms of his hands, a sensation that was impossibly delicious.

And apparently, it felt as good from Melody's end.

She pulled his shirt free from the waist of his pants, slipping her hands underneath and sliding her fingers up along the muscles of his chest as they knelt there together on her bed.

"You have no idea how long I've wanted to touch you like

this," she whispered. "All those weeks of watching you run
around with hardly any clothes on..."

Cowboy had to laugh. All this time, he'd thought she'd become
immune to damn near everything he'd thought he had working in
his favor.

He ran his hands lightly down her stomach, marveling at the
way it seemed to bloom from her body. The rest of her was still
slender. It was true, she'd put on a few extra pounds since Paris,
but he'd thought she was a bit too skinny before. She felt good
beneath his hands—so soft and utterly, thoroughly feminine. He
strained to see her in the darkness, but though his eyes had tried
to adjust, he still couldn't see a damn thing.

She kissed him as she tugged at his shirt, breaking off to say,
"I'm feeling very much as if I'm the only one naked here."

"That's because you are. And, to be honest, I like it. There's
a real hint of a master-slave thing to it," he teased. He lowered
his head to draw one hard bud of a nipple into his mouth as his
hand explored lower, sweeping beneath the taut curve of her
stomach, his fingers encountering her soft nest of curls. Talk about
a turn-on. She was ready for him, slick with heat and desire, and
as he touched her, first lightly, then harder, deeper, she clung to
him.

"Master and slave, huh?" Her voice was breathless. "In that
case—slave, take off your clothes."

Cowboy cracked up. Damn, he couldn't get enough of this girl.
He yanked his shirt over his head, then kissed her, pulling her
back with him onto the bed, careful, so careful to be gentle.

He felt her fingers fumble with the buckle of his belt, and he
tortured himself for a moment, just letting her knuckles brush
against him as she worked to get him free. There was no way
she'd ever figure out how to unfasten that belt—certainly not in
this blanket of darkness, and probably not even in the light.

"Jones..."

He reached down with one hand and released the catch.

"Thank you," she murmured.

It took her next to forever to unfasten the button. And he was so aroused, it took her another eon to work the zipper down, and then...

She didn't touch him. Damn, she didn't touch him! She dragged his pants and his shorts down his legs instead, leaving him screaming with need, aching for her touch, and loving every minute of the way she always kept him guessing.

Melody pulled off his boots one by one, and he wished for the zillionth time that it wasn't so damned dark. He would've loved to have watched.

He propped himself up on his elbows as he helped her pull his legs free from his pants. "Honey, do you have a condom?"

She froze. "You're not kidding, are you?"

"No. I...just want to protect you and the baby."

He felt her sit down next to him on the bed, felt her touch his leg, her fingers trailing up from his calf to his knee to his thigh. "Most guys wouldn't think past the fact that they couldn't get me more pregnant than I already am."

Her fingers did slow figure eights on his thigh. He reached for her, but she heard him start to move and backed away. He felt her fingers again, this time down near his ankle. He'd never realized that being touched on the ankle could be such a mind-blowing turn-on. He tried to moisten his dry lips. "Most guys wouldn't have gotten totally paranoid by reading every book in the library on pregnancy."

"Most guys wouldn't have bothered." She kissed him on the inside of his knee, her mouth soft and moist and cool against the fiery heat of his skin.

Cowboy reached for her again, but again, she wasn't there. He had to move slowly, searching for her carefully in the pitch black. He didn't want to knock her over with quick moves and flailing arms. Besides, he liked this game she was playing too damn much to want it to end.

But it was going to end. In just a handful of hours, the sun was going to creep above the horizon, and this night *was* going to end. And he was going to crawl out of Melody's soft bed and walk out of her room, out of this house. He was going to pack up his tent and be gone. Game over.

It was ironic. The fact that there was an end in sight was quite possibly the only reason Melody was making love to him tonight. It was possible that it was only because he'd already told her that he wouldn't stay that she could let herself have this time with him.

But with each kiss, each touch, each caress, *he* was wishing that he could keep this crazy game alive forever.

Forever.

She touched him again, and this time he was ready for her. His fingers closed around her arm and he gently pulled her up, finding her mouth with his, her body with his fingers, entangling their legs, the heaviness of his arousal against the roundness of her belly.

She moved languidly, lazily, kissing his neck, his ear, that delicate spot beneath his jaw that drove him crazy and made him want nothing more than to bury himself inside her forever.

Forever.

In the past, the word had scared him to death. It meant a deadly sameness, a permanent lack of change. It meant stagnation, boredom, a life of endless reruns, a slow fade from the brilliant colors of fresh new experiences to the washed-out gray of tired and old.

But Cowboy could be a SEAL forever without ever fearing he'd fall victim to that fate. Even if he ever got tired of parachuting out of jet planes, Joe Cat would have Alpha Squad doing HALO jumps—jumping out of planes at outrageously high altitudes, yet not opening the chute until they reached a ridiculously *low* altitude. And if he got tired of that—and he'd have to do one whole hell of a lot of 'em ever to be blasé about the adrenaline-inducing sensation of the ground rushing up to meet him—there was always Alpha Squad's refresher courses in underwater demolition, or Arctic, desert and jungle survival, or...

The truth was, he could be a SEAL forever because he never knew what was coming next.

Cowboy had always thought he'd feel the same about women. How could he possibly agree to spend the rest of his life with only one, when he never knew for certain who might be walking into his life at any given moment? How could he survive the endless stagnation of commitment even as temptation walked toward him every time he turned a corner?

But as he lost himself in the sweetness of Melody's kisses, he found himself wondering instead how he could possibly survive the constant disappointment of searching for her face in a crowd—despite the fact that he knew damn well she was two thousand miles away. How could he survive turning corner after corner, coming face-to-face with beautiful women, women who wanted to be with him—women he wanted nothing to do with, women whose only real faults were that they weren't Melody?

She pulled away from him slightly, opening herself to his hand, lifting her hips to push his fingers more deeply inside her. Her own fingers trailed down his side, moving across his stomach, almost but not quite touching him.

"You're driving me insane," he breathed.

"I know." He could hear the smile in her voice.

"I want you so badly, honey, but I'm terrified I'll hurt you." His own voice was hoarse.

She pulled back. "Do you mind if I get on top of you?"

Mind? Did she actually think he would *mind?* But then he realized that she was laughing at his stunned silence.

"But first..." She touched him, and his mind exploded with white-hot pleasure as she kissed him most intimately. "Do you think if I keep doing this while calling you Harlan," she wondered, "you'll learn to associate positive emotions with the use of your first name?"

Cowboy didn't know whether to laugh or cry.

"Harlan," she said. "Harlan. Harlan. Harlan. You know, I never really thought about it before, but I *like* that name."

He could barely speak. "I like it, too."

Melody laughed. "Wow, that was easy. I think I may have just developed a powerful brainwashing technique. Better not let any enemies of the U.S.A. get their hands—so to speak—on this, or we'll all be in trouble."

"Yeah, but it wouldn't work with anyone else but you."

Melody was quiet for a moment. "Well, that was really

sweet,'' she said. He could tell from her voice that she didn't believe him.

He pushed himself up on one elbow. "Melody, I'm serious."

She pushed him back down, straddling his thighs. "Let's not argue about this now," she told him, reaching for something. He heard the sound of a drawer opening, and then she moved back. "Let's just...pretend that we might've been able to make this thing between us work."

"But—"

"Please?" He felt her touch him, covering him with a condom.

"Mel, dammit, if you could look into my eyes—"

"Hush up and kiss me, Jones."

It was an order he couldn't refuse. And when she shifted herself forward, and in one smooth, languorous motion, surrounded him with her tight heat, he couldn't do more than groan her name.

He wanted more. He wanted to thrust deeply inside her. He wanted to flip her onto her back and rock her, hard and fast, the way he knew she liked it. He wanted to turn on the light and gaze into her eyes. He wanted to watch her release, see the incredibly sexy look on her beautiful face as he took her higher than she'd ever been before.

Instead, he lay on his back. "Mel, I'm afraid to move." His voice was a paper-dry whisper in the darkness.

"Then I'll move," she whispered back, doing just that.

The sensation was off the charts. Cowboy clenched his teeth to keep from raising his hips to meet her. It was possible that he'd never been more turned on in his entire life. Not in the bathroom of the 747. Not in Paris. Not anywhere.

"But I want—"

She pushed herself a little bit farther onto him, and he heard himself groan. "Come on," she urged him, "I promise I won't let you hurt me. I promise there are pregnant women everywhere around the world, making love just like this, right this very minute...."

Her long, slow movements brought him almost entirely out of her before he glided deeply back in.

And it was then, as Cowboy pushed himself up to meet her in this, the sweetest of dances, that he knew the truth at last.

He wanted to come home to this woman every night for the rest of his life.

He wanted forever, and he knew that that forever with Melody would be as fascinating and endlessly exciting as his future with the SEALs, because, bottom line—he loved her.

He *loved* her.

And he knew right at that moment that in Paris, when Melody had kissed him goodbye and told him not to write, not to call, not to see her anymore, she'd been both very, very wrong *and* very, very right. She had been wrong in not giving them a chance to be together. She had been wrong not to let their passion deepen. But she had been right when she'd told him that real love was so much more than the hot flood of lust and relief. Because while his feelings for her had been born of danger and attraction and the powerful rush of being trusted and needed so desperately, it wasn't until he was here, in everyday, average Appleton, U.S.A., that those feelings had truly started to grow.

He loved her, but not because she needed him. In fact, one of the reasons he loved her so very much was because she refused to need him.

He loved her laughter, her point-blank honesty, her gentle kindness. He loved the faraway look she would get in her eyes when she felt their baby kick. He loved the fierceness with which she supported her sister. He loved the sheer courage it must have taken for her to stand up in front of the conservative Ladies' Club of Appleton to announce her pregnancy. He loved sitting on her back porch and talking to her.

He loved the heavenly blue of her eyes and the sweetness of her smile.

And he especially loved making love to her.

"Oh, Harlan," she breathed as he felt her release, and he knew without a single doubt that he would indeed forever associate sheer pleasure with his name.

He'd been clinging rather desperately to the edge of the cliff that controlled his own release, and as Melody gripped him tighter, as he filled his hands with her breasts, he felt himself go into free fall, felt the dizzying, weightless drop.

And then he exploded in slow motion. Fireballs of pleasure rocketed through him, scorching him, making him cry out.

Melody kissed him, and the sweetness of her mouth took him even further.

And then, with Melody's hands in his hair, with her head on his shoulder, with their unborn child resting between them, Cowboy began his ascent back to the surface of reality.

He was leaving in the morning. She didn't want to marry him, didn't need him, didn't love him. There were no decompression stops, although he wasn't sure it would have mattered either way. There wasn't anything he could have done to protect himself from the painful truth.

As much as he wanted her, she'd be happier without him.

Melody rolled off him, then snuggled next to him, drawing up the covers. "Please hold me," she murmured.

Lt. Harlan Jones pulled her in close, fitting their bodies together like spoons.

He would hold her tonight. But tomorrow, he would let her go. He knew he could do it. He'd done impossibly difficult things before.

He was a U.S. Navy SEAL.

Chapter 15

Alpha Squad was back in Virginia. Someone at the base apparently disapproved of the SEALs' disagreement with FinCOM, because the Quonset hut to which they'd been reassigned was several very healthy steps down from the first one they'd been given. And *that* had been no palace.

As Cowboy went inside, the door creaked on rusty hinges and a spider damn near landed on his head. He could see daylight through part of the corrugated-metal roof.

Whatever top brass had placed them here hadn't simply disapproved of their disagreement with FinCOM—he no doubt disapproved of SEALs in general. But that was no big surprise. This wasn't the first time they'd run into narrow-minded thinking.

Wes was on the phone. "Computers and rain don't mix, sir," he was saying. His tone implied that *sir* was merely a substitution for another, far less flattering word. "We have close to half a dozen computers we need up and running, plus a series of holes in the roof that will not only make it very chilly, *but,* when it starts to rain—which according to the forecast will happen within the next few hours—will make it very wet in here. As a matter of fact, there are already several permanent-looking puddles on the floor. Sir."

Built during World War II, this place looked as if it hadn't been used since the Vietnam conflict.

"We've been waiting on that request for a week, sir. Meanwhile, our computers are still in their boxes and we're sitting here with our thumbs up our—"

Joe Cat and Blue were on the other side of the gloomy room, deep in discussion.

"Well, yippee-yi-oh-kai-ay! Look who's back!" Cowboy looked up to see Lucky O'Donlon grinning down at him through the biggest hole in the roof.

Harvard was up there, too. "Get your butt up here, Junior. Aren't you some kind of expert when it comes to fixing roofs?"

"No—"

"Well, you are now. You're always claiming that with a little time and a library, you can learn to do anything. Here's your chance to prove it. And if that's not a compelling enough reason, how about this? As last man back from leave, you've won yourself the honor."

"Jones. Welcome back."

Cowboy turned to see Joe Cat coming toward him. He shook his captain's hand. "Thank you, sir."

Wes hung up the phone with a crash. "No go, Skipper. Apparently, there's no other location for us on the entire base."

Bobby joined them, bristling. "This place is huge. That's a load of—"

"Hey, I'm just saying what they told me." Wes shrugged. "We can request repairs, but it's got to go through channels and you know what that means. We'll still be able to stargaze from our desks three weeks from now."

"I say we forget about channels and fix this place ourselves," Lucky called down from his perch on the roof.

"I'm for that, too, Cat," Harvard chimed in. "We can get the job done better in a fraction of the time."

Cowboy squinted up at the roof. "Can we patch it, or will we have to replace the whole damn thing?" This was good. He could get into the distraction of creative problem solving. It would take his mind off the woman he'd left behind in Appleton, Massachusetts.

Melody hadn't thrown herself at his feet and begged him not to go. She'd only taken a few minutes away from the frantic housecleaning she was helping Brittany do in anticipation of a visit from Social Services. Britt's request to adopt Andy Marshall was actually being considered. Melody had been so focused on Britt's need to make everything as perfect as possible, she'd barely noticed when he left.

She'd kissed him goodbye and told him to be careful. And then she'd gone back to work.

Cowboy had passed a billboard advertising Ted Shepherd's candidacy for state representative on his way out of town. The man's pasty face, enlarged to a giant size, made him feel sick with jealousy. He'd had to look away, unable to gaze into the man's average brown eyes, unable to deal with the thought that this could well be the man Melody would spend her life with. This could be the man who would raise Cowboy's child as his own.

If he'd had a grenade launcher in his luggage, he would have blown the damn billboard to bits.

"Jones, I understand congratulations are in order." Joe Cat slapped Cowboy's back, bringing him abruptly back to the present. "When's the big day?"

The big...?

"Yeah, you gonna invite us to the wedding?" Lucky asked. "Damn, I feel like singing a verse of 'Sunrise, Sunset.' I can't believe our little Cowboy is actually old enough to tie the knot."

"You want us to wear dress whites, or should we cammy up?" Wes asked. "Dress whites are more traditional, but the camouflage gear would probably go better with the shotgun accessories."

Beside him, Bobby broke into a chorus of "Love Child."

Cowboy shook his head. "You guys are wrong—"

"Yeah, you know, that's probably the only way *I'm* going to go," Lucky said. "Trapped in the corner with no way out."

"Yo, Diana Ross," Harvard called from the roof. "S-squared."

Bobby obediently sat down and shut up.

"The rest of you guys back off," Harvard continued. "Junior's doing the right thing here. Maybe if you pay attention, you might actually learn something from his fine example."

Cowboy looked up at Harvard through the hole in the roof. "But I'm not marrying her, H." He looked around at the other guys. "I'm going to be a father in a few weeks, but I'm not getting married."

Blue McCoy, a man of few words, was the first to break the silence. He looked around at the rest of Alpha Squad. "This just goes to show we should learn to mind our own business." He turned to Cowboy. "I'm sorry, Jones," he said quietly.

But Wes couldn't keep his mouth shut. "Sorry?" he squeaked. "How could you be sorry? Jones's luck is rocketing off the scale. In fact, the way I see it, O'Donlon's just lost the right to his nickname. From now on, I'm calling *Jones* Lucky."

Cowboy shook his head, unable to respond, unable even to force a smile. By all rights, he should have been agreeing with them and celebrating his freedom, but instead he felt as if part of him would never feel like celebrating again. "I'm gonna go check out this roof," he told Joe Cat.

The captain had a way of looking at a man that made you feel as if he could see clear through all the bull and camouflage to the heart and soul that lay beneath. He was looking at Cowboy that way right now.

"I'm sorry, too, kid," he said before nodding and dismissing him.

Cowboy escaped out the door, searching for the easiest way up to the curving metal roof. There was a drainpipe on the southwest corner of the building that looked pretty solid. In fact, as he approached, Lucky was using it to climb down.

"Kudos to you, Jones," he said, wiping the remnants of rust from his hands onto his pants. "How about getting together tonight over a cold beer? You could share the secrets of your success." His smile turned knowing. "I remember that girl, Melody.

She was something else. And she was on top of you like a dog in heat right from the word go, wasn't she?''

Something inside Cowboy snapped, and snapped hard. He knocked Lucky down into the dust. "Just shut the hell up!"

Lucky was instantly on his feet, crouched and ready in a combat stance. "What the—"

Cowboy rushed him again, and this time Lucky was ready for his attack. They landed together, hard, in the dirt. Cowboy's elbow hit a rock and he welcomed the pain that shot through him. It was sharp and sweet, and it masked the pain in his heart.

But Lucky didn't want to fight. He kneed Cowboy hard in the stomach. While Cowboy was struggling to regain his breath, Lucky scrambled free. "You crazy bastard! What the hell's wrong with you?"

Cowboy pulled himself to his feet, breathing hard, moving menacingly toward the other SEAL. "I warned you if you badmouthed her again, I'd kill you."

Wes had stuck his head out the door to see what was causing the commotion. "Senior Chief!" he bellowed after taking one quick look.

Harvard was across the roof and down that drainpipe in a flash. "Back off," he shouted to Cowboy, stepping directly between the two men. "Just back off! Do you hear me, Jones? You hit him again, and your butt is going to be in deep trouble!"

Cowboy stood, bent over, hands on his knees, still catching his breath.

Harvard turned and glared at Wesley and Bobby, who both stood watching by the door. "This doesn't concern you!"

They disappeared back inside.

"What the *hell* is this about?" Harvard asked, looking from Cowboy to Lucky.

"Beats me, H." Lucky brushed dirt from his shoulder. "The psycho here jumped me."

Harvard fixed his obsidian glare on Cowboy. "Junior, you have something to say?"

Cowboy lifted his head. "Only that if O'Donlon so much as breathes Melody's name again, I'll put him in the hospital."

"Damn, I feel like a kindergarten teacher," Harvard muttered, turning back to Lucky. "O'Donlon, were you really stupid enough to be dissing his woman?"

"His *woman...?*" Lucky was genuinely confused and not entirely unamused. "Jones, you just got through telling us that you're not going to marry...the one who shall remain nameless because I don't want to have to put *you* in the hospital."

Harvard swore pungently. "It's obvious that right here we've got a live showing of *Dumb and Dumber, Part Two.*"

"I don't get it," Lucky said to Cowboy. "If you're so hot for this girl, why the hell aren't you marrying her?"

Cowboy straightened up. "Because she doesn't want me," he said quietly, all of his anger and frustration stripped away, leaving only the hurt behind. God, it hurt. He looked at Harvard. "H., I tried, but...she doesn't want me." To his absolute horror, tears filled his eyes.

And for maybe the first time in his entire life, Lucky was silent. He didn't try to make a joke. Harvard looked at the blond-haired SEAL. "Jones and I are going take a walk. That okay with you, O'Donlon?"

Lucky nodded. "Yeah, that's uh... Yeah, Senior Chief."

Harvard didn't say another word until they'd walked halfway across the exercise field. By then, thank God, Cowboy had regained his composure.

"Jones, I have to start by apologizing to you," Harvard told him. "This whole snafu's my fault. I told the guys you were going to marry this girl. I guess I just assumed you'd do whatever you had to, to convince her that marrying you is the right thing. Which leads me to my main point. I'm honestly surprised at you, Junior. I've never known you to quit."

Cowboy stopped walking. "Bottom line, what do I really have to offer her? Thirty days of leave a year." He swore. "I grew up with a father who was never there. With only thirty days each year, there's no use pretending I could be any kind of a real father to my kid—or a real husband to Melody. This way, we're all being honest. I'll be the guy who comes to visit a few times a year. And Mel will hook up with someone else. Someone who'll be there for her *all* the time.''

Harvard was shaking his head. ''You've talked yourself into believing this is a lose-lose situation, haven't you? Open your eyes and look around you, boy. Your captain's in the exact same boat. It's true Veronica and his kid miss him when he's gone, but with a little effort, they're making the situation work.''

''Yeah, but Veronica is willing to travel. I couldn't ask Melody to leave Appleton. It's her home. She loves it there.''

''Junior, you can't afford *not* to ask.''

Cowboy shook his head. ''She doesn't want me,'' he said again. ''She wants an average guy, not a SEAL.''

''Well, there I can't help you,'' Harvard said. ''Because even if you quit the units tomorrow, you're never going to be mistaken for an average guy.''

Quit the units tomorrow...

He could do that. He could quit. He could move to Massachusetts, set up permanent residence in that tent outside Melody's house....

But he didn't want to quit. Except that was exactly what he'd done. Harvard was right. In what could possibly be the most important fight of his life—the fight to win Melody—he'd surrendered far too easily.

He should have told her he loved her before he left. He should be there right now, down on his knees, still telling her that he loved her, telling her that this time it was real. No matter what she said, he knew it was real. And she loved him, too. He'd seen it in her eyes, tasted it in her kisses, heard it in her laughter.

Yeah, she might not know it yet, but she definitely loved him. He should have realized it a full day ago, from the way she'd held him so tightly up at the quarry.

Cowboy looked at Harvard. ''I've got to go back to Massachusetts right away. A weekend. That's all I need. Just two and a half days.''

Harvard laughed. ''Come on. I'll go with you. We'll go talk to Joe.''

"Thank you, Senior Chief."

"Don't thank me yet, Junior."

Joe Catalanotto sighed. "I can't do it, Jones. It's going to have to wait a week or so." He gestured to the television in the corner of his office. "I've been monitoring a situation in South America for the past day and a half. A plane's been hijacked. Two hundred forty-seven people on board." Sure enough, the TV was tuned to CNN. "Any minute now, this phone's gonna ring, and Alpha Squad's going to be ordered over to Venezuela to help create order out of chaos." He shook his head. "I'm sorry, kid. I need you with the team. Best I can tell you is to let your fingers do the walking. Make a phone visit, but do it now. Get your gear ready to go, too. Because once we get the word to move, there won't be time."

Cowboy nodded. "And if you're wrong, sir?"

Cat laughed. "If I'm wrong, I'll give you an entire week. But I'm not wrong."

As if to prove his point, the telephone rang.

Cowboy scrambled for the door. He threw it open and made a dash for the nearest telephone. He punched in his calling-card number and then Melody's number. Please, God, let her be home. Please, God...

The phone rang once, twice, three times. All around him, he could hear the sounds of Alpha Squad getting ready to move. On the fourth ring, the answering machine picked up.

"Come on, Cowboy!" Wes shouted. "You don't even have your gear together yet!"

Brittany's recorded voice came on, followed by the beep.

"Melody, it's me, Jones." God, he had no clue what to say. "I just wanted to tell you—"

Beep. Damn, he paused too long and the answering machine, mistaking his silence for a disconnected line, had cut him off.

"Come on, Cowboy! Move!"

"I love you!" he shouted into the receiver. *That* was what he should have said. KISS. Keep it simple. Bottom line. But it was too late to call her back.

Cowboy hung up the phone with a curse.

* * *

Melody was dreaming. She knew she was dreaming because Jones was with her, and they were back in the Middle East, hiding from the soldiers who were patrolling the city.

"Close your eyes," Jones told her. "Keep breathing, shallowly, softly. They won't see us. I promise."

Her heart was pounding, but his arm was around her, and she knew at the very least, if she died, she wouldn't die alone.

"I love you," she whispered, afraid if she didn't say it now, she'd never get the chance.

He motioned for her to be silent, but it was too late. One of the soldiers had heard her, then turned and fired his gun. The bullet slammed into her with wrenching force. Pain exploded in her abdomen.

The baby! Dear God, she'd been shot, and they'd hit the baby.

Her legs felt wet with blood, but Jones was fighting the enemy soldiers. He was firing his own gun, driving them away.

Another knife blade of pain seared through her, and she cried out.

Jones turned toward her, touching her, and his hands came away red with her blood.

He looked at her and his eyes were so green, even in the darkness. "Wake up," he said. "Honey, you've got to wake up."

Melody opened her eyes to see the first dim light of dawn creeping in through her windows. She'd been so tired last night, she hadn't even taken the time to draw the curtains.

Pain knifed through her, real pain, the same pain she'd dreamed. She gasped, turning to reach for the lamp on her bedside table. She switched it on, and with shock realized that her hands had left behind a smear of blood.

She was bleeding.

She pulled back the covers to see that her nightgown and the sheets below were stained bright red.

Brittany was still at work. She wouldn't be home until after seven.

Pain made the room spin.

"Jones!"

But Jones wasn't there to help her, either. Melody didn't know *where* Jones was. He'd called and left a message on the machine over two weeks ago. She'd tried to call him back, but was told he was unavailable and would remain that way for an undetermined amount of time.

He was out of touch on some mission, risking his life doing God knows what. She'd spent the past two weeks scared to death and kicking herself for not being honest with him. She should have told him that she loved him while she had the chance.

Please, God, keep him safe. Every time Melody thought about him, she said that silent prayer.

The pain gripped her again, and she cried out. God, what was happening? This wasn't labor. She wasn't supposed to *bleed* when she went into labor....

Her door was pushed open. "Mel?"

Brittany. Thank God, she'd gotten home from work early.

"Oh, dear Lord!" Brittany saw the blood on the sheets. She picked up the phone, dialed 911, smoothed back Melody's hair, feeling her forehead, checking her eyes. "Sweetie, when did the bleeding start?"

"I don't know. I was sleeping…God!" The pain made her see stars. "Britt, the baby! What's happening with the baby?"

But Brittany spoke into the phone, rattling off their address. "We need an ambulance here stat. I've got a twenty-five-year-old woman in the ninth month of her first pregnancy, experiencing severe abdominal pain and hemorrhaging."

Melody closed her eyes. Please, God, keep both Jones and her baby safe and alive…

"Yes, I'm a nurse," Brittany responded. "I suspect placental abruption. We'll need fetal monitors and an ultrasound ready and waiting at the hospital. Yes. I'll have the door open. Just get here!"

"Jones, you better get down here." Harvard's voice sounded tight and grim over the telephone line. "There's a stack of messages for you that's four inches high."

Cowboy's heart leaped. "From Melody?"

"Junior, just get *down* here."

Fear flickered inside him. "H., what's the deal? Is Mel all right? Did she have the baby?"

"I don't know for sure. It looks as if the first few messages are from Melody, but the rest... Jones, Mel's sister has been calling nearly every hour for the past two days. I recommend you get down here and call her back ASAP. She's left a number at the hospital."

A number at the hospital. Cowboy didn't even say goodbye. He hung up the phone and ran.

The temporary barracks he was sharing with the other unmarried members of the team were a good half mile from the leaky-roofed Quonset hut that housed Alpha Squad's office. Cowboy was still wearing his clunky leather boots and his heavy camouflage gear, but he covered the distance in a small handful of minutes.

As he burst through the door, Harvard handed him both the pile of messages and a telephone. The sheer number of message slips was enough to terrify him. Brittany had, literally, called every hour on the hour since early Monday morning.

Cowboy's hands were shaking so badly, he had to dial the number twice. Harvard had backed away, giving him privacy. He sat down at the desk, shuffling through the pile of messages as, up in the County Hospital in Appleton, Massachusetts, the phone was ringing.

"Hello?"

It was Brittany's voice. She sounded hoarse and worn-out.

"Britt, it's Jones."

"Thank God."

"Please tell me she's safe." Cowboy closed his eyes.

"She's safe." Brittany's voice broke. "For now. Jones, you've got to come up here and talk her into having a C-section. I think one of the reasons she's refusing to do it is because she promised you that you could be here when the baby was born."

"But she's not due for another two and a half weeks."

"She had a partial placental abruption," Brittany told him.

"That's when the placenta becomes partially separated from the uterus—"

"I know what it is," he said, cutting her off. "Did she hemorrhage?"

"Yes. Early Monday morning. It wasn't as bad as I first thought, though. She was taken by ambulance to the hospital and her doctor managed to get her stabilized. Both she and the baby are being monitored. If there's the slightest change in either of their conditions, they're going to *have* to do a C-Section. She *knows* that. But right now, the doctor has told her that the baby's in no real danger, and she's determined to hold on as long as possible."

Cowboy drew in a deep breath. "May I talk to her?"

"She's sleeping right now. Please, Lieutenant, I don't think she's going to agree to have this baby until you get up here. But if she starts hemorrhaging again, there's no guarantee that this time they'll be able to get her to stop. They'll be able to save the baby, but they'll lose the mother."

Cowboy looked down at the phone messages in his hand. There were four from Melody, all dated close to the day he'd left for South America. The first three were just notices that said she'd called. The last actually had a message. It was written in quotes, and the receptionist who answered the phone had put a smiley face next to the words, "I love you."

Cowboy stood up. "Tell her our deal's off," he told Britanny. "Tell her not to wait for me to have the baby. Tell her I'll be mad as hell if I get up there and that baby's not hanging out in the hospital nursery. Tell her I'm on my way."

He hung up the phone, and Harvard silently appeared. The senior chief handed him papers signed by the captain, granting him as much personal emergency leave as he needed.

"There's an air force transport heading up to Boston in twenty minutes," Harvard told him. "I've called in some favors from some people I know—they're holding the flight for you. Bobby's out front with a jeep to drive you to the airfield."

Cowboy held up the message that Melody had left. "She loves me, H."

"This is news to you, Junior?" Harvard laughed. "Damn, I knew that last year in the Middle East." He followed Cowboy to the door. "Godspeed, Jones. My prayers are with you."

Cowboy swung himself up and into the jeep, and with a squeal of tires, he was away.

"She was given an amniocentesis so we could assess the baby's lung development." Brittany was talking in a whisper as she came into the room. Melody kept her eyes closed. "All of the tests have indicated that this baby is ready for delivery. His estimated weight clocked in at over eight pounds. But Melody insists that unless the baby is in danger, she's not going to deliver him any earlier than December 1st. You've got to convince her that her stubbornness is putting her life in danger."

"The worst part about being in the hospital is that everybody always talks about you as if you weren't in the room." Melody opened her eyes, expecting to glare up at her sister and some new doctor she'd enlisted.

Instead, she found herself looking directly at Harlan Jones. He was wearing camouflage pants and a matching shirt, and he looked as if he'd come directly from the jungle.

"Hey," he said, smiling at her, "heard you've been raising a little too much hell around here."

She recognized that smile he was giving her. It was his "I'm going to pretend everything's all right" smile. In truth, he was scared to death.

"I'm fine," she told him. As she watched, Brittany quietly left the room.

He sat down next to her. "That's not what I hear."

She forced a smile of her own. "Yeah, well, you've been talking to Nurse Doom."

He laughed. She realized he was carrying a clipboard in his hands, and he held it out to her now. "Sign these forms," he told her. "Have the C-section. It's time to stop playing games with your life."

Melody lifted her chin. "You think that's what this is? Some game? Everything I've ever read stressed the importance of carrying a baby to term. Or at least carrying for as long as possible. The baby's not in danger. I'm not in danger. I see no reason to do this.''

Jones took her hand. "Do this now because until this baby is born, there *is* a risk that you will bleed to death,'' he said. "Do this because although the chances of that happening are very slim, so were the chances of your having a placental separation in the first place. You don't have high blood pressure. You aren't a smoker. There's no real reason why this should have happened. Do this because if you die, a very large part of me will die, too. Do this because I love you.''

Melody was caught in the hypnotizing intensity of his gaze. "I guess you got my message.''

"Yeah," he said. "But you only got part of mine. I had literally ten seconds before I had to leave and I blew it. What I meant to say on your answering machine was that I want you to marry me, not for the baby's sake, but for *my* sake. Purely selfish reasons, Mel. Like, because I love you and I want to spend my life with you.''

He cleared his throat. "And I was going to tell you that I knew there was a part of you that could love me, and that I was going to keep coming back to Appleton, that I was going to court you until you *did* fall in love with me. I was going to tell you that I wasn't going to quit, and that sooner or later, I'd wear you down—even if you only married me to shut me up." He handed her the clipboard. "So sign these release forms, have this baby and marry me.''

Melody's heart was in her throat. "Do you really understand what you're asking me to do?''

He looked out the window at the dreary late-afternoon light. "Yeah," he said, "I do. I'm asking you to leave your home and come live with me near naval bases, moving around God only knows how many times in the course of a year. I'm asking you to give up your job, and your garden, and your sister and Andy, just to be with me, even though some of the time—hell, most of the time—I'll be gone. It's a bad deal. I don't recommend you take it. But at the same time, honey, I'm praying that you'll say yes."

Melody looked at the man sitting beside her bed. His hair was long and dirty, as if he hadn't showered in days. He smelled of gasoline and sweat and sunblock. He looked spent, as if he'd run all the way from Virginia just to be here with her.

"Trust me," he whispered, leaning close to kiss her softly. "Trust me with your heart. I'll keep it safe, I swear."

Mel closed her eyes and kissed him. Harlan Jones wasn't the average, run-of-the-mill, home-every-day-at-five-thirty type she would have chosen if the choice could be made with pure intellect. But love wasn't rational. Love didn't stick to a plan. And truth was, she loved him. She had to take the chance.

"You are going to get *so* sick of me telling you to be careful," she whispered.

"No, I'm not."

Melody signed the medical procedure consent forms. "Do you think Harvard would agree to be our best man?"

Jones took the clipboard from her hands. "I want to hear you say yes."

She gazed up at him. "Yes. I love you," she told him.

Tears filled his eyes, but his smile was pure Jones as he leaned forward and kissed her.

Epilogue

Melody Jones sat in her new backyard, watching her neighbors, her friends and her new family gather to celebrate her wedding.

It was only February, but the South was having a mild winter, and the daffodils in her garden were already in bloom.

The growing season in Virginia was at least three months longer than in Massachusetts. She loved that. She loved everything about her new life. She loved this little rented house outside the naval base where Alpha Squad was temporarily stationed. She loved waking up each morning with Jones in her bed. She loved holding their son, Tyler, in her arms as she rocked him to sleep. She even loved the late-night feedings.

Brittany sat down next to her. ''The papers came through,'' she said. ''Day before yesterday. Andy's my kid now.'' She laughed. ''God help me.''

Melody embraced her sister. ''I'm so happy for you.''

''And I'm so happy for you.'' Brittany laughed again. ''I'm not sure I've ever been to a party before with so many incredible-looking men. And all those dress uniforms! I nearly fainted when I went into the church. I suppose you get used to it.''

Melody grinned. "No," she said, "you don't."

Across the yard, Jones had Tyler on one shoulder. He swayed slightly to keep the baby happy as he stood talking to Harvard and his father, the admiral. As Melody watched, he laughed at something Harvard said and the baby started. Jones gently kissed the baby's head, soothing him back to sleep.

As Melody looked around her yard, she realized that Brittany was right. Nearly all of the men there were SEALs, and they were, indeed, an unusual-looking group.

Jones looked across the yard and met her eyes. The smile he gave her made her heart somersault in her chest. It was his "I love you" smile—the smile he saved for her and her alone. She smiled back at him, knowing he could read her love for him as clearly in her eyes.

Despite her best intentions, she had gone and married the least everyday, ordinary, average man that she'd ever known. No indeed, there was absolutely nothing normal about a man called "Cowboy" Jones. He was one hundred percent out of the ordinary—and so was his incredible love for her.

And she wouldn't have it any other way.

* * * * *

To a MacAllister Born

JOAN ELLIOTT PICKART

JOAN ELLIOTT PICKART

is the author of over eighty-five novels. When she isn't writing, she enjoys watching football, knitting, reading, gardening and attending craft shows in the town square. Joan has three all-grown-up daughters and a fantastic little grandson. In September of 1995, Joan travelled to China to adopt her fourth daughter, Autumn. Joan and Autumn have settled into their cosy cottage in a charming small town in the high pine country of Arizona.

THE MacALLISTERS

LEGEND
- • Adopted
- ◇ Child of Affair
- ---- Affair
- = Ryan MacAllister's partner
- *Ryan

To my daughter Paige,
my very own Tempe, Arizona, fire fighter

I'm a proud mummy, Peep

Chapter One

Jennifer Mackane stretched leisurely, then snuggled deeper beneath the blankets on the bed with a sigh of contentment.

She wasn't scheduled to work today, or tonight, at Hamilton House, she mused, and would be able to spend the free hours with her precious Joey. They'd straighten up around the house and run errands, then indulge in dinner at Joey's favorite fast-food restaurant.

She'd have the luxury of tucking a fresh-from-his-bath Joey into bed that night and reading him a story as he drifted off to sleep. Bliss. Sweet bliss.

A faint aroma of freshly brewed coffee reached Jennifer, and she knew the automatic timer on the machine had produced the hot, beckoning brew.

No, she thought. She'd stay in bed a while longer,

be sinfully lazy. Then again, the coffee smelled so deliciously tempting.

"Oh, who am I kidding?" she said, laughing. "That coffee is calling my name."

She threw back the blankets and left the bed, poking her feet into enormous yellow slippers that boasted the head of a smiling Big Bird.

Joey was so proud of those slippers he'd given her for Christmas last year, she mused. He'd gone shopping with his Uncle Brandon and Uncle Ben, the outing producing the bizarre slippers as Joey's gift to his mom.

Jennifer had shot dagger-filled looks at Brandon Hamilton and Ben Rizzoli when she'd opened her present, and had seen the merriment and mischief dancing in their dark eyes. But she'd become accustomed to the pair's nonsense while the three of them had grown up together. Here in the pretty little town of Prescott, nestled high in the mountains a hundred miles above Phoenix, they'd enjoyed an idyllic childhood.

Jennifer thudded her way toward the kitchen as she smoothed her red flannel nightshirt down to her knees. Big Bird's heads bobbed up and down with each step she took.

Joey would be checking to see that she was wearing these silly creations, she knew, despite the fact that it was nearly a year since he'd given them to her.

In the large kitchen of the old, three-story Victorian house, Jennifer poured herself a mug of hot coffee, then opened the refrigerator to find the carton that would provide the splash of milk.

She hesitated and frowned, her gaze falling on the bridal bouquet on the bottom shelf of the refrigerator. She added milk to the coffee, retrieved the bouquet, then settled at the kitchen table, staring at the lovely flowers as she took her first sip.

She could clearly recall the shock and dismay she'd registered when the bouquet had come sailing through the air at Megan and Ben's wedding reception yesterday and somehow landed in *her* hands. She'd stared at it in wide-eyed horror, as the other women in the assembled group cheered for her, telling her she was now officially destined to be the next bride.

"No way," she had said, poking the flowers with one finger. "Not a chance."

She had planned to quietly slide the bouquet behind the stack of wedding gifts on the table at the reception and forget it. But Joey had been jumping up and down with excitement, declaring his mom to be a great pass catcher, just like whomever he had said caught the football from some quarterback he'd named. Joey had insisted on holding the touchdown bouquet all the way home.

Jennifer got to her feet, went to one of the cupboards and rummaged through it until she found a vase. She filled it halfway with water, then returned to the table and began to carefully dismantle the bouquet, sticking the flowers into the water.

They would now be just flowers in a vase, she decided, with no old wives' tale connotations connected to them. Not that she actually believed in the who-ever - caught - the - bouquet - is - the - next - bride theory, but why take unnecessary chances?

She had no intention of remarrying, and having the bridal bouquet take up residence in her refrigerator even overnight was long enough, thank you very much.

"There," she said, admiring her work. "They're flowers in a vase, nothing more. The spell is broken. End of story."

"Hi, Mom," a sleepy Joey said, coming into the kitchen. He peered under the table at Jennifer's feet.

"Hello, sweetheart," Jennifer said, her heart warming at the sight of her sleep-rumpled, five-year-old son in his Rugrats pajamas. "How's my big boy this morning? Ready for some breakfast?"

"Guess so." Joey slid onto a chair opposite her, yawned, then frowned. "Whatcha do to the flowers you caught?"

"They needed water to stay fresh so we could enjoy them," Jennifer said.

"Oh. Well, you still get to be the next bride like everyone said. Can you have a chocolate wedding cake if you want to when you're the bride? Aunt Megan and Uncle Ben's cake tasted kinda yucky. You should pick chocolate for yours."

"Sweetheart," Jennifer said, "I'm not going to have a wedding cake because I'm not getting married."

"Yes, you are," Joey said, his voice rising. "Everyone at the party said so after you caught the flowers. You'll be a bride like Aunt Megan was and…well, first you gotta find somebody to be the groom guy, then I'll have a daddy like Sammy. That's how it works, Mom. It does."

Jennifer felt a chill sweep through her and tighten into a cold fist in her stomach.

"Joey," she said gently, praying her voice was steady, "you've never said you wanted a daddy. We're a team, you and me, the two of us. We're doing great together, don't you think?"

"Yeah, sure, Mom, but..." Joey shrugged. "It would be nice to have a daddy like Sammy does. They do men stuff together."

"Well, you do...men stuff with Uncle Ben and Uncle Brandon, and even Uncle Taylor when he comes up from Phoenix. They take you fishing, camping, hiking—all kinds of things."

"Yes, but..." Joey sighed.

"But what, sweetheart?" Jennifer said, leaning toward him.

"When I'm done doing men stuff with Uncle Ben, and Uncle Brandon, and Uncle Taylor, I have to give them back. I don't get to keep them, Mom. I don't have a daddy all the time like Sammy does."

"I see," Jennifer said softly, struggling against threatening tears. "But you know that's because your daddy is in heaven with the angels, Joey. I can't change that, sweetheart."

"You could be a bride like you're supposed to be 'cause you caught the flowers," Joey said, nearly yelling. "All you need is a guy to wear a suit and tie and buy you a yellow ring like Uncle Ben got Aunt Megan. How come you won't do that, Mom?"

"Joey, I realize that you don't understand and that you're getting angry at me because you don't. When you're older, bigger, this will make sense to you."

Joey scowled and dropped his chin to his chest. "No, it won't."

Jennifer stared at her son, her heart aching.

She had known, somewhere in the back of her mind, that this discussion would take place one day, she thought miserably.

When Joey was three years old, he'd asked why he didn't have a daddy, but had readily accepted the explanation that his father was in heaven with the angels.

Now, at five years old, Joey was comparing his family to that of his best friend, Sammy, and deciding it came up very short.

She'd worked so hard at being both mother and father to her son, and was eternally grateful to Ben, Brandon and Taylor for stepping in as father figures for Joey whenever they could.

But now her little boy wanted his *own* daddy, just like Sammy had. His uncles just weren't enough.

Oh, Joey, I'm so sorry, Jennifer thought, blinking back tears. What he wanted, she would never give him. She could not—would not—marry again. All she could do was weather this emotional storm of Joey's and hope, pray, it would soon pass.

Added to that heartfelt prayer was the ongoing one that Joey would never learn the truth about his father. *No one* knew the true facts of her past with Joe Mackane, and, heaven help her, no one ever would.

"Well," she said, forcing a cheerful tone into her voice, "you must be a hungry boy. How would you like pancakes made in the shape of animals?"

Joey's head popped up. "Yeah. Cool. I want a horse and elephant and hippopotamus."

Jennifer laughed and got to her feet. "A hippopotamus? Goodness, I don't know if I'm that talented a pancake artist, my sweet, but I'll give it my best shot."

Joey slid off his chair. "I'll pour my own milk into a glass. I need milk for my bones and teeth."

"Indeed, you do, sir," Jennifer said, taking a bowl out of a cupboard. "You'll grow up big and strong like...like your uncles."

And be a fine, upstanding man like your uncles, with no hint of the lack of morals and values of your father, she mentally tacked on, as she began to prepare the pancake batter.

Joey looked so much like her—it was as though Joe had had nothing to do with the child's creation. Joey had her wavy, strawberry-blond hair and fair complexion. His eyes were a sparkling green, and his features resembled hers. Anyone could tell that he was her son.

No, there was no hint of Joe Mackane in Joey, thank God, and there never would be as she continued to teach him the important lessons of integrity and honesty. Ah, yes, honesty. That was definitely something Joe never possessed, nor knew the meaning of.

Joe had been killed in a construction accident a week before Joey was born. In heaven with the angels? Jennifer mused. No, not even close. He wouldn't have begun to qualify for admission. But that was something her son would never know.

* * *

After cleaning the kitchen after breakfast, during which she'd received a passing grade for her pancake hippopotamus, Jennifer showered and dressed in jeans and a green sweater that matched her eyes.

While Joey was putting away scattered toys in his room, Jennifer opened the drapes on the windows in the living room, then frowned.

There was a man standing on the sidewalk in front of the house. He was tall, extremely handsome, with dark, auburn hair, rugged features, wide shoulders, and long, muscular jeans-clad legs. His hands were shoved into his jacket pockets, and he was staring at the top of the house, apparently unaware of her sudden appearance in the window.

What was he doing there? Jennifer wondered. Who was he? If he was a thief casing the place, he wasn't being very subtle about it.

All right, he had two minutes to be on his way, or she was going to march out there and confront him.

Jennifer narrowed her eyes.

Maybe that was dumb. Friendly, small-town Prescott or not, it was probably foolish to demand an explanation from a perfect stranger.

Perfect? Well, on a score of one to ten, the man was an eleven as far as looks and build went—but that was beside the point. She was a woman alone with a small, vulnerable boy to protect.

No, she'd give it another minute, then call Sheriff Montana and tell him about the stranger who was still—darn him—scrutinizing her home, her safe haven. He would handle this in the proper manner.

Okay, buddy, she thought, it's now one minute and counting.

Jennifer's breath caught as her gaze .connected with the stranger's. He smiled, sketched .a salute, then spun around and walked down the sidewalk.

A frisson of heat coursed through her and settled low in her body. She wrapped her hands around her elbows, then moved to the edge of the window, watching until the man disappeared from view.

Dear heaven, she thought, that smile of his should be registered as a lethal weapon, along with the loose-limbed, oh-so-sexy way he walked.

It had been many years since she'd had a sensual response to a member of the opposite sex. It was unsettling, to say the least, and very unwelcome.

It was also borderline crazy. She'd had a physical reaction to a man she didn't even know, and who might very well be a thief contemplating breaking into her house to steal her worldly goods, such as they were.

What on earth was the matter with her? she thought, shaking her head. On that horrifying day of Joe's funeral, when she'd learned the truths that had shattered her world, she'd begun the process of building a wall around herself.

Never again, she had vowed, would a man awaken her sexuality. Never again would a man touch her heart or her body. Never again would she love someone who was capable of destroying her.

"Mom," Joey yelled, running into the room, "I found my favorite dinosaur. It was under my bed. Cool, huh?"

Jennifer drew a steadying breath, then turned to smile at her son.

"Very cool," she said. "Oh, it's very dusty, too. Let's wash it off in the kitchen sink. There's nothing worse than a dusty dinosaur."

That evening, Jennifer settled onto the sofa in the living room in front of the crackling fire in the hearth, and picked up the mystery novel she was in the process of reading. Joey was fast asleep, having nodded off during the tale of *Peter Pan.*

She tucked her legs up close to her on the puffy cushion, spread an afghan she had knitted across her lap, and opened the book to the page that boasted a brightly colored bookmark Joey had made her for Mother's Day.

After reading one sentence, the image of the stranger who had stood in front of her house that morning superimposed itself over the words on the page.

"Darn you," she said, snapping the book closed. "Would you just go away and leave me alone?"

She sighed and shook her head as she set the book next to her, then stared into the leaping flames of the fire.

The anticipated, carefree day with Joey had been a disaster. Everywhere the two of them had gone, she found herself looking for that man, while at the same time registering excitement and fear.

The stranger had haunted her through the seemingly endless hours of the day. And with the thoughts of him came the disturbing remembrance of the rush of heated desire that had suffused her when he'd smiled.

"Oh-h-h, I'm driving myself crazy," Jennifer said aloud, throwing up her hands.

Okay, enough of this, she admonished herself. She was getting a grip right now. She'd analyze this bizarre behavior of hers, figure out why she was acting so unlike her norm, then be done with it.

"Fine," she said, tapping one fingertip against her chin. "Wait…a…minute. Of course. That's it."

She was the victim of a series of events that had taken place in rapid succession.

First, she'd attended the beautiful wedding of her dear friends, Ben and Megan, who were obviously deeply in love.

While she had neither the intention nor the desire to remarry, the romantic event had no doubt poked a bit at her subconscious and emphasized the lack of a special man in her life—even though she didn't want one…

Second, she'd caught the wedding bouquet, and had been surrounded by people declaring over and over that she would soon fall in love and be the next bride.

Third, Joey had expressed his sadness over not having a father, which had made her heart ache for her son.

If one added up all those events that centered on romance, love, a husband, a daddy that Joey wouldn't have to give back…well, it was no wonder she'd overreacted the very next time a handsome man directed a smile at her.

Thank goodness, she'd figured it out. She felt so

much better. It was amazing what a little inner dialogue could do to get a person squared away.

With a decisive nod, Jennifer picked up the book, found her place on the marked page and began to read.

Just before four o'clock the next afternoon, Jennifer entered Hamilton House, the hotel where she was manager of the dining room.

The beautiful building had been completely restored by her childhood friend Brandon Hamilton, after he'd dropped out of the fast lane in New York and returned to his roots in Prescott.

The large lobby was exquisite, transporting a person back to the turn of the 19th century. The Victorian furnishings, the original cabbage-rose carpeting, the gleaming piano by the front windows—everything was perfect.

Along the far wall was a simulated old-fashioned, cobblestone street, complete with lampposts to light the way. Open-fronted specialty shops beckoned to be explored.

One of the shops, Sleeping Beauty, offered feminine apparel and luscious bath accessories. The store was a smaller version of the one in Phoenix that was owned by Taylor Sinclair's wife, Janice.

Jennifer waved at Ryan, who was on duty behind the reception desk, then headed down the hallway that led to the dining room.

For the next hour, Jennifer was busy as she checked the reservation book for the evening ahead, spoke with the dinner and pastry chefs, reviewed and approved an order the wine steward wished to place, and conferred with the manager of house-keeping regarding the condition of the high-quality, linen tablecloths and napkins that were used in the dining room.

At five o'clock she was at her post behind the podium by the doors, ready to welcome the first guests arriving for dinner.

The flow of patrons moving in and out kept her bustling back and forth as she sat the guests at their tables and presented them with oversize menus.

A little after seven o'clock, Jennifer returned to the podium yet again, then smiled automatically as the doors to the dining room opened.

And then she stopped breathing.

Her smile disappeared, her eyes widened and her heart began to beat in a wild tattoo.

It was him, she thought frantically. *The man.* He was now beyond magnificent, in a dark blue sport coat over a white shirt and blue tie, and gray slacks. But it was most definitely him.

The stranger who had stood on the sidewalk in front of her house and might very well have decided on the best method to break in.

The man who had smiled at her, causing a desire to swirl within her, and who had haunted her thoughts ever since.

Dear heaven, what was he doing here? Had he followed her? Was *she* the reason he had studied her house? Was she being stalked by a raving lunatic?

Jennifer looked quickly around the room. What should she do? Scream at the top of her lungs? Grab the receiver to the telephone on the podium and call Sheriff Montana?

No, no, she had to calm down. She was surrounded by people, was safe...for the moment, at least. She'd just bluff her way through this until she could formulate a sensible plan.

"Good evening," she said to the man, unable to produce even the smallest smile. "May I help you?"

Jack MacAllister walked slowly toward the podium, his gaze riveted on the woman who had spoken to him.

It was her, he thought incredulously. The beautiful lady in the window of the intriguing Victorian house.

The woman who had not been far from his mental vision ever since he'd seen her yesterday morning as he'd stood on the sidewalk in front of her home.

She was even more lovely up close. Her eyes were green—incredibly green, and her hair was a silken tumble of strawberry-blond waves to just above her shoulders. Her features were delicate, her lips made for kissing. What he could see of the pale green dress she was wearing gave hint of lush breasts beneath the soft material.

And for some unknown reason, she was staring at him as though she expected him to leap over the podium and strangle her with his bare hands.

All he had done was walk into the dining room of the hotel, but, heaven only knew why, he was scaring this breathtaking feminine creature to death.

He'd never caused *that* kind of reaction in a woman before.

"Good evening," he said, stopping in front of the podium and producing his best, hundred-watt smile.

"I apologize if I startled you when I opened the doors."

"Startled me?" she said, more in the form of a squeak.

"Well, yes—I mean, you look rather…frightened."

"Frightened?" She splayed one hand on her breasts. "Me?"

"Look," Jack said, frowning as he extended one hand toward her, "I don't know what I did to—"

She took a step backward. "Don't come any closer. I might appear frightened, but I'm not. No, sir, not one little bit. I'm wise to you, mister. I have a great many friends in this town, including the sheriff, and you'll never get away with it—not in a million years."

"Huh?"

She glanced quickly around the room. "Just—just…" She flapped one hand at him. "Shuffle off to Buffalo. Get out of Dodge. Give up on whatever your diabolical scheme is before you end up in the clink."

"Huh?" Jack said again, totally confused.

"Hey, there you are," a deep voice said.

"Brandon—" Jack and the woman said in unison.

Brandon Hamilton strode to the podium. "Jennifer, I'd like you to meet Jack MacAllister, a good buddy of mine. Jack, this lovely lady and I have been friends since before we could walk and talk. This is Jennifer Mackane."

"It's a pleasure to meet you, Ms. Mackane," Jack said, grinning.

Chapter Two

Before Jennifer was forced to respond to Jack MacAllister's greeting, the dining room doors once again opened.

When she saw Brandon's wife, Andrea, and his great-aunts, twin sisters Prudence and Charity, enter the room, she nearly flung herself at them for a group hug.

"Hi," she said weakly, then snatched up a pile of menus. "Your table is ready. Let's go." She shook her head slightly. "I mean, would you follow me, please?"

Rushing from behind the podium, she bumped smack-dab into Jack, and the menus went flying in all directions.

"Oh, I'm terribly sorry, Mr. MacAllister," Jennifer said, not looking directly at him. "My, my, clumsy me. I'll just pick these up and—Brandon, you have the corner table by the windows. I'll be with you in just a second.''

Jennifer squatted to collect the scattered menus, only to have Jack hunker down next to her and retrieve two of them.

''I'll give you a hand,'' he said.

Jennifer's head snapped up, and she found herself only inches from Jack. He was looking directly at her, a small smile on his lips.

Chocolate fudge sauce, she thought. That was the color of Jack MacAllister's eyes. Delicious, chocolate fudge sauce. Good grief, he was handsome—so ruggedly male, as though his features had been chiseled from rough stone.

There were tiny lines by his eyes, and she guessed he was maybe thirty-five or thirty-six. His hair was thick, an auburn shade reminding her of a glossy Irish setter.

His nose was straight, his jaw square, his lips masculine but soft, as though waiting for a kiss....

Jennifer, get a grip, she ordered herself, averting her eyes from Jack's. There was that heat again, that damnable heat, swirling low within her, pulsing, causing a warm flush to stain her cheeks.

Jennifer stood, clutching the menus to her chest. Jack rose and offered two more to her.

''Thank you,'' she said, nearly snatching them out of his hand. ''Brandon, why are you still here? I thought you were going over to your table.''

''We will, sweetie pie,'' Aunt Charity said, ''just as soon as we figure out what in the blue blazes is the matter with you.''

"Yes, dear," Aunt Prudence said. "You do seem a teeny bit flustered this evening. Is something wrong?"

Jennifer looked at the elderly aunts. Although they were twins, their mirror image was the only similar thing about them.

Aunt Prudence was wearing a sedate gray dress with a high neck and long sleeves. Aunt Charity was decked out in yards of royal blue taffeta, the dress reminiscent of a turn-of-the-19th-century dance hall costume.

Andrea was standing next to tall, dark and handsome Brandon. Her maternity dress was peach, which accentuated her lovely, silky dark hair. She had an expression of concern on her pretty face.

"I'm fine," Jennifer said, producing a passable smile. "I just overreacted to something I shouldn't have overreacted to, that's all. My imagination got the better of me and…I'm fine now."

"Hold it," Jack said, snapping his fingers. "The lightbulb just went on over my head. You saw me on the sidewalk in front of your house yesterday morning. *Staring* at your home. Casing the place, one might think. Am I getting this straight? Then I showed up here, and that scared the bejesus out of you. Right?"

Jennifer lifted her chin. "That's correct, Mr. MacAllister. Your behavior unsettled me. I apologize for…" She frowned. "No, I don't. I had just cause to question your intentions."

"You betcha," Aunt Charity said. "There was a stranger gawking at your house, for mercy's sake. That would shake up any single, unmarried, unattached, not-even-dating-anyone woman who has a little boy to protect.''

"Thank you for sharing, Aunt Charity," Jack said, smiling at her.

"Just stating the facts, hotshot," Aunt Charity said, obviously pleased with herself.

Jennifer closed her eyes for a moment and squeezed the bridge of her nose as she drew a deep breath and let it out slowly. Then she raised her head and forced a smile into place.

"Welcome to the dining room of Hamilton House," she said, looking at a spot above the assembled group. "May I show you to your table?"

Jack chuckled. "Why certainly, Ms. Mackane. Do lead on."

"Call her Jennifer," Aunt Charity said. "She's a member of our family, and so are you now, Jack. Jennifer, call Jack...Jack."

"That's Jack MacAllister," he said, grinning at Jennifer. "Not Jack the Ripper."

"Mmm," she said, glaring at him.

Jennifer marched across the room to the designated table. When the others joined her, she shoved the stack of menus at Brandon, who grabbed them before they fell to the floor again.

"Enjoy your dinner," Jennifer said, then hurried away.

Everyone settled into their chairs, and Brandon passed out the menus.

"MacAllister," Brandon said, laughing, "you've only been in town a couple of days and you've already caused trouble. New York City is probably celebrating your permanent departure, and the citizens of Ventura, California, are shaking in their shorts.''

"Hey, I'm innocent," Jack said. "All I was doing was admiring a dynamite example of historical architecture—which is badly in need of some tender lovin' care, by the way. I didn't intend to shake up the lovely Jennifer. She sure has a temper to go along with that red hair of hers.''

"She's a handful, all right," Aunt Charity said, peering at her menu. "Has been ever since she was a little girl. It would take a very special man to be a match for our Jennifer.''

"And a father for Joey," Aunt Prudence said.

"I assume Jennifer is divorced," Jack said.

"No, dear," Aunt Prudence said. "She's a widow. Her Joe was killed in a construction accident a week before Joey was born. Jennifer returned to Prescott to raise her son. Her parents relocated to Phoenix shortly thereafter due to Jennifer's mother having severe arthritis. Jennifer is living in their family home.''

"It's a lovely house," Andrea said, "but it's an awful lot for Jennifer to keep up, I'm afraid.''

"I see," Jack said slowly. "How old is Joey?''

"Five," Aunt Charity said. "He's cute as a button. Looks just like his mama.''

Jack frowned. "That's a good many years to mourn a man, no matter how great he might have been. Aren't there any eligible bachelors in this town?''

"Oodles," Aunt Charity said. "Jennifer seems determined never to remarry. Heaven knows, we've done our darndest to fix her up with the cream of the crop around here.'' She paused. ''Maybe we should leap into action again, Pru. After all, Jennifer did catch Megan's bouquet at the wedding.''

''Indeed, she did,'' Pru said, smiling.

''Oh, man, here we go again,'' Brandon said, chuckling. ''Poor Jennifer.''

''Sounds to me like the lady knows her own mind,'' Jack said. ''She likes being single. End of story. The same holds true of me. All the matchmaking in the world wouldn't get me to change my stand on the issue. I'm a bachelor and intend to remain one.''

''Wanna bet, big boy?'' Aunt Charity said, leaning toward him.

''You'd better shut up, MacAllister,'' Brandon said, shaking his head. ''Aunt Charity and Aunt Pru are pros at this matchmaking bit. I was a confirmed bachelor, too, remember?''

''And so was Ben,'' Andrea said, smiling. ''As well as Taylor.''

''Yep,'' Brandon said, nodding. ''And now we're all married. Don't get too mouthy on the issue, Jack. You never know what the future holds.''

''I know what it holds for me on the subject of marriage,'' Jack said. ''It ain't gonna happen.''

''Yes, dear,'' Aunt Pru said, patting his hand. ''We hear you.''

''Ah, how the mighty will fall,'' Andrea said, smiling. ''You did tell us the fascinating tale of the baby bet business that took place within the MacAllister clan, Jack. Your cousin, Forrest, was the reigning champion for eons—then *kaboom*, he was dethroned, so to speak.''

"Yep," Brandon said. "That's how the story went. The same could hold true for the remaining eligible males in a bachelor bet. Look at how many of us have taken the fall." He glanced quickly at Andrea. "And very happily so, my sweet."

"Nice save, Hamilton," Andrea said, laughing.

"I'll be pleased to take your money in a bachelor bet, Brandon." Jack leaned back in his chair and crossed his arms over his chest. "So would my younger brother, Richard, I imagine. My sister is single, too, if you want to add bachelorettes to the soup."

"I want a piece of this action," Aunt Charity said, rubbing her hands together.

"I do believe," Andrea said thoughtfully, "that our new sheriff, Cable Montana, would be in the camp with you and your brother, Jack."

"The numbers grow," Jack said, nodding. "There are simply men in this world who have no intention of marrying…ever."

"I know," Brandon said, grinning at Jack. "I was one of them."

Jack flattened his hands on the table and leaned toward Brandon.

"The difference between us, buddy," Jack said, "is that I'll never change my stand on the issue."

"Yes, dear," Aunt Prudence said, smiling sweetly. "So you said."

Jack chuckled, sat back again and shook his head.

"You're all smiling like Cheshire cats," he said. "You obviously believe I'm full of hot air. Oh, easy pickings, that's what you are. Money in my pocket. How long before I can collect this bachelor bet? Do

I have to be a hundred and two and still single before you pay up?"

"We'll work out the details of that part of the bachelor bet later, big boy," Aunt Charity said. "Here comes our waitress. Let's eat. I'm starving to death while I'm sitting here."

"So are we," Andrea said, patting her protruding stomach. "Baby Hamilton is doing gymnastics to let me know she's hungry."

"She? She?" Brandon said, raising his eyebrows. "Have you finally accepted the fact that I'm right? That we're having a girl? A daughter?"

"Sure, she has," Jack said. "I told you that when Forrest finally lost the baby bet, the baton was passed to the daddy-to-be. The fathers have been right every time since. If you say it's a girl, Brandon, then it's a girl. Your wife is a smart lady, and realized that the baby bet has proven itself. You're having a girl."

"And smart person that I am," Andrea said, "I'm putting my money on your falling in love and losing the bachelor bet, Jack."

Over the next hour, Jennifer carried out her hostess duties by rote.

She was furious at herself. She'd behaved like an idiot in front of Brandon's friend Jack MacAllister. Granted, she had just cause to have been frightened of Jack.

But then? Oh, good grief. Had she dismissed the incident as a misunderstanding, regained her composure and performed in a professional manner?

Oh, no, not her. She'd been caught up in a mishmash of lingering anger, along with acute feminine awareness of Jack's blatant masculinity. She'd turned into Ms. Fumble Fingers, dropping the menus, then added Shrew-of-the-Year to her titles while showing the group to their table.

Jennifer stepped behind the podium and stared at the reservation book, not really seeing the schedule of diners yet to arrive.

Even now, she thought, Jack MacAllister seemed to be somehow reaching out and touching her from way across the room. He was just so...there, and just so...male, and just so...

Heat feathered down her back, then wove into her to pulse low in her body. She shook her head in self-disgust, then looked at Jack from beneath her lashes.

Why? she wondered frantically. Why did that man have such a powerful and unsettling impact on her? He was just an ordinary man, for Pete's sake.

Well, no, that wasn't entirely true. She'd already conceded that Jack was an eleven on a scale of one to ten. He was so ruggedly handsome, so perfectly proportioned, and that thick, dark auburn hair of his was just begging to have feminine fingers sift through it.

And his eyes? Oh, those chocolate fudge sauce eyes mesmerized her and made it difficult to breathe.

Jennifer, stop it, she ordered herself, shifting her gaze back to the book. She was getting a grip—right now. All she had to do was bid Jack a pleasant goodbye as he left the dining room, and that would be that. She'd never see him again.

She frowned.

Wait a minute. Was he a guest at Hamilton House? If so, how long would he be staying in Prescott? Would he be popping into the dining room for dinner night after night? It stood to reason he'd be registered at his friend's hotel, but for how many days?

It didn't matter, she thought, lifting her chin. She'd been thrown off-kilter by Jack MacAllister for reasons she couldn't begin to fathom. But she was on full-alert now, her protective walls firmly in place. She was hereby immune to the spell-weaving Mr. MacAllister, even if he smiled that knock-'em-dead smile of his.

And the minute she got home tonight she was throwing away the flowers from Megan's bridal bouquet. Unsuperstitious or not, she wasn't taking any more chances.

Very good. She was back in control. Everything was fine. Thank heavens all of this ridiculous nonsense was at an end.

Jack listened absently as Aunt Charity related a tale of Brandon, Ben, Taylor and Jennifer's mischievous deeds when they were children growing up together in Prescott.

Ah, here we go, he thought. Some people had just entered the dining room, which meant—yes, there it was...Jennifer's smile. It lit up her face and caused those marvelous green eyes of hers to sparkle to the point where he was dazzled from across the room.

He'd watched her move through the tables with elegant, natural grace. She was femininity personified, and the heat throbbing low in his body told him that he was very aware of that fact, both mentally *and* physically. The fascinating Ms. Mackane was turning him inside out.

Which didn't make one bit of sense.

Jennifer was the type of woman he steered clear of, big time. She was, as the saying went, encumbered—with a five-year-old son, a home, a life-style that virtually shouted that the missing ingredients were a husband and father. No way. That was *not* his scene, not even close.

He'd also learned that Jennifer wasn't seeing anyone, wasn't into the singles' dating scene. She did not, therefore, know how to play the no-strings, no-commitment game.

Jennifer didn't wish to remarry, which was a point in her favor. A shaky point. He'd heard that bit before, but when a guy came along who collected a hefty paycheck, lo and behold, how quickly that tune could change.

Nope, he wanted no part of the lovely Jennifer. She was more than a pleasure to look at, was feisty and funny, and dynamite when she got her temper in a roar, but he would cut a wide path around her during the remainder of his stay in Prescott.

Jack watched as Jennifer led a couple to a small table in the center of the room. The man spoke to her, and Jennifer laughed as she handed the pair their menus.

A flash of heat rocketed through him as he heard the lilting sound of Jennifer's laughter. He shifted slightly in his chair and frowned.

Damn, he thought. Jennifer was pushing his libido buttons again. Why was she capable of doing that?

He controlled his actions and reactions toward women. *He* set the tempo, called the shots, and exited stage left at the first hint of possessiveness on the part of the woman in question.

He treated women with respect, showed them a good time, but he didn't particularly trust them.

He sure didn't know why Jennifer Mackane was able to hang him out to dry, but he'd had enough of it. She was upsetting his peace of mind and driving his raging body over the edge.

Why the hell was this happening to him—?

"Right, Jack?" Brandon said, snapping Jack back to attention.

"What?" Jack said. "Oh, sorry. I was off somewhere, I guess."

"She's thirty-three," Aunt Charity said, "but she looks younger, don't you think?"

"Who?" Jack said, an expression of pure innocence on his face.

"Give it up, hotshot," Aunt Charity said. "I've been sitting here watching you watching Jennifer through this entire meal."

"Me?" Jack said, raising his eyebrows. "Well, I may have glanced at her a time or two, but there's no harm in looking at the scenery, Aunt Charity."

"That's true, dear," Aunt Prudence said, "but you need to do more than look at our Jennifer. You should, as the gentleman I'm certain you are, speak with Jennifer privately and sincerely apologize for frightening her while you studied her home."

"I thoroughly agree," Andrea said decisively.

"Buy her some candy from the snazzy shop in

the lobby,'' Aunt Charity said, then paused. "On second thought, buy me some, too. I love the stuff.''

"Hey, I didn't scare Jennifer intentionally," Jack said. "It was a simple misunderstanding, that's all.''

"Which needs to be put to rest properly," Aunt Prudence said.

"You're dead meat, buddy," Brandon said, smiling. "Don't argue the point any further, because you'd be wasting your breath. Apologize to Jennifer when you get the chance, and be done with it.''

"Mmm," Jack said, glaring at Brandon.

"What I was saying to you when you were daydreaming," Brandon went on, "is that you're going to design our house while you're in Prescott. I was bringing the aunts up to date on that.''

"Oh. Sure. Right," Jack said, nodding. "That's what I'm going to do, fantastic architect that I am. I'll have those plans to you and Andrea before I head to Ventura for the MacAllister reunion. Man, Christmas is going to be a zoo with the whole clan together.''

"It sounds like fun," Andrea said.

"I think the kids outnumber the adults by now," Jack said. "The MacAllisters are into having babies, that's for sure. I'll have to learn how to talk to munchkin-type people, since I'm going to be part of the MacAllister architectural firm in Ventura. No more New York City rat race and brutal winters. Maybe I'll even learn how to surf.''

"You did the smart thing by leaving New York," Brandon said. "I've never been sorry I dropped out of the fast lane." He smiled warmly at Andrea.

"Coming home to Prescott was the best thing I ever did."

"Thank you, love," Andrea said, matching his smile.

"Jennifer's hair is naturally curly," Aunt Charity said. "No fancy perms or globby makeup for our girl."

"Aunt Charity, would you cut it out?" Jack said. "I'm not interested in all the little details about your Jennifer. She has an interesting house that I'd love to do some restoration work on, and that's it. Period."

"I'm just chatting," Aunt Charity said, batting her eyelashes at him.

Jack shook his head and laughed.

"Maybe flowers would be a better gift of apology for Jennifer," Aunt Prudence said, pressing one fingertip to her chin. "Mmm. No, the chocolates are best, because Jennifer has fresh flowers at the moment. She caught the bridal bouquet at Megan and Ben's wedding."

"So you said," Jack said, rolling his eyes heavenward. "Which means Jennifer is to be the next bride and blah, blah, blah. I hope she'll be very happy with whatever guy she snags."

"That's the problem," Aunt Charity said. "We can't get Jennifer into snagging mode. Been working on that for years."

"So, it's settled, then?" Aunt Prudence said, leaning toward Jack. "You'll purchase some dainty chocolates for Jennifer?"

Jack raised both hands in a gesture of defeat. "Yes, I'll do it. I'll buy the bribe and humbly apologize to Ms. Mackane. Can we change the subject now?''

''Yep,'' Aunt Charity said. ''I'm ready for a sinful dessert. Bring it on.''

The dining room at Hamilton House closed at eleven o'clock, then preparations were made for breakfast the next morning.

Just before midnight, Jennifer turned off the lights, locked the doors to the dining room, then walked along the hallway to the quiet lobby of the hotel.

She waved goodbye to the clerk on duty behind the registration desk, then headed toward the front doors, buttoning her coat as she went.

As she passed one of the high-back chairs, a figure rose, startling her and causing her to gasp and stumble a bit.

''I'm sorry,'' Jack said. ''I didn't mean to frighten you.''

Jennifer frowned. ''Oh? You seem to be making it your life's work as far as I can tell.''

Jack closed the distance between them and extended a gold foil covered box toward Jennifer.

''My peace offering,'' he said, smiling. ''A token of sincere apology for upsetting you by staring at your house. Sweets for the sweet, and all that.''

Jennifer looked at the box, Jack's face, the box, then narrowed her eyes as she met Jack's gaze again.

''Aunt Pru and Aunt Charity put you up to this, didn't they?'' she said.

''Well…'' Jack said slowly.

Jennifer sighed and took the offered box of chocolates. "All right. So be it. I accept your apology, and the whole business is forgotten. You didn't have to stay up until midnight to do this."

Jack shrugged. "I'm a night owl." He paused. "May I walk you to your car?" *What?* he thought incredulously. *Where did that come from?* His intention had been to hand over the dumb candy, then head to his room and the soft bed that was waiting for him.

Jennifer laughed, and a bolt of heat shot through his body, causing him to frown at his now-familiar reaction to the lilting sound.

"You really don't want to volunteer to walk me to my car, Mr—Jack," Jennifer said. "It's parked in the driveway at my house. Thank you for the candy. My son, Joey, and I will enjoy it. Good night."

"Wait a minute," Jack said, as Jennifer started to move around him. "How are you getting home if you didn't drive to work?"

"I walked. Since you're so familiar with the location of my house, you know it's only a few blocks away, and the weather is surprisingly mild for mid-November in Prescott." Jennifer shrugged. "So, I walked."

"Are you nuts?" Jack said, his voice rising. "You can't stroll along the sidewalk at midnight. You'll get mugged before you go ten feet."

"I certainly will not," Jennifer said, matching his volume. "This is Prescott, Arizona, not...wherever it is you're from."

"New York City, and I don't care if this *is* cute

little Prescott. You've got no business walking home alone at this hour.''

"I do it all the time.''

"Well, you're not doing it tonight,'' Jack said, taking her elbow. "Let's go.''

Jennifer jerked her arm free of Jack's grasp.

"You are, without a doubt, one of the pushiest, rudest men I have ever met,'' she said. "You may be Brandon's friend, but that doesn't mean that *I* have to like you—which I don't. Good night, Mr. MacAllister.''

Jennifer marched toward the front doors of the hotel. Jack fell in step beside her, causing her to stop as she placed one hand on the door latch.

"Now what?'' she said.

"I'm going for a midnight walk, that's all,'' Jack said, smiling at her. "If I happen to meander in the direction of your house…sue me.''

"You're really exasperating, do you know that?'' Jennifer said. "Fine. Whatever. I'm not wasting any more of my time arguing with you. Your death, however, will not be on my conscience.''

"What death? I thought you said it was safe out there on the streets.''

"Oh, it is. However, you're not even wearing the sport coat you had on at dinner. This is not shirt-sleeve weather. If you get pneumonia and croak, it will serve you right.''

Jack chuckled. A shiver slithered down Jennifer's back as she heard the sexy, male rumble.

"I don't suppose,'' he said, "that you'd wait while I went to my room for a jacket, would you?''

"Not a chance.''

"Didn't think so."

"End of story," Jennifer said, lifting her chin. "Goodbye."

Jennifer pushed open one of the doors and left the hotel.

Jack followed right behind her.

Chapter Three

The night was clear, crisp and incredibly quiet.

A million stars twinkled in the black-velvet sky, creating a silvery beacon to show the way as Jennifer and Jack turned the corner and left the lights of downtown Prescott behind.

Jack shoved his hands into his trouser pockets and hunched his shoulders against the chill as he matched Jennifer's long-legged stride along the sidewalk.

He was out of his tiny mind, he thought, mentally shaking his head. He probably *would* catch pneumonia and croak, which would be his just desserts for this ridiculous performance.

There he was, slowly freezing to death, as he escorted a woman—one who didn't wish to be escorted—home at midnight. Yep, he was definitely certifiably insane.

But…well, what could he say? A foreign sense of protectiveness had consumed him when Jennifer had announced she was about to walk home alone. There was no way he could just stand in the warmth of the hotel lobby and watch her set out on her own.

Oh, man, he was cold. He needed to do something to shift his attention from the fact that the blood was freezing in his veins. *So, MacAllister, talk to Jennifer.*

"Well, here we are," he said.

"Mmm," Jennifer said.

"Sure is quiet."

"Mmm."

"I'm used to New York, you know, the city that never sleeps."

"Mmm," Jennifer said again.

Jack sighed in defeat and trudged on.

Jennifer slid a glance at Jack, then looked quickly back down at her feet. She was being rude, she knew, by refusing to engage in the simplest conversation. But she just couldn't chatter like a magpie. Not yet. Not until she regained at least a modicum of control over her raging emotions.

She was acutely aware—again—that Jack's powerful male presence was causing heat to thrum within her despite the chill of the night.

But something more unsettling her now. When she'd realized that Jack intended to see her safely to her door even though he didn't have a jacket to wear, she'd had to struggle against very unwelcome tears.

Dear heaven, how long had it been…if ever…since she'd felt protected and watched over by a man?

How long had it been…if ever…since she had been made to feel special and important due to the actions of a man?

How long had it been…if ever…since she'd been able to relax and just be, because someone else had stepped in and taken charge?

Jack's stubborn insistence on walking her safely home had touched a place deep within her, and she'd been nearly overwhelmed by the emotions that gesture had evoked.

Oh, Jennifer, stop, she ordered herself.

Jack MacAllister wasn't Prince Charming riding to the rescue of a damsel in distress. He was a smooth operator who was accustomed to having his way with women, a man who rarely heard "no," she figured, from a member of the opposite sex.

They had engaged in a battle of wills of sorts, on the subject of her going home alone, and Jack obviously couldn't deal with losing the war. So there he was, freezing his tush off in order to proclaim himself the victor. What a dunce.

"Cold?" Jennifer said, glancing over at Jack.

He chuckled. "You'd better believe it. This was a pretty dumb thing to do, but my big-city instincts kicked in and… Well, I was obviously wrong. This town is buttoned down so tight, we haven't even seen a stray dog."

"You're admitting that I was right?" Jennifer said, surprise evident in her voice.

"Yep."

"Oh." She smiled. "Fancy that."

"What did you think? That I was on a big macho trip here? It's hard to be a hero when there aren't any dragons to slay." Jack laughed. "What I am is a six-foot popsicle."

Jennifer stopped walking, and Jack skidded to a halt.

"Jack, this is silly," she said, smiling. "Why don't you turn around and head back to the hotel. Jog or something to get there as quickly as possible. I appreciate your gentlemanly gesture here, but as you can see, it really isn't necessary."

"Hey, we're almost to your house," he said, matching her smile. "A jacket of Joey's obviously wouldn't fit me, but if I beg, maybe you'll loan me a blanket for my return journey in the wilds."

"I'd be happy to."

Jack nodded as he continued to look directly into Jennifer's eyes, now clearly visible in the silvery glow of the stars.

Neither of them moved. They hardly breathed. Time lost meaning. Heat began to curl and swirl within them, gaining force, pulsing low.

A sudden chill coursed through Jennifer, a wave of fear, of knowing she was losing control of the very essence of herself.

"No," she whispered, then spun around and hurried down the sidewalk.

Jack shook his head slightly to shake off the strange, sensuous spell that had been woven over him. "Man," he said, then took a much-needed deep breath.

He glanced quickly in the direction Jennifer had

gone, then sprinted after her, catching up as she turned onto the cobblestone walk leading to her house. She was fumbling in her purse for her key while holding the box of chocolates in her other hand.

"Jennifer—" Jack started.

"No," she said, going up the steps of the wide front porch.

She unlocked the door and entered the house with Jack right behind her. "I'll get you a blanket," she said, her back to him as he entered the house and shut the door behind him.

"Jennifer, wait a minute," he said. "We need to talk about what happened a minute ago."

She spun around, her green eyes flashing. "No, we do not," she said, her voice not quite steady. "There's nothing to talk about."

"But you felt it, I know you did. The heat, the pull, the—"

"Lust," she said, lifting her chin. "Let's give it the tacky title it deserves, shall we? That's what it was—lust. And as far as I'm concerned, the incident is forgotten. I certainly don't wish to discuss it."

Jack frowned, then shook his head slowly. "No, that wasn't lust," he said thoughtfully. "Nope. No way. I know lust when I'm caught up in it and that…whatever it was that took place between us was something very, very different."

Jennifer dropped her purse and the candy box onto the sofa facing the fireplace, where embers of a dying fire still glowed. Her coat joined the lot moments later.

"Whatever," she said, looking at Jack again.

"You have your opinion. I have mine. It really doesn't matter because the subject is closed."

"What are you afraid of?" Jack said, studying her intently. "I mean, hey, I'm a tad shook up myself here, because I've never experienced anything quite like that before. But I'm not *afraid* of it. I want to know what it was."

"Well, I don't," she said, wrapping her hands around her elbows. "Jack, please, let it go. It's late, I'm tired, and I have to be up early in the morning to get Joey ready for kindergarten."

Jack swept his gaze over the large room that was furnished with worn but comfortable chairs and a sofa. The tables were oak and had seen better days.

"Where's your baby-sitter?" he said.

"When I'm on this shift at the hotel, Joey sleeps at Mildred Clark's house next door. Mildred is a wonderful woman who is like a grandmother to Joey. In fact, he calls her Grandma Clark and… Oh, forget it. Why am I explaining all this to you?"

Jack smiled. "Because I asked?"

"Don't smile," she said, nearly yelling. "Don't you dare smile that smile at me."

"Huh?" he said, definitely no longer smiling.

Jennifer pressed one hand to her forehead for a moment. "I'm losing it. I really am. This is insane. I don't behave this way. What on earth is the matter with me?"

"Gotcha," Jack said, pointing at her. "See? You *do* want to know what that strange spell was that came over us out there in the cold, dark night. Whatever it was is what on earth is the matter with you. Get it?"

"What I'm going to get, mister," she said, "is a blanket for you. Then you are marching yourself out of here. Get it?"

"Got it."

"Good."

Jennifer nodded decisively, then left the room, returning minutes later with a blanket.

Jack burst into laughter. "You're kidding," he said. "You're sending me packing wrapped in a Winnie-the-Pooh blanket?"

"You'll be cute as a button," she said, shoving the brightly colored blanket at him. "Goodbye."

Jack tucked the blanket under one arm. "Okay. I'm gone. Lock up behind me."

At the door, Jack hesitated and turned. Jennifer was right behind him; their toes were nearly touching.

"I think—" he said quietly. "I truly believe…that you have the same questions and want the same answers that I do. It's all very confusing, don't you think?"

"I—"

"Shh."

Jack slid his free hand to the nape of Jennifer's neck, lowered his head and claimed her mouth with his.

Jennifer's eyes flew wide open in shock, but in the next instant her lashes drifted down as heat suffused her. Of their own volition her arms floated upward, then her hands encircled Jack's neck.

She savored the feel, the taste, the wondrous sensation of Jack's lips on hers, and offered no resistance as his tongue slipped into her mouth to seek and find her tongue.

Jack dropped the bulky blanket and gathered Jennifer close to his body, deepening the kiss as desire rocketed through him. He raised his head a fraction of an inch, then slanted his mouth in the opposite direction, drinking in the tantalizingly sweet taste of Jennifer. Heat coiled low and tight within him, arousing him almost to the point of pain.

Jennifer, his mind hummed. He'd known, just somehow known that it would be far, far more than just a simple kiss. It would be ecstasy.

Jennifer was responding to him, holding nothing back, returning his kiss with total abandon. He felt ten feet tall because Jennifer was, in this moment stolen out of time, his.

Jack groaned in pure male pleasure as he pressed Jennifer even more tightly against him, relishing the feel of her lush breasts being crushed to his chest.

Oh, his mind thundered, how he wanted her, wanted to make love with Jennifer Mackane through the remaining hours of the night.

The rumbling sound of Jack's sensual moan penetrated the mist encasing Jennifer, bringing her back to reality with a *thud,* jarring her from the rosy, sensuous place she'd floated to.

She broke the kiss, jerked out of Jack's embrace, then took a shaky step backward as she drew a steadying breath.

Jack shook his head slightly. "Whew. That was— You are... Whew."

"That was," Jennifer said, hearing the thread of

breathlessness in her voice, "a mistake, should never have happened."

"Why not?" Jack said, frowning. "It was sensational—*and* equally shared."

"I…" Jennifer started, then threw up her hands. "Yes, all right, I can't deny that I…took part in that kiss."

Jack smiled. "Kisses. Plural."

"Whatever," she said, hugging herself. "The fact remains that it—they, those kisses—were a mistake. I don't behave like this…ever. I don't know what came over me, but I'd appreciate it if you'd forget that this incident ever took place."

"Incident?" he said, raising his eyebrows. "Lady, it was a happening, an event, that defies description. Forget it? No way. Are you telling me that you can honestly *forget* how you felt, how you responded to me?"

"Yes. No. I…Jack, please, just go. I'm embarrassed and upset and— Just leave."

"Hey," he said gently, "don't be so hard on yourself. You're a young, healthy, beautiful woman, with wants and needs that are nothing to be ashamed of. We felt it—both of us. The desire—not lust, desire. There's nothing wrong with that."

"Yes, there is," she said, her voice rising, "because I don't want any part of feeling that heat, that need, that… No. I have no room for all that in my life—not anymore. Not now. Not ever again."

"Why are you doing this to yourself?" Jack said, matching her volume. "So, okay, you loved your husband, but, my God, Jennifer, it's been five years since that man died. He wouldn't want you to grieve for a lifetime, to cease to exist as a woman. You can't mourn him forever.''

"You don't understand.''

"No, I sure as hell don't," he said, restlessly raking a hand through his hair. "What I do understand—what I know—is that you want me as much as I want you.''

"No," she whispered, shaking her head.

Jack sighed in exasperation, then leaned down and grabbed the blanket from the floor. "I'm leaving now, Jennifer," he said, "but this discussion isn't over. There's something happening between us, and I want to know what it is. I'll be back.''

Jack turned and left the house, closing the door with a tad more force than was necessary.

Jennifer walked to the door on trembling legs, snapped the lock into place, then rested her heated forehead on the cool, smooth wood.

Dear heaven, she thought frantically, what had she done? She'd responded to Jack's kisses like some wanton hussy, had pressed her body to his, had felt his arousal surging full and heavy against her and had inwardly rejoiced in the knowledge that such a magnificent man wanted her. *Her.*

Sensuous images had flitted through her passion-laden mind of clothes disappearing by magic, of tumbling naked onto her bed and reaching eagerly for Jack, bringing him to her to fill her emptiness, to awaken her sleeping femininity with glorious lovemaking.

I'll be back.

Jack's fiercely spoken words echoed in her head, and she spun around, her eyes darting across the room in a near-hysterical search for somewhere to hide.

"To hide from Jack?" she said aloud, as tears stung her eyes. "No, heaven help me, to hide from myself."

This was her fault. She wasn't who she really was when she was with Jack. She didn't know why— just did *not* know why, but she *did* know she would be certain never to be alone with Jack MacAllister again.

Exhaustion swept over her like a heavy curtain, and she stumbled across the room, turning off the lights as she went. A short time later she slipped into bed, a weary sigh escaping from her lips as her head touched the soft, welcoming pillow.

Sleep. She needed to sleep, to escape from the turmoil in her mind, to put hours of distance between herself and what had transpired with Jack in her living room.

Sleep, she thought foggily. Then morning would come and everything would be fine in the light of the new day.

When sunlight tiptoed into Jennifer's bedroom the next morning and nudged her awake, she stirred, opened her eyes slowly…and thought of Jack.

With a muttered "Damn him," she threw back the blankets on the bed and stomped into the bathroom for her shower.

Dressed in jeans, a navy-blue sweatshirt and her Big Bird slippers, she entered the kitchen twenty minutes later in a less-than-chipper mood. With a mug of hot coffee in one hand, she began to assemble Joey's breakfast with the other, a frown on her face.

"Mom," Joey said, coming into the kitchen.

"What!" Jennifer snapped. Then her shoulders slumped. "Oh, Joey, I'm sorry. I sound like a grumpy bear. Good morning, sweetheart. Did you sleep well?" She paused. "How did you get into the house?"

"You didn't answer my knock at the front door, and the doorbell's broke, and I had to use the key from under the mat to get in."

Jennifer set her mug on the counter and lifted Joey into her arms. "I apologize," she said, then kissed him on the nose. "I didn't start my day with my best foot forward, but I'm fine now. I'll fix you breakfast, then walk you to school."

"'Kay," he said, wiggling to get down.

Jennifer set him on his feet.

"But don't hold my hand when we turn the corner by the school, Mom," Joey said, sliding onto his chair at the table. "That's baby stuff, and I'm big now."

"Yes, you certainly are getting big," she said quietly. "Very quickly, too. You'll be grown and gone before I know it."

Joey frowned. "Gone where? I belong here with you. I'm never going to leave you, Mommy. Never, ever, never. 'Cause if I did, you'd be all alone." He straightened in his chair and smiled. "No, you wouldn't. Not if you were the next bride 'cause you caught the flowers. Then you'd have a groom guy and you wouldn't be alone at all."

To Jennifer's dismay she was assaulted by the

memory of being held so tightly in Jack's embrace, wrapped in the safe, strong cocoon of his arms as he kissed her.

"Don't start *that* again, Joey. I am *not* going to be the next bride. I'll be just fine when I'm alone after you're grown up. Clear?"

"No," he said, sticking out his bottom lip in a pout. "I'm going to talk to Uncle Ben and Uncle Brandon about this. I'm going to tell them that you're breaking the rules about catching Aunt Megan's flowers. You told me I should never break rules, Mom."

"Oh, my stars," Jennifer said, rolling her eyes heavenward. "I don't believe this. We are now changing the subject. What do you want for breakfast? Cereal? Toast? Eggs?"

"Hot dog with mustard."

"Why not?" she said, throwing up her hands.

"And potato chips," Joey added.

"Don't push your luck, sir. I'll trade you potato chips for a banana."

"And orange soda."

"Milk."

Joey sighed. "'Kay."

Jennifer began to prepare the agreed-upon breakfast as Joey chattered about beating Grandma Clark at Candy Land the previous evening.

Jennifer laughed. "Poor Grandma Clark. You played Candy Land again? She can probably do it in her sleep by now."

"Huh?"

"Never mind."

"Guess what, Mom. It's my turn to feed the gerbil at school today. That is so cool. Can I have a gerbil of my own? I'll keep it in my bedroom.''

"Oh, ugh, no," Jennifer said, smiling. "Those things remind me of mice. Just enjoy the one at school.''

"Can I have a dog? Know what? Sheriff Montana told me he might get a dog. If I had a dog, then my dog and Sheriff Montana's dog could be friends. Wouldn't that be really great?''

"One hot dog with mustard, plus a banana," Jennifer said, placing a plate in front of Joey. "There—you have a dog.''

"That's a hot dog," Joey said, giggling.

"A dog is a dog. I'll get your milk.''

Jennifer crossed the room and took a carton of milk from the refrigerator. As she turned again, she saw Joey jump from his chair. "Where are you going?" she said.

"Somebody is knocking at the front door," he said, running from the room.

"So early?" she said, frowning. "Wait, Joey. Don't open the—darn it.''

Jennifer hurried after Joey as quickly as her Big Bird slippers would allow, the carton of milk still in one hand. Joey flung open the door, and Jennifer stumbled slightly before coming to a halt behind him.

"Hi," Joey said.

"Hi. I'm Jack MacAllister, a friend of your mom's. You must be Joey. I borrowed your blanket last night and I came to return it. I also brought some fresh cinnamon rolls from Hamilton House as a thank-you gift for allowing me to use your Pooh bear.''

Jack shifted his gaze slowly to look at Jennifer. ''Good morning, Jennifer,'' he said, smiling. ''May I come in?''

''Sure,'' Joey said, stepping back and bumping into his mother.

Jack entered the house, and Joey slammed the door.

Jack swept his gaze over Jennifer, chuckling as he gave special attention to her feet. ''Love the slippers,'' he said, grinning at her. ''Milk? Great,'' he added, nodding toward the carton in her hand. ''That will hit the spot with these cinnamon rolls. Come on, Joey. Let's dig into these goodies while they're still warm.'' He dropped the blanket onto the sofa.

As Joey and Jack headed for the kitchen, Jennifer just stood where she was, Big Bird slippers on her feet, a carton of milk in her hand.

''My life,'' she said, a rather bemused tone to her voice as she stared into space, ''is suddenly out of control.''

Chapter Four

Jennifer headed toward the kitchen, then stopped, staring down at her silly slippers.

She should make a detour to her bedroom, she thought, and change into her tennis shoes. No, forget it. Jack had already seen her funny feet, and besides, she'd never do anything to hurt Joey's feelings.

Joey, she thought, starting toward the kitchen again. He shouldn't eat one of those enormous cinnamon rolls from Hamilton House. He'd be on such a sugar rush, he'd be bouncing off the walls the entire morning at school.

"New York City," Jack was saying when Jennifer entered the kitchen.

"Wow. Cool," Joey said. "They have big apples there, or something."

Jack laughed. "Or something. But I'm moving to

Ventura, California. I just stopped off in Prescott to visit my buddy Brandon. I'm going to be a member of MacAllister Architects, Incorporated.''

"Why?" Joey said, then took a bite of the gooey roll.

"Why?" Jack frowned. "Well, because I was ready for a change, and it will be nice to be working with family.''

"Whoa, Joey," Jennifer said, bringing a knife to the table where the pair sat. "Half a cinnamon roll for breakfast. You can have the rest later.''

"'Kay," Joey said, as Jennifer cut the roll in two.

"You'll join us, won't you, Jennifer?" Jack said.

"I don't eat breakfast," she said, not looking at him. "A cup of coffee is all I have.''

"Then bring your cup and sit down," Jack said.

"Yeah, Mom," Joey said. "You should do that because we have company.''

"Mmm." She glared at Jack. "Very *early* company." She paused. "Oh, all right. Would you like some coffee, Jack?''

"Yes, thank you," he said, smiling. "Sounds great. I take it black.''

"Dandy," she said, spinning around and nearly falling over her slippers.

Don't think, she ordered herself as she went to the coffeemaker. She would *not* entertain any thoughts, any memories—absolutely none—about what had happened between her and Jack the previous night.

She would not allow her bones to dissolve when Jack MacAllister smiled at her.

She would pay no attention to the flutter of heat that was now swirling and pulsing through her body.

She couldn't care less if Jack had removed his jacket to reveal a sweater that was the exact shade of his chocolate fudge sauce eyes.

She could handle this. No problem. Jack was just a man, who was sitting at her table stuffing his face with a cinnamon roll. A gorgeous man. A man whose shoulders looked a mile wide in that sweater. A sweater that encased strong arms that had held her so tightly, so safely in his embrace. An embrace that had included kisses that were ecstasy in its purest form and—

That's enough, she ordered herself. Get a grip.

She plunked a mug of coffee in front of Jack, retrieved her own from the counter, then poured a glass of milk for Joey. She sat down next to her son at the table and put the glass in front of him.

"Every drop, sweetie," she said.

"'Kay," Joey said, then looked at Jack again. "How come you had my Pooh blanket? Did you leave yours in New York City?"

"Something like that," he said, smiling. "I used your blanket like a coat, because I wasn't wearing mine and it was cold."

"Oh," Joey said, nodding. "Do you have a dog?"

"No," Jack said, then took a bite of roll. "Mmm. Delicious."

"Do you have a little boy?" Joey asked.

"No," Jack said.

"Do you have a wife lady?"

"No," Jack said.

Joey leaned forward. "Do you have a suit and tie?"

"Joey," Jennifer said quickly, feeling a flush of embarrassment heat her cheeks, "eat your breakfast. It's getting late."

"I have a suit and tie," Jack said. "Why did you ask me that?"

"Well, because you need to have a suit and tie if you're going to be a—"

"Time to go," Jennifer said, getting to her feet.

Joey glanced at the clock on the wall. "No, it's not. The big hand isn't at the top, Mom."

"Oh." Jennifer sighed and sank back into her chair.

"Back up, Joey," Jack said. "I'm definitely missing something here. I need to have a suit and tie to be a...what?"

"A groom guy," Joey said.

"Oh, good grief," Jennifer muttered.

"See, my mom caught Aunt Megan's wedding flowers and that means my mom is going to be the next bride, but she needs a groom guy if she's going to be a bride. Then I'd have a daddy I don't have to give back." Joey paused. "Just like Sammy has. See?"

"More coffee, Jack?" Jennifer said, looking at a spot about four inches above his head.

"No, I'm fine," Jack said, his gaze riveted on Joey. "Let me make certain I understand this, Joey."

"Oh, let's not," Jennifer said.

Jack ignored her comment. He leaned back in his chair and crossed his arms over his chest.

"I think I get the picture, Joey," he said, "except for the part where you have to give the daddy back."

"Oh," Joey said. "That's Uncle Ben, Uncle Brandon and Uncle Taylor. We do men stuff together, but…" He shrugged. "When we're done doing men stuff, I have to give them back."

"Ah," Jack said, nodding slowly.

"Sheriff Montana might be a good groom guy 'cause he's thinking about getting a dog," Joey went on. "But I don't know if Sheriff Montana has a suit and tie." He frowned. "The thing is, though, my mom doesn't want to be the next bride."

"Ah," Jack said again.

"That's breaking the rules of catching the flowers," Joey said.

"Indeed," Jack said.

"*I* can't break rules, so I don't think my mom should get to. Do you?"

"My, my, look at that big hand on the clock, Joey," Jennifer said. "Run and brush your teeth and get your jacket. Then I'll walk you to school."

"'Kay."

Joey hopped from the room on both feet, announcing that he was Tigger. As he exited, the coffee mugs jiggled and clinked on the table.

"That is one terrific kid," Jack said, smiling at Jennifer. "Man, he's neat."

"Yes, well, I think he's pretty special," she said, tracing the rim of her coffee mug with one fingertip. "He's all boy, that's for sure. Full of energy… Of course, as a typical five year old, he has definite opinions about things, and doesn't hesitate to ex-

press them. You have to discount a great deal of
what he says because he has a tendency to blither
on and on, whether he knows what he's talking
about or not. Therefore—''

''Whoa,'' Jack said, raising one hand. ''You've
made your point. You want me to forget everything
that Joey said about your being the next bride, and
whether I have a suit and tie so I can be the groom
guy. Right?''

Jennifer met Jack's gaze. ''Yes,'' she said, nodding. ''Joey has suddenly become obsessed with the
idea that he wants a father. But he also wants a dog,
so...'' She shrugged. ''This, too, shall pass.''

''I don't know about that,'' Jack said seriously.
''He seems pretty adamant about having a daddy.
Uncles just aren't enough.''

Jennifer sighed. ''Having Brandon, Ben and Taylor spend time with Joey is the best that I can do.''

''Is it?'' Jack said quietly, looking directly into
her eyes.

''Yes, it definitely is.''

They continued to gaze at each other, and with
the ticks of time came memories of the previous
night. Memories of kisses shared and hearts racing.
Memories of a soft body pressed to a rugged body.
Memories of heated desire that licked throughout
them like all-consuming flames.

Jennifer tore her gaze from Jack's and stared into
her mug, willing her heart to quiet its wild tempo.

''Why did you come here this morning?'' she
said, not looking at him.

''To return the blanket. To meet Joey. To see if
you were all right after last night.''

"Of course I'm all right," she said, getting to her feet. "Because what happened last night is forgotten."

"Oh, come on, Jennifer, give me a break," Jack said. "You haven't forgotten it any more than I have."

"Believe what you wish," she said, starting across the room. "But you're not capable of reading my mind."

"No, I'm not," he said, "but I can sure as hell read what I just saw in your eyes a minute ago. Desire, Jennifer. Simmering desire."

Jennifer thudded her mug onto the counter and turned to glare at Jack. "Would you just leave it alone?" she said. "What happened was a mistake, should never have taken place. It's over. Done. Finished. Just forget it, Jack."

"No."

"Oh, you're exasperating," she said, throwing up her hands. "Fine. Don't forget it. I don't care. But I've erased it all from my memory bank."

"Is that a fact?"

"Yes," she said, lifting her chin. "It most certainly is."

"I see. You've totally forgotten how perfectly you fit against me when I held you in my arms? How it felt when I kissed you, and you returned those kisses in kind? You've forgotten the sensuous spell that comes over us whenever our eyes meet? You've forgotten that you wanted me as much as I desired you?"

"Stop it," Jennifer said, then glanced quickly at

the doorway that Joey had disappeared through. "Why are you doing this, Jack?"

He stood, then closed the distance between them. "I told you why. I want answers to the questions of what is happening between us. I'm an architect, Jennifer. I deal in facts, details. I don't like feeling confused. I don't rest until all the pieces to the puzzle are in place."

"And then you move on to the next challenge."

"Well—"

"I'm ready, Mom," Joey said, zooming back into the kitchen.

"Okay, sweetie," Jennifer said. "Say goodbye to Jack because he's leaving now."

"No, I'm not," Jack said. "I'll join you two on the walk to school."

"Cool," Joey said.

"No," Jennifer said.

"Why not, Mom?" Joey said, frowning.

"Yeah, Mom," Jack said, grinning. "Why not?"

Jennifer opened her mouth, hesitated, then snapped it closed again.

"Fine," she said, shaking her head. "We'll all walk to the school."

"Great," Joey said, jumping up and down. "Just like the three bears. Baby Bear, Mommy Bear and—"

"Joey," Jennifer said, "did you remember to put the cap back on the tube of toothpaste?"

"It doesn't have a cap, Mom. You bought me the push-the-button kind."

"Oh, so I did. I'll get my jacket."

Jack shrugged into his own jacket as Jennifer hurried from the room.

At the front door, Jennifer patted her pocket. "Okay, I have my house key," she said. "We're ready to go."

"It's none of my business," Jack said. "But…"

"What?" she said a tad sharply.

"Do you usually make this trek in the morning," Jack said, raising his eyebrows, "wearing your spiffy Big Bird slippers?"

Joey dissolved in a fit of laughter. And an embarrassed-beyond-belief Jennifer went to her bedroom to change into her tennis shoes.

The day was clear and crisp, the sky a bright blue dotted with puffs of white clouds. As the trio made their way along the sidewalk, Joey gripped one of Jennifer's hands and one of Jack's. The energy-filled child hopped on his right foot, then his left, then swung both feet in the air, using the adults as part of his human trapeze. Their combined laughter danced through the morning air.

Baby Bear, Jennifer's mind echoed. *Mommy Bear. And…Daddy Bear.* This was the type of outing she'd daydreamed about having someday with her husband and child. This was how it should have been, but hadn't been—would never be.

She glanced quickly at Jack, who was smiling down at Joey. Why had Jack insisted on joining her and Joey on the walk to school? she wondered. What sneaky motive did he have for making such an effort to be buddies with her son? What was Jack MacAllister after?

Good grief, listen to her. She sounded so hard, so bitter, so mistrusting. Well, fine. Better safe than sorry. She'd rather be squinty-eyed suspicious, than wide-eyed innocent and vulnerable.

She was, however, probably overdoing it a bit. Jack was on a vacation of sorts and was just filling idle hours. He was accustomed to the fast pace of New York City and was no doubt becoming bored in dinky Prescott. He had the opportunity to go for a walk with a cute, happy little boy and had decided to tag along with Baby Bear.

And Mommy Bear? her mind nudged. Did Jack see this stroll as a way to spend time with her, too? Yes, he probably did. He was determined, for heaven only knew what reason, to discover what was happening between them.

Why? Why should whatever was happening between them matter to a man like Jack? A man who could obviously have the amorous attention of any stunning, sophisticated woman who crossed his path.

Why? He was bored. That was it. She'd heard him telling Joey that he was on his way to Ventura to join the family architectural firm and had stopped in Prescott to visit Brandon. Jack probably hadn't realized this town was so small, but was too polite to cut his stay short.

So, he'd zeroed in on her for something to do? Oh, that was rotten. Really crummy.

Jennifer sighed.

There she went again, thinking the worst, drawing dark conclusions about men. She hadn't realized that was where her mind had settled during the past five years. Hadn't known, because Jack MacAllister was the first man in all that time to touch the woman within, to awaken the feminine part of her she'd put so firmly to sleep.

Oh, she didn't like this—not one little bit.

She didn't want to be awakened from her safe, protective slumber.

Nor did she wish to deal with the bitter, suspicious woman she was discovering she had become. A woman her husband's lies had made her.

Even more, she had no desire to acknowledge the...well, the desire itself that Jack had evoked within her—that incredible heat, that longing to mesh her body with his and make sweet, slow love for hours.

In short, she wanted to turn back the clock to before she'd seen Jack standing on the sidewalk staring at her house.

"One...two...three—" Joey yelled, then laughed in delight as Jennifer and Jack swung him through the air.

She was indulging in childish thinking, Jennifer's mind rushed on. She was doing a "Joey," could remember how he wanted to push the clock forward when he'd run out of patience waiting for his birthday to arrive.

She could *not* turn back the clock, any more than Joey had been able to move it forward. She *had* seen Jack, met Jack, been held and kissed by Jack. She had no choice but to deal with him.

And deal with him she would, by golly, by making it crystal clear, once Joey was safely deposited at the school, that she preferred not to spend any more time with one Mr. Jack MacAllister, thank you very much. There. It was settled, once and for all.

"Here we are," Jennifer said when they reached the school, she leaned down to give Joey a quick kiss on the cheek.

"Mom-m-m-m," he said. "Don't kiss me at school."

"Sorry," she said, smiling. "I lost control. I'll be right here by the gate to walk you home when the bell rings, sweetie. 'Bye for now."

"'Bye," Joey said. "'Bye, Jack."

"See ya, sport," Jack said.

"When?" Joey said.

"Off you go," Jennifer said. "You don't want to be late getting into your classroom."

"When will I see you again, Jack?" Joey said.

"Joey, the gerbil is hungry," Jennifer said. "It's your turn to feed him. Remember?"

"Oh, yeah. Cool. 'Bye."

Joey took off at a run across the schoolyard and disappeared into the building.

That little guy, Jack thought, was a heart stealer. Joey was so incredibly open and honest, he just stepped up and said whatever was on his mind. Kids were amazing, that was for sure, and Joey Mackane was extra special, no doubt about it.

What an awesome role it would be to be father to a child like Joey, a boy who would see his daddy as a hero and want to be just like him. Whew. Heavy stuff.

He'd never given much thought to being a father. Of course, it flickered through his mind now and again when he was with friends and family who had kids. But he'd always dismissed the idea out of hand, because with the child came the wife. The woman. The marriage. The commitment. The waiting to discover the *real* agenda of that feminine half of the partnership.

He'd been burned too many times by women who finally showed their true colors. The materialistic demands began. She wanted this, she wanted that...it never ended.

Oh, yeah—love me, love my paycheck, Jack thought dryly. Hell.

"Well," Jennifer said, bringing Jack from his thoughts, "Joey is all squared away for a few hours."

"Yep," Jack said, nodding. "He really is a neat kid, Jennifer. You should be very proud of the job you've done raising him alone."

"Thank you," she said, nodding her head slightly.

"So," Jack said, "what do you do after you've walked Joey to school?"

"Go to bed."

"Oh?" he said with a burst of laughter. "That sounds like it might be very enjoyable."

"Mmm," Jennifer said, glaring at him. "What I meant was, I go home and sleep for a couple of hours so I'm rested enough to enjoy the afternoon with Joey, then work the evening shift at the hotel."

Jack nodded. "Do you have other shifts at different times?"

"Yes, I rotate, and I have a schedule in place with Grandma Clark. Joey and I are so lucky to have her. My parents live in Phoenix because of my mother's arthritis. I grew up in the house where Joey and I are living." She paused. "So, I'm off. Have a nice day, Jack."

"I'll walk you home."

"Are we back to my getting mugged on the wild streets of Prescott?"

Jack chuckled. "No, we're back to I enjoy your company and I'd like to walk you home. I may even snag another one of those cinnamon rolls before I tuck you into bed."

"I beg your pardon?" she said, her eyes widening.

"Just kidding," he said, laughing. "At least I know you're listening to what I'm saying. Some women smile and nod in all the right places, but they're actually thinking about the sale at Neiman Marcus, or whatever."

"I've never even been inside a Neiman Marcus store," Jennifer said, starting down the sidewalk.

"But you'd like to be able to shop at a classy place like that," Jack said.

"That should have been a question, not a statement," she said, glancing at him as he fell in step beside her. "The answer to the question would have been, I've never given it a thought. It's beyond my budget, so why dwell on shopping in stores like that?"

"Yeah, well, if someone handed you a credit card for Neiman Marcus, you'd manage to spend your share of the green stuff."

"Nope," she said, shaking her head. "I don't use credit cards. If I can't afford to pay cash for something, then I can't have it now."

"You're kidding."

"No, I'm not, Jack."

"Amazing," he said, shaking his head.

"I don't know why," Jennifer said. "It makes very simple sense to me."

"But… Never mind."

"I get the feeling that you don't quite believe me, Jack."

"I didn't say that," he said. "I'm digesting what you said."

Jennifer shrugged, and they walked without speaking further.

Strange, she thought. She and Jack didn't know each other well enough for a sudden silence like this to be so comfortable. Yet it was. It was as though she'd known Jack for a long time, which was ridiculous.

Of course, nothing about her reactions to Jack MacAllister were even close to normal. Heavens, no. The sensual impact he continually had on her was absurd. Her incredible *awareness* of him was borderline insane, as was the quickening of her pulse each time he smiled that devastating smile of his.

And at the top of the This Is Nuts list was the fact that she'd returned his kisses with such heated abandon that the mere memory brought a flush to her cheeks.

Jack MacAllister was dangerous. Unsettling. Upsetting. Magnificent.

Oh, Jennifer, shut up, she admonished herself.

Jack chuckled suddenly, and Jennifer looked over at him questioningly.

"Groom guy, huh?" he said. "According to Joey, all it takes to be a husband is a suit and tie."

"Ah, the innocence of a child," Jennifer said, then sighed. "What a shame that Joey will have to travel the rocky road of adulthood. I'd like to wrap him in a cocoon and protect him forever, but I can't."

"No, you can't. Some people have rockier roads than others. Maybe Joey will be one of the lucky guys."

"I hope so. At least there are *some* tough truths I can keep from hurting him."

"Such as?"

"Oh, just…things. Here's my house. Do you want another cinnamon roll and cup of coffee?" Great, Jennifer thought, shaking her head in self-disgust. What had happened to making it clear that she didn't want to spend any more time with Mr. MacAllister?

"Sure. Thanks. Then I'll be on my way so you can get some sleep."

Jack followed Jennifer up the front walk leading to the porch. What truths was Jennifer determined to protect Joey from? he wondered. It hadn't been an idle statement on her part, because there had been a fierceness to her voice when she'd said it. She'd then avoided answering his question as to what she meant.

The lady had secrets.

Oh, yes, she was intriguing as well as desirable. There were many layers to Jennifer Mackane. She was like a mysterious, alluring package, waiting to be unwrapped to reveal what was within.

And for some unexplainable reason, he knew he wouldn't rest until he'd discovered who Jennifer Mackane really was.

Chapter Five

Jennifer cleaned up the kitchen after breakfast, while Jack treated himself to another cinnamon roll and a mug of hot coffee. He chatted about how he would be drawing the plans for Brandon and Andrea's dream house while he was staying in Prescott.

The couple had purchased a piece of land, he said, and had a contractor ready to get started. If the weather cooperated, the home could very well be completed by the time the Hamilton baby arrived in March.

Jennifer sank into the chair across from Jack, a dishcloth in one hand. "A new baby and a new home at the same time," she said wistfully. "Isn't that wonderful? Brandon and Andrea must be pinching themselves in an attempt to believe it's all true." She sighed. "Goodness."

"They're excited, all right," Jack said, nodding. "Now Brandon is bugging Andrea to decide on a name for their daughter."

"They know they're having a girl?" Jennifer said. "I wasn't aware of that. I thought Andrea had decided not to have an ultrasound."

"Ah, madam," Jack said, smiling, "you don't know the history of the MacAllister baby bet business. Brandon and Andrea qualify because they're close friends of yours truly—a MacAllister.

"Besides that, I have a cousin named Andrea over in California. Andrea MacAllister Stewart, to be precise, who is married to John. They have two sets of twins—Matt and Noel, and Jeff and Kate."

"My stars, they're busy parents."

"Yep. Anyway, Andrea Hamilton doesn't need a fancy test to determine if she is having a boy or a girl, because Brandon said a daughter is on the way, and so says the baby bet. It's a given."

"Wait, wait," Jennifer said, laughing. "I don't want to miss one word of this." She wiped up the table where Joey had been sitting, went to the sink to rinse out the cloth, then plunked back into the chair. "Okay, I'm ready. What's the scoop on the baby bet?"

Jack explained the famous MacAllister baby bet as Jennifer listened in delight.

"Such fun," she said, when he'd finished his tale. "It must be marvelous to be part of such a big family."

Jack nodded. "We sure had a lot of good times while we were growing up. I've been away for years living in New York, and I'm looking forward to being involved with the clan again.

"My folks retired to Florida, but they're flying in for the enormous MacAllister reunion that's being held at Christmas. That is going to be a zoo. Kids will be coming out of the woodwork."

"Super." Jennifer paused. "Well, you made a believer out of me. I'll buy some pink yarn and knit a blanket for baby girl Hamilton. I wonder what name Andrea and Brandon will pick for their daughter?"

"I don't know," Jack said, "but I hope between that project and the long list of decisions regarding the new house, they'll forget about the dumb bachelor bet nonsense they're talking about."

"This gets better and better," Jennifer said, laughing. "What's the bachelor bet?"

"Well, see, Brandon was a confirmed bachelor, as were your friends Ben and Taylor."

"They're all married now."

"Exactly," Jack said, nodding. "Brandon is yapping his head off about a bachelor bet, saying that I won't last at being footloose and fancy-free, and nor will my brother, Richard. There's someone else, too... Oh, yeah, the sheriff here in Prescott."

"Cable Montana?" Jennifer said. "The women in town are swooning over him, but as far as I know, he hasn't dated anyone since he moved here." She laughed. "Let me guess—Aunt Charity said she wanted in on the bachelor bet."

"Got it in one," he said, laughing with her. "She was rubbing her hands together, anticipating her winnings. Crazy people. What they haven't figured out yet is how old we have to be—and still single—before *we* can collect our money from *them*.''

''What a hoot,'' Jennifer said.

She leaned back in her chair and folded her arms beneath her breasts.

''So, you're a confirmed bachelor, huh?''

''In spades.''

''Why?'' she said, smiling and raising her eyebrows.

Jack chuckled. ''Why? You sound like Joey.''

''I guess I do,'' she said, her smile fading. ''Well, forget I asked, because it's none of my business. I don't intend to ever remarry, but I don't wish to get into a lengthy discussion as to why I feel that way.''

''I assume you're still mourning your husband, Joey's father.''

Jennifer shrugged.

Jack leaned toward her. ''I said it before and I'll say it again, Jennifer. Five years is enough—too long, in fact, to grieve for a man, for what once was. It's time to move on with your life. I realize that I'm overstepping here, but, damn it, Joey wants a father. Don't you yearn for a special man in your life?''

''No,'' she said firmly. ''I don't.''

''Damn,'' he said. ''You're one stubborn lady. You're making a tremendous mistake.''

''Oh? I do believe there is a double standard in effect here, Mr. MacAllister. It's apparently perfectly acceptable for you to be a confirmed bachelor, for reasons known only to yourself. But I'm making a big mistake by taking the same stance?''

''That's different,'' he said, frowning.

"Aha," Jennifer said, pointing a finger in the air. "One set of rules for men, another for women? Your mind-set is from the wrong century, Jack."

"You have a son to think about," he said, his voice rising.

"So I should marry the first thing that comes along in a pair of pants so Joey will have a father?" she said, matching his volume. "Not in this lifetime, mister."

They glared at each other for several long moments, then Jack smiled.

"What?" Jennifer said, still glowering at him.

"Who's going to be the groom guy in the suit and tie—the daddy bear—if you don't adjust your attitude?"

"Oh, good grief," she said, laughing in spite of herself. "This is so ridiculous. We're arguing like people who have known each other for a long time, when the truth of the matter is, we hardly know each other."

"Don't we?" Jack said seriously, his voice very low, very rumbly, and very, very male.

A whisper of heat slithered through Jennifer, and her smile disappeared. She was pinned in place by the sound of Jack's voice and the compelling depths of his chocolate-fudge-sauce eyes.

Memories of the kisses shared with him rushed over her. Her heart began to beat in a wild tempo, and the heat began to pulse low in her body.

Heaven help her, she thought frantically. She wanted this man with an intensity that was so frightening, it was like nothing she'd experienced in her entire life. She couldn't move, could hardly breathe and—

No.

She tore her gaze from Jack's and drew a trembling breath. She started to rise, praying her legs would support her, but Jack trapped one of her hands under one of his on top of the table.

"Jennifer, don't run from me," he said, his voice slightly husky. "Don't run from me, or from whatever it is that's happening between us. I would never do anything to hurt you."

Jennifer snapped her head up to look at him again, her green eyes flashing. She pulled her hand away from beneath his.

"Oh, really?" she said, an edge to her voice. "What a joke. You're passing through town. You see me as a challenge because I'm not falling all over you like your city women. So, what the heck, you'll keep after me until you get me into bed to satisfy your male ego and fill your idle hours, then go merrily on your way. But you would never do anything to hurt me? Give me a break, Jack."

Jack's jaw tightened slightly with anger and he narrowed his eyes. "I don't deserve that," he said. "You're making very unfair assumptions about me that aren't even close to being true."

He paused, then frowned as he studied her for a long moment.

"You're acting like a woman who has been...betrayed, terribly hurt, rather than like a widow grieving for the loss of perfection she had with her husband, the father of her son."

"That's enough," Jennifer said, getting to her

feet. "Now you're the one who is making assumptions."

Jack rose, met Jennifer as she came around the table, and gripped her shoulders. "Jennifer, wait a minute," he said quietly. "I don't want to argue with you. Let's back up. Okay?"

"Good idea," she said coolly. "We'll rewind this video to before you stood on the sidewalk staring at my house, then rewrite the script so that you walked down a different block and didn't have dinner at Hamilton House last night. Therefore, we never met."

"I wasn't thinking of reversing this scenario *that* far," he said, smiling. "You just erased me."

"Yep," she said, appearing quite pleased with herself. "I certainly did. Goodbye."

"Ah, but you're forgetting something," he said, his smile broadening. "It is a well-known fact that men in this country have a strange need to monopolize the remote control. It's in our genes or something. Therefore, *I'm* the one who decides where to halt this flick."

"Oh?"

"Indeed. I've pushed the button, and we are now back to last night in your living room and… Enough said."

Jack lowered his head and captured Jennifer's lips in a searing kiss that stole the very breath from her body.

No, no, no, she thought. *But… Oh, dear heaven, yes, yes, yes.*

She encircled Jack's neck with her arms and stepped into his embrace as he dropped his hands from her shoulders and wrapped his arms around her. He deepened the kiss even more, parting her lips, finding her tongue with his own.

Ah, Jennifer, Jack thought. It had been too long since he'd kissed her, an eternity since he'd been able to savor her sweet taste and aroma, the feel of her slender body pressed to his.

He'd never get enough of this woman; he needed, wanted more, much more. He was succumbing— very willingly at the moment—to the spell Jennifer was weaving over, around and through him.

He ached with the heated desire to make love with Jennifer Mackane.

Jack ended the kiss slowly, reluctantly, then sifted the fingers of one hand through Jennifer's silken hair as she rested her head on his chest.

They stood there, waiting for hearts to quiet and breathing to return to normal. They simply stood there, each lost in private, jumbled, sensual thoughts.

Then Jennifer sighed a sad-sounding sigh, a weary sigh that held the echo of tears.

"I can't do this," she whispered, still not moving. "I can't just listen to the needs of my body and ignore my emotions. I can't, Jack."

"I understand," he said, his voice hushed. "I won't push you, Jennifer, nor ask more of you than you're capable of giving. But I sincerely mean it when I say I want to know what's happening between us."

"Why is it so important to you?"

"I don't know. I guess because I've never felt,

experienced, anything like this before. It's so different, so...I want answers."

"I don't."

"What are you afraid of, Jennifer?"

She sighed again. "Wakening what I've put so firmly to sleep...the essence of my femininity and all the wants and needs and driving, reckless actions that overpowering passion can result in. I can't. I won't."

"All right," he said, nodding slowly. "We have different agendas. I want the answers, you don't. You're in control of your—what did you call it?— the essence of your femininity. Okay. That's fine. You'll make certain that what is slumbering within you stays deeply asleep, no matter what I do or say. Am I getting this the way it is?"

"I, well... Yes."

He eased her away from him, and she lifted her head to meet his gaze.

"So, if I spent time with you," Jack went on, "in order to find my answers, to set things to rights within myself, it wouldn't upset you, hurt you in any way, because you have a firm handle on where you're coming from."

"Well, I don't know if—"

"Makes sense to me." He paused and nodded. "Sure, this is fine. So, I have a proposition for you."

Jennifer's eyes widened. "You what?"

"I'm not propositioning you in the way you're thinking," he said, taking a step backward and shoving his hands into his pockets. "What I'm hereby proposing to you will fall within the guidelines of what we've each determined to be where we are."

"You're losing me," Jennifer said, frowning.

"I need to spend time with you before I end up nuttier than a fruitcake trying to figure out why you're capable of weaving spells over me."

"I weave spells over *you?*" she said, splaying one hand on her chest.

"Big time. For all I know, it's a flash in the pan, and will burn itself out and be gone, *kaput.* I'll be back to normal. You'll be dandy while I'm hanging around because you've already cemented your program."

"Huh?"

"Hence, my proposition," he said. "This is one dynamite house that you live in."

"Now we're talking about my house?" Jennifer said, her voice rising. "I can't keep up with you."

"Pay attention. This house needs repairs, and my hands are itching to work on a historical structure like this one. You buy the supplies, I'll be the labor—free of charge."

"Oh, I don't think—"

"Good. Don't think it to death. Just agree. It's a win-win situation. I'll figure out why you've blitzed my mind and body, your house gets some tender lovin' care, and you're perfectly safe through the whole bit because your essence is asleep, or whatever. Get it?"

"Not really," she said, shaking her head slightly.

"Well, you're tired," Jack said. "Once you've rested, you'll understand the whole deal. I'll shove off so you can get to bed. We'll connect later so I can really have a go at examining this house. Then we'll decide which repairs have priority." He

moved forward and dropped a quick kiss on her lips.
''See you later.''

Jack grabbed his jacket from the back of the chair
in which he'd been sitting, then strode from the
room.

Jennifer blinked, then frowned. That man, she
thought, was like a steamroller operating at maximum speed. Had she just agreed to allow Jack to
make much-needed repairs on her home? No, she
certainly had not. Had she?

Jennifer sank back into her chair, the fingertips of
one hand floating up to rest on her lips.

Oh, mercy, kissing Jack was wonderful. He made
her feel so vibrantly alive, so womanly and desirable. She couldn't think rationally when he kissed
her. She could only feel, savor—want more and
more and more.

''Jennifer Mackane,'' she said with a sigh, ''you
are treading in dangerous territory. What on earth
are you doing?''

Well, she was grabbing a handful of...life. She
was allowing her femininity to awaken and glory in
its existence. She was filling her senses to overflowing with the taste, feel and exquisite male aroma of
Jack.

And that was really, *really* dumb.

Jennifer plunked one elbow on the table and
rested her chin in the palm of her hand. Well, maybe
not *really* dumb, just borderline dopey.

Jack seemed to have a better handle on where she
was than she did. He'd spelled it all out for her—
how she couldn't be hurt by spending time with him
because she was in control.

What was wakening within her, she could put back to sleep when she chose to do so.

That made sense. That was true. And that meant she could spend time with Jack, be held in his arms, be kissed by him, then bid him a breezy *adieu* when he left Prescott for his new life in California.

Kissed, she thought dreamily. Held in those strong, yet gentle arms. Make sweet, sweet love through the night with Jack MacAllister.

Jennifer sat bolt upward in the chair. "Oh, now wait just a minute here," she said aloud.

Just how could she guarantee she wouldn't end up with a broken heart? She didn't have a clue as to the answer to that question.

All she could do was make certain she *was* retaining control of herself.

At the first hint that she might be growing more fond—yes, that was a good word—*fond* of Jack than was allowed within her emotional safety zone, she'd send him packing and resume her life as it had been before he entered her serene existence.

Her lonely existence.

No, no, now stop it, she admonished herself silently. She was alone, but not lonely. She had Joey, a challenging career, oodles of wonderful friends who were like a family to her.

But...

Yes, all right, sometimes, just once in a while, when Joey was asleep and the night stretched before her, she was a tad lonely. That was perfectly normal.

It didn't mean that she wanted a serious relationship with a man. And heaven knew she never intended to remarry. No, she just sometimes had the need to feel wanted and womanly.

And Jack was doing that.

Just for a while. Hours stolen out of time. Then he would be leaving town…and that would be that.

There was no way at all she could be hurt by any of this, because she was in control.

And Joey? She would make it perfectly clear to her son that Jack was here on vacation and would soon be leaving. Jack was *not* a potential suit-and-tie guy who would qualify to be a groom, a daddy bear. But Joey would benefit from another male influence in his life, even for the short term.

"Fine," she said, getting to her feet. Everything was hunky-dory, and the frosting on the cake was that her house was going to get some much-needed repairs.

She had absolutely nothing to worry about.

"Nap time," she said cheerfully as she left the kitchen.

Chapter Six

Jack settled onto a bench in the town square, then stretched out his legs and crossed them at the ankles. He unbuttoned his jacket to further enjoy the warming sun that was rising higher in the brilliant blue November sky.

He deserved an award, he thought, folding his arms over his chest, for having delivered some of the fastest talking blither ever produced by man. He'd rattled off his rationale to Jennifer without coming up for air, explaining why it was perfectly safe and sound for them to spend time together.

Why had he done that?

He'd been mentally scrambling, had been on the edge of panic that she'd tell him she didn't want to see him again. For reasons he couldn't begin to fathom, the idea of her sending him packing had caused a cold fist to tighten in his gut.

So, he'd steamrolled her, laid a bunch of malarkey on her, then hightailed it from her house before she had a chance to figure out what in the heck he'd actually said.

Why had he done that?

Jack sighed, shook his head, then dragged both hands down his face. He slouched lower on the bench and shoved his hands in his jacket pockets.

Actually, he mused, what he had rattled off to Jennifer wasn't all nonsense.

He *did* want to know what was happening between them. He didn't deal well with confusion and unanswered questions.

And no, he didn't wish, nor intend, to hurt her. If she was as in control of her emotions as she claimed to be, his presence shouldn't represent any potential harm to her mental health and well-being.

And yes, he really did want to do some repairs on that dynamite house of hers.

So, hey, what he'd said at warp speed had all been true. And to top it off in grand style, he would get to spend more time with neat little Joey.

Jack smiled as he replayed in his mind the earlier conversations with Joey.

"A groom guy," he said aloud, chuckling. "A daddy bear."

That kid was something. Cute. Smart. Knew who he was and what he wanted—a father. Well, according to Jennifer, Joey wasn't going to get one.

Jack narrowed his eyes.

Jennifer's adamant stance on never remarrying

was producing another slew of unanswered questions. There was something off-kilter there.

His assumption that Jennifer was still mourning her deceased husband was beginning to set off warning bells in his mind, indicating that there was a great deal missing from that picture.

Jennifer just wasn't coming across as a grieving widow. No, she seemed…angry—even close to bitter somehow. Why? What was the true story behind her marriage to Joe Mackane? She'd built strong walls around her heart, had put her femininity—or however she'd described it—to sleep, to be assured that no man would ever get emotionally close to her again. Why?

Why? Why? Why? Now *he* sounded like Joey.

Little heart-stealer Joey Mackane.

It was sure going to be tough saying goodbye to that nifty kid when it came time to head to California.

And the nifty kid's mother?

How would he feel when he walked away from Jennifer for the last time?

Sudden images of the kisses shared with Jennifer flashed through Jack's mental vision. The remembrances of her taste and aroma, of her being nestled against him, rushed over him, causing heat to coil painfully in his body.

"That's all," Jack said, getting to his feet. "Go for a walk, MacAllister. Don't think, just walk."

Jack spent the remainder of the morning in his room at Hamilton House working on the plans for Andrea and Brandon's house. He ate lunch with the couple in their apartment on the fifth floor of the hotel so he could show them what he had done and hear more of their ideas regarding their dream home.

"I love the lowered ledge near the ceiling in the kitchen," Andrea said, her eyes sparkling with excitement.

"It's called a pot wall, or sometimes it's referred to as a plant shelf," Jack said. "It gives you more of an opportunity to decorate a kitchen than you would normally have to make it uniquely yours."

"Perfect," she said.

"I'd like the back patio bigger," Brandon said. "We want room for the kids to play, plus be able to barbecue and eat out there."

"Got it," Jack said, nodding.

"Kids?" Andrea said, smiling at Brandon. "As in more than one?"

"Well, sure," Brandon said, matching her smile. "We'd spoil an only child rotten. Besides, she'd be lonely without a sibling to play and squabble with."

"Makes sense to me," Andrea said.

"At least she'll have a mother *and* a father," Jack said quietly.

"Why the serious expression?" Brandon said. "You grew up with a mother and father, Jack."

"I wasn't referring to me, Brandon," he said. "I was thinking about Joey Mackane. Do you know what he said? He likes doing 'men' things with his uncles, but it's not the same as having a father because…well, because he has to give the uncles back."

"Oh-h-h," Andrea said. "I'm going to cry. That is so sweet, but so sad. Poor Joey. He's obviously reached the age where he really misses having a father.''

''A daddy bear,'' Jack said, ''to go along with the baby and mommy bears. He wants the whole nine yards, like his best friend Sammy has.''

Brandon leaned back in his chair and crossed his arms over his chest. ''Sounds to me like you've spent quite a bit of time with Joey,'' he said.

''And, therefore, with Jennifer,'' Andrea said. ''They are, after all, a package deal.''

''Don't get in a roar,'' Jack said, raising both hands. ''I stopped by their house to return the Winnie-the-Pooh blanket, and took some cinnamon rolls with me for their breakfast. It's no big deal.''

''Pooh blanket?'' Andrea said.

''Oh, well, Jennifer loaned it to me because when I walked her home last night I wasn't wearing my jacket and it was a tad chilly.''

''You walked Jennifer home last night?'' Andrea said.

Jack frowned. ''You're starting to sound like a parrot, Andrea, echoing everything I'm saying.''

''Just gathering the facts, sir,'' she said, smiling brightly.

''Right,'' Jack said dryly, giving her a dark look. He shifted his gaze to Brandon. ''What do you know about this Joe Mackane who Jennifer was married to?''

Brandon lifted one shoulder in a shrug. ''Nothing. Jennifer and Joe were married somewhere in Colorado. A year or so later, Jennifer moved back to Prescott with a newborn Joey, after Joe was killed in a construction accident. None of us ever met Joe Mackane.''

''It's such a tragic story,'' Andrea said. ''I can't imagine the horror of losing my husband, much less a week before our baby was born... I don't believe that Jennifer has ever really gotten over it. She refuses to even go out on casual dates, let alone remarry and give Joey the father he wants. She must have had a very special, very wonderful relationship with her husband.''

''Or a really lousy one,'' Jack said.

''What?'' Brandon said, frowning.

''Think about it,'' Jack said. ''You're all assuming that Jennifer's marriage was a match made in heaven. What if it was just the opposite? What if it was such a living hell that she has vowed never to get into a serious relationship with a man again?''

''You're forgetting something, Jack,'' Brandon said. ''Jennifer named Joey after his father. A mother wouldn't do that if the guy was a louse.''

''She might do it as a smoke screen,'' Jack said, ''to provide evidence that she had a happy existence with the man, when the truth might be the flip side of the coin. Does Jennifer talk about Joe? Relate stories about the terrific things they did together, shared as a couple?''

''No,'' Brandon said slowly, shaking his head. ''She doesn't. She never mentions him, and changes the subject if someone brings up the topic of her marriage. We all assumed that it's too painful for her to discuss Joe.''

''After five years?'' Jack said, his voice rising. ''Come on, Brandon, get real. It doesn't add up.

Jennifer is too strong to be living that much in the past. It doesn't fit who she is.''

"You feel you know her that well to make that statement?" Andrea said, raising her eyebrows.

Jack shifted his gaze to the pencil he was holding, fiddling with it as though it were the most fascinating thing he'd ever seen.

"Yeah, I know her that well," he said quietly. "And I also know that something doesn't click here. Jennifer is definitely being influenced today by events that transpired in the past, but they're not necessarily memories of sweet bliss with Joe Mackane. Maybe I'm wrong, but I just don't think so."

"Interesting," Brandon said, staring into space.

"It's also upsetting," Andrea said. "The circumstances, the timing, of Joe's death were bad enough. It's even worse to entertain the idea that Jennifer's life with the man was a nightmare. Think of the pain she has bottled up inside her, if what you're saying is true, Jack. It's really heartbreaking."

"This doesn't make sense," Brandon said. "Jennifer has terrific parents, plus Ben, Taylor and I are like brothers to her. Andrea, Aunt Charity and Aunt Pru love her, too. Jennifer could have come to any of us and shared the truth about… No, I think you're out in left field on this, Jack."

"Maybe Jennifer *did* confide in her parents," Andrea said.

"No," Brandon said, "she didn't. Not with a negative story, anyway. Her father told me several years ago that it was obvious from Jennifer's behavior that no man would ever begin to be able to take Joe Mackane's place in her heart.'' He shook his head. "No, I just can't buy your theory, Jack.''

"I could be wrong,'' he said, nodding.

"But what if you aren't?'' Andrea said, leaning toward him. "If Jennifer doesn't deal with the pain of her past, she'll never experience the joy of a future with a special man.''

Andrea paused and sighed. "How are we going to discover the truth, so that, somehow, if what Jack is saying is how it really is, we can help her?'' she said.

"Don't look at me,'' Brandon said. "I don't have a clue. What are we supposed to do? March up to Jennifer and demand she spill the beans about her marriage to Joe Mackane? Yeah, right.''

"No, the ticket is to pay attention to what Jennifer says and does,'' Jack said. "It's the little, subtle things that have given me the evidence I already have. The more I observe, the clearer the picture will be.''

"That works for me,'' Andrea said. "Then, if it's really apparent that she is harboring dark, painful secrets, we could sit her down, explain that we love her, and offer to listen. Maybe if she talked it through, it would allow her to be free of it all, to move forward with her life.''

"Just remember that Jennifer and Joe might have been so incredibly happy,'' Brandon said, "that she honestly doesn't wish to settle for less with someone else. I don't care if it's been five years or fifty since Joe died. If what they had together was close to perfection, then Jennifer has every right to live out her days with those memories.''

"That's true," Andrea said.

"That stinks," Jack said, frowning, "and I don't believe for a second that Jennifer was on cloud nine with Mackane."

"Okay," Andrea said. "We agree that we don't know the truth. We agree that we care enough about Jennifer that we need to explore the issue further. The problem is…how? You said we should pay attention to the little, subtle things that Jennifer says and does, Jack. We're all busy people. We're not with Jennifer that often."

"*I* will be," Jack said.

"Oh?" Brandon said.

"I'm going to do some repairs on her house," Jack went on. "Jennifer will buy the supplies, and I'm free labor. Those kind of historical structures fascinate me as an architect. I'll report back to you, let you know if I discover anything of importance."

"A question," Brandon said, holding up one finger. "Why?"

"Why what?" Jack said.

"Why the interest in Jennifer?" Brandon said. "Why are you so concerned that she might be a…a victim of her past, so to speak? Why are you doing this?"

"That's none of our business, honey," Andrea said, patting one of Brandon's hands.

"It's not?" he said. "Yes, it is."

"No, it is not," Andrea said firmly. "If Jack has feelings for Jennifer, cares for her, realizes that she's a wonderful and special woman who deserves to be truly happy…well, that's none of our business."

"Hey, now wait a minute," Jack said. "I never

said I had *feelings* for Jennifer, or *cared* for her, for crying out loud. You're making this sound like a— a man and woman thing, when it's actually a…a…" His voice trailed off, and he frowned.

"Yes?" Andrea said, an expression of pure innocence on her face.

"It's…it's a humanitarian endeavor," Jack said. "Yes, that's what it is. I'm a nice guy who hates to think that a lovely, rare woman like Jennifer might be—what I mean is… Ah, hell, forget it."

"Mmm," Andrea said, smiling sweetly.

"Do you want me to report back to you about what I learn or not?" Jack said gruffly.

"Oh, of course we do," Andrea said.

Jack got to his feet and began to roll up the house plans. "I'm outta here," he said. "Jennifer is probably back home after collecting Joey from school, and I can take a look at her house. It was Joey's turn to feed the class gerbil today. He was really excited about it. Man, he's a neat kid." He paused. "Keep thinking about ideas for your house. Catch you later."

"See ya," Brandon said.

"Goodbye, Jack," Andrea said. "And thank you for *everything.*"

"Yeah, sure."

As Jack strode across the room, then left the apartment, Andrea folded her hands on her large tummy and smiled.

"This is *my* bedroom," Joey said, grabbing Jack's hand and attempting to hurry him forward. "It's neat-o."

"You betcha it is," Jack said.

He swept his gaze over the all-boy room and nodded in approval. There was a bookcase constructed of boards painted in bright, primary colors and supported by cinder blocks. The shelves were jampacked with toys and books. Dinosaurs smiled from the bedspread and curtains, and model airplanes were suspended from the ceiling by ribbons. Joey's dresser was red with white pull-knobs.

"This is actually the parlor," Jennifer said. "My bedroom is in what should be the formal dining room with double doors. Since there's a full bath down here, I've closed off the upper floors to save money on the heating bills."

"Makes sense," Joe said, nodding.

"When I was a teenager," Jennifer went on, "I had the third floor all to myself. It's under the eaves, so when we go up there, you'll have to be careful not to bump your head." She laughed. "I used to pretend I had my own apartment. I felt so grown up and sophisticated."

"Can I live up there by myself when I'm big, Mom?" Joey said.

"Sure," she said, smiling at him. "You'll be able to talk to all your girlfriends on the telephone without me hearing you."

"I don't like girls too much," Joey said, wrinkling his nose. "They scream and holler when they see a worm, and they never want to get their clothes dirty. They just stand around and don't do nothing."

"Anything," Jennifer corrected automatically.

"That's what I said," Joey said. "They don't do nothing."

Jack chuckled. "Joey, my friend, I realize this is hard to believe, but you *will* change your mind about how you feel about girls."

"When you're twenty-five," Jennifer said quickly, causing Jack to hoot with laughter.

The trio completed the tour of the entire house, then Joey ran out into the backyard to play on his swing set. Jennifer and Jack went into the living room, where Jennifer sat in an easy chair, and Jack sat on the sofa.

"This really is a fantastic house," Jack said. "They sure knew how to design and build them way back when."

"It's lovely, but it's an awful lot to keep up," Jennifer said.

"Mmm," he said, nodding. "Well, my work is cut out for me, and I'm eager to get started. The stairs inside have dried out over the years and need repair. The shutters outside the windows are hanging on by a hope and a prayer. The front steps are sagging, as well as some of the boards in the porch itself. Then there's the—"

"Enough," Jennifer said, smiling. "Let's face it. My house is terminally ill."

"No, it's not. It just needs some tender lovin' care, and I'm just the guy to do it." Jack paused and looked directly at Jennifer. "I'm very good at tender lovin' care, Jennifer."

Jennifer's heart did a funny little two-step and a curl of warmth swept through her body. "Yes," she said softly, "I'm sure that you are…good at…" Her voice trailed off.

They continued to gaze at each other, assaulted by sensual memories as well as the heat of desire.

"Jennifer."

The sound of her name—*the simple sound of her name*—being spoken by Jack in a voice gritty with heightening want and need that matched her own caused Jennifer to shiver and tear her gaze from his.

"We agree, then?" Jack said.

Jennifer snapped her head around to look at him again, her eyes widening.

"To what?" she said.

To making love, sweet Jennifer, Jack thought rather hazily. Sweet, slow love for hours and hours—

He cleared his throat. "To my fixing up this place. You buy the supplies, and my labor is on the house—excuse the pun."

"Oh, yes, of course," she said. "And I appreciate it more than I can tell you."

"It will be my pleasure." Jack glanced around the room. "This home is a fine old lady."

Jennifer laughed. "Don't let Aunt Charity and Aunt Pru hear you call it an 'old lady.' They remember when it was built."

"Those two are something, aren't they?" Jack said, matching her smile. "They may be twins, but their personalities are as different as day and night." He paused and narrowed his eyes as he studied Jennifer. "They're on the same wavelength about one thing, though. Believing that everybody should be married. I gather they're really into matchmaking."

"Oh, they are, but they gave up on me several years ago, thank goodness."

"Don't be so certain of that," he said, still looking at her closely. "They're zeroing in on the fact that you caught that bridal bouquet."

"Good grief," she said, rolling her eyes heavenward. "Those flowers have caused me nothing but trouble. Joey got it in his head that since I caught the bouquet, all I need to do is find—"

"A groom guy," Jack finished for her, "who has a suit and tie. The daddy bear."

"I hope Joey won't make himself unhappy because he doesn't have a daddy like his friend Sammy. There are some things in this life that I just can't give him."

"Do you think that Joe Mackane would have been a good father to his son?" Jack said.

Jennifer averted her eyes and picked an imaginary thread from her jeans. "Well, I...I have no way of knowing that, do I?" she said, then sighed. "Yes, I do. Joe would not have been a— Never mind."

Dear heaven, she thought, what was she doing? She'd said enough that Jack now knew she didn't believe that Joe would have been a loving and devoted father to Joey. She'd never even hinted at such a thing to anyone before. Why now? Why Jack?

"I see," Jack said quietly. "How did Joe measure up in the husband department?"

Jennifer got to her feet. "I'd prefer not to discuss this further. Why don't I give you some money so you can shop for what you need to get started with the repairs? That's more efficient than my attempting to purchase what I don't know the first thing about. Good idea? Yes, it is. Certainly. Therefore—"

"Jennifer," Jack said, rising from the sofa. "I didn't mean to upset you by bringing up the subject of Joe."

"I'm not upset," she said, fidgeting. "I...I simply don't wish to talk about him. It serves no purpose."

"I agree," he said, nodding. "But his having an emotional hold on you serves no purpose, either."

"He doesn't," she said, her voice rising.

"Doesn't he?" Jack said quietly, starting toward her. "Well, that's very good news. That means that when I kiss you, you're kissing *me*. Not a ghost of another man. Me."

Jennifer watched Jack approach, trepidation, excitement and anticipation intertwining and tumbling through her.

He came closer...and closer...and...

Jack stopped in front of Jennifer, framed her face in his hands and lowered his head slowly, so very slowly, toward hers.

"Me," he said, then his mouth melted over hers.

Jennifer encircled Jack's waist with her arms as she returned the searing kiss in total abandon.

Kissing Jack, her mind hummed. Not a ghost of Joe. No, never that. Kissing Jack MacAllister. And it was heavenly.

The room disappeared as a sensual mist encased them, carrying them to a passion-filled place where they wished to stay, savor, want more, so much more. Heat pulsed and coiled and thrummed within them, heightening their desire to a near-frantic pitch.

A whimper of need caught in Jennifer's throat.

A groan rumbled in Jack's chest.

The back door slammed, and Joey's voice reverberated through the air. "Mom! Guess what!"

Jennifer and Jack jerked apart, then spun around to face the direction that Joey would appear. They each drew steadying breaths, willing their bodies back under control.

Joey ran into the room and came to a halt in front of the adults. "Mom," he said, then frowned. "What's the matter? You look funny."

"I do?" she said.

"Yeah." Joey cocked his head and looked at her intently. "Like when we run home from school. Your face is all pink and stuff."

"Oh, well, I guess I have the heat too high in here," Jennifer said.

No joke, she thought. She was on fire, desire still coursing throughout her. Dear heaven, her son had almost caught her kissing Jack, being held and caressed by Jack. This was terrible, just absolutely terrible.

"You went outside to play without your jacket, Joey," she said.

Joey shrugged. "You didn't tell me to put it on."

"You know you're to wear it in this weather," she said. "I shouldn't have to tell you." She sighed. "Remember next time. Okay?"

"'Kay. Guess what?"

"What?" Jennifer and Jack said in unison.

"I jumped off my swing from high up and didn't even fall on my butt. Great, huh?"

"Marvelous," Jennifer said, managing to produce a smile. "Just be careful when you do that."

"Jennifer, do you—" Jack started, then cleared

his throat when he heard the gritty quality of his voice. "Do you have a metal measuring tape?"

"Yes," she said. "Joey, would you get it for Jack, please? It's in the toolbox in the pantry."

"Sure," he said, then was off and running.

Jennifer turned to look at Jack, a deep frown on her face. "Do you realize what just happened?" she said, keeping her voice hushed. "Joey was seconds away from seeing us when we were..." She shook her head. "I can't believe that I was so irresponsible, so—"

"Human?" Jack said, matching her frown. "We weren't doing anything wrong, Jennifer. Joey is old enough to understand that you're a woman, as well as being his mother."

"Oh, listen to the child expert here," she said, planting her hands on her hips. "Joey is scouting around for a groom guy, remember? He'd believe he'd hit pay dirt if he saw us kissing. Get your suit and tie ready, MacAllister. Joey would have you signing on the dotted line to be the daddy bear."

"We'd just explain to him that people might kiss each other without having plans to get married." Jack nodded. "He's a smart kid. He'd understand."

"Wrong," Jennifer said, shaking her head. "You're very, very wrong."

"Got it," Joey said, zooming back into the room.

"Thanks, sport," Jack said, taking the measuring tape from Joey. "Let me ask you something, Joey. What does it mean when two people kiss each other?"

"Jack, for crying out loud," Jennifer said.

"You mean old people like you and Mom?" Joey said.

Jack chuckled. "Yes, old people. Not your friends at school."

"Oh, well, when old people kiss," Joey said, "they get a baby. I saw Uncle Brandon kiss Aunt Andrea when we all went on a picnic, and now they're going to have a baby." He frowned at Jack. "How come you don't know 'bout kissing and babies, Jack?"

Jack felt a foreign flush of heat creep up his neck, then glowered at Jennifer when she laughed.

"Yeah, Jack," she said. "How come?"

"I guess I forgot," he said. "Old people forget things sometimes."

"Oh-h-h," Joey said, nodding. "Well, if you forget something else, I'll tell you, 'cause I know a bunch of stuff."

"So you do," Jack said dryly.

"Do you want to kiss my mom and make a baby, Jack?" Joey said, jumping up and down. "That would be neat-o. You could be the groom guy, my daddy and—"

Jack reached out and planted his hand on Joey's head in mid-jump, causing the little boy to stop his pogo stick routine. "How would you like to help me measure some things, Joey?"

"Cool." Joey paused. "Why?"

"Why. Well, because I'm going to do some repairs around here. You know, fix what needs to be fixed."

"Sammy's daddy fixes up their house," Joey said. "That's daddy work."

Jennifer examined the fingernails of one of her hands. "Need a shovel, Jack?" she said pleasantly. "To dig yourself in a little deeper?"

"Could you help me out here?" he said.

"Nope," she said. "This is between you and Joey. Men stuff. You know what I mean? I'm going to see what's in the freezer that I can defrost for Joey and Grandma Clark's dinner. Have fun, you two."

As Jennifer left the room, Joey began to jump up and down again. "What are we going to measure first, Jack? Can I hold the tape? Can I pull it out? Can I tell you the numbers? Can I—"

"Sure, sure," Jack said, staring at the doorway Jennifer had disappeared through. "Whatever."

Had he just been set up? he wondered, narrowing his eyes. Had Jennifer very cleverly manipulated him into a scenario where he was once again a groom guy candidate in the eyes of her son?

Was one of her many secrets a hidden agenda to actually put the past behind her and snag a husband for herself, a father for Joey?

Did Jennifer have a well-thought-out master plan that he wasn't aware of?

That certainly would follow the rotten pattern of behavior of every woman—every damn one—he'd ever been involved with.

"Jack?" Joey said, tugging on Jack's arm.

"Oh. Right. Ready to get to work?"

"Yep."

"Could you get a piece of paper and a pencil from your bedroom?" Jack said.

"Yep," Joey said, then ran from the room.

No, Jack thought, looking at the empty doorway again. Jennifer wasn't like the others. Not Jennifer. She was real and honest, didn't play games. Not Jennifer.

Why not Jennifer? a little voice in his mind asked ruthlessly. She was a woman, wasn't she? Members of the female species were clever and sneaky, and always thinking, thinking, thinking.

Jennifer had a house that was badly in need of repair. And? Bingo. There he was, about to repair it. But that had been *his* idea. Hadn't it? Or had he somehow been made to *believe* that it was? Hell, he didn't even know anymore how the fix-it-up project came into being.

Man, oh, man, he was a muddled mess.

He'd sat in Brandon and Andrea's apartment and talked a blue streak to convince them that Jennifer wasn't necessarily being held in the grip of the past by memories of blissfully happy times with Joe Mackane, but possibly by remembrances of a disaster of a marriage.

Jennifer needed to let go of those ghosts and get on with her life.

But how did he know, how could he be really certain, that she wasn't already doing that? How did he know for sure that she, along with Joey, wasn't checking him out to see if he qualified to be the groom guy, the daddy bear?

Every woman he'd ever trusted had betrayed that trust with the revelation of what she really wanted. And it was never just him, the man, the person. Hell, no. It was what his money could buy said woman, the materialistic loot, the life-style she coveted.

Why should Jennifer Mackane be any different from the women who'd come before her?

But—but Jennifer was Jennifer and...

"Ah, hell," he said, dragging one hand over the back of his neck.

"You can't say 'hell' in our house," Joey said, reappearing at Jack's side.

"Sorry."

"Here's a piece of paper," Joey said. "I couldn't find a pencil so I brought a red crayon. Red crayons are good."

"Fine," Jack said. "I'm an award-winning architect who will be writing down measurements with a red crayon. Why the hell not? It makes about as much sense as the rest of my life at the moment."

"You can't say 'hell' in our house," Joey repeated.

"Sorry," Jack said again. "Be patient with me, Joey. I'm old, remember? Not only that, but I'm very, *very* confused."

Chapter Seven

Jennifer stood by the front windows in the living room, watching Joey and Jack stack supplies close to the house on the grass near the edge of the sidewalk.

Joey had pleaded to be allowed to accompany Jack on the shopping trip, and Jennifer had finally agreed, with the stipulation that Joey wear his seat belt while riding in the vehicle.

With the pair's departure had come the silence within the big, empty house. With the silence had come niggling, negative voices in Jennifer's mind—voices that gained more and more volume—regarding her decision to spend time with Jack.

She sighed and shook her head. She was driving herself crazy. The longer Joey and Jack were gone, the more doubts she had that she could handle being in close proximity to Jack for the measured amount of days—and nights—he'd be in Prescott.

Fear that she was making a terrible mistake reached through her like icy tentacles. She could very well be playing emotional roulette, she concluded, and that was a very dangerous and foolish thing to do.

She had Joey to consider, too. She had to be concerned about his obviously growing attachment to Jack. She had to make crystal clear to her son that Jack was only in Prescott temporarily, then hope Joey wouldn't fantasize otherwise. Joey had to comprehend that when Jack left, they'd never see him again.

By the time she'd showered and dressed for work, Jennifer mused, still looking out the window, she'd done a complete reversal of her original decision.

She could not, would not, share any more desire-evoking kisses with Jack MacAllister. She had no choice as far as seeing him—the agreement regarding the repairs on the house was a done deal.

But she'd mentally place Jack in the same category as Brandon, or Ben, or Taylor. A brother type, a buddy, a pal. Jack would no longer be an attractive man, but a platonic friend.

As Jennifer stood there drinking in the sight of Jack, her heart was racing and the new familiar heat was pulsing in her body. She wanted to rush out the door and into his arms, feel his lips on hers, savor the power and masculinity of his magnificent body.

"Oh, Jennifer," she said aloud wearily, "make up your mind, would you, please?"

What she had to do was deliver, like a mantra,

the same speech to herself that she would give to Joey: Jack was here temporarily. Jack would leave. She would never see Jack MacAllister again.

And while he was in Prescott, she was going to grab a handful of life and live it to the maximum, rejoice in her womanliness, tuck each precious memory of what she shared with Jack safely away.

There, she thought dryly. She'd made up her mind. Again. Until when? The next time she was alone too long, the house was too quiet, the nagging voices in her mind spoke more loudly than her present resolve?

Oh, yes, she was definitely driving herself crazy.

As Joey and Jack started toward the porch, Jennifer went to the front door and opened it.

"Hi, Mom," Joey said, running into the house. "We got great stuff. Guess what? Jack bought me my very own hammer, 'cause I'm going to be his helper."

"Wow," Jennifer said, smiling at her excited son. "Your very own hammer. That's very special."

Jack entered the house, and Jennifer closed the door behind him. She gave him a quick smile, then redirected her attention to a chattering Joey, who was telling her in great detail about everything he and Jack had purchased.

Jack unbuttoned his jacket while his gaze was riveted on Jennifer. Beautiful, he thought. The burnt-orange dress she was wearing was a perfect color for her, and the simple style accentuated the womanly curves of her figure.

And her face as she listened to Joey! So open, so honest, so radiant with pure, motherly love.

How could he have doubted the *realness* of this woman? How could he have relegated her to the dubious ranks of all the other women he'd known? How could he have done such a crummy thing?

This was Jennifer, for heaven's sake, who was like no woman he had ever met before. She didn't have a sneaky agenda regarding him, wasn't after his money, his social status. Hell, no, not Jennifer Mackane. Sure, he'd just met this woman, but he *knew* her, deep down in his bones, in his heart.

"Well, I see you're ready for work," he said. "I'll take off and be back in the morning to get started on this place."

"I'll stay home from school so I can help you, Jack," Joey said.

Jennifer laughed. "Nice try, mister. You'll go to school in the morning, as usual."

"There's plenty to do around here, Joey," Jack said. "You'll get to use your new hammer as much as you want to, no doubt about it."

"'Kay." Joey sighed. "I guess."

Jennifer shifted her gaze to Jack. "Are you planning on having dinner at Hamilton House this evening?" she asked.

"No, Andrea wants Mexican food, says she's craving hot sauce, or whatever."

"Oh." For Pete's sake, she admonished herself. She'd felt it, the wave of disappointment that she wouldn't see Jack during the hours she'd be on duty in the dining room at the hotel. What a ridiculous, adolescent reaction.

"There are some great Mexican restaurants in town," she said. "I'm sure you'll have a delicious meal." She paused. "Well, see you in the morning."

"Right." Jack didn't move.

"Goodbye," Jennifer said.

"Right." He still didn't move.

"Jack?" she said.

"Oh! Yeah, right. Have a nice evening. See ya tomorrow, Joey."

"'Bye, Jack," Joey said.

Jack left the house and strode down the walk to his vehicle, parked at the curb. He got in and drove away, forcing himself not to look back at the house before it disappeared from his view.

He hadn't wanted to leave, he thought incredulously. It was as though his feet had suddenly become cemented to Jennifer's living room floor, making it impossible for him to walk out the door.

He didn't want to have dinner with Brandon and Andrea; he wanted to spend the evening at Jennifer's with her and Joey. They'd eat, clean the kitchen, play a board game or something, with Joey in front of a warm, welcoming fire in the hearth, then...

Ah, yes, then Joey would be put to bed and the remaining hours of the night would belong to Jack and Jennifer. He'd gather her into his arms and kiss her until they couldn't breathe. He'd see her incredible green eyes take on a smoky hue as her desire for him grew, along with his for her. Then they'd...

"Shut up, MacAllister," he said gruffly. "Just shut the hell up." He paused. "And remember that you're not allowed to say 'hell' in Jennifer's house."

What a stupid scenario he'd just whipped up. Jennifer was on her way to work at Hamilton House. If he'd hung around, he would have ended up spending the hours with Joey, and watching Grandma Clark knit, or crochet or whatever, until she toted the kid to her house to put him to bed.

Man, he was losing it.

The MacAllister clan was in for a big surprise. When he arrived in California for the family reunion, they'd all discover that poor Jack was totally bonkers. They'd ship him off to the funny farm, never to be heard from again.

"That's where I'm headed, all right," he said, smacking the steering wheel with the heel of one hand. "Right over the edge of sanity."

Jennifer smiled as she waved good-night to the clerk behind the reservation desk, then slowed her step as she crossed the lobby of the hotel. She made a production out of buttoning her coat as she went, enabling her to slide glances at the high-back chairs to see if Jack was going to materialize and offer to walk her home.

As she fiddled with the last button, she finally accepted that he was nowhere to be seen. With a sigh, she left the hotel, admitting reluctantly the emotional letdown she was registering over Jack's absence.

She'd been disappointed when she learned Jack wouldn't be eating dinner in the dining room that evening. Now she was rapidly getting a full-blown case of the blues because he hadn't stayed up late to escort her home.

She was sinking below adolescent behavior. At

the rate she was going, she would end up pitching a screaming fit like Joey did on occasion when things didn't go the way he'd decided they should.

"Oh, me. Oh, my," she said aloud as she trudged along the sidewalk. Her life was suddenly so confusing and complicated. She had established a routine for her and Joey, an existence that varied little from one day to the next.

Week after week.

Month after month.

Year after year.

It was calm, predictable and…boring? Blah?

Lonely?

Well, she certainly hadn't thought so…until now. Until Jack.

But her mental condition was not entirely Jack's fault. No, the majority of her unrest was due to her own indecisiveness.

She'd decide that she was going to go for the sexual gusto with Jack while he was in town, then— *blam*—she'd get cold feet and vow not to see him again other than in a platonic relationship.

Jennifer continued to walk, her mind racing.

It was time to take a stand, to make a choice, then stick to it, before she worked herself into a complete nervous breakdown.

"Yes," she said decisively, then frowned. The problem was that she had no idea if she was going to take her firm stand on Plan A or Plan B. Darn, her mind was still running in circles as though she were a close relative of the gerbil in Joey's classroom, racing around in its never-ending exercise wheel.

"Get a grip, Jennifer," she muttered. "Get a brain. Get a life."

Ah, there was the key word. *Life*. Her life. The one she was suddenly questioning.

The mother part of her was filled to overflowing with her beloved Joey. He was her sunshine boy, who continually gave her so much, made her so complete and happy in her maternal role simply by being.

But the woman?

The woman wanted Jack.

With earthy, real, burning desire, she wanted to make love with Jack MacAllister, mesh her body with his, be filled with him, giving, receiving, becoming one entity as they savored the ecstasy of their intimate union.

Oh, yes, yes, yes, she wanted—

"Hello, Jennifer."

She gasped as she came to a sudden teetering halt in front of the steps to the porch of her house, having walked there by rote, not even realizing that she'd arrived home.

Jack rose in the shadows beyond the dim light cast by the lamppost at the curb. He had been sitting on the steps and now stood, tall and magnificent.

Jennifer spoke his name, vaguely aware that it would sound like a greeting, but knowing it was actually the conclusion of her sensuous thought.

"Jack."

"I'm sorry if I startled you," he said quietly.

"What are you doing here?"

"I need to talk to you," he said, his expression unreadable in the nearly total darkness. "I didn't want to insult your intelligence again by hanging around the hotel and offering to escort you safely home, so I waited for you here.''

''Oh. What—what did you wish to speak to me about?'' Jennifer said.

''Could we go inside?''

''Yes. Yes, of course.''

Jennifer retrieved her key from her purse and hurried past Jack, not looking at him.

She was flustered, she knew, and admonished herself for her ridiculous thought that she'd somehow conjured Jack up by having admitted how much, how very much, she wanted to make love with him.

She managed to draw what she hoped was an unnoticed steadying breath as she unlocked the door and entered the house with Jack right behind her.

Jack moved around her, and as she closed the door and turned to face him, he stepped in front of her, trapping her against the door, his hands on either side of her head. Jennifer's eyes widened in surprise, and the key and her purse dropped unheeded to the floor.

The glowing embers of a waning fire in the hearth cast a soft, golden glow over the room. Jack looked directly into Jennifer's eyes, and her breath caught as she stared into the depths of his eyes, those incredible chocolate fudge sauce eyes.

''We have to talk,'' he said, his voice low, ''because if I don't straighten out this mess called my mind, I'm going to lose what's left of my sanity.''

''I—''

''Hear me out,'' he said gruffly. ''Please.''

Jennifer nodded.

"You can't deny—or, at least, I hope you won't—that something is happening between us. One minute, I'm determined to discover what it is. The next, I have doubts about that being a smart thing to do. I bring my past into the present and decide to put a lot of distance between us before...but then I see you and I can't bring myself to do that. See? I'm going nuts."

"So am I," Jennifer said softly.

"What?"

"I want to run as far away from you as possible, Jack. I want to run into your arms. You terrify me because you're awakening a part of me that I vowed would stay asleep forever. Yet you excite me because you make me feel so vitally alive and womanly... I'm going crazy, too, and I can't go on like this. I just can't."

"I'll be damned."

"You can't swear in this house," Jennifer said, trying to produce a smile that failed to materialize.

"Sorry. Then we agree that we need to agree? What I mean is, we have to reach a decision about this situation that is acceptable to both of us?"

"Yes," she said. "Could we sit down?"

"In a minute. I'm thinking."

"I need to think, too, but I can't do that when you're so...so close to me because... Well, I just can't. This isn't fair, Jack. This conversation calls for clear and level heads."

"Yeah, okay."

Jack brushed his lips over Jennifer's, then stepped back to allow her to move away from the door.

Jennifer retrieved her keys and purse from the

floor, removed her coat and set everything on the back of the sofa. She waited until Jack had chosen to sit in one of the chairs by the hearth, then sat opposite him in another, the fireplace separating them.

"I should turn on a lamp," she said, starting to rise again.

"No, don't," Jack said. "I'll put another log on the fire."

The fresh log Jack put in place crackled, then caught fire. Both Jennifer and Jack stared into the hypnotizing flames, each lost in jumbled thoughts.

Jennifer shifted her eyes to sweep her gaze over the room, realizing that because of the brighter light in the hearth, the space beyond where she and Jack sat was now completely dark.

It was as though it wasn't there, she thought. All that existed was the glowing circle encasing the two of them in a golden hue. There was nothing beyond this space. Nothing. And for some unknown reason, there was a rightness about that—a peaceful sense of how it should be.

"Jennifer," Jack said, drawing her from her reverie. He leaned forward, resting his elbows on his knees and linking his fingers. "We agree that something is happening between us that is far from ordinary. We also agree that not knowing what to do about it is driving us both nuts."

"Yes," she said softly.

"Neither of us is interested in a serious, long-term relationship," Jack went on. "I'll be leaving Prescott in a month or so, and starting a new life in

California. We have a set length of time to be together, if we choose to be.''

''I'm aware of that.''

''Since we know all of this is temporary, there's no way either of us can be hurt if we…well, I don't mean to sound tacky…but if we go for it.''

''I understand what you're saying.''

''Good. I'm not forgetting about Joey, either,'' Jack said. ''We'd be sure to remind him that I'm leaving before Christmas. We'll listen carefully to what he says, be certain that he isn't fantasizing about me being the groom guy or the daddy bear.''

''I'm glad you realize that Joey is an intricate part of this—this decision,'' Jennifer said, smiling slightly. ''That means a great deal to me.''

''Hey, he's a terrific kid. I wouldn't want to do anything to upset him. Not ever.''

''Thank you, Jack.''

''Which brings us back to square one—the two of us.'' Jack sank back in the chair and dragged a hand through his hair. ''I'm so afraid that I'll present this in such a way that it will come across as sordid to you, when I know it wouldn't be. It truly wouldn't.''

He stared up at the ceiling for a long moment, then met Jennifer's gaze again. ''Okay, here goes,'' he said, then drew a steadying breath. ''Jennifer, I want you. I want to make love with you. Holding you, kissing you, is heaven itself, but I want more. I ache for you, Jennifer.''

''I—''

''It's not lust, it's desire,'' Jack rushed on. ''Plus, I enjoy being with you. You're complicated as hell—oh, sorry—as heck, but you're fascinating, too, and fun, upbeat, and, heaven knows, you're beautiful.''

He smiled. ''Actually, it was your Big Bird slippers that tipped me over the edge.'' His smile faded. ''Am I making sense?''

''I—''

''During the weeks I have left here in Prescott, we could share so much,'' he said, as though she hadn't spoken. ''All kinds of things. And during those weeks we'd be lovers, too. Then, when it's time for me to go, we'll each have memories. We won't be emotionally hurt by this, because we're being up front and honest about how things stand.''

''I—''

''There you have it. I desire you more than any woman I've ever met. I've presented my case.'' Jack frowned. ''I sure wish you'd talk to me, for crying out loud.''

Get a life, Jennifer told herself. Feel beautiful, special, cherished and desired.

Awaken your essence for a few weeks, then put it back to sleep gently when time runs out.

No tears. No heartache. No pain.

Just lovely memories to relive in quiet moments when she was once again alone.

''Jennifer?'' Jack said. ''Say something. Please.''

And so, she did.

With a soft smile on her lips and an inner sense of being incredibly and wondrously alive, Jennifer spoke.

She said one word that she knew would change

everything. She would never be quite the same again.

She said it with conviction, while trepidation hovered around the edges of her resolve.

She said it with courage that held a hint of fear.

She gazed directly into Jack MacAllister's mesmerizing eyes and said, "Yes."

Chapter Eight

Relief, joy, excitement and desire tumbled through Jack with such force that he was unable to sit still for one second longer.

He got to his feet at the same moment that Jennifer did, and they each moved forward to meet in front of the blazing fire.

Jack framed Jennifer's face in his hands and studied her intently. "Are you sure about this?" he said. "It's so very important that you're absolutely certain this is right for you."

"Oh, heavens," she said, smiling. "Reaching this decision was difficult enough without reexamining it under an emotional microscope."

"But—"

"Shh. No, don't." Jennifer's smile disappeared. "Jack, these weeks together will be like a gift I'm giving to myself, maybe selfishly so, but I intend to have this time with you. When it's over, when you leave, I'll be fine because I know this is temporary. It's perfect, really, because I'm not willing to commit myself to a permanent relationship.''

''I couldn't have said it better myself,'' Jack said. ''We're in complete agreement.''

Jennifer nodded.

''Good,'' he said, lowering his head toward hers. ''That's good.''

Jack captured Jennifer's mouth in a searing kiss, parting her lips and finding her tongue with his own. He dropped his hands from her face to encircle her body with his arms, and she melted into his embrace, wrapping her arms around his neck.

He raised his head a fraction of an inch to draw a quick breath, then slanted his mouth in the opposite direction as he claimed her lips once again.

The heat of desire burned within them. They were on fire, the want and need of each other consuming them.

They didn't think, didn't *need* to think, about the decision they'd made—not anymore. The turmoil of confusion was gone. They were free to just feel, savor, anticipate what was yet to come.

Jack broke the kiss, then murmured close to Jennifer's lips. ''I want you, Jennifer, so damn much.''

''Yes,'' she whispered. ''I want you, too, Jack.''

''Make love with me…here…by the fire.''

''Yes.''

They stepped back to allow room to shed their clothes, hurrying, the distance between them too great. Then they were naked, each standing still, allowing the other to visually trace every inch of what was within their view, what would be theirs.

"You're so lovely," Jack said, his voice raspy, "so beautiful."

"You're magnificent," Jennifer said.

Jack shook his head slightly to clear the sensual mist consuming his mind. "Wait," he said. "I want to protect you."

He fumbled with his jeans that lay on the floor and found his wallet, aware that his hands were trembling as he retrieved the foil packet. He returned as quickly as possible to Jennifer and drew her into his arms, kissing her deeply.

They sank onto the carpet in front of the crackling fire, stretching out next to each other. For a long, heart-stopping moment, they gazed into each other's eyes.

Then Jack lowered his head to claim Jennifer's mouth as he splayed one hand on her stomach, his weight supported on his other forearm.

He moved from her lips to one of her breasts, drawing the soft flesh into his mouth, laving the nipple with his tongue. Jennifer closed her eyes with a sigh of pure pleasure as sensuous sensations swept through her.

They kissed, caressed, explored, discovered the mysteries of each other, rejoiced in what was revealed to them. Lips followed where hands had traveled…and passions soared.

They were in a world that was only as big as the golden circle of light from the fire; a private world—their world—where no one else was granted entry.

It was ecstasy far beyond what either had ever known before.

"Jack, please," Jennifer said finally. "I need...please."

"Yes."

He moved over her and into her, slowly, watching her face for any hint of pain, knowing instinctively that it had been many years since her body had been filled with the very essence of a man.

Jennifer smiled. It was a soft, gentle, womanly smile...and Jack was lost. He thrust into her, bringing to her all that he was, and she received him in the moist heat of her femininity.

He began the rocking rhythm, and she matched him beat for beat in perfect unison. He increased the tempo, harder, faster, thundering, as they climbed higher and higher, reaching...reaching...

"Jack!" Jennifer said as she was flung into glorious oblivion.

He joined her there a second later, a groan rumbling deep in his chest.

They hovered, then floated back slowly. Jack kissed her, then moved off her, tucking her close to his side as he collapsed next to her, spent, sated.

"Oh, my," Jennifer whispered.

"Oh, yeah," Jack said.

"I've never felt so... There aren't words to describe how..." Jennifer smiled. "I think I'll just shut up."

Jack chuckled. "Okay." He paused and frowned. "I didn't hurt you, did I? It's been a long time since you've— What I mean is..."

Jennifer smiled at him. "I think *you* should just shut up."

"Good idea."

"Mmm," she said, her lashes drifting down.

"Don't go to sleep," Jack said, then yawned. "It wouldn't be too great if Joey came bouncing in the door in the morning and found us here."

Jennifer's eyes flew open again. "Don't even think such a thing. Jack, we must be very careful around Joey. He mustn't even see us kissing."

"No joke," he said, chuckling. "He'd tell the world that he saw us making a baby. Hey, you kiss, you get yourself a kid."

"Yep, that's how it's done," Jennifer said, laughing. She sobered in the next moment. "Joey is so innocent. I'd give anything to protect him from the world as it really is." She paused. "I suppose every mother feels that way."

"Some more than others." Jack rolled to his side, supporting his weight on his forearm so he could look directly at Jennifer. "It would depend on the mother's past experiences—if she'd been badly hurt, or had just sailed through life without having endured any emotional bumps and bruises."

"Mmm," Jennifer said, frowning.

"If the mother—that woman—" Jack went on, "was bitter, no longer trusted easily, she'd have to be careful that she didn't...I don't know... brainwash her child, make him wary of reaching out to people."

"I would never do that to Joey, even though—Never mind. It's getting awfully late, Jack.

I hate to end this wonderful night, but I have to get some sleep so I can function tomorrow.''

"Back up a minute," he said. "What were you going to say?"

"Nothing."

Jennifer moved away from Jack, then got to her feet and began to gather her strewn clothes.

What was she hiding? Jack thought, watching her. He'd bet a buck it had something to do with Joe Mackane. Would Jennifer ever trust Jack enough to share her past with him?

Whether she did or not shouldn't matter, considering the temporary status of their relationship. They were living for the moment, with no plans for a future together. Their pasts held no importance in the overall scheme of things.

No, it shouldn't matter how deeply Jennifer's trust of him went. But it did. She'd given him the gift of her body, shared the most intimate act there was between a man and a woman. Why couldn't she trust him with her innermost secrets, as well?

"Jack?" Jennifer said, her clothes bundled up in her arms.

"What? Oh. Yeah, I'm getting it in gear."

He rolled to his feet and dressed quickly, shrugging into his jacket as he stood by the front door.

"I'll see you later," he said. "I won't come back until I know that Joey's in school so there won't be a hassle about him wanting to stay home and help me with the repairs with his mighty hammer."

Jennifer nodded. "Fine."

Jack slid one hand to the nape of Jennifer's neck and kissed her. "Thank you, Jennifer. I mean that sincerely—thank you,'' he said quietly, then turned and left the house, closing the door behind him with a soft *click*.

''And *I* thank *you*,'' Jennifer whispered, staring at the door, ''for making me feel so special, so womanly, so incredibly alive.''

With a wistful sigh and a gentle smile on her lips, Jennifer headed for bed.

The next morning, Jack slid onto a chair at a table in the dining room at Hamilton House. He smiled and greeted Andrea and Brandon, Aunt Charity and Aunt Prudence.

''I'm running a little late,'' he said. ''I slept longer than usual.''

''It's probably because of the altitude here in Prescott,'' Andrea said. ''Being a mile high makes many people tired until they adjust to it.''

''Yep, that's it, I imagine,'' Jack said, picking up the menu that had been left for him by the waitress. ''The altitude.''

''So?'' Brandon said. ''Report, Jack. Do you have any information to share with us about Jennifer?''

''Yeah, big boy,'' Aunt Charity said. ''What have you learned? Andrea and Brandon filled Pru and me in on your theory that Jennifer was unhappy with Joe Mackane. We all assumed the opposite because she named Joey after his father. We figured Jennifer refused to even date because she was holding fast to memories of sweet bliss with her husband.''

''Which is fine to a point,'' Prudence said, ''but there comes a time when a person should move forward with their life… It was distressing enough to us that Jennifer seemed to be living in the past when that past had been, to her, near perfection. To think it might have been just the opposite is heartbreaking. If that's true, we must help her free herself of those memories of misery.''

''I think I'll have pancakes,'' Jack said, signaling to the waitress.

Brandon drummed his fingers impatiently on the tablecloth as Jack placed his order, then sipped the hot coffee the waitress had poured into his cup. ''Come on, MacAllister,'' Brandon said. ''What, if anything, do you have to tell us?''

Jack frowned as he stared into the coffee cup. Damn, he thought, he was suddenly very uncomfortable with the idea of *reporting* on whatever subtle little clues he'd picked up regarding Jennifer's marriage to Mackane.

He now knew Jennifer did not believe that Joe Mackane would have been a devoted and loving father to Joey. He didn't know why she felt that way, only that she did.

He could make this group's day—this committee-to-save-Jennifer-from-herself—by passing along that tidbit. But he was registering a sense of protectiveness and possessiveness about Jennifer, about the special world the two of them created when they were together, a place where no one else was allowed to enter.

Was he being totally selfish? A really rotten guy? If what he divulged to Andrea, Brandon and the aunts made it possible for them to help Jennifer, she could very well embrace the thought of a future with a special man—a husband for her, a father for Joey.

Damn, he hated the idea of some other guy touching Jennifer, holding and kissing her, making love to her in the secret, dark hours of the night. Really, *really* hated that thought.

Ah, hell, he was boggling his mind again. Why was he doing this to himself? He and Jennifer had reached an understanding about the temporary, no-strings-attached status of their relationship. They'd discussed it like mature adults and reached ground rules that were acceptable to both of them.

He should be kicking back and enjoying the time he had left with Jennifer while he was in Prescott. But, oh, no, not him. Now he was *thinking* again, and turning his beleaguered mind into scrambled eggs.

"Pancakes," the waitress said.

Jack jerked in his chair as he was brought back to attention, then moved his coffee cup out of the way so a huge plate could be placed in front of him. He had, he realized, staring at the tower of pancakes, lost his appetite.

"All set?" the waitress said.

"Yes. Fine," Jack said. "Thank you."

"Are you back with us now, buddy?" Brandon said. "You were so deep in thought, I swear they could have dropped a bomb in here, and you wouldn't have noticed."

"Yeah, well…" Jack's voice trailed off, and he busied himself buttering the pancakes and dribbling syrup over them from a small china pitcher.

"There he goes again," Brandon said, throwing up his hands. "Zoned."

Andrea nibbled absently on a piece of toast as she

studied Jack. "There's something troubling you, isn't there, Jack," she said finally.

Jack took a bite of pancakes, chewed, swallowed, then sighed. "Look," he said, sweeping his gaze over everyone at the table. "How would you feel if a group of people were discussing you in a very personal manner behind your back? People you believed were your friends and cared about you very deeply. It's pretty tacky, you know what I mean?"

"But we're doing this because we *do* care about Jennifer," Brandon said. "Hey, you were the one who brought up the possibility that Jennifer had a lousy marriage. This was your plan, MacAllister. Now you're on our case because we agree that we should pursue it because Jennifer is part of our family and we love her. What's with you?"

"Honey, calm down," Andrea said to Brandon. "Jack is obviously having second thoughts about reporting what he may have discovered about Jennifer's past. We have to respect that."

"No, we don't," Brandon said. "How are we going to help Jennifer if we don't know if she needs us to help her?" He frowned. "Did that make sense?"

Aunt Charity narrowed her eyes as she stared at Jack. "Something's cooking in the kitchen. Okay, big boy, what's going on?"

Jack pushed his plate away, unable to take another bite of the sweet, gooey breakfast.

"Nothing is 'going on,' Aunt Charity," he said. "I just… Ah, hell, forget it. Can we just cancel this whole plan? Forget I ever brought up the subject of Jennifer's past, her marriage to Mackane?"

"No," Brandon and Aunt Charity said in unison.

"I'm a tad confused, Jack dear," Aunt Prudence said. "Our hearts are in the right place on this matter, as I believe you know. Don't you feel that Jennifer is worth whatever efforts we might make on her behalf?"

"Is Jennifer worth—" Jack began. "Aunt Prudence, Jennifer is one in a million—a very rare, special and wonderful woman. She's real, honest, open and is a terrific mother to a fantastic little boy who…" He glanced at Andrea, who was smiling at him. "What's *your* problem?" he said gruffly.

"*I* don't have one," Andrea said. "*I'm* not the person at this table who is acting like a protective knight of the Round Table, or whatever, in regard to Jennifer. Nope, not me."

"Give it a rest," Jack said gruffly. "I just don't think it's appropriate to analyze every little thing a person does or says, when they have no clue you're doing it."

"It's based on love, dear," Aunt Prudence said.

Jack stared up at the ceiling for what felt like a long moment, then shook his head as he looked at the group again. "Okay," he said wearily. "I'm outnumbered. I give up. Jennifer let it slip that she didn't believe Joe Mackane would have been a loving and devoted father to Joey."

"Oh, my stars," Aunt Prudence said. "How very distressing."

"A dud as a daddy, huh?" Aunt Charity said. "What about as a husband? Get a scoop on that?"

"No," Jack said, getting to his feet. He dug into

the pocket of his jeans, then dropped several bills onto the table. "I have things to do. See ya."

He turned and strode across the dining room.

Jack walked along the sidewalk, mentally grumbling as he headed for Jennifer's house. He shouldn't have told Andrea, Brandon and the aunts what Jennifer had said about Mackane not being good father material for Joey, he admonished himself. That was Jennifer's private business, and not for public knowledge.

Then again, the public, in the form of the four people at the table at Hamilton House, weren't nosy nobodies. They loved Jennifer, wanted only the best for her.

If Jennifer had, indeed, had a miserable marriage with Joe Mackane, it would be those same four caring people who just might be able to help her let go of the painful memories and move forward.

Who was *he* to be spilling the beans regarding Jennifer and Joe? *Jennifer and Joe.* Erase that. He didn't like the sound of their names as a couple echoing in his mind. *Jennifer and Joe. Joe and Jennifer.* No. No way.

Forget it. ·

It was supposed to be Jennifer and *Jack.*

Jack nearly stumbled at the impact of his last rambling thought. Where in the hell had that come from? The way it had flowed in his head made it seem as though *Jack* was next in line for being the groom guy, the daddy bear.

Not a chance.

Slow down, MacAllister, he ordered himself. He

was being too hard on himself. Of course he'd think in terms of Jennifer and Jack because, for now, they were together, and would be until he left Prescott to begin his new life in California.

So there was nothing wrong with mentally linking his name with Jennifer's for the time being. They were, after all, engaged in an affair.

Jack frowned and shoved his hands into his jacket pockets as he trudged on. *Affair,* his mind echoed. That was a rather pitiful word to describe what he was sharing with Jennifer. Affairs were centered on sex, on physical gratification, with no emotional involvement.

No, he wasn't having an *affair* with Jennifer Mackane. It was more than that—richer, deeper, meaningful. They hadn't engaged in sex, they'd made love.

And there *were* emotions involved. He cared for Jennifer, respected her. It mattered—hell, yes, it mattered—that he never did anything to hurt Jennifer, never made her cry.

Fine. That was fine. There were no dangerous emotions lurking in the shadows, threatening to sneak up on him, to cause him to wake up one morning and discover that he'd committed the ultimate act of stupidity and fallen head-over-heels in love with Jennifer.

Nope. Couldn't happen. He and Jennifer knew where they stood in regard to their…their relationship. Everything was under control.

Jennifer's house came into view, and Jack quickened his step, aware of a sense of anticipation over seeing Jennifer, kissing her, hearing her laughter.

As for the I Spy number he was engaged in for Andrea, Brandon and the aunts…well, he'd figure that out later, decide what was the right thing to do.

Yeah, he'd tackle that problem later, because right now he was within minutes of holding Jennifer Mackane in his arms.

Chapter Nine

On Saturday morning, Jennifer lay in bed blissfully indulging herself by reliving the events that had taken place since she and Jack had first made love on Tuesday night.

So-o-o wonderful, she thought dreamily. The lovemaking she and Jack had shared every night since then had been incredibly beautiful, like nothing she'd experienced before or even imagined possible in her most fantasy-filled daydreams.

But that intimacy was only a part of what had made these days and nights so special, so meaningful. She'd been warmed to the very tips of her toes as she'd watched Joey and Jack working together on the repairs of the house.

Jack was so patient with Joey—answered her son's endless questions, allowed Joey to take an ac-

tive part in the project, which undoubtedly was
slowing Jack down.

There was lunch together, too, the three of them
sitting at the kitchen table, chatting and laughing as
they consumed the meal she had prepared.

Joey now wanted his sandwich cut just like
Jack's, the same number of ice cubes in his glass as
Jack had in his, and carefully spread his napkin over
one knee precisely the way Jack did.

Joey hung on Jack's every word, had reversed his
recent stand that bubbles in his bath were for babies
when Jack declared bubble baths to be a majorly fun
event.

Jennifer frowned and shifted restlessly on the bed.

Was Joey becoming too attached to Jack? Was
her little boy headed for heartbreak whenever Jack
left, even though he was reminded, when the opportunity presented itself, that Jack was leaving for
California before Christmas?

Was Joey listening to what was said to him, but
refusing to really *hear* that Jack would be walking
out of their lives forever in just a few weeks?

Forever, Jennifer's mind echoed. Jack would be
gone...forever.

A chill swept through her and she pulled the blankets to beneath her chin.

Jennifer, don't, she ordered herself. She knew
Jack was leaving, knew that what they were now
sharing was temporary. She *knew* that.

Jack's definite departure was, in fact, the reason
she'd had enough courage to enter into a relationship with him in the first place. There was no danger
of Jack asking more of her than she was prepared

to give, because he wouldn't be there to pressure her.

She knew all that.

Then why did the image of Jack saying goodbye for the last time cause such a cold emptiness to suddenly consume her? The future—the days, weeks, months, years—loomed before her with such a bleak sameness, as if something of vital importance was definitely missing.

Oh, dear heaven, what was happening to her? Was she, not Joey, the one whose heart would be shattered when Jack said his final farewell?

"No, no, no," she said, flinging back the blankets and sitting up on the edge of the bed. "Don't be ridiculous. I'm fine. In control. Know the facts. I'm hunky-dory. A-okay."

"Who are you talking to, Mom?" Joey said, coming into the bedroom.

Jennifer shoved her feet into her slippers. "Big Bird. I talk to my slippers when you're not around to listen to me. Big Bird is a great audience." She smiled at her son. "How's my big boy this morning? Ready for some breakfast, my sweet?"

Joey crawled up onto the bed and lay down. "I'm not hungry," he said. "My stomach hurts on my belly button."

Jennifer frowned and turned to place her hand on Joey's forehead. "You're a little warm," she said. "Why don't you snuggle in there and see if you can go back to sleep for a bit? I'll bring you some juice, then you try to snore. Okay?"

"No, Mom, I want to help Jack when he comes," Joey whined.

"Jack won't be here for a while. It's very early, you know. I imagine he's still snoozing away in his bed in Uncle Brandon's hotel. You have plenty of time to get some more rest."

"But I'm his partner, Mom," Joey said, his eyes filling with tears. "We do men stuff together fixing up the house. What if I'm asleep when he comes? Jack needs me to hand him nails and everything. He really does. I want to be with Jack, Mommy."

"Shh, sweetie, don't get upset," Jennifer said, tucking the blankets around him. "I'll wake you up when Jack arrives."

"Promise?" Joey said, then sniffled.

"I promise."

"'Kay."

"Stay awake long enough to drink some juice, and I need to take your temperature, too. I'll be right back."

"'Kay."

An hour later, Jennifer was dressed in jeans and a white fisherman's-knit sweater. She sat on the edge of her bed, watching Joey sleep. His cheeks were flushed and his slumber was restless.

Should she call Ben? she wondered. Joey's Uncle Ben Rizzoli was Joey's doctor, and she knew he wouldn't mind if she disturbed him at home on a Saturday morning.

Well, maybe Ben wouldn't welcome the intrusion of a ringing telephone, considering that he and Megan were on their honeymoon, for all practical purposes.

The couple was planning on an official wedding

trip in the spring, but they *were* newly married and— No, she'd see how Joey was feeling when he woke up, and bother Ben only if it was absolutely necessary.

Jennifer smoothed the blankets over Joey, brushed his moist hair from his forehead, then after one last lingering look at him, wandered out of the bedroom and down the hallway.

In the living room she opened the drapes on the front windows. As she now did every morning when she performed the ritual, her gaze zeroed in immediately on the spot on the sidewalk where she had first seen Jack MacAllister staring at her house.

The remembrance of that morning always brought a sense of joy with it, along with a flash of embarrassment as she mentally relived her performance in the dining room at Hamilton House when Jack made his ''stalking'' appearance that evening.

''I'm Jack MacAllister. Not Jack the Ripper,'' she said in a deep voice, then laughed. ''Oh, I was such an idiot. What a show I put on.''

Her glance was drawn once again to the spot on the sidewalk where Jack had stood on that life-changing morning. Her smile faded as she stared at it, suddenly acutely aware that the space was empty. Jack wasn't there, and in a handful of weeks would never be there again.

Jack would be gone, taking with him the warmth of his smile, his compelling chocolate fudge sauce eyes, the rich timbre of his voice and chuckle, the strength and gentleness of his arms, his magnificent body that carried her away to glorious heights of ecstasy when they made love.

"He isn't mine to keep," Jennifer whispered. "Like Joey says, I have to give him back."

Jennifer lifted her chin and ignored the sting of tears in her eyes.

Fine. That was how it should be. If Jack had moved to Prescott, instead of just being a temporary visitor, she never would have engaged in any kind of relationship with him at all.

That would have been too risky, far too emotionally dangerous. She might very well have fallen in love with him over time, lost her heart to him, which was something she'd vowed she'd never *ever* do with any man again.

And Jack might have fallen in love with her, then pushed her to make a commitment to forever—even asked her to marry him, for heaven's sake. She would have been forced to break off her relationship with him, ending what they had in heartache and, possibly, anger.

Jennifer looked at the empty sidewalk and nodded.

So be it. This was how it should be—the only way it could be. Yes, she'd miss Jack for a while when he left, but that was to be expected. She'd have her lovely memories to hold her in good stead in the months and years ahead.

"Mommy!" Joey yelled, jerking Jennifer from her thoughts.

She turned and ran across the room and down the hall to her bedroom. "I'm here, sweetie," she said, coming to a teetering halt by her bed.

"My tummy is jiggly," Joey said.

"Oops." Jennifer scooped Joey into her arms.

"We know what that means. You're going to give back that juice you drank."

After Joey had redistributed the juice, Jennifer washed his face, then settled him once again in her bed. "Does your belly button still hurt?" she said, sitting down next to him.

"My whole stomach hurts really bad," Joey said, then burst into tears. "It hurts worse than anything in the whole wide world."

"Well, it's time for me to call Uncle Ben and ask him what we should do about that tummy, Joey."

"Tell Uncle Ben to fix it 'cause I gotta help Jack, Mommy."

"I will. I'll tell him." She kissed Joey on the forehead, then got to her feet. "I'll be back as soon as I've spoken with Uncle Ben."

"'Kay. Oh-h-h, it hurts," Joey said, thrashing on the bed.

A cold fist of fear tightened within Jennifer, and she turned and ran from the room. As she entered the living room, a knock sounded at the front door.

"Jack," she whispered, coming to a halt.

She hurried to the door and flung it open.

"Good morning, lovely lady," Jack said, smiling. "I'm reporting for duty to—"

Jennifer grabbed Jack's arm and dragged him into the house, slamming the door closed behind him. "Joey's sick," she said. "I have to call Ben."

"You're pale as a ghost," Jack said, frowning. "How sick is Joey?" He shrugged out of his jacket and tossed it onto the back of the sofa. "What's wrong with him?"

"He has a really terrible stomachache," she said,

her voice trembling. "I've never seen him in this kind of pain, Jack."

"Okay," Jack said. "Go call Ben. Where's Joey?"

"In my bed."

"I'll stay with him while you call. Go."

"Thank you. Thank you, Jack."

As Jack headed across the room, Jennifer went into the kitchen and looked at a sheet of paper tacked to the wall above the telephone. She lifted the receiver and punched in the number.

"Be there, Ben," she said as she heard the phone at the other end ringing. "Please be home."

"Hello?"

"Oh, Ben, thank goodness," Jennifer said, pressing one hand to her forehead. "This is Jennifer. Joey has a terrible pain in his stomach, and I—"

"Whoa," Ben said. "Slow down. Take a deep breath and get a grip. I need to ask you some questions."

"Yes. Okay. I'm calm."

"Good. Jennifer, did Joey say where the pain was in his stomach?"

"Where? Well, at first he said his belly button hurt, but now it's his whole stomach. He has a fever and he upchucked and—"

"Halt. This is important. Did Joey have the pain first, before he became nauseated?"

"Yes," Jennifer said, nodding.

"Oh, boy. It's textbook classic."

"Textbook classic what? What's wrong with him?"

"Didn't you have your appendix out when we

were kids? I seem to remember playing checkers
with you while you were recuperating.''

"Yes, I was ten.''

"Did Joey's father have his removed?''

"Oh, I don't know, Ben, I— No, wait, yes, he
did. He said that he was in high school and couldn't
play football for several weeks.''

"That cooks it,'' Ben said. "The genetic factor
plays a heavy role in appendicitis.''

"Dear heaven.''

"Look, I'll meet you in the emergency room at
the hospital, rather than at my office. That will save
a lot of time.''

"Are you going to operate on Joey? Take out his
appendix?'' Jennifer said, nearly shrieking. "He's
just a baby, Ben.''

"No, he's not. He's a strong, healthy boy who
has all the classic symptoms of a hot appendix. I'll
know for sure when I examine him. I'm not a surgeon, you know, Jennifer, but I'll be with him every
minute if it comes to that. Do not—do *not*—give
Joey any more to eat or drink. Got that?''

"Yes. I hear you.''

"Wrap Joey up and bring him in. I'll meet you
at the hospital. Drive carefully, Jennifer. Keep your
cool. I realize that you're facing this alone, but—''

"No, no, Jack is here.''

"Jack? Oh, Jack MacAllister? That friend of
Brandon's? I met him the other day. Nice guy. Well,
good, you're *not* alone. You and Jack can do this
together. See you in a few minutes. 'Bye.''

"'Bye.''

Jennifer hung up the receiver, drew a shuddering breath, then ran from the room.

Jennifer paced restlessly around the waiting room in the hospital, glancing often at her watch, then the clock on the wall.

Jack entered the small, nicely furnished area, carrying two foam cups.

"Coffee," he said. "Come and sit down, Jennifer, and drink this. Okay?"

"No, thank you, Jack. I'm stressed enough without getting the jitters from too much coffee." She shook her head. "I can't believe this is happening. Joey was fine yesterday, and now he's in surgery having his appendix removed. He was so frightened by the pain and by all that took place after we arrived here. I felt so helpless. I still do."

Jack set the cups on one of the tables, then closed the distance between them. He pulled her close, and she wrapped her arms around his waist as she laid her head on his chest.

"I'm not handling this very well," she said. "Joey has always been so healthy, has never had anything beyond an occasional cold or bout of the flu. And now? He's being operated on, for God's sake, and I'm falling apart."

"Hey," Jack said, rubbing her back gently, "don't be so hard on yourself. This is a scary deal. I would have done anything to stop the pain Joey was in as we drove over here. I felt powerless. It didn't matter how big and strong a man I might be— my size and strength were worthless."

"Then you *do* understand how I feel."

"Damn straight, I do," Jack said. "Joey and I are supposed to be pounding nails together right now, having a great old time. I hate what he's going through, Jennifer. I really hate it."

He paused. "But, hey, everything will be fine. Ben is a top-notch doctor, and he personally chose the surgeon for Joey. Everything is under control." He chuckled. "Except us. We're coming unglued."

"Ah, the joys of parenthood," Jennifer said, smiling. "You don't know what will happen from one minute to the next." She lifted her head to meet Jack's gaze. "You were wonderful with Joey during the drive over here. You were so calm, talked to him, got him to relax at least as much as he could, considering the pain he was in. I do believe that you're a natural-born father."

Alarm bells went off in Jack's head and he stiffened slightly as he looked at Jennifer. What was this? he thought. A little push, a hint at what might very well be Jennifer's hidden agenda?

Had she changed her previous mindset about never remarrying?

Was she zeroing in on him to be her next husband and a father for Joey?

Had she shifted gears on him, and he'd been too dumb to realize it?

Damn it, was Jennifer Mackane like all the other women he'd been involved with? Was she now hell-bent on getting what *she* wanted from him?

"Yeah, well," he said, no hint of a smile on his face. "I operate with kids under the same guidelines that Joey does with his uncles. I give them back."

"Mmm," Jennifer said, frowning. "Joey certainly isn't very happy with that premise these days.''

"Well, I'm very satisfied with mine regarding children. When I move to California, there will be MacAllister kids coming out of the woodwork. I'll borrow a few when the mood strikes, then return them when I've had enough and they're driving me nuts.''

''Has Joey been a pest while you've been working together on the house?''

''Hey, no way,'' Jack said. "Not for a second. I've enjoyed spending time with him.''

''Doing 'men' stuff,'' Jennifer said, smiling again.

''Yep. However, I must admit that the *man* stuff I do with you when we're alone is much more to my liking.''

''Hush,'' Jennifer said, feeling a flush of heat stain her cheeks. ''We're in a busy hospital, and someone might hear you.'' She sighed and eased out of Jack's arms. ''Back to reality. We're in a hospital and my son is being operated on. What's taking so long?''

Jennifer began to wander around the room again, her troubled gaze alternating among the clock on the wall, her watch and the doorway.

Jack slouched into a chair and studied her. He wished he could peer into Jennifer's brain, find out what she was really thinking. Man, he hated having these sudden doubts about Jennifer, hated even entertaining the idea that she might not be who she presented herself to be.

Maybe her words had just been an idle remark, a

compliment. She thought he was a natural-born father and had told him so. End of story. No big deal.

Or was it?

Jack took a deep breath and let it out slowly, puffing his cheeks. Enough of this. For now, he'd just concentrate on waiting for word of how Joey was. That was plenty on his plate at the moment.

Besides, he reasoned, so what if Jennifer had taken a fresh look at her future and decided that, yes, sir, Jack MacAllister would do a dandy job as a husband for her and a father for Joey? It didn't mean squat if she'd changed her views on the subject of commitment because in a few weeks he'd be long gone, anyway.

Ah, hell, who was he kidding? It *did* matter. He wanted, *needed* Jennifer to be as real and honest as he believed her to be.

Just once in his life, he would like to be able to savor memories of time shared with a woman, not look back with anger and self-disgust at his own gullibility.

No, it was even more than that. He wanted and needed to be able to cherish his memories of Jennifer Mackane.

"I should have asked Ben how long this would take," Jennifer said, interrupting Jack's racing thoughts. "Oh, darn, why didn't I? Maybe a nurse would know. Yes. I'll go ask a nurse."

"You're going to be very upset if you're not in this room when Ben comes," Jack said quietly.

Jennifer sighed and sat down on a sofa. "Yes, you're right."

"Always."

Jennifer laughed. "Is that a fact?"

"Guaranteed."

"Oh, Jack, thank you," she said, smiling at him warmly. "You've been fantastic through all of this. I'd be out of my mind if I was caged up in this room alone."

"You have a lot of friends in Prescott," he said. "You could have called someone to come over here and wait with you."

"I suppose. But I probably wouldn't have. I'm set on automatic independence." She paused. "When I was speaking with Ben on the telephone at the house, he said something to me that keeps popping into my head."

"Oh? What?"

"I told Ben that you were there with me, and he said it was good that I wasn't alone. 'You and Jack can do this together,' he said."

Jack straightened in the chair and narrowed his eyes as he looked at Jennifer. "What point are you trying to make here?" he said, a slight edge to his voice.

Jennifer shrugged. "Only that I might have fallen into a pattern of behavior of being *too* independent, of not allowing myself to ask for help, to lean a little, to seek comfort from time to time from those who care about me. I'll have to give that some very serious thought when things calm down again."

"You do that," Jack said, lunging to his feet and glaring down at her. "Who knows, Jennifer? You might decide to swoop up that bridal bouquet you caught and go find yourself a groom guy, a daddy bear. How does that strike you, Ms. Mackane?"

"For heaven's sake, Jack," she said, frowning in confusion. "Where did all that nonsense come from? And why do you seem so angry all of a sudden?"

"I…" Jack stopped speaking, closed his eyes for a moment, and shook his head before looking at Jennifer again. "I'm sorry. Forget I said that. This waiting is hard on the nerves, and I'm stressed. Just erase that last bit I barked at you. Okay? Can you do that?"

"I…I guess so," Jennifer said, getting to her feet. "But you made me sound like a woman on a husband hunt, or some such thing. My goodness, Jack, don't you know me better than that by now? How could you even imply that I— Oh!"

Jennifer gasped as Jack closed the short distance between then, gripped her upper arms…and kissed her.

But…she thought hazily. She needed to understand why Jack had said such nasty things to her with a strange and bitter edge to his voice that she'd never heard from him before. She…really needed…to understand because… Oh, never mind.

Don't think, Jennifer, Jack mentally pleaded. *Don't dwell on the rotten junk I said to you. Just feel. Just feel. Don't think.*

"I hate to interrupt, but…" Ben said with a chuckle as he entered the room.

Jennifer and Jack jumped apart, then spun around to face Ben.

"Joey?" Jennifer said, clasping her hands tightly beneath her chin.

Ben looked at Jennifer, then Jack, then back at

Jennifer, then chuckled again. "I'll be damned," he said, grinning.

"Ben!" Jennifer yelled. "Joey?"

"He's fine, fine, fine," Ben said. "Came through like a champ. His appendix definitely needed to get out of there, but we got it in plenty of time. We'll keep him here for two, maybe three, days, depending on how he does. He'll have to take it easy for a couple of weeks. I'd keep him home from kindergarten, if I were you, to be assured he doesn't run, jump—well, be an active little boy. Okay?"

"Yes, I understand. May I see him now, Ben?" Jennifer said.

"Mosey on over to the pediatric wing," Ben said. "Joey will be in his room in about half an hour."

Jennifer kissed Ben on the cheek, then Jack shook the doctor's hand. "Thank you," Jennifer and Jack said in unison.

"You're welcome. I'll see you later." Ben crossed the room and stopped at the doorway. "Go back to doing what you were when I interrupted. I'd write a prescription for that jazz if I could. It cures a lot of ills. 'Bye."

"'Bye," Jennifer said, then added to Jack, "So much for keeping our relationship a secret." She paused. "Well, so be it. The important thing is that Joey is all right. Let's go to the children's wing and wait for him in his room. Okay?"

"Absolutely," Jack said, pulling her close. "But first, I believe that people should always follow doctor's orders."

"Do tell," Jennifer said, smiling.

"I show much better than I tell," he said, lowering his head toward hers.

"Prove it."

"I will."

And he did.

Chapter Ten

Joey Mackane was *not* a happy patient.

He had a nagging headache from the anesthesia, his tummy hurt, he did not like the intravenous needle that had been inserted and taped into place on the back of his hand, nor the bars on the sides of his bed that made him feel, he whined, like a "dumb baby." The hospital smelled funny, and he wanted to go home. *Now*.

It was a very long, exhausting day.

Jennifer selected several books from the cart a candy striper produced, but Joey pouted and complained through the reading of each one that he'd heard that story before and it was dumb, dumb, dumb.

Jack went to the hospital gift shop and returned with a coloring book and crayons, but Joey rejected the offering, stating that his crayon box at home had a sharpener attached. Crayon boxes without sharpeners were really dumb.

In the early evening, the surgeon and Ben paid a visit and the I.V. was removed from Joey's hand.

After the doctors had gone, a nurse arrived with a dish of green Jell-O. She swung the table over in front of Joey and placed the dish and a spoon in front of him. "Enjoy," she said, smiling, then left the room.

"I hate dumb green Jell-O," Joey said, flinging one hand through the air. The dish went flying, splashing green jelly over the blanket on the bed.

"Oh, Joey," Jennifer said, getting to her feet from the chair next to the bed. "That wasn't a nice thing to do. We'll have to get a different blanket now and— Please, sweetheart, calm down. Okay?"

"No, no, no," Joey yelled. "I hate this place. I hate green Jell-O. I hate you, too, Mom, 'cause you won't take me home right now. I hate you. I hate you."

It was too much, it really was. The worry, the stress, the seemingly endless hours attempting to make Joey happy caught up with Jennifer in an emotional rush. She spun around as tears filled her eyes, and pressed trembling fingertips to her lips.

"That's it," Jack said. He rose from the chair he'd been slouched in across the room and strode to the bed, moving past Jennifer to bend over and look directly into Joey's eyes.

"Listen up, my friend," he said sternly. "I've sat in this room all day while you've whined and fussed, and I've had enough. I know what you've been through isn't fun, but you're going to be fine. There are kids in this hospital who are very, very sick, Joey, but you aren't one of them. You'll be as good as new in time to celebrate Thanksgiving.

"I thought you were my pal, my partner," he continued. "What happened to the big boy who has been helping repair things at the house all week? All I can see is a kid who is whining like a baby."

Jennifer turned around. "Jack, don't. Joey is—"

"Joey is going to shape up right now," Jack went on, still looking at the little boy. "Aren't you, sport? You're also going to apologize to your mother for saying that you hate her. Are you my buddy, or not?" He extended his hand toward Joey. "Make up your mind."

Joey looked at Jack's hand, at his face, then back at his hand. He lifted his own little hand and placed it in Jack's big one. "I still want to be your buddy, Jack," Joey said quietly.

Jack wrapped his fingers around Joey's hand. "And?" Jack said. "What do you have to say to your mother?"

"I'm sorry, Mommy," Joey said. "I don't hate you. I love you more than the whole wide world. I hate green Jell-O, but that's okay, 'cause you didn't cook it for me. I won't act like a baby brat anymore. I promise."

"Oh, Joey," Jennifer said, sniffling. "I love you, too, so much. I know this has all been very frightening for you and—"

"Actually," Jack interrupted, releasing Joey's hand, "it's very cool, sport. You get to eat in bed and watch television, and you don't have to do your chores while you're here. I'm going to ship you out and crawl in that bed myself.''

Joey laughed. "You can't do that, Jack. This is *my* bed. Can I do the remote control for the TV?''

Jack picked up the remote from the side table and handed it to Joey. "Go for it," Jack said. "You can channel surf until they tell you it's time to go to sleep. I'm taking your mom home now because she's really tired."

"'Kay." Joey's attention was riveted on the television mounted on a platform high on the far wall. He whizzed through the channels. "Zoom. Zoom."

"Jack," Jennifer said, glaring at him, "I'm staying with Joey until he falls asleep."

"No, you are not," Jack said, folding his arms over his chest. "Have you looked in the mirror lately? You're pale, have dark smudges beneath your eyes and—Jennifer, you're dead on your feet. Kiss Joey good-night, then I'm taking you home."

Jennifer narrowed her eyes and planted her hands on her hips. "How dare you try to take control of my life, my decisions, my—my person, like some kind of dictator on a macho trip?" she said none too quietly. "You have no right to—"

"Mom," Joey said, "could you yell at Jack kinda quieter, please? I can't hear the TV."

"Yeah," Jack said, grinning at Jennifer. "Yell at me kinda quieter. You *are* in a hospital, you know. There are rules about quieter yelling."

"Oh, good grief," Jennifer said, dropping her face into her hands. "I don't believe this."

"Zoom. Zoom," Joey said, still zipping through the channels on the television.

Jack eased Jennifer's hands from her face with a gentle touch, and she lifted her head slowly to meet his gaze.

"I'm not attempting to control your life, Jennifer," he said quietly. "I'm taking a stand here because I care about you. I'm trying to do what's best for you as I see it."

He paused. "And for Joey, too. If someone didn't pull the plug on his behavior, he would have kept it up and been completely convinced that he was miserable. This isn't a macho trip, it's a caring trip. Okay?"

Fresh tears filled Jennifer's eyes and she sighed. "'Kay."

"Good," Jack said. "Kiss Joey good-night."

Jennifer did as instructed, then Jack and Joey exchanged a high five.

"I'll call Grandma and Grandpa in Phoenix," Jennifer said to her son, "and tell them what happened and what a brave, big boy you are."

"Don't tell them 'bout the baby bratty part," Joey said, frowning.

"No, I won't sweetheart. Good night."

"'Night, Mom. 'Night, Jack."

"See you tomorrow, buddy," Jack said.

"Zoom. Zoom," Joey said, his attention once again on the television.

In Jennifer's living room, Jack stood just inside the closed front door, but didn't remove his jacket when Jennifer tossed her coat over the back of the sofa.

"I take it that you're still mad as hell at me,"

Jack said. "You haven't said even one word since we left Joey's room."

Jennifer sank onto the sofa, leaned her head back and stared at the ceiling. "I don't know what I'm feeling," she said softly. "Mad as hell at you for taking control of the situation? Experiencing warm fuzzies for your caring enough to do it? I just don't know. It's all very confusing, and I'm much too tired to even attempt to figure it out."

"Would you like me to go so you can get some rest?" Jack asked, remaining by the door.

Jennifer got to her feet slowly, then turned and looked at Jack. "What if I don't know the answer to that, either?" she said.

"We flip a coin?" he said, smiling. Then his smile faded and he shoved his hands into his jacket pockets. "I don't want to leave you tonight, Jennifer, if my vote counts for anything. It's been a long, grueling, pretty frightening day, but…well, we did it, we got through it…together. I want to finish this day with you, hold you until you fall asleep, know for certain that you're getting the rest you need. I'm not pushing for making love—I just want to hold you close, be with you. Be here *for* you."

And she, Jennifer thought, with a flash of panic, she was… Oh, God, slowly but surely falling in love with Jack MacAllister. He was chipping away, piece by emotional piece, at her protective wall, crumbling it into dust.

No, no, no, this mustn't happen. She'd promised herself, vowed, she'd never love again, never trust a man enough again to lose her heart to him.

To fall deeply in love with Jack MacAllister…if

she hadn't already…oh, she didn't want to know the true depths of her blossoming love for him. Jack was guaranteed heartbreak because he was walking out of her life in a handful of weeks. To be gone forever.

She had to send him away. *Now. Right now.* She had to rebuild her wall quickly, quickly, and ignore whatever messages her heart might be whispering. She had to protect herself from Jack and—heaven help her—from herself.

"Jennifer?" Jack said. "Talk to me. Do you want me to leave?"

Yes! her mind screamed.

"No," she heard herself say, an echo of tears in her voice. "No, I don't want to…to be alone."

Jack nodded, then began to unbutton his jacket while still looking directly at Jennifer. Quicksand, he thought suddenly. He was being pulled deeper and deeper into Jennifer's life, her world.

Emotional quicksand, that was what it was, and he wasn't doing one damn thing to free himself.

He was, in fact, doing exactly the opposite. He'd felt the knot in his gut dissolve when Jennifer had said she wanted him to stay. He'd made his heartfelt statement, then waited with a sense of dread that she'd send him away to spend a lonely night at Hamilton House.

What was he doing? He'd experienced flashes of doubt regarding Jennifer's true agenda, wondering if he'd once again misjudged a woman and was being played for a fool.

But in between? Hell, he was scrambling for the right words to express his honest caring, his sincere desire to stand by her side during this crisis with Joey.

Zoom, he thought dryly. His brain was doing what Joey was with the television remote. Zooming around with no rhyme or reason, making no sense, driving him crazy.

"I need to call my parents," Jennifer said, bringing Jack back to attention.

Jack shrugged out of his jacket and set it next to Jennifer's coat on the back of the sofa. "Okay," he said. "Do you want me to start a fire in the hearth, or would you prefer to go right to bed and get some rest?"

"I'm too wired to sleep. A fire would be nice." Jennifer paused. "Are you hungry? Those sandwiches you brought us from the hospital cafeteria weren't great. I could fix us some—"

"No," he said. "I'm fine. Don't worry about me, Jennifer. We're concentrating on you tonight, and that doesn't include your cooking anything."

"This is *my* night?" she said, smiling slightly. "Like I won the lottery or something?"

"Or something," he said, chuckling. "Go call your folks, but leave out the part about Joey acting rotten. You promised him you wouldn't blow the whistle on him."

Jennifer cocked her head to one side and studied Jack intently.

"What?" he said finally.

"How did you know that the time had come to get firm with Joey? I'm his mother, and I was practically standing on my head in an attempt to please him, make him happy, and failing miserably. You just knew what needed to be done. How? Why?''

Jack shrugged and walked to the fireplace. He hunkered down in front of it, opened the screen and began to place kindling on the grate.

"You are *definitely* a natural-born father," Jennifer said, starting across the room. "I'll go telephone my parents."

Jack's head snapped around and he watched Jennifer disappear from view. He looked at the grate again, then threw some kindling onto it with more force than was necessary.

There it was again, he thought, that zinger of Jennifer's that he was a natural-born father, only this time she'd added an emphatic *definitely*. Damn it, where was she going with that nonsense? What foundation was she putting in place?

Ah, MacAllister, give it a rest, Jack told himself, setting a log on the kindling. He'd had a long day, too, and had been scared to death during that drive to the hospital with a crying Joey.

The wait during the surgery hadn't been a picnic, either. He was beat, and had no business now attempting to get a handle on what Jennifer might be after. He wasn't going to think about it any more tonight. Not tonight.

Jack struck a match, started the fire, then closed the screen. He moved backward to lean against the sofa, knees bent, his wrists dangling over them. He stared into the now leaping flames and began to feel himself relax, his muscles loosen.

That Joey was something, he thought, smiling. He'd had Jennifer jumping through hoops for hours on end at the hospital. Any kid would continue to push buttons on a parent that he hadn't been allowed to push before.

Well, he'd called a halt to Joey's performance. Enough had been enough. Joey had seemed almost relieved to be told to knock it off, had been more than ready to be his usual, smiling self. *Zoom. Zoom.* Give a kid a remote control and all was right in the world of being five years old.

How *had* he known that it was time to pull the plug on Joey's act? How had he, bachelor *extraordinaire,* sensed that a firm stand was needed to get Joey squared away?

Jack frowned. Well, hell, maybe he *was* a natural-born father. A father. That was a role he never intended to have because it would include getting married, being a husband, actually believing he'd chosen the right woman to be his life's partner.

Nope. No way. Not with his track record of misjudging the honesty, the *realness,* of every woman he'd ever been in a relationship with. He was a complete dud when it came to being able to see the true colors of members of the female species.

Including Jennifer Mackane?

Don't go there, he ordered himself. Not tonight. He wasn't diving into that muddled part of his brain when he was weary to the bone. He was just going to sit here and enjoy the fire. Enjoy being with Jennifer. Be here for her after her long, exhausting day.

"What a lovely fire," Jennifer said, coming back into the room. "Would you like some brandy?"

Jack accepted the small snifter that Jennifer was

offering him, then she sat down next to him on the floor, holding a snifter of her own.

"When I talked to my dad," she said, "he reminded me that he'd left a bottle of brandy on the top shelf of one of the kitchen cupboards. He said it sounded like it was time to open it and relax after the day I'd had."

"Smart man." Jack lifted his snifter. "Cheers, and all that good stuff."

Jennifer clinked her glass against Jack's, then they each took a sip of the amber liquid.

"Nice," Jack said, nodding. "Very smooth."

"Goodness," Jennifer said, then coughed. "This is potent. One little sip warmed me all the way down to my toes." She laughed. "My mother asked me if Joey was being a good patient. I did a couple of 'Well, um... Well, sort of...' and my mom fell apart laughing."

"Why?"

"She said I might have been ten when I had my appendix out, but I acted about three years old. I fussed, fumed, and—to quote—was an Olympic-form brat. That went on until my father told me that babies went to bed very, very early and that could be arranged for me when I got home from the hospital. I turned into little Miss Sunshine in the next instant."

Jack chuckled. "So, Joey inherited that gene from you, huh?"

"I'm afraid so," she said, smiling. "My father put an end to my pitch-a-fit, just like you did with Joey. You fellas sure are wise."

"Right," Jack said, an edge to his voice. He took

a deep swallow of the brandy. "Natural-born fathers."

Jennifer looked at Jack and frowned. "You sound angry all of a sudden, Jack. Did I miss something here?"

Jack sighed. "No, forget it. I'm just tired." He extended one arm toward Jennifer. "Come here."

She scooted close to him, and he caressed her arm as she rested her head on his shoulder. They finished the rich brandy in silence, then Jack set the snifters on the floor next to him. They still didn't speak as they stared into the flames, allowing themselves to be semi-hypnotized—not thinking, just relaxing.

"Mmm," Jennifer said finally. "This is much better. I think I may live, after all. What a grueling day."

"Yep."

"Thank you for everything, Jack. I can't begin to express—"

"Then don't try," he interrupted, "because it isn't necessary." He kissed her on the forehead. "I was where I wanted to be today. I'm where I want to be tonight. Enough said."

"Okay."

This is *my* night, Jennifer thought, suddenly recalling her earlier conversation with Jack. Well, she wasn't going to spend it beating herself up for having lost her heart to Jack MacAllister. Nor would she use these hours to determine just how deeply she was in love with him.

That she was going to cry in the lonely, dark hours of the night when Jack was gone was now a given. But how badly shattered her heart would be was something she didn't have the energy to deal with now.

No, this was *her* night to do with as she wished, to put her wants and needs absolutely, positively first.

And she wanted to make love with Jack.

Jennifer lifted her head from Jack's shoulder and turned to look at him. "Jack?" she said softly.

He met her gaze. "Hmm?"

She placed one hand on his cheek, then raised up enough to capture his lips with hers. Jack jerked in surprise, then slid one hand to the nape of her neck and returned the kiss with equal intensity.

Heat rocketed through him and his desire soared instantly. He had to force himself to break the kiss, then drew a ragged breath.

"Jennifer," he said, his voice rough, "don't. You're exhausted. Let's not start something here that can't be finished."

"But you said it was my night," she said. "Mine. This is what I choose to do with it. I want you, Jack." She paused. "Of course, if *you're* too tired, then—"

Jennifer's words were smothered by Jack's mouth covering hers in a melting kiss that stole the very breath from her body. She wrapped her arms around his neck, sinking her fingertips into the lush thickness of his hair, urging his mouth harder onto hers.

She was filled with immeasurable joy—a sense of completeness—that was accompanied by raging passion she made no attempt to quell.

She was falling for this man, her heart sang. She was falling in love with Jack MacAllister, who was real, and honest, and everything he claimed to be. Surely he would never betray her, lie to her. After all, she knew his truths, knew he would be leaving soon.

This night was hers.

She would bask in the wondrous glory of making love with a man with no secrets, no weapons of duplicity to destroy her with.

The memories would be hers to cherish once Jack was gone. Memories of a relationship that she would not have to bury deep within her to keep the pain from ripping her to shreds.

Oh, yes, this night was hers.

Jennifer shifted her hands to push lightly against Jack's chest, ending the passionate kiss. She got to her feet and, her gaze never leaving his, removed her clothes. She stood naked before him, the light from the dancing flames in the hearth cascading over her like a golden waterfall.

Jack's heart thundered as he strove for control. He made himself sit where he was, drinking in the vision of loveliness standing before him.

There she was, he thought hazily. Jennifer. *His* Jennifer. She was rendering herself totally vulnerable, trusting him, believing in him, knowing he would never hurt her.

And *he* trusted and believed in *her*.

Ah, yes, he truly did, because this was Jennifer, a woman like none he'd ever known before. An honest woman. A real woman. She didn't have a secret agenda, wasn't attempting to take from him more than he was willing, or able, to give.

No, not Jennifer.

She was simply Jennifer Mackane, exactly as she was, as he knew her to be.

And he loved her.

Jack stiffened, every muscle in his body tensing as the realization of his emotions slammed into his mind.

No! he thought frantically. How had this happened? When had he lost the tight command over his heart?

He had to get out of there, out of this house, put as much distance as possible between him and Jennifer as quickly as he could.

Run, MacAllister.

Run, before Jennifer discovered the true depths of his feelings for her, had the power to demolish him, strip him bare of all his defenses.

Go. Run. Now!

"Jack?" Jennifer said, her voice quivering slightly as a shadow of uncertainty clouded her features. "Don't...don't you want me?"

Ah, hell, Jack thought, he couldn't fight the spell Jennifer had cast over him. He couldn't leave her now, causing her to question his desire for her.

He couldn't do that—not to the woman he loved.

Jack rolled to his feet. "Want you? You'll never know how much."

Jennifer smiled. "Then show me."

Jack tore off his clothes, flinging them aside, then closed the distance between him and Jennifer. He took her into his arms, then lowered her to the floor and lay next to her. His mouth melted over hers, and a groan of need rumbled in his chest.

Jennifer splayed her hands on Jack's back, relishing the feel of his taut muscles beneath her palms.

Power. Strength, her mind hummed. But infinite tenderness, gentleness. Magnificent. Oh, how very magnificent was this man.

"Jack, please," she whispered, close to his lips. "I can't bear it. I need you. I want you…now."

"Yes. I've got to protect you, though, so—"

"No, no," she said, her hold on him tightening as a sob caught in her throat. "Don't leave me. It's all right. It's the wrong time of the month. It's safe. Don't leave me. Come to me, Jack. *Please.*"

All rational thought fled Jack's mind. He moved over her and thrust into her with one powerful surge, filling her.

It was wild. Earthy. Rough and real. The rhythm was pounding, the cadence thundering.

They were flung into oblivion seconds apart, holding fast to each other as they shattered into brilliant pieces. They lingered there, etching memories indelibly in their minds.

When they returned to reality, they didn't speak. They lay close, limbs entwined, sated and contented.

Jack moved finally to pull an afghan from the sofa to cover their cooling bodies.

Then with Jennifer's head nestled on Jack's shoulder, they slept.

Chapter Eleven

Jennifer peered into the oven, nodded in approval as she looked at the turkey, then closed the door. She turned to the counter and began to cut tomatoes into cubes for a salad while she hummed off-key.

Thanksgiving day, she thought. It was time to take a quiet moment and count her blessings—a pleasant task that would probably take more than all her fingers and toes to complete.

The sound of laughter reached her where she worked in the kitchen, and she smiled, knowing her home was filled with people who were important to her, people she loved.

Out in the living room, probably chattering like a magpie, was Joey, her precious son. It had been ten days since the frightening event of his surgery, and Joey was practically as good as new. He'd return to school on Monday, no doubt ready to relate his great adventure to anyone who would listen to the exciting tale.

Her beloved parents had driven up from Phoenix for the special day, and it was wonderful to see them. Andrea and Brandon were here, Aunt Prudence and Aunt Charity, Megan and Ben.

And Jack.

Jack, Jack, Jack, Jennifer thought, tossing a handful of tomato chunks into a bowl. The intensity and depth of her feelings for him grew with every passing day…and night, despite her knowing they had no future together.

She was an idiot. And she would pay a heavy price when Jack left Prescott, which he most certainly would.

All she knew for sure was that now, right now, she was happier, more fulfilled and complete, than she had ever been in her life. While Jack didn't know how she felt about him, she certainly did, and she was savoring every moment, every memory while Jack was still there.

The piper would come to collect his due when Jack was gone. She knew that, but still, she felt as she did.

"Football, football, football," Andrea said, coming into the kitchen. "We actually had some conversation going out there for a bit, but so much for that. The men are now watching other men clobber each other. What a silly game that is."

Jennifer laughed. "Don't let my mother hear you say that. She's a devoted fan of that nonsense. I told her that she likes to see guys wearing tight pants. She just smiled, and did *not* deny it.''

''Aunt Charity is watching the game, but Aunt Prudence is talking to Megan. I bet Aunt Charity takes a good look at those nifty male tushes, too.''

''I'm sure she does,'' Jennifer said, smiling.

''What can I do to help you with dinner?''

''Nothing. It's all under control. With each of you bringing a part of the meal, there isn't that much for me to do. The turkey is cooking right on schedule. You and baby-girl Hamilton can just sit down at the table there and relax.''

''Baby-*girl* Hamilton?'' Andrea said, settling onto one of the chairs at the kitchen table.

Jennifer nodded. ''No doubt about it. Jack told me about the MacAllister family baby bet and how Brandon qualifies because he's a close friend of a MacAllister. Brandon says you're having a girl, so—''

''I know, I know,'' Andrea said, laughing. ''They made a believer out of me, too. I'm concentrating on the bachelor bet now. There are three candidates for marriage in the running—Jack, his brother Richard, and our own Sheriff Cable Montana.''

''So I've heard. Jack told me.''

''It would seem that Jack has kept you up to date on a lot of things, Jennifer.''

''Yes, well, I've been meaning to talk to you about Jack, but I never see you alone for long enough at the hotel.''

''Oh?''

Jennifer covered the salad bowl, put it in the refrigerator, then crossed the room and sat down opposite Andrea at the table.

"I'm all ears," Andrea said.

"No, you're all tummy," Jennifer said. "How are you feeling these days?"

"Fat," Andrea said. "Don't change the subject. What did you want to discuss with me regarding Jack?"

Jennifer took a deep breath and let it out slowly. "Okay," she said, "here goes. I know Ben must have told you that he saw Jack and me kissing in the waiting room at the hospital the day of Joey's surgery. And we were…kissing. Actually, you see, Jack and I are involved in a… What I mean is, we're— Now I realize it's very foolish because he'll be leaving soon, and I'll never see him again, but I don't care because I've never been this happy, and I'm holding fast to what I'm sharing with Jack for as long as it's mine to have."

Jennifer lifted her chin. "I don't want to hear that I'm headed for heartache because it's all temporary. I know the facts and I've accepted them, so don't worry about me. I just felt that since Ben told you what he'd witnessed at the hospital, I should explain that no one need be concerned that I'll be a basket case when Jack goes. Sad? Yes. Missing Jack? Oh, yes. But I'll be all right in time."

Jennifer nodded. "There. That covers it, I guess. Oh, wait. There's Joey, too. He's very fond of Jack, idolizes him, but we remind him that Jack will be leaving before Christmas. Joey seems to understand that. So, that's it. That should answer any questions you might have after Ben reported what he saw."

"I see," Andrea said slowly. "There's just one little thing you ought to know."

"What is it?" Jennifer said, frowning.

"Ben never said one word about seeing you and Jack kissing," Andrea said, laughing.

"Oh, good grief," Jennifer said. "I don't believe this. I was certain that he would go racing right over to the hotel and... Don't men know how to gossip?"

Andrea shrugged. "Some don't, apparently. Ben is a very private person, you know. Look how long he kept silent about the fact that he might lose his sight at some point in the future."

"That's true," Jennifer said, nodding. "Well, I just blithered my little heart out for no reason."

"I'm glad you told me, Jennifer, and I'm sincerely happy for you. I'm a bit worried, too, that you'll be hurt by this relationship because it will all be over soon."

"Nope. Won't happen. I won't be hurt."

"I hope you're right." Andrea paused, then nodded. "This explains why Jack... Yes, it makes sense."

"What are you talking about?"

"Well, I'll confess that we all had been discussing you a bit, wondering why you refused to even date. Jack presented a theory—this was early on, right after he'd met you—that maybe you weren't grieving for the happiness you'd had in your marriage with Joe Mackane, but were protecting yourself because that union had been...well, totally miserable."

Jennifer felt the color drain from her face. "Jack said that?"

"Yes, and it was something none of us had ever thought of," Andrea said, "due to the fact that you named Joey after his father."

"Yes," Jennifer whispered. "Yes, I did."

"Anyway, Jack got us all upset with that new thought and he promised to report back on any clues he got while he was repairing your house. Please don't be angry, Jennifer. This was all done because we care so much about you."

Jennifer nodded, still gazing at Andrea. Yes, she thought frantically, all of them *did* care about her, but, dear heaven, no, she didn't want anyone to know the truth about her and Joe Mackane.

"The thing is," Andrea went on, "Jack suddenly clammed up, wouldn't say a word, said it was actually none of our business. It was baffling because it had been his idea in the first place. Now everything makes sense."

"It does?" Jennifer said.

"Well, sure. Jack was becoming personally involved with you. Whatever had kept you from dating for the past five years was no longer standing in your way. But Jack, gentleman that he is, wasn't about to show up for breakfast at Hamilton House and announce to all of us that there was no longer any cause for concern about you because he was sleeping with you."

Jennifer's earlier pallor was replaced by a flush of embarrassment.

"I never said that we were—" she started.

Andrea laughed. "Hey, it's all right. I'm a big girl, know the facts of life. Of course you're sleeping with Jack." Her smile faded. "But, oh, Jennifer, I don't want to see you brokenhearted when he leaves.''

''I'll be fine,'' Jennifer said quietly. ''I really will. This time with Jack is like a gift I'm giving myself. I feel so womanly, so alive, so—''

''In love?'' Andrea said gently.

''Oh, no, no, I...'' Jennifer sighed. ''Well, truth is, I think I'm falling in love with Jack. I certainly didn't intend for that to happen, believe me, but I've accepted the reality of it and am prepared to handle it when he's gone.''

''Does Jack know how you feel about him?''

''Heavens, no,'' Jennifer said. ''There's absolutely no point in his knowing. In fact, it might be disastrous if he knew. He could very well break things off between us and leave for California earlier than he planned if he thought things were getting...sticky, shall we say, between us. No, he mustn't find out the depths of my feelings. I don't want to lose what time I have left with him—not one minute of it.''

''Oh, dear me,'' Andrea said, shaking her head. ''This sounds so emotionally...dangerous for you.''

''Worry not, my friend,'' Jennifer said, getting to her feet. ''I'm in control. All is right with the world. I've got to check on my turkey.''

As had been agreed, Brandon had brought a long, folding table from one of the conference rooms at the hotel, as well as enough chairs to seat Jennifer's guests. The table was set up in the living room behind the sofa that faced the fireplace.

Jennifer's parents had surprised her with a lovely

centerpiece of flowers in fall colors that looked perfect on the off-white linen tablecloth.

Jack's contribution to the event had been several bottles of top-of-the-line wine that Jennifer poured into crystal glasses. The table was filled with a variety of food, and delicious aromas floated through the air.

Jennifer sat at the head of the table with Jack on her right and Joey on her left, his plastic glass containing apple juice.

"A toast," Jennifer said, lifting her glass after everyone was seated. "To family."

"Hear! Hear!" Brandon said.

Jennifer clinked her glass against Joey's, then turned to repeat the ritual with Jack. He met her gaze and she smiled as their glasses touched. She forced herself to break the warm, visual contact with him, then spoke to her father, who sat at the opposite end of the table.

"Would you say grace, please, Dad?" she said.

Dishes were soon being passed and several conversations taking place at the same time. The noise level was high, the mood festive.

To family, Jack thought, mentally repeating Jennifer's toast. Yes, that was who was gathered around this table—friends who were so close and caring they were a family. It had been a great many years since he'd taken part in a traditional Thanksgiving like this one.

Family.

Jack slid a glance at Jennifer, then Joey, as he began to eat. He loved them. There was no point in attempting to deny it, nowhere to hide from the momentous truth of it. He loved Jennifer as a man loved a woman. He loved Joey as a father would a son.

The unanswered question was…what was he going to do about it?

Jennifer didn't have a clue as to his true feelings for her. He would leave for California just before Christmas as planned, with Jennifer none the wiser.

And that *should* be that. End of story.

But it wasn't, and he knew it.

He hadn't intended to fall in love with Jennifer Mackane, nor have his heart well and truly captured by her son, and he was angry as hell at himself that he had let it actually happen. A cold fist tightened in his gut as he once again questioned his inability to see the real agenda hidden by a woman.

But the thought of leaving Jennifer and Joey, walking out of their lives, never seeing them again, caused his stomach to clench yet again each time the image of their last goodbye flashed in his mind's eye.

Family.

His was waiting for him on the coast—the huge MacAllister clan, plus close friends who were included in the group. He'd be surrounded by those who loved him, overrun by little kids eager to spend time with fun-loving Uncle Jack. He'd have more than enough people to fill his idle hours.

Yet…

None of them would be Jennifer. None of them would be Joey.

His family. *His* wife.

Jack choked on a sip of wine as the word *wife* echoed loudly in his mind.

"Goodness," Jennifer said, reaching over and patting him on the back.

"It just went down the wrong way," he said, smiling slightly.

"I must say, Jack," Jennifer's father said, "that the old homestead looks great. I understand you're the one to thank for that."

"I helped Jack fix junk, Grandpa," Joey said. "We did men stuff together."

"So I heard," his grandfather said. "And a fine job you did, too, Joey. Have you and Jack finished with all your projects around here?"

"Yep," Joey said. "We're all done. Jack helped me make a birdhouse while I was 'cuperating from my operation, so it took him longer to do the house stuff 'cause he had to do it alone, but we're done now. Right, Jack?"

"Right, sport," Jack said. "We're a good team, you and I."

"Well, in my opinion," Jennifer's father went on, "this would be an excellent time to sell this place. It's spruced up and ready to go on the market."

"You're kidding," Jennifer said, halting her fork halfway to her mouth. "Sell our family home?"

"It's too big for you, Jennifer, and too difficult to maintain," her father said. "It's yours to do with as you wish, but your mother and I would like to see you and Joey living in something smaller, newer. Maybe a town house, where all the outside mainte- nance is taken care of by an association."

"But...but I grew up in this house," Jennifer

said, setting her fork back onto her plate. "And I could never accept money that belonged to you and Mom."

"Dear," her mother said, "your father and I have fond memories of the many years we lived here. All we're saying is, it's perfectly fine with us if you'd like to sell this rambling old place. Things change, and it's often best to let go of the past and look to the future."

"I don't know what to say," Jennifer said.

"Just think about it," her father said. "Thanks to…Joey and the help Jack gave our young man in repairing this place, it's market ready."

"Now you're talking," Aunt Charity said. "Let go of the past and look to the future. That's excellent advice, Jennifer."

"Yes, it is, dear," Aunt Prudence said.

"Joey?" Jennifer said. "Do you have an opinion about this?"

"If we moved someplace else," Joey said, "could I take my swing set?"

"Yes, of course," Jennifer said.

"'Kay." Joey shrugged, then shoveled in a mouthful of potatoes.

"It would complicate my life," Jennifer said. "I have such a good setup with Mildred Clark next door to tend Joey while I'm working."

"Mildred left yesterday to visit her daughter in Toledo," Aunt Charity said, "and won't be back until after the new year. Your routine is already blown to Timbuktu."

"Well, yes, I know," Jennifer said, "and I

haven't solved that problem yet, but... Goodness, actually sell this house?''

"Want us to vote on it, Jennifer?" Brandon said. "You won't have to get in a dither about it. We'll decide for you, wonderful folks that we are."

Jennifer laughed and shook her head. "No, thank you, Brandon. I need to give this some very serious thought. Let's change the subject to *your* house."

"Funny you should bring that up," Brandon said, smiling. "I just happen to have brought along the plans that Jack drew for us."

"Which you will all gush over, like it or not," Andrea said, smiling, "or Brandon will pout."

"You betcha I will," he said. "It's going to be a fantastic house. The contractor is ready to roll, and we break ground next week."

"Oh, congratulations," Jennifer said, smiling warmly. "That's so exciting."

"Well, Jack," Aunt Charity said, "sounds to me like you've wrapped up all your projects. What are you going to do with yourself, hotshot?"

Jack slid his hand across Jennifer's knee beneath the table. She jumped slightly at the sudden, tantalizing touch, and felt her eyes widen.

"Gosh, Aunt Charity," Jack said. "I don't know. I'll think of *something*."

"Thought you might, big boy," Aunt Charity said, cackling merrily.

Jennifer reached beneath the table and smacked Jack's hand where it still rested on her knee, causing him to burst into laughter.

"What's funny?" Joey said, frowning.

"Nothing, sweetheart," Jennifer said, hoping her

cheeks weren't as flushed as they felt. "Brandon, don't forget that you're taking turkey sandwiches to Cable Montana when you leave. I invited him to join us today, but he said that since he was single, he'd stay on duty and free up one of the married deputies."

"Nice save, Ms. Mackane," Jack said quietly, grinning at her.

"Hush, hush," Jennifer whispered, shooting him a quick glare.

Jack laughed again.

"What's funny?" Joey repeated louder.

"Not—a—thing," Jennifer said firmly.

"Ah, yes, Hunk-of-Stuff Montana," Aunt Charity said. "He's one of the candidates in the bachelor bet."

"Oh, boy," Jack said, frowning and shaking his head. "Here we go."

"I do believe," Aunt Charity said, tapping one fingertip against her chin, "that I'll plead senility and admit that I made a mistake when I put my money on Jack getting married. Yes, I'm officially withdrawing my wager."

Jack scowled and leaned forward so he could see Aunt Charity, who was farther down the table.

"Why?" he said.

"You're just not husband material, hotshot," Aunt Charity said. "Nope, I'm not blowing my cash by betting on you."

"I'm not husband material?" Jack said, his voice rising. "Why not? What in the—" he looked quickly at Joey "—heck is wrong with me?"

"Charity, dear," Aunt Prudence said, "I'm well

aware that our Jack wouldn't be what one might prefer to have in a husband, but I'm not certain that Thanksgiving dinner is the proper place to discuss it.''

"You feel the same way, Aunt Pru?" Jack said, then slouched back in his chair. "I don't believe this. Anyone else want to get on this bandwagon?"

"Well, now that you mention it," Brandon said, staring into space.

"Hey, I demand an explanation," Jack said. "This is really rotten stuff you're laying on me here."

"Jack would be a good groom guy," Joey said. "He has a suit and tie, and everything."

"Thank you, Joey," Jack said. "I appreciate your support."

"Uncle Brandon could teach you how to kiss so you could make a baby, Jack," Joey said.

"Oh, okay," Jack said, chuckling.

"Nope," Aunt Charity said. "Jack isn't going to be a groom guy, Joey."

"I repeat," Jack said. "Why not?"

"You moved in the fast lane in New York City for too long, big boy," Aunt Charity said. "Brandon got out of that scene in the nick of time, but you're hopeless. You're a love-'em-and-leave-'em type, no doubt about it." She shook her head. "Can't see you mowing the lawn, taking out the trash, changing diapers. You're off to California to make whoopee with the beach bunnies."

"What's 'whoopee?'" Joey said.

"I certainly am not," Jack said. "I haven't given

one thought to the beach. Or the bunnies. I'm really getting insulted here."

"Don't know why," Jennifer's father said. "Not everyone is cut out for marriage, Jack. That's just the way it is sometimes."

"I'll have you know, all of you," Jack said, sweeping one hand through the air, "that I would be a dynamite husband." He nodded decisively. "I'm kind, thoughtful, would honor my wedding vows until the day I died. I could change a diaper if I had to…sure, I could do that. I'm handy around the house, could learn to pick up my socks and—"

Jack stopped speaking and glanced around the table. Everyone, except Jennifer, was smiling at him. Jennifer was simply staring at him with wide eyes, a rather stunned expression on her face.

"I've been had," Jack said, shaking his head. "I fell for it hook, line and sinker. You're a devious woman, Aunt Charity."

"Just checking up on my twenty bucks," she said, looking extremely pleased with herself.

"I'm still not convinced that Jack is cut out to be a husband," Brandon said.

"Don't count your money yet, Aunt Charity," Megan said. "Just because Jack feels he'd be a good husband doesn't mean he wants to be one."

"Bingo," Jack said, acknowledging Megan. "Got it in one."

"That doesn't work, Megan," Ben said. "We men can be so dense on the subject of marriage that we oftentimes don't know that we want that kind of commitment, when in actuality we do."

"Oh, brother," Jack said, rolling his eyes heavenward.

"Spare me."

"Would anyone like some pumpkin pie?" Jennifer asked, but no one paid any attention to her.

"You're right, Ben," Brandon said. "I'm a clearcut example of that theory."

"And look at you now," Andrea said, smiling as she patted her protruding stomach.

Brandon dropped a quick kiss on her lips. "I'm a happy man," he said. "Ecstatic. Over the moon and—"

"Give it a rest, Hamilton," Jack said gruffly.

"This is all very interesting," Jennifer's father said, stroking his chin, "and just confusing and complicated enough that I believe I'll pass on putting money on the bachelor bet in regard to Jack. I couldn't be certain which way to bet. Yes, this is *very* complicated."

Tell me about it, Jack thought. His poor muddled brain was dissolving into dust.

Marry Jennifer Mackane? Be a groom guy? A daddy bear? Oh, man, what a terrifying thought.

Or…or was it?

"Pumpkin pie with whipped cream?" Jennifer said, raising her eyebrows. "As in, we're changing the subject and concentrating on dessert? The topic of marriage has been known to give some people indigestion."

"Some people?" Jack said, no hint of a smile on his face. "Meaning you? I suppose you're with Brandon, agreeing with him that I'd make a lousy husband."

Jennifer turned her head slowly to meet Jack's frowning gaze. "No," she said quietly. "I think you'd make a wonderful husband, Jack." She paused. "Providing you found the right woman."

I have, damn it, Jack's mind yelled. *You! I love you, Jennifer Mackane. What's it going to take for you to trust and believe in me enough to love me in return?*

Oh, heaven help him, he *did* want to marry this woman, spend the rest of his life with her. And with Joey. And the children that he and Jennifer would create together while making sweet, sweet love in the darkness of night.

Jennifer switched her attention to the group. "Pie?" she said, her voice not quite steady.

"Yes," Andrea said quickly, "it's definitely time for pumpkin pie."

Jennifer got to her feet, picked up her plate and Joey's, then hurried into the kitchen.

Get a grip, Jennifer, please, she begged herself, putting the plates on the counter. She was rapidly losing the control that she'd assured Andrea she had.

Jack MacAllister in the role of a husband? Oh, yes. To a woman other than her? Oh, no. No, no, no. She couldn't bear the thought of his pledging his love forever to another woman.

She wanted Jack's forever to be with *her.*

Love, trust—they were emotions she'd sworn never again to have in regard to a man, but she wanted desperately to put her faith in Jack. To believe that he was different.

"Oh, Jennifer," she whispered, "you foolish, foolish woman. Now you want it all—and none of it is yours to have."

Chapter Twelve

Jack stood in front of the fireplace in Jennifer's living room, staring into the leaping flames. His hands were shoved into the pockets of his slacks and a deep frown knitted his brows.

That afternoon and on into the evening following the Thanksgiving dinner were a blur, he realized. No one had commented on the fact that he was acting strangely, so he must have performed in a halfway normal manner.

But the truth of the matter was, he'd been withdrawn, centered on his own raging thoughts.

Everything was happening too quickly, not allowing him time to adjust, to come to grips with the new and startling direction his life was taking.

He was in love for the first time. He'd forgotten the painful lessons about trusting too easily, believing that a woman was actually who she presented herself to be.

Oh, yes, he was, indeed, deeply in love with Jennifer Mackane.

Even more unsettling was the realization that he wanted to spend the rest of his life with her. Marry her, for God's sake. Be a groom guy for Jennifer, and a daddy bear for Joey.

Jack shook his head and sighed wearily. He needed to be alone, to get a handle on all this. The thought of a lifelong commitment terrified him, yet the idea of walking out of Jennifer's life forever was too chilling to bear.

"I'm a wreck," he said under his breath. "I'm totally losing it."

Jennifer stood at the entrance to the living room and stared at Jack, seeing the slump of his shoulders and hearing his deep sigh. He muttered something she couldn't make out, but she knew it was further evidence that he was troubled, upset.

He had been preoccupied since dinner, a fact of which no one but her, apparently, had been aware.

Had the silly conversation about the bachelor bet disturbed him? Jennifer wondered. Had Jack felt cornered when everyone focused on whether or not he was husband material?

Was he angry at himself for adamantly stating that he was very capable of being a good husband and father, when he had no desire whatsoever to function in either of those roles?

Oh, she didn't know what was on Jack's mind, knew only that he hadn't been himself since dinner.

The way to discover what was bothering him was to come right out and ask.

But she couldn't—wouldn't—do that.

She, too, had functioned on two levels since the Thanksgiving meal. Outwardly she had been cheerful, pleasant, an attentive hostess.

But another part of her had been struggling with the newfound truth that she wanted to spend the rest of her life with Jack MacAllister. Be his wife, the mother of his children, watch him perform in the role of Daddy Bear for her beloved Joey.

She wanted it all, and had fought against threatening tears throughout the seemingly endless hours that everyone was at the house, as her mind screamed unrelentingly that none of it was hers to have.

No, she couldn't ask Jack what was troubling him. It was too risky. Suppose, just suppose, that despite his own preoccupation he'd been aware of hers? What if he returned the question, wanted to know what had been wrong with *her* in the hours following dinner?

So much for communication between a man and a woman, Jennifer thought dryly. She was breaking one of the important rules of being in a relationship, but she had no choice but to keep silent.

Jennifer lifted her chin and walked farther into the living room. "Joey's asleep," she said, forcing a lightness to her voice. "He had such fun today, but he's thoroughly worn out."

Jack turned from staring into the flames and looked at Jennifer. "That's good," he said. "I mean, it's not good that he's worn out, but it's good that he's asleep, getting his rest and... Never mind.''

Jennifer sat down on one end of the sofa. ''Would you like some coffee, Jack? Brandy? There's some of that wine you brought left, too.''

''No. No, I'm fine, thank you.''

You are not fine, Jack MacAllister, Jennifer thought. Oh, what, what, what was troubling him?

''I—I hope you enjoyed yourself here today, Jack,'' she said.

Jack slouched onto the sofa, rested his head on its back and looked at the ceiling. Jennifer slid a glance at him and registered the distance he'd put between them. A cold knot tightened in her stomach.

''It was really great,'' Jack said, still staring at the ceiling. ''It's been years since I've been part of a traditional Thanksgiving celebration. It was...very nice.'' He paused. ''Tiring, though. All that chatter and... Wipes a person out.''

''Well...''

Jack turned his head to look at Jennifer. ''Aren't you exhausted?'' he said.

''Well...''

He lunged to his feet, and Jennifer jerked in surprise.

''Sure you are,'' he said. ''Listen, I'm going to shove off and let you relax, then get to bed early. Okay? Yeah, good idea.''

Oh, Jack, Jennifer thought, feeling the sting of tears in her eyes once again. *What is wrong?*

She got to her feet.

''All right,'' she said, hoping, praying that her voice was steady.

"I—I'm going to drive down to Phoenix tomorrow, Jennifer," Jack said, directing his attention to the fire again. "I've never been there, and I'd like to take a look at some of the historical buildings. I might…might stay a couple of days. It's a big city. Lots for an architect to take in. You know?"

Lame, MacAllister, he thought. But he needed some time alone to make sense of the jumbled mess his mind had become.

"Yes," Jennifer said softly. "Phoenix is very big city. Very big."

Jack nodded, then strode across the room to the front closet and retrieved his jacket. Jennifer walked toward him slowly and met him at the front door.

He dipped his head and brushed his lips over hers. "I'll call you, or come by, when I get back to Prescott," he said.

Jennifer nodded, unable to speak past the ache of tears in her throat.

Jack looked directly at her, an intense but unreadable expression on his face. He lifted one hand and drew his thumb gently over her cheek.

"Ah, Jennifer, I…" he started, then stopped speaking and shook his head. "Good night."

"'Night," Jennifer managed to whisper.

Jack left the house, closing the door behind him with a *click.* Jennifer snapped the lock into place, then leaned her forehead against the smooth wood and allowed the pent-up tears to flow.

Jennifer was scheduled to work days starting on the Monday following Thanksgiving, requiring her to be at the hotel at seven a.m. and leave at 4:00 p.m.

Due to Mildred Clark's vacation, Jennifer made arrangements to drop Joey off at Sammy's house in the early morning.

Joey would attend a day-care center adjacent to his school after kindergarten was dismissed, a fact Joey was reserving judgment on until he—to quote—checked it out for fun stuff to do.

As Jennifer seated the breakfast patrons, she made a silent wish that this Monday would be one of the days Andrea, Brandon and the aunts would decide to eat in their own apartments upstairs in the hotel.

She did not want to explain to the observant quartet why she had purple smudges beneath her eyes from lack of sleep. She was also certain that her plastic-feeling smile would not fool the caring foursome.

Jennifer sighed, acutely aware of her bone-deep fatigue. She'd tossed and turned the night Jack announced he was going to Phoenix. And she'd tossed and turned every night since, her sleep coming in short doses that produced muddled, yet definitely disturbing, dreams.

Jennifer frowned and stared into space, recalling how happy she had been as the Thanksgiving festivities began, and how miserable she'd been by the time the special day was over.

This was a practice run, she supposed, for when Jack packed up his vehicle and headed for California in just a few weeks. And, oh, mercy, it was awful, just terrible, and lonely beyond belief.

Well, no, she reasoned in the next instant, this was

different than that final leaving would be. Jack's sudden decision to go to Phoenix had not been on the schedule.

There was something troubling Jack, and she'd made no attempt to communicate with him, to discover what was causing his turmoil, due to her fears that he might demand similar answers from her.

Jack's exodus to the valley with so much left unsaid between them was admittedly as much her fault as his.

She was once again being pulled back into the painful memories of the past, nearly numb with the fear that Jack would somehow hurt her, shatter her, with what he refused to share. She was losing her trust and belief in him, those newly found emotions slipping through her fingers like grains of sand.

Jennifer smiled automatically as a couple entered the dining room and made the appropriate, pleasant remarks as she led them to their table and handed them their menus. When she returned to the podium, she narrowed her eyes and stared into space again.

No, by golly, she was *not* going to step backward into the dark world where she'd existed with Joe Mackane. She'd moved into the sunshine with Jack MacAllister and was stronger for it, free of the hideous ghosts of lies and betrayal. She would not be beaten by old fears.

If Jack contacted her upon his return from Phoenix—oh, please, let Jack contact her when he got back to Prescott—she was going to sit him down and talk to him, for heaven's sake. If she truly believed in him, trusted him, then it was time to prove it—not only to him, but to herself as well.

That baring of her soul wouldn't change the outcome of her relationship with Jack. She knew that. He would still leave Prescott before Christmas. All that they'd shared would be over, forever. She was prepared to deal with that.

But she would handle it as a woman changed, as one who had grown, become stronger, had reached into the dark shadows of her past and retrieved the very essence of who she was to be complete now, whole.

But she couldn't say that final goodbye to Jack with dignity and grace if she didn't step up and square off against whatever it was that was now taking place. Whatever was wrong with Jack—and, therefore, with them—had to be addressed.

It had to be done in order for her to be who she wished to be. Free of the horror of the past. A woman of strength, courage and purpose. A woman who would cry when Jack left, but one who would have the fortitude to dry those tears and move forward with her life.

"Hi, Jennifer."

Jennifer jerked at the sound of a woman's voice. "Hello, Deborah," Jennifer said, smiling. "I haven't seen you in ages. How are you?"

"Busy," Deborah said. "I'm meeting some clients who are staying here at Hamilton House. We're having breakfast, then I'm going to show them some houses. They're ready to retire and have decided that Prescott is the place to settle and enjoy."

Jennifer glanced at the reservation book. "Yes, here you are. A table for three. Do you want to wait here for your people, or be seated now?"

"I'll sit and have some coffee," Deborah said. "I'm facing a lot of hours on my feet today. I wish I still had the energy I did when you and I were in high school together. Anyway, my clients are the Reynolds. You can send them in my direction when they arrive."

"Very good."

Jennifer led Deborah to a table, gave her a menu, and placed two more on the table for the expected couple. "Enjoy your breakfast," Jennifer said, then started away.

She stopped, took a deep breath and returned to stand next to Deborah. "I want to sell my house and I'd like you to have the listing."

Deborah's eyes widened. "You want to sell—You're kidding. You grew up in that house. I can still recall the hours we spent together in your nifty room on the top floor when we were in high school. Remember how we pretended we were in our own apartment in whatever exciting city struck our fancy that day?"

"Yes, I remember," Jennifer said, "but the house is too big for me and Joey, and is impossible to maintain. Thanks to a—a friend, everything is repaired right now, spruced up. This is the time to sell... It was my folks' idea and...well, I'm going to do it. I want a nice-size town house with a back-yard big enough for Joey's swing set. I hope you can find us something."

"Well, I'm definitely surprised," Deborah said, "but thrilled to have the listing. I shouldn't have any trouble selling a beautiful historic home like yours. I'll call you to set up a time when I can come

by and do a walk-through and settle on an asking
price. Okay?''

"Fine," Jennifer said. "Thanks."

"Thank *you*," Deborah said, smiling. "You made
my day. I'm a happy Realtor."

And she, Jennifer thought, walking away, was as
stunned as Deborah. During the long days and nights
since Thanksgiving dinner, her subconscious must
have been busily dwelling on her parents' suggestion that the family home be sold. She'd been so
centered on Jack, she'd had no idea that part of her
was working through the question of whether or not
to sell the house.

Well, fine. So be it. Being involved in a muddled
mess of a relationship was good for something other
than sleepless nights. She would have driven herself
crazy wondering what to do about her home, but had
now discovered she'd made the decision already.
She'd just opened her mouth and told Deborah to
put the house on the market.

And it felt right. It truly did. It was one more step
forward, instead of lingering in the past.

Oh, yes, indeed, she was changing and growing,
gaining an inner strength she had no idea she possessed.

And when—well, *if* Jack MacAllister showed up
on her doorstep after driving back up the mountain,
they were going to talk, by golly, openly and honestly, even if she had to bar the door and keep him
in her living room until she'd had her say.

Jennifer nodded decisively, and when the next
people entered the dining room, her smile was genuine.

* * *

The evening Jack returned to Prescott, he stood across the street from Jennifer's, one shoulder propped against a large tree as he stared at the house.

He'd managed to avoid seeing Andrea, Brandon and the aunts when he'd returned to Hamilton House, thank goodness.

A quick glance into the dining room, then some idle chitchat with the guy on duty at the registration desk gained him the information that Jennifer was working days and had left the hotel at four o'clock.

So here he was, skulking in the shadows. Any second now, he thought, the cops were going to arrive, blue lights flashing, sirens wailing, after receiving a report of a suspicious-looking man who was hugging a tree.

Jack glanced again at his watch, which he could see clearly in the glow of the street lamp. Five more minutes, he decided. It had been ten minutes since the light in the bedroom he knew to be Joey's had been extinguished. He was waiting to be certain the little boy was sound asleep before he knocked on Jennifer's door.

It wasn't that he didn't want to see Joey, because he did, he really did, but this wasn't the time for a fun romp with Joey—not by a long shot.

Jack dragged both hands down his face and sighed wearily. Man, he was beat. Hadn't had a decent night's sleep since before Thanksgiving. In the hotel room in Phoenix, he'd done more pacing and thinking than sleeping, and when he had managed to doze off, it had been a restless slumber.

Enough was enough, he'd finally concluded. He couldn't go on like this. The time had come to have a serious discussion with Jennifer, to sit her down, to tell her that he was in love with her.

It wouldn't be what she wanted to hear, that was for damn sure, but he was going to unburden his beleaguered brain, be certain that she listened, even if he had to block the doors of the house with furniture.

It could very well be that Jennifer would tell him to take a hike, to hit the road, to get out of her life. His declaration of love might rob him of the remaining weeks left to be with her.

But that was a risk he was going to have to take because the jumble of emotions within him was more than he could handle.

And the fact that he wanted to be Jennifer's groom guy and Joey's Daddy Bear? A husband and father? Every time he focused on that realization, his mind just stopped. That was due, he knew, to the cold-fist-in-his-gut feeling that he'd never get that far in baring his soul to Jennifer.

He'd broken the rules of their no-strings, no-commitment relationship. Man, had he ever. Jennifer liked the agreed-upon status quo, the end of which would be a breezy "See ya, Jack" as he set off for California.

Oh, yeah, he was about to burst Jennifer's blissful bubble, gum up the works big time. Jennifer wanted no part of a forever with him because…

Jack frowned and straightened from his slouching pose against the tree.

…Because Jennifer Mackane had secrets from her

past that were dictating her present, and robbing her of a future.

And she didn't trust and believe in him enough to share those secrets with him. That hurt. That really ripped him up.

He'd overcome his own self-doubts about his ability to really trust Jennifer, to be certain she didn't have a hidden agenda, but she hadn't returned in kind that kind of heartfelt, emotional trust. Damn.

Jack looked at his watch again, then drew a deep breath, letting it out slowly. "Okay, MacAllister," he said aloud. "This is it. Get geared up to be sent packing."

Chapter Thirteen

When the knock on the front door reverberated through the living room, Jennifer jumped to her feet, then sat down abruptly as a wave of dizziness assaulted her. She blinked, placed one hand on her racing heart, then rose again slowly.

Jack was here, she thought, walking toward the door. She knew, just somehow knew, that he was standing on her front porch. So, okay, fine. This was it. Truth time.

"I'm not home," she said under her breath. "Oh, Jennifer, get a grip. You can do this. You *have* to do this."

She lifted her chin, squared her shoulders and opened the door.

"Hello, Jennifer," Jack said quietly.

Jennifer drank in the very sight of him. She'd

missed him so much, she wanted to fling herself into his arms and—

"Jennifer?"

"Oh! Yes, hello, Jack," she said, stepping backward. "Come in."

Jack moved past her, took off his jacket and dropped it onto a chair, then went to stand in front of the fire, where he rubbed his hands together.

Jennifer stared at him, then jerked herself back to attention and closed the door. She returned to her spot on the sofa, acutely aware that her legs were trembling and her heart was racing.

Jack turned from the fire and met her gaze. "How are you, Jennifer?" he said. "And Joey? How's Joey?"

"We're both fine. Did you enjoy your trip down to Phoenix?"

"No."

"You didn't?" Jennifer said, frowning. "Then why did you stay away so long?" She paused and shook her head. "Oh, listen to me. I might as well come right out and say that I missed you. I did…miss you."

"I missed you, too." Jack stared at the ceiling for a long moment, then looked at Jennifer again. "What I'd like to do is take you in my arms and kiss you until we can't breathe. Then? Then we'd make love for hours, not talking, definitely not talking—just…just feeling."

Go for it, MacAllister, Jennifer thought giddily, as a frisson of heat whispered through her.

"But I can't do that, Jennifer, because we *have*

to talk. There are things that need discussing, can no longer be ignored.''

''I know,'' she said quietly, clutching her hands in her lap.

''We made a pact of sorts,'' Jack went on, ''that contained the ground rules of our relationship. We had an understanding that no one could get hurt because we both knew the facts, acknowledged that all this was temporary.''

''Yes.''

''Well, Jennifer, I broke the rules, and I can't go on with everything bottled up inside of me. It's driving me nuts. I have to be honest with you, tell you the truth, knowing full well that by doing so you might choose to end things between us right now.''

''I...I don't understand, Jack. I mean, I broke the rules, too, but I don't for one minute believe that you broke the same rules that I broke and— Oh, I'm not making any sense.''

''What rules did you break?'' Jack said, frowning.

''What rules did *you* break?'' she said, matching his expression.

''Hell, this isn't getting us anywhere,'' he said, his voice rising.

''Shh. You'll wake up Joey, and this is obviously an adult conversation.''

''No joke.'' Jack shook his head. ''Whew. This is rough going. Okay. Jennifer, I've been hurt in the past, disillusioned time after time because of my choices in relationships, because of the women I trusted and believed in. I was wrong, duped, every damn time. They all had hidden agendas, something they wanted from me...materialistically, socially, whatever. None of them were real. None of them were who they presented themselves to be. Never again, I vowed. Never, never again.

"Then I met you. I waited, watched, listened for your…your program, for what you were really after by agreeing to engage in a relationship with me."

"But I—"

"Please." Jack raised one hand. "This is difficult enough. Let me finish."

Jennifer nodded, her eyes holding Jack's.

"As each day…and night…went by," he continued, "I began to realize that you *didn't* have a secret agenda. You *are* real. You *are* honest. You *are* who you present yourself to be."

"Yes. Yes, I am, but you sound angry about it. This is very confusing, Jack."

"You think *you're* confused? I'm eligible for Olympic Gold in that category," he said, splaying one hand on his chest. "Why? Because you made me break my promise to myself, forget the past and what I'd supposedly learned from it. Because you…because you're you and… Damn it, Jennifer, I fell in love with you!"

"You did? Oh, you did not." Jennifer's eyes widened. "You did?"

"I did. I am." Jack dragged a hand through his hair. "In love. With you. That's the part of the rules I broke." He paused. "Ah, hell, what a mess. If you want to end things between us right here, right now, I'll understand because—"

"No," she said, her voice unsteady. "This all terrifies me at the same time that it makes me happier than I've ever been in my entire life. I intended to tell you how I felt if you came to me when you returned from Phoenix. I was so afraid you'd leave for California sooner than planned, but I knew I had to tell you. I'm falling in love with you, too.''

''I—''

''It doesn't mean that I think we have a future together, or anything like that,'' Jennifer rushed on. ''But I couldn't keep silent any longer because I wouldn't be true to myself if I did. I—''

''Wait a minute,'' Jack said, slicing one hand through the air. ''Wait just a damn minute here. You're saying that you're falling in love with me?''

''Yes,'' she whispered.

''On the surface, that sounds like two pieces of a puzzle fitting together, doesn't it? But there's a hell-uva big piece missing.''

''There is? What piece is missing? You're confusing me again, Jack.''

''Trust and belief, Jennifer. Your trust and belief in me is *not* in this picture. I've told you about my past, about why I was determined not to become seriously involved with a woman again. I spelled it all out for you. But you? You have secrets, Jennifer. There is something about your marriage to Joe Mackane that made you vow never to love again, never to remarry. There's a whole section of yourself that you won't allow me to touch, share.

''You say that you're falling in love with me,'' he continued, ''but how can that be true when you don't trust and believe in me enough to tell me what happened between you and Joey's father? Maybe you had the greatest marriage imaginable and couldn't fathom being able to come close to that kind of perfection again, so you didn't intend to even try. But I don't think that's the case—not even close. Tell me, Jennifer. Tell me about your existence with Joe Mackane.''

Jennifer nervously crossed her arms and held her elbows for a moment, then dropped her hands to her lap again. "No."

Jack sat down next to her, shifting so he could lay one arm across the top of the sofa behind her. He covered her hands with his other hand, and she turned her head to meet his gaze.

"Ah, Jennifer, don't you see?" he said. "Your past is standing between us like a solid wall. We can't acknowledge, can't…embrace the fact that we're meant to be together, let alone gather the courage to think about what the future might hold… Talk to me. Share with me. Trust and believe in me the way I do you."

"Are you testing me?" Jennifer said with a sudden flash of anger. "Is this one of those 'If you really love me, you'll do this' things?"

Jack looked away and stared into the fire for a long moment, then met Jennifer's gaze again. "Yes, I guess I am testing you," he said. "I'm so unsure of myself on the subject of being in love. I know that I love you, but, oh, man, it scares the hell out of me. I'm trying desperately to get a handle on my emotions here, be comfortable with them, welcome them. I'm no expert on love, but I do realize that this secret of yours is too big, has too much power. We're fragile, Jennifer, very fragile in this new place we've found ourselves. There's no room in here for your ghosts. Do you understand what I'm saying?''

Jennifer drew a wobbly breath. "Yes. Yes, but… Oh, God, no one knows what happened with Joe. I haven't told anyone—not even my parents. I have to protect Joey from the truth. He must *never* discover the true facts about his father."

"Do you think I'd ever do anything to hurt Joey?"

Jennifer looked into the depths of Jack's dark eyes. "No," she said softly. "No, you wouldn't."

"And you?" Jack said. "Can you envision me hurting you, Jennifer?"

"No."

"Then tell me about Joe Mackane."

Jennifer got to her feet and moved to stand in front of the fire. She stared into the flames, her hands once again wrapped protectively around her.

Please, Jennifer, Jack pleaded silently, staring at her. *Please talk to me.*

They couldn't do anything until the ghosts—the barrier—created by Jennifer's past were gone.

Talk to me, Jennifer, please.

"When I graduated from college," Jennifer said quietly, still staring into the fire, "I took a position as the manager of a small hotel in Colorado. When I'd been there about six years, a construction crew came to town to do the finishing work on a retirement home project. There was a lounge—a bar in the hotel that was popular with the local people. Joe and the other men in the construction crew came into the bar on a regular basis."

Jennifer turned slowly to look at Jack, and he frowned as he saw that the color had drained from her face.

"Joe swept me off my feet," she said, her voice flat and low. "He made me feel beautiful, special, like the most important woman on the face of the earth. I was so…so unsophisticated and inexperienced and…I fell in love with him—or believed I was in love—and two weeks after I met him we were married. I was twenty-seven years old, but a young, unworldly twenty-seven, and Joe was thirty."

Jack nodded.

"I wanted a church wedding with my parents present, wanted to be married here in Prescott, but Joe said he couldn't get time off from work and he'd meet my mother and father later. We were married by a justice of the peace with office workers as witnesses, then moved into a tiny apartment."

Jennifer stopped speaking and stared into memory-filled space.

"And?" Jack prompted, hardly breathing.

"After a month of wedded bliss," Jennifer went on, "Joe said the job he was on was completed and he'd taken a new assignment out of town, two hundred miles away. He'd only be able to get home on the weekends. I wasn't happy about it, but I put on a brave face—wanted to be the perfect, supportive wife.

"I kept busy at work and lived for the weekends when Joe would be home," she said. "But he began to make excuses why he couldn't come—they were working overtime, he had the flu…whatever. I had to wait for him to telephone me, because he said there was no phone in the boarding house where the crew was staying."

Jack narrowed his eyes.

"I was lonely, so lonely," Jennifer said, shaking her head. "Then I found out that I was pregnant. Oh, how thrilled I was about the baby, could hardly wait to tell Joe. I was determined not to share my news over the telephone. It was too special, too wonderful. Or...so I thought."

"What happened?" Jack said quietly.

"Joe was gone for over a month after I discovered I was pregnant. When he finally came home, I fixed his favorite dinner, put candles on the table, dressed up so prettily for him. As we ate, I told him about the baby. He...he was furious. He said I was supposed to have made certain I wouldn't get pregnant. He didn't want any part of being a father, and I should terminate my pregnancy immediately."

"Ah, Jennifer," Jack said. "I'm so damn sorry."

"Oh, that's just the tip of the iceberg, Jack," she said, a sudden bitter edge to her voice. "This story gets even better. I refused to end the pregnancy, and Joe came home less and less, often staying away two months or more at a time. He wouldn't touch me when he did show up because he said I was fat, disgusting."

"Why—why didn't you divorce him?"

Jennifer pressed her fingertips to her temples. "I couldn't admit to myself that I'd made such a terrible mistake marrying Joe. I convinced myself that he'd change his attitude once he saw and held our baby."

"Jennifer," Jack said, extending one hand toward her.

"No," she said, her voice trembling. "Let me

finish. I'm hanging on by a thread here. Don't—don't comfort me, or I'll fall apart.''

"Don't say any more," Jack said, getting to his feet. "This is too painful for you. It's okay, Jennifer. We'll just leave it in the past where it belongs. We won't allow it to stand between us.''

"No, I'm going to get it all out," she said, her eyes filling with tears. "I need to. It's been festering within me for so long, consuming a part of me that I want back. Yes, I need to do this.''

"All right," Jack said, remaining on his feet.

"A week before the baby was born," she said, looking directly into Jack's eyes, "one of the men from Joe's construction crew came to the apartment. He told me that Joe had been killed when a wire holding a high platform let go and Joe fell to the ground. I was devastated. My parents flew up to be with me and we were informed that funeral arrangements had already been made. I didn't question that. I was numb—in shock.

"On the day of the funeral it rained," she said. "I don't know why I'm telling you that, except that at the time it seemed to represent my life—so bleak and dark. After the graveside service, a woman in her late forties asked to speak to me alone. My parents went on to the car, and I stood there with that stranger, that woman, next to Joe's casket.''

"Who was she?" Jack said, his heart racing.

A sob caught in Jennifer's throat. "Joe's wife! Are you getting this, Jack? *She was Joe's wife.* She sneered at me, said I was a stupid child, just one more in a long string of affairs that Joe had had. She didn't care if he played around, she said, because he always came home to her. And then she laughed, Jack. She laughed. She said Joe had really done it up big this time by actually going through with a marriage ceremony. He did love a challenge, she said, and had probably gotten a real kick out of seeing if he could pull it off.''

''That lousy son of a—'' Jack started, then shook his head.

''The baby was a joke on Joe, the woman said, still laughing that horrible laugh,'' Jennifer said, ''and it would have served him right to get stuck with child support. She left me standing there in the rain. I could hear her laughter as she walked away— heard it in my nightmares for months afterward… My world was shattered. It had all been lies, a joke, a game. I was so ashamed. How could I have been so gullible, so foolish, so—''

''Jennifer, don't,'' Jack said. ''It wasn't your fault. You couldn't have known that Joe—''

''*I trusted and believed in him,*'' she said, tears spilling onto her pale cheeks, ''*and he destroyed me.*''

''Damn it,'' Jack said, rubbing a hand over his face.

''I vowed, as I stood there in the rain staring at Joe's casket, that no one, *no one,* would ever know the truth. No one would know my shame. And even more important, I would protect my child from the truth of the kind of man his father really was.''

''And so you named your son after his father,'' Jack said, ''to indicate a—a memorial of love and respect and… You named the baby Joey.''

''Yes,'' Jennifer said, dashing the tears from her

cheeks. "But when I look at my son, say his name, I have no thoughts of Joe, of what he did, who he really was. Joey is mine. He has no…no connection to Joe Mackane. None. Joey will never learn the truth about his father."

A sob caught in Jennifer's throat and fresh tears filled her eyes. She lifted her chin and drew a deep, shuddering breath.

"So, did I pass your test, Jack?" she said, tears once again streaking her cheeks. "Did I get high enough marks? Are you satisfied now?"

"Oh, Jennifer."

Jack closed the distance between them and pulled Jennifer into his embrace, holding her tightly. She buried her face in his shoulder and wrapped her arms around his waist as she struggled not to cry.

"I'm so sorry," Jack said. "I shouldn't have pushed you to relive that pain. I've been so selfish, deciding how things should be between us, demanding that you…Jennifer, please forgive me for putting you through this ordeal. I love you, and I've hurt you, and I'm so damn sorry."

Jennifer raised her head to look at Jack, and he nearly groaned aloud as he saw the tears glistening on her pale cheeks and shimmering in her beautiful, green eyes.

"No, you didn't hurt me, Jack," Jennifer said, her voice trembling. "You were right. The past is over. It's the present and—and the future that matters. I do trust and believe in you. I do…love you."

Jack attempted to reply, but sudden, overwhelming emotions closed his throat. He shook his head slightly, then captured Jennifer's lips in a heartfelt kiss that he hoped would convey the words he was unable to speak.

Jennifer returned the kiss in total abandon, joyously aware that she was, at long last, free of the haunting, painful memories that had plagued her for so many years. She was free to live and free to love.

And as unbelievable and wondrous as it seemed, Jack loved her in return.

Jack gently broke the kiss, then wiped away Jennifer's tears with a stroke of his thumbs.

"Pretty heavy stuff, huh?" he said, his voice raspy.

"*Very* heavy." She smiled, then sniffled. "Very special. Very scary."

"Yep. Look, I have a suggestion to make," Jack said. "I'm sure as hell not saying this is how it has to be, because my dictator days are over after what I just did to you. But, I just think...maybe we shouldn't discuss the future yet—not yet. Let's give ourselves time to adjust to the idea that we've fallen in love. How does that sound?"

No, Jennifer thought. It was wrong. It meant she still had a secret, was still keeping something of great magnitude from Jack that might cause him to reconsider and end things between them now. She needed to tell him that she wanted it all—a forever with him. Wanted to be his wife, wanted him to be a father to her son.

"Okay?" Jack said. "Jennifer?"

"Yes, all right," she said. "We'll live in the present for now, savor it and how we feel about each other, because we're free of the past."

"We'll live one day at a time."

"There aren't that many days left before you're scheduled to leave for California, Jack."

"There's plenty of time," he said, lowering his head toward hers. "Plenty—" he brushed his lips over hers once "—of time—" twice "—my love." Then his mouth melted over hers in a feverish kiss.

A shiver of foreboding coursed through Jennifer, but was quickly replaced by the rushing current of desire that consumed her.

Chapter Fourteen

*T*ime.

It was such a small word, Jennifer thought, staring at the calendar on the kitchen wall. It had only four letters and rhymed with lime, and slime, and chime and...

Time, her mind echoed over and over. Time...time...time...

It was moving too fast. It hardly seemed possible that it had been nearly three weeks since the night she had told Jack the truth about Joe Mackane.

Three weeks since she and Jack had declared their love for each other.

Three glorious weeks of sharing, caring, making love.

Three weeks with not one word spoken by either of them about the future.

Time was rapidly ticking away, while screaming the fact that there were only ten days left until Christmas, the holiday that Jack was scheduled to spend in California with his family. She'd been so centered on Jack that she now realized she hadn't heard word from Deborah about putting the house on the market.

Jennifer sighed, glanced at her watch, then began to pace restlessly across the kitchen.

Up until this very moment, she'd wanted time to stop, leaving her suspended in the wondrous world that revolved around Jack and Joey.

But right now? she thought, looking at her watch again. She wanted the next four minutes to fly, instead of dragging by second by second the way it was.

In four more minutes—no, in three minutes and thirty-five seconds—she would hurry down the hallway to the bathroom and check the results of the home pregnancy test she'd taken.

"Oh, dear heaven," she said, stopping her trek and pressing her fingertips to her aching temples. Stay calm, she ordered herself. She was *not* pregnant. Her body was off-kilter, reacting to stress and fatigue. She'd taken the test to reassure herself of that fact, to put the ridiculous notion to rest once and for all.

She—was—not—pregnant.

She was exhausted, the pace at work having increased to a near-frenzy. Hamilton House was booked solid through the holidays, the nightly number of patrons in the dining room growing.

There were also endless private parties being held

in the conference rooms, events that required Jennifer to check and double-check a multitude of details, ensuring everything was ready.

There was Christmas shopping to complete, gifts to wrap, cards to be addressed and mailed. One entire, memory-making evening had been spent with Jack and Joey, buying a tree, setting it up in front of the living room windows, then decorating it as they played carols on the stereo.

Adding to her fatigue was the fact that she hadn't been sleeping well. In the dark, quiet hours of the night, the underlying tension and stress hovering around her and Jack reared its nagging head and screamed her doubts and fears over Jack and his intentions.

Despite his declaration of love, did Jack still plan to walk out of her life before Christmas? Was her love, her trust and belief in Jack MacAllister misplaced? Was he going to shatter her hopes, her dreams, her heart by leaving her forever?

Oh, Jack said he loved her, but did he wish to spend the rest of his life with her? Did he want to be her husband, and a father for Joey?

The questions were there, always there, demanding more attention with each passing day.

No wonder her body was out of whack, she thought, throwing up her hands. She'd had several dizzy spells because of the building stress she was under. Her appetite was nonexistent, and when she did eat she became queasy.

But no, she wasn't pregnant. She was a woman in love who had to know what the future held. What was called for here was another serious discussion with Jack.

"Definitely," she said decisively, then looked at her watch. "Okay. Time is up."

She marched from the kitchen, her eyes narrowed as she envisioned sitting Jack down that night after Joey was asleep and telling Mr. MacAllister that enough was enough. They had to talk about their future together—or lack of same.

She'd wasted precious money buying the pregnancy test kit, Jennifer thought as she approached the bathroom. She didn't have a nickel to spare during the holidays aside from what she spent on presents for everyone on her long list.

With a cluck of self-disgust, she entered the bathroom and went to the vanity where she'd placed the pieces of the kit.

And then she stopped breathing.

Her heartbeat pounded painfully in her ears. Tiny black dots danced before her eyes, and she gripped the edge of the sink with both hands as she stared at the little plastic device.

"Oh, God," she whispered, "no. It's wrong. A mistake. This isn't true." She drew a wobbly breath, and a bubble of hysterical laughter escaped from her lips. "Yes, it is. I'm pregnant. I'm carrying another baby who might not be welcomed by its father. Dear heaven, what am I going to do?"

With trembling hands, Jennifer collected the pieces of the kit, stuffed them into the box, then hurried back down the hallway. In the kitchen she shoved the box into the trash basket, hiding it under a layer of debris.

Then she sank onto a chair at the table, rested her elbows on the place mat and dropped her face into her shaking hands.

Jack's baby, her mind thundered. She was pregnant with Jack MacAllister's baby. How had this happened? They were always careful. Jack protected her every time they made love and—

Jennifer raised her head and her eyes widened. *One night.* There had been one night when she had clung to Jack, hadn't wanted him to leave her even for a moment. It had been after the horrifying ordeal of Joey's surgery. She had been physically exhausted and emotionally drained, had wanted only to escape to the blissful place Jack took her when they made love.

She had almost forgotten about that passion-filled night. She now remembered that she'd told Jack it was all right, it was the wrong time of the month for her to become pregnant—and that had been true. But her body obviously hadn't been paying attention to the calendar.

And she'd conceived Jack's child.

Jennifer sank back in the chair and splayed her hands on her flat stomach. Jack's baby, her mind whispered. No, it was *her* baby. Her secret. She was not going to tell Jack about this child unless he came to her and asked her to marry him. She wouldn't trap him into proposing to her, thus sentencing herself to a lifetime of wondering if he truly wished to be by her side.

If Jack packed up and left, went to California per his original plan, he would never, ever know that this child existed.

And the serious discussion with Jack that she'd scheduled on the agenda for this evening? Oh, yes, they'd have that talk, but she'd keep a tight rein on her emotions, be very certain that she didn't blurt out her news of the baby. She'd wait to hear what Jack had to say.

Wait…while she hoped and prayed that he'd ask her to be his wife. Then, and only then, would she tell him about this baby.

Jennifer stiffened as she heard the sound of the front door, accompanied by Joey's chatter. She got to her feet, produced what she felt was a passable smile and went into the living room.

"I bought your Christmas present, Mom," Joey said, jumping up and down. "It's wrapped and everything. You can't peek at it, either."

"Oh, it's beautiful," Jennifer said, smiling. "Why don't you put it under the tree?" She looked at Jack, who was shrugging out of his jacket. "You survived shopping with Joey, I see."

Jack tossed his jacket onto a chair, then turned to look at Jennifer, a frown on his face. "Yeah, it was fun," he said. "Joey has champagne tastes on a beer budget, though." He paused. "We bumped into a woman named Deborah while we were in one of the stores. She recognized Joey and asked me to give you a message."

"Oh?"

"She said you knew she'd been called out of town on a family emergency, but she had just gotten back and hoped to show your house to prospective buyers very soon."

Jennifer shrugged. "Okay. That explains why I

haven't heard from her. Thank you for telling me. Why don't you two gentlemen wash up, because I have a casserole in the oven for dinner and it should be ready in about five minutes.''

"'Kay,'' Joey said, running from the room.

Jack walked slowly toward Jennifer, his frown still firmly in place. "You didn't tell me that you'd definitely decided to sell this house,'' he said, sweeping one arm through the air as he stopped in front of her.

"I didn't?'' Jennifer said, matching his frown. "I thought I'd mentioned it. I made up my mind right after Thanksgiving, but you were in Phoenix and... Oh, well, nothing has happened about it because Deborah was called away. But she's back now so...'' She shrugged again.

"You're awfully casual about such a major decision in your life, Jennifer. If you sell this house, you'll need a new place to live.''

"Well, yes, that's generally how it goes, but to tell you the truth, I've been so busy I haven't given the whole subject much thought.''

"To tell me the truth,'' Jack said, his frown deepening. "Interesting premise. Damn it, Jennifer, don't you think I had the right to know that you intended to sell your home and start over somewhere else? Just where do you believe that somewhere will be?''

"I don't have a clue,'' she said, planting her hands on her hips. "Nor do I have the slightest idea what you're pitching a fit about. I'm obviously missing something here. Would you care to enlighten me, Mr. MacAllister?''

"Washed my hands," Joey said, racing back into the living room. "I'm hungry. Can we eat now?"

"Yes, of course." Jennifer shot a glare at Jack before directing her attention to her son. "You can help me set the table while Jack washes his hands." She spun around and headed for the kitchen. "Come on, Joey."

He was definitely losing it, Jack thought as he walked slowly down the hallway to the bathroom. He'd felt his tension building as each day went by, bringing him closer and closer to the time he was scheduled to leave for California. There was a knot in his gut that kept coiling more and more tightly.

In the bathroom, Jack scrubbed his hands, dried them, then studied his reflection in the mirror mounted above the sink. It wouldn't have surprised him to see that he'd grown a couple more heads, each containing a brain that was focused on a different subject.

One part of him was in heaven. Being with Jennifer, knowing she loved him as he loved her, was fantastic, out of this world. During the past weeks they'd operated as a family—Jennifer, Jack and Joey. Mommy bear, daddy bear and baby bear. Perfect. He was so content and happy in his roles that his feelings defied description.

But there was another part of him that felt like a ticking bomb that was counting down the days, hours, minutes, seconds until he had to gather his shaky courage and ask Jennifer to marry him. He wanted her and Joey to leave Prescott, come to California with him, be part of the new life he would start there.

What if Jennifer refused his proposal? What if she said no? What if she smashed his heart to smithereens and sentenced him to a bleak, empty, lonely existence without her?

And then there was the third brain, the ugly one that refused to completely disappear. It had a voice, that brain, that taunted him, told him not to let down his guard like a fool, but to be on alert for the possibility that Jennifer did, indeed, have a secret agenda.

It had been that part of his mind that had reacted to the previously unknown news that Jennifer had decided weeks ago to sell this house.

Why hadn't she told him? Was she envisioning a huge new home on the coast, with him picking up the tab? Was she breathing a sigh of relief that her days of standing on her feet for long hours as the manager of the dining room at Hamilton House would soon be over if she became a lady of leisure at his expense?

"Damn," Jack said aloud, dragging both hands down his face. How could he even entertain such rotten thoughts about the woman he loved? The woman he *knew* was real and honest. The woman he trusted and believed in.

He'd been so sure that he'd put his past behind him, just as Jennifer had, but there was a dark shadow left within him that still claimed a part of his soul.

"What are you going to do, MacAllister?" he said, leaning toward the mirror. "Walk out of her life, or ask her to go with you?"

Jack left the small room and headed for the

kitchen, his thoughts tumbling one into the next, creating a jumbled maze of confusion.

He loved Jennifer Mackane and intended to spend the rest of his life with her.

But why hadn't she told him she'd put her house on the market?

Jennifer believed in him, trusted him with her heart—the very essence of herself—and with her precious son.

Or was the total abandonment of her lovemaking and her urging him to spend time with Joey part of a master plan to snag herself a financially secure husband and a devoted father for Joey?

Ah, hell, he couldn't go on like this. Not only was he running out of time on the calendar, he was slowly but surely losing his sanity, as well.

Tonight. Yes, tonight after Joey was asleep, he was going to have a serious discussion with Jennifer. Tonight, decisions would be made that would determine the course of their futures. This was the night.

Jack entered the kitchen to find Jennifer talking on the telephone and Joey hopping up and down like a pogo stick beside her, a big smile on his face.

"All right," Jennifer said into the receiver. "Forty-five minutes. I'll try to get some dinner into him before you pick him up. 'Bye."

Jennifer replaced the receiver and looked at Joey. "Halt," she said. "Sit. Eat."

"'Kay," Joey said, then ran to the table and slid onto his chair.

"What's going on?" Jack said.

"That was Sammy's mother on the phone," Jennifer said, not looking directly at Jack. "The families on their block are going Christmas caroling, and they invited Joey to go, then spend the night with Sammy.''

"Oh," Jack said, nodding.

"Hurry, hurry," Joey said. "I gotta eat and pack my stuff.''

"We'll have to bundle you up good," Jennifer said. "It's starting to snow outside. Isn't that fun, Joey? Singing Christmas carols in the snow.''

"Neat-o," Joey yelled. "Cool.''

"Cold," Jennifer said. "You keep your mittens on, young man.''

"'Kay.''

They consumed the meal hastily, then Jennifer left the kitchen with Joey to help him pack for the sleep-over and to put on the layers of clothes for the outing.

Jack began to clear the table. As he scraped the food from a plate into the trash, he frowned as he saw that the liner in the basket was full. He pulled it free, tied a knot in the top and headed out the back door, flipping on the backyard light as he went.

The snow was falling in big, wet flakes, turning everything into a winter wonderland.

As Jack swung the bag up to place it in the large container provided by the city, the bottom of the liner struck the edge and split, spilling trash onto the ground that was becoming rapidly covered with snow.

"Ah, hell," he said, hunkering down to scoop up the debris. Then his outstretched hand stilled and his heart began to race in a wild cadence. With visibly shaking fingers he picked up the box that announced in bold letters Home Pregnancy Test Kit. He shook the contents onto the ground, looked at the plastic device, then flipped the box over to read the chart on the back.

"Positive," he said. "Holy hell, Jennifer...Jennifer is pregnant."

A red haze of fury and heartfelt pain assaulted him, making it difficult to breathe. He flung the scattered trash into the container and slammed the lid, his breathing labored, his motions jerky. He cleaned his hands with the freshly fallen snow, then attempted to dry them on his damp jeans.

Then he turned and stared at the house that suddenly seemed to be miles away, out of his reach, disappearing into oblivion and leaving only the dark, chilling emptiness of betrayal behind.

You're a natural-born father, Jack.

We're in this together, Jack.

It's the wrong time of the month. It's safe. Don't leave me. Come to me, Jack. Please.

You're a natural-born father...natural-born father...natural-born...

"No!" Jack said, his voice raspy. "Oh, God, Jennifer, no."

Lies. It had all been lies. Jennifer Mackane was like all the others. She'd had a secret agenda the entire time they'd been together, had set out to trap him and—

The back door of the house was flung open, and Joey poked his head out. "'Bye, Jack," he said. "I'm going singing in the snow now."

"What? Oh, have a great time, sport."

"See ya," Joey said, then slammed the door.

"See ya," Jack said quietly.

He started toward the house, struggling to put one foot in front of the other. He felt drained, and had to tell himself to breathe in, then out.

He entered the kitchen, vaguely aware that he was tracking wet snow onto the clean floor. He closed the door, leaned against it, then drew a shuddering breath.

"'Bye," Jennifer called in the distance. "Have fun. I love you, Joey."

Jennifer was smiling when she returned to the kitchen, but frowned when she looked at Jack. "My goodness," she said, "you're all wet. What have you been doing?"

"I—I took out the trash," Jack said quietly.

"Oh. Well, thank you. Why don't you go in by the fire and dry off? I'll take care of this mess from dinner and join you in a few minutes. You might catch a cold if you stand around in those damp clothes."

"Once a mother, always a mother," Jack said gruffly, starting across the room. "Right, Jennifer?"

"I..." she said.

"I'll be in the living room."

Jennifer watched Jack disappear from view, then began to clean the kitchen. Jack was still acting strangely, she thought. Was he brooding about her not telling him she'd decided to sell her house? Why was he making such a big deal out of something she'd simply forgotten to mention?

Maybe she was reading too much into Jack's behavior. He was cold and damp at the moment and was probably grumpy because of it. She was so jangled, due to discovering that she was pregnant, that she wasn't capable of thinking clearly. Yes, that was it. *She* was the one who was upset—not Jack.

When she joined him in the living room, he'd be his usual chipper self. And she'd tell him that they needed to have a very serious discussion.

What she would *not* tell him was that she was carrying his baby—*unless* he first asked her to marry him.

What transpired with Jack this evening would determine her entire future.

When the kitchen was clean, Jennifer drew a steadying breath, then went into the living room. Jack was standing in front of the fireplace, staring at the leaping flames. She settled onto the end cushion of the sofa, then splayed one hand on her stomach for a moment.

"Jack," she said, "we need to talk."

He turned slowly toward her, a closed expression on his face.

"Yes," he said, nodding, "we do. Go ahead. I'm listening."

"Well, time is running out," Jennifer said, clasping her hands in her lap. "There's only a week or so left before you'll be leaving for California."

"Yep," he said, folding his arms over his chest. "I've promised everyone that I'll be there for Christmas, for the reunion."

"Yes, I know." Jennifer paused. "Jack, these weeks we've had together have been wonderful. We agreed not to discuss the future, but the days are passing so quickly that the future is becoming the present."

· "Mmm," Jack said, nodding.

"You're scheduled to leave, and I need to know what you're thinking about us, about…" Jennifer threw up her hands and sighed.

"At the risk of sounding like Aunt Prudence," Jack said, "you want to know if I have honorable intentions regarding you. Right?"

"That's one way to put it, I guess," Jennifer said, frowning slightly.

"Isn't there something you need to tell me at this point, Jennifer?" Jack said, narrowing his eyes.

"No," she said slowly. "Only that I love you very much."

"Damn it, Jennifer," Jack yelled, shifting his hands to his hips, "knock it off, would you? Enough is enough. I know what your agenda is, so give the game-playing a rest."

"I don't know what you're talking about," Jennifer said, getting to her feet. "Why are you so angry? Why are you shouting at me?"

"You heard me say that I took out the trash. Didn't it occur to you that my clothes and hair were awfully wet for a quick run to the trash container and back?"

"I—"

"The bag broke, spilling trash into the snow," Jack said, his volume still on high. "I picked up the junk—and guess what I found? A handy-dandy, home pregnancy test kit with a plastic deal that was still registering the big news."

"Oh, dear heaven." Jennifer sank back onto the sofa as her knees began to tremble.

Jack strode forward and braced one hand on the

arm of the sofa, the other on the top, trapping Jennifer in place. She leaned back instinctively as Jack loomed above her, a muscle ticking in his jaw.

"When did you plan to tell me that you're pregnant with my baby?" he said, his voice low and harsh. "Were you holding your trump card until you found out if I intended to ask you to marry me? And if I'd said, 'Well, it's been a helluva fine time, sweetheart, but I'm outta here,' were you going to whip your newsflash on me? Push my buttons, yank my strings like I was a marionette? Try to force me to marry you? When, Jennifer? When did you plan to inform me that you're carrying my baby?"

Jennifer flattened her hands on Jack's chest and shoved him away. He straightened, and she scrambled to her feet, immediately spinning around to face him, her green eyes flashing.

"I wasn't going to tell you at all," she said, nearly yelling, "unless you asked me to marry you. I had no intention of doing what you're accusing me of doing."

"Yeah, right," he said, his voice ringing with bitterness. "You put your house up for sale so you'd be ready, footloose and fancy-free when it came time to go to California with me. Ah, yes, *me,* the 'natural-born father' of the century. You've been sliding that little zinger in every chance you got. And if I refused to marry you despite your being pregnant? Well, hey, just go to plan B. Hire a sharp attorney and soak me for every dime you could get in child support."

"No!" Jennifer said, shaking her head. "If you didn't love me enough to want me to be your wife, to stay by your side until death parted us, then you would never have known about this child. It would be *my* baby. Mine. Just as Joey is mine with no connection to Joe.''

''Damn it, Jennifer, you're insulting my intelligence. Oh, that's a hoot. My intelligence. I was such a fool, just like I've been with every woman I've ever been involved with. I even fell for your 'It's the wrong time of the month for me to get pregnant' crap. You're slick, Jennifer, very good. You had me under your spell, knew it, and everything fell right into place for you.''

''No, Jack, you're wrong,'' Jennifer said, unwelcome tears filling her eyes. ''How can you say such horrible things to me? I thought you loved me, believed in me, trusted me, as I did you. You're betraying my love and trust in your own way, just as Joe did in his. Dear God, Jack, don't do this to us.''

''Don't try to lay a guilt trip on *me*,'' he said. ''*You're* the one who's so conveniently pregnant. I'm just the idiot who bought into your phony facade. Well, nice try, lady, but you lose. Oh, you'll get your child support money, but you're not snaring me in your matrimony trap.''

Jack laughed, the sound sharp and humorless. ''Want to know the kicker? I'd planned to ask you to marry me. I wasn't sure what I was going to do, but I know now that I wouldn't have been able to leave for California without you and Joey. Well, forget it, Ms. Mackane. I'm going to the coast *alone*.''

''Fine. You do that,'' she said, wrapping her hands around her elbows. ''Don't bother to send child support checks, because I'll tear them up. I don't want anything from you, Jack MacAllister. Nothing.''

"You can't keep my child from me if I decide that I want to be part of his life. That decision will be mine—not yours. I'll make that clear to your attorney when I'm contacted about how much I'm to shell out to you every month.''

"Stop it!'' Jennifer shrieked, shaking her head. "You're destroying everything we've had together.'' Tears spilled onto her cheeks. "You're not even leaving me the memories I thought I could cherish. I trusted you, Jack, believed in you and, equally important, I believed that you trusted me. I—'' A sob caught in Jennifer's throat, choking off her words.

"Don't bother turning on the tears,'' Jack said. "They won't work this time. I'm leaving, Jennifer. I'm leaving this house, this town.''

He looked up at the ceiling for a moment, struggling to regain control of his emotions. He looked at Jennifer again, and when he spoke his voice was a hoarse whisper. "Damn it. Why couldn't you have been real?''

Jack snatched up his jacket from where he'd tossed it onto the chair and strode to the door.

"Jack,'' Jennifer said, tears echoing in her voice.

He stopped, his back to her, one hand gripping the doorknob.

"I *am* real,'' Jennifer said. "I know that I didn't set out to get pregnant, despite what you believe. I know that my love for you is genuine. None of that matters to you now, but I'll seek solace in those truths. I won't keep you from being a part of your child's life if you choose to be, but I will *not* accept one penny from you. I have to think of Joey, too. Would you meet him after school tomorrow and walk him home, say a proper goodbye? Don't break his heart, too, by just disappearing from his world.''

''Yeah, I'll walk him home tomorrow.''

''Thank you. You won't have to see me again. Just leave Joey on the porch after you bring him home. I'm back on the evening shift at the hotel starting tomorrow, but I imagine you'll be gone by the time you might join Andrea and Brandon and the aunts for dinner.'' Another sob caught in Jennifer's throat. ''Goodbye, Jack.''

Jack's hand on the doorknob began to tremble and he muttered an earthy expletive. He yanked open the door and left the house, slamming the door closed behind him.

Jennifer gave way to her tears, allowing them to flow freely down her face and along her neck. The distance to the sofa was too far to walk, would require more energy than she possessed.

She sank to her knees on the floor, wrapped her arms around herself and wept from the very depths of her soul as her heart shattered into a million pieces.

Chapter Fifteen

"No!" Joey burst into tears and flung his arms around Jack's neck. "I don't want you to leave, Jack. Please don't go away. I don't want to have to give you back the way I do Uncle Brandon and Uncle Ben. No, no, no."

Jack rose from his hunkered position on the sidewalk leading to the porch of Jennifer's house. He lifted Joey into his arms as he straightened, holding him tightly.

As Joey buried his face in the crook of Jack's neck and cried, a knot tightened in Jack's gut and an achy sensation burned his throat. "Don't cry, sport," Jack said, his voice husky. "You knew I would be going to California before Christmas. I have a lot of miles to drive."

"You don't have to go," Joey said, his voice

muffled. "You can draw pictures of houses here. You can stay with me and my mommy, Jack. You can. We could be a real family, just like Sammy has, and you could kiss my mom so we could get a baby, and—"

"Joey, stop it," Jack said.

This bundle in his arms was tearing him apart, Jack thought miserably. He'd known this farewell was going to be rough but, oh, man... He was exhausted, had hardly slept the night before as he'd replayed that final scene with Jennifer over and over in his mind. He was emotionally drained, sliced and diced, and now Joey was pouring salt in his raw wounds.

"Come on, partner," Jack said. "Don't cry."

"I have to cry 'cause I'm sad," Joey said, then sniffled.

Jack set the little boy on his feet and pried his arms free. "Okay, you're right," Jack said. "There's nothing wrong with crying when you're sad. But that doesn't mean that the tears will change how things are. I really do have to go, Joey."

Joey swiped his nose across the sleeve of his jacket, then glared at Jack. "No, you don't," Joey said. "You want to leave, that's what. You like me and my mom, but you don't love us, 'cause if you did you'd stay with us. I love you, Jack, and my mom does, too. I know she does, 'cause she smiles at you all the time with the special smile that makes her eyes happy. How come you don't love us back?"

"I..." Jack started, then stopped speaking and shook his head. He *did* love Joey, as much as any man could love his own son. And Jennifer? He loved the woman he'd believed she was before her duplicity came to light. "Go into the house, Joey. It's cold out here."

"No."

"Yes. Go on. I'll never forget you, sport. You'll always be my buddy."

Joey stomped toward the house, his unhappiness emphasized by every heavy step he took. Jack watched until Joey had gone inside and slammed the door, then turned and walked slowly away, his heart aching.

I love you, Jack, and my mom does, too…smiles at you all the time with the special smile that makes her eyes happy.

I trusted you, Jack, believed in you and, equally important, I believed that you trusted me.

We could be a family, just like Sammy has.

I won't keep you from being a part of your child's life if you choose to be, but I will not accept one penny from you.

I don't want to have to give you back the way I do Uncle Brandon and Uncle Ben.

I know that I didn't set out to get pregnant, despite what you believe. I know that my love for you is genuine.

Jack stopped and pressed his fingers to his temples.

How long would he be tormented by Jennifer and Joey's words?

How long would he hear their voices, and see both of them so vividly in his mind?

How did a man forget a little boy who had captured his heart?

How did he live with the pain of being betrayed by the only woman he had ever loved?

Jack sighed and started off again, finally arriving at Hamilton House. When he entered the lobby of the hotel, he saw Andrea standing by the huge, decorated Christmas tree by the front windows. He quickened his step, not wanting to engage in a conversation with her—or anyone, for that matter.

"Jack?" Andrea said.

Damn, he thought, halting in his tracks. "Hi," he said quietly as he turned to face her.

Andrea came over to where Jack stood and frowned as she studied his face. "What's wrong?" she said finally. "You look like you just lost your best friend."

"Got it in one," Jack said, attempting to produce a smile, but failing miserably. "Two of them, in fact." He paused. "Listen, I'm heading out, leaving for California as soon as I get packed. I have a Christmas present for Joey in my room, and I was wondering if you would give it to him for me?"

"Why can't you do it yourself?" Andrea said.

"Because I've already said goodbye to him."

"I didn't realize that you were planning on leaving so soon, Jack. I mean, I thought that you and Jennifer were..." Andrea's voice trailed off.

"Yeah, well, things aren't always what they appear to be, are they?" he said, an edge to his voice. "To be more precise, people aren't always who they present themselves to be."

Andrea narrowed her eyes. "Are you referring to Jennifer?"

"Never mind," Jack said wearily. "There's nothing to be gained by rehashing the whole thing. I made a mistake. End of story."

"Yo, MacAllister," Brandon called. He crossed the lobby to join Jack and Andrea. "What's happening?"

"Jack is leaving this afternoon," Andrea said.

"You are?" Brandon said. "Why?"

"Because he's convinced he made a mistake by falling love with Jennifer," Andrea said.

"Hey, wait a minute," Jack said. "I never said that I was in love with Jennifer."

"Oh, for Pete's sake," Andrea said, "how dumb do you think we all are? Any idiot who sees you two together would know you love each other."

"*I* could even tell," Brandon said. "And I have a tendency to be a tad slow on the uptake about these things. The way Jennifer looks at you, smiles at you, Jack? Oh, yeah, she loves you—and, I will add, you love her."

"Just drop it, okay?" Jack said. "Don't go there. It's complicated and... Bottom line? It's over."

"Because Jennifer wasn't who she presented herself to be?" Andrea said.

"Yes!" Jack said, none too quietly. "I have to go pack."

"Don't—you—move," Andrea said.

"Uh-oh," Brandon said. "You're really in for it now, buddy."

Andrea pointed to a grouping of chairs in the lobby. "Sit, Mr. MacAllister."

"Hell," Jack said, then strode to one of the chairs and slouched at the edge of it. He unbuttoned his jacket and glared at Andrea and Brandon as they sat down opposite him. "Where's the bare lightbulb?"

"It can be arranged," Andrea said. "All right, give me one example of how Jennifer isn't who she presented herself to be."

Jack leaned forward and rested his elbows on his knees. "Okay. Try this on for size. Do you know that Jennifer plans to sell her house?"

"Yes," Andrea said, nodding. "She gave the listing to Deborah, who hasn't had time to put up a sign on Jennifer's lawn because there was a family emergency. Deborah is back now, though."

"Oh," Jack said. "Yeah, well, I bet Jennifer didn't happen to mention where she intends to live once her house is sold."

"I'll take that bet," Brandon said. "Jennifer told Deborah she wanted a town house for her and Joey so the outside maintenance would be taken care of."

"Oh," Jack said, frowning. "She said that?"

"Yes, Jack, she did," Andrea said, staring at him intently. "And if she said it, then it's true. Jennifer places a tremendous amount of importance on honesty."

"Right," Jack said dryly, leaning back in the chair again.

"Jack, let me tell you something," Andrea said. "I confronted Jennifer on Thanksgiving, asked her if she was in love with you. She said she was falling in love with you, but wasn't planning on telling you because she was afraid you'd leave Prescott earlier than scheduled. She wanted to share every possible moment she could with you. Jennifer knew that you'd leave before Christmas, but she was willing to run the risk of having her heart broken. She allowed herself to be totally vulnerable because of how much she loved you. She assured me that she would handle it just fine when you left, but I've been so worried that she wouldn't…''

Jack's gaze was riveted on Andrea, and his heart thundered, echoing in his ears.

''Oh, Jack, don't you see?'' Andrea said gently. ''Jennifer's love for you is so real, so pure and honest, that her own potential heartache was unimportant compared to what she was sharing with you. Jennifer wasn't who she presented herself to be? She isn't capable of being anyone other than herself. She just doesn't know how.''

Jack drew Andrea's softly spoken words deep within himself, then waited for the cacophony of voices, bringing the doubts, the evidence of betrayal, the pain.

But they didn't come.

The cold chill within him was replaced by an incredible warmth, a soothing touch of peace and understanding that caressed his mind. Though it had taken some very special friends to knock some sense into him, in his heart and soul he knew the truth about Jennifer. And the error of his ways.

''Dear God,'' he said, his voice husky with emotion, ''what have I done? I accused Jennifer of—I was so sure that she had— My fears created by my past had a louder voice than the truth of Jennifer's love for me and…I've lost…*I've lost the only woman I've ever loved.*''

"That's what I thought once myself," Brandon said quietly, "but I was wrong. Women in love are incredible creatures, Jack." Brandon got to his feet, then extended one hand toward Andrea to assist her from the chair. "You blew it?" Brandon said. "Then fix it, buddy."

"Go to her, Jack," Andrea said. "Give Jennifer a chance to forgive you."

Jennifer threw back the blankets on the bed with a disgusted click of her tongue. She shoved her feet into her Big Bird slippers and left the bedroom, unable to sleep and refusing to lie there and toss and turn for another moment.

Four-thirty in the morning, she thought, entering the living room, and she'd only had snatches of sleep. She couldn't go on like this. She was consumed by images of Jack, memories of Jack. His smile. His touch. His masculine aroma and rumbly chuckle. His beautiful chocolate fudge sauce eyes. His—

"Jennifer, shut up, please," she said aloud.

After her eyes adjusted to the darkness, she wandered over to the Christmas tree, then her glance fell on the drapes covering the remainder of the windows not filled by the tree.

Look at the sidewalk, Jennifer, she told herself. *See that it's empty. Jack isn't there. He'll never be there again. He's gone...forever.*

Jennifer brushed aside the curtain, then gasped at the same moment she felt her heart begin to beat a rapid tattoo.

Jack was standing on the sidewalk! There he was,

in the same spot she'd first seen him so many weeks ago. Jack was there.

He was hunched against the cold, his hands shoved into the pockets of his jacket. It was snowing lightly, and the street lamp cast an eerie glow in the snow-filled darkness.

Jennifer dropped the curtain and pressed trembling hands to her cheeks. Get a grip, she told herself. There was no way on earth that Jack MacAllister was really standing on that sidewalk at four-thirty in the morning in the freezing cold. Her imagination and heartfelt desire to see Jack had conjured up an image of him that wasn't real. Jack was in California, no doubt sleeping soundly after the long drive to the coast.

"Rest, Jennifer, you need rest," she said. "You're slipping over the edge."

She turned from the drapes, then hesitated.

All right, she thought. Just one more teeny, tiny peek to prove to herself that she was once again in control. Jack was *not* standing on that sidewalk. And after that nonsense was settled, she was going back to bed.

She moved close to the curtains and opened them just enough to peer out with one eye. "Oh, dear heaven," she whispered, "he's still there."

Her breath caught as the ghostly figure of Jack pulled one hand from his pocket, waved, then pointed toward the front door of the house.

As though her head did not belong to her, it nodded in agreement, and the mirage on the sidewalk started toward the house.

Jennifer dropped the edge of the curtain and

smoothed her nightshirt neatly over her hips. Poor Joey, poor new little baby, she thought rather hysterically. Their mother is a cuckoo.

Jennifer snapped on a lamp, then went to the front door and unlocked and opened it. The next instant she slapped both hands over her mouth to stifle a scream.

Filling the doorway was an enormous furry brown teddy bear wearing a suit and tie.

"May I come in? Please?" the bear said. "I'm frozen solid."

Jennifer heard a funny-sounding giggle, then realized it had come from her. "Well, certainly," she said, stepping back. "Never let it be said that I allowed a bear to freeze to death on my front porch."

The bear entered the room, and Jennifer closed the door.

As she turned, she saw Jack set the bear on the floor, then straighten and smile at her. "Hi," he said.

"If you think that I intend to carry on a conversation with a figment of my imagination," Jennifer said with an indignant sniff, "you're crazy. Correct that. *I am* crazy and I've had enough of this malarkey. I'm going back to bed. Goodbye."

"Jennifer, wait," Jack said, raising one hand. "You're not imagining that I'm here. I'm real."

"Don't be ridiculous. Why would you be standing on my sidewalk, transforming yourself into a six-foot Popsicle at four-thirty in the morning?"

"Actually," Jack said, "I've been out there since about three o'clock. I couldn't sleep, needed to see and talk to you the minute you woke up so…" Jack shrugged. "It seemed like a good idea at the time but, damn, I'm cold."

Jennifer reached out tentatively with one finger and poked Jack in the chest. "Merciful saints," she said, her eyes widening, "you *are* real."

"Could I start a fire in the hearth so I can defrost?"

"Go for it," Jennifer said, then looked at the bear. "I suppose that bear is really here, too."

"Yep."

Jack went to the fireplace and began the process of making a fire. Jennifer studied the huge bear for a long moment, shook her head slightly, then followed Jack across the room and sank onto the sofa.

As the flames began to crackle in the hearth, Jack closed the screen and turned to look at Jennifer, all traces of his smile gone.

"I had to see you, Jennifer," he said quietly. "Talk to you. I've come here to tell you how much I love you and to beg your forgiveness for what I did. I said some lousy things to you, hurt you terribly, which is something I had vowed never to do. I was wrong, so damn wrong, and I'm more sorry than I'll ever be able to express to you in words."

Jennifer sank back against the sofa cushion, her gaze fixed on Jack.

"I was so determined," Jack went on, "that you put your past to rest, be free of your ghosts, that I wasn't aware that I hadn't finished dealing with my own. When I found out that you planned to sell this house, then discovered that you were pregnant, I was flung back in time—couldn't see, or think, beyond the memories of all the women who had duped me."

"But I—"

"But you," Jack interrupted, "are not like any of those women. You're open, and honest, and exactly who you present yourself to be. I know…now…that you didn't set out to trap me into marriage by getting pregnant. I know now that your decision to sell this house wasn't part of a secret agenda, a master plan of deception. You put the pain of your past behind you—and I have finally done the same. Oh, Jennifer, I love you so much. I want to spend the rest of my life with you, with Joey, with our baby you're now carrying, and three or four more little MacAllisters."

Tears filled Jennifer's eyes, and she had to remind herself to breathe.

"I guess you're wondering about that bear," Jack said. "He's sort of…tangible evidence of what I'm attempting to say to you. I want to be a groom guy, wearing a suit and tie. I want to be the daddy bear when we create a family. I trust and believe in you, Jennifer, I swear I do… Jennifer, please forgive me. Please. Say you will, and say you'll be my wife. *Oh, God, Jennifer, please.*"

Jack opened his arms to her.

Jennifer flew off the sofa and into his embrace. He staggered slightly from the impact, then wrapped his arms around her so tightly that it was as though he'd never let her go again.

"Yes," Jennifer said, "I forgive you. Yes, I'll marry you. Oh, Jack, I love you beyond measure."

"Thank you," he said, drawing a deep breath of relief. "Will you move to California with me?"

"Of course." Jennifer paused. "There's just one thing that we need to discuss."

"What is it?"

"How many little MacAllisters did you say we should produce?"

Jack chuckled, and Jennifer shivered at the wonderful, familiar, masculine sound.

"One at a time, my love," he said. "How's that?"

"Perfect."

Jack lowered his head and captured Jennifer's lips in a kiss that spoke of commitment, of pain dealt with and dismissed for all time, of love that was rich and deep, honest and real.

"You're kissing my mom!"

Jennifer and Jack jerked apart, breaking the kiss, but Jack continued to hold Jennifer close to him.

Joey jumped up and down in excitement. "You are," he said. "You're kissing my mom, Jack. We're going to get a baby. We're going to be a family. Right? I won't ever have to give you back, will I, Jack?"

"No, Joey," Jack said, smiling. "You won't ever have to give me back."

"Neat-o!" Joey yelled. "Wow! Look at that big teddy bear. Cool."

"You can have him," Jack said, "because I'm going to be a *real* groom guy and daddy bear." He shifted his gaze to Jennifer again. "We're going to be together."

"Forever," Jennifer whispered, smiling through her tears. "Forever."

*   *   *   *   *

SPECIAL EDITION™

PRESCRIPTION: LOVE by Pamela Toth

Montana

When city slicker Zoe Hart arrived in Thunder Canyon, she wasn't expecting sexy local physician Christopher Taylor to sweep her off her feet the way he did. But would Zoe opt to stay with the man who made her pulse race like no other?

THE OTHER SIDE OF PARADISE
by Laurie Paige

Seven Devils

There's an instant attraction between Mary McHale and her new boss, Jonah Lanigan, but Mary's eerie similarity to the Daltons who live on the next ranch takes her away. She must decide whether to stay with her new-found family or follow her heart…

FAMILY MERGER by Leigh Greenwood

Millionaire Ron Egan's teenage daughter was pregnant and beautiful Kathryn Roper seemed to be the only bridge between Ron and his daughter. But should Kathryn and Ron ignore their powerful yearnings for each other…?

Don't miss out!
On sale from 16th June 2006

0606/18a

SILHOUETTE®
Sensation ™

SUSPICIOUS by Heather Graham

When police officer Jesse Crane returned to his Florida home town, he was shocked to discover a rash of mysterious killings. Lawyer Lorena Fortier, who was working undercover at an alligator farm with mysteries of its own, was the key he needed—and wanted—to solve the case. Her beauty intrigued him, but mixing business with pleasure was never a good idea—or so he thought.

ROMANCING THE RENEGADE
by Ingrid Weaver

Payback

Timid bookworm Lydia Smith had no idea she was the daughter of a legendary gold thief, but sparks flew when dashing FBI agent Derek Stone recruited her to find a lost shipment of gold bullion. Together they uncovered her secret past…and a chance for love worth treasuring.

ONE MAJOR DISTRACTION
by Linda Winstead Jones

When Flynn Benning and his team went undercover in an all-girls school to crack a robbery and murder case, he hardly expected to fall for school chef Tess Sanford. Although Flynn was keen on keeping his relationships casual, Tess was not a casual kind of woman. But once Flynn finished his mission, this one major distraction was sure to change his ways…

On sale from 16th June 2006

Available at WHSmith, Tesco, ASDA, Borders, Eason, Sainsbury's and most bookshops

www.silhouette.co.uk

SILHOUETTE®
Sensation™

0606/18b

AKA GODDESS by Evelyn Vaughn

The Grail Keepers

Modern-day grail keeper Maggie Sanger was on a quest, charged with recovering the lost chalices of female power. But when her research was stolen and suspicion fell on her ex-lover, Maggie was challenged to uncover the truth about the legacy that she'd been born into—and the man she once loved.

EMBRACING DARKNESS by Margaret Carter

Until she met Max Tremayne, Linnet Carroll had led an ordinary existence. But Max claimed to be a 500-year-old vampire…and Linnet believed him. Now they needed to join together to hunt down the renegade vampire responsible for the deaths of Max's brother and Linnet's niece. Even if they succeeded, would this mismatched couple ever be able to have a life together?

WILD WOMAN by Lindsay McKenna

Bombshell: Sisters of the Ark

Pilot Jessica Merrill's risk-taking actions had earned her the nickname Wild Woman. Now she'd been charged with retrieving the powerful Native American totem from the madman who would use it to gain immortality. But Jessica's doubtful partner, Mace Phillips, was less enthusiastic about the mission. It was up to her to save the tribe—and show Mace that sometimes you had to take wild chances to get what you wanted…

On sale from 16th June 2006

Available at WHSmith, Tesco, ASDA, Borders, Eason, Sainsbury's and most bookshops

www.silhouette.co.uk

❤ SILHOUETTE®
INTRIGUE™

ROCKY MOUNTAIN MANHUNT
by Cassie Miles
Colorado Crime Consultants

When Kate Carradine woke up with no memories of who or where she was, only one thing was clear: someone was trying to kill her—and she had to go into hiding. Then suddenly, a sexy stranger materialised, offering his protection. But would Liam MacKenzie accept her once she regained her memory, or would he long for the wild woman he'd rescued?

DENIM DETECTIVE by Adrianne Lee
Cowboy Cops

Sheriff Beau Shanahan's life fell apart when his mistrust led to his family's demise. And then his wife returned—with a killer on her trail and the belief that their baby was alive. Would his mistakes cost him the two people he loved the most…again?

OUT FOR JUSTICE by Susan Kearney
Shotgun Sallys

Kelly McGovern suspected the town was covering up her brother's murder, and the one man the townsfolk didn't trust was the only one she wanted watching her back. Between dodging bullets and town interrogations, could she convince dangerous rebel Wade Lansing their attraction needed some private investigation of its own?

THE SEDGWICK CURSE by Shawna Delacorte
Eclipse

Donovan Sedgwick's great-grandfather had loved a woman with an obsession that had left them both dead and their families cursed. Now, a century later, Taylor MacKenzie invaded Donovan's life, questioning the Sedgwick curse and looking too beautiful to resist. When a rash of murders began, it seemed the past was repeating itself. But, this time, were Taylor and Donovan destined to love…or destined to die?

On sale from 16th June 2006
www.silhouette.co.uk

Perfect for the beach, these **BRAND NEW** sizzling reads will get your pulse racing and the temperature rising!

PLAYING GAMES by Dianne Drake
On air she's the sexy, sassy radio shrink – off air she's mild-mannered Roxy Rose. Both have only one desire – the sexy handyman next door.

UNDERCOVER WITH THE MOB
by Elizabeth Bevarly
Jack Miller isn't the type you bring home to mum, which is exactly why Natalie should stay clear of him. But her attraction to him is undeniable, as is her need to uncover his story.

WHAT PHOEBE WANTS by Cindi Myers
Men think Phoebe is a pushover, but now she's refusing to take orders from anyone – especially hunky Jeff Fisher. Because now it's all about what Phoebe wants.

On sale 2nd June 2006

Available at WHSmith, Tesco, ASDA, Borders, Eason, Sainsbury's and all good paperback bookshops

www.millsandboon.co.uk

Can secrets unite a family – or tear them apart?

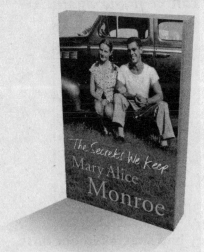

The Blakely family is broken and scattered as matriarch Mary June refuses to face the truth of her past and a legacy of tragedy. She and her husband Preston have paid the price for years of unspoken emotions – one son is lost forever, another, Morgan, has not been home in over a decade.

When Morgan unexpectedly returns to help care for his sick father, the family begins to face their demons. Then Mary June reveals the heart-breaking family secrets she and Preston have kept for forty-seven long years.

21st April 2006

MIRA

Through days of hard work and troubles shared, three women will discover that what was lost can be found again...

Tessa MacCrae has reluctantly agreed to spend the summer helping her mother and grandmother clean out the family home. They've never been close, but Tessa hopes that time away will help her avoid facing the tragedy of her daughter's death and the toll it's exacting on her marriage.

At first, the summer is filled with all-too-familiar emotional storms. But with the passing weeks each of their lives begins to change. And for the first time, Tessa can look past the years of resentment.

'This much-loved family saga of insecurity and tragic loss is compulsive.'
—*The Bookseller*

19th May 2006

"I was fifteen when my mother finally told me the truth about my father. She didn't mean to. She meant to keep it a secret forever. If she'd succeeded it might have saved us all."

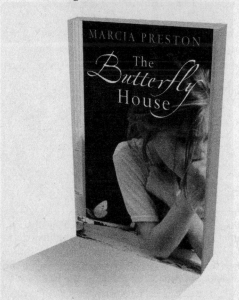

When a hauntingly familiar stranger knocks on Roberta Dutreau's door, she is compelled to begin a journey of self-discovery leading back to her childhood. But is she ready to know the truth about what happened to her, her best friend Cynthia and their mothers that tragic night ten years ago?

16th June 2006